Emily Calb

TARGET: THE GIRL

DORIAN BOX

FRICTION
PRESS

Acclaim for *The Hiding Girl*

Book 1 of the Emily Calby Series

"Dark and gritty ... an exceptional, heart-pounding story full of raw emotion, deep-seated fear, and an undercurrent of hope and innocence. Deeply atmospheric ... without peer in contemporary mysteries/thrillers." — *Publishers Weekly BookLife Prize Semifinalist*

"In Emily, Author Dorian Box has created a rarity—a teenage protagonist that is at once sympathetic, vulnerable and largely fearless ... This sharp characterization within a fast-paced work of suspense makes The Hiding Girl one of the year's most exciting series openers." — *BestThrillers.com (Best Psychological Thriller of 2021)*

"The story that author Dorian Box has created for Emily Calby is nothing short of thrilling, but it's The Hiding Girl's masterful interplay of character, setting, and theme, along with its fast-pace and high emotional stakes that makes it a real page-turner." — *IndieReader Discovery Award for Fiction*

"You root for the lead, Emily, and stick with her throughout. Engaged me from the first page." — *Feathered Quill Medal Winner for Mystery/Suspense*

"A unique mix of hope, shattered innocence, pain, fear, and vulnerability ... a great, suspenseful read." — *Readers' Favorite Award for Suspense Fiction*

"Stunning, captivating, heartbreaking but also heartwarming ... The characters were so alive, believable, with heart and warmth, humor and love ... This book is certainly on my 'best ever books' list." — *NetGalley*

"A fantastic book that completely demolished my expectations. ... This novel is fast-paced and action-packed but it has a profound human element that sets it apart from other novels in its genre." — *BookishFirst*

Acclaim for *The Girl in Cell 49B*

Book 2 of the Emily Calby Series

"A groundbreaking, nail-biting and wondrous legal thriller." — *BestThrillers.com*

"[S]tandout sequel from Dorian Box featuring a fierce female main character, a perfectly planned and paced plot, and a strong sense of theme. ... Emily is a brilliant character ... Her character continues to grow and mature in captivating ways and the series keeps diving deeper and deeper into important morals, messages, and motifs. ... Every scene is meaningful, which makes the book a true page turner." — *IndieReader (starred review, IR Seal of Approval)*

"[A] must-read thriller ... engrossing ... memorable. ... By adding all the right ingredients of emotions, action, corruption, justice, courtroom drama, and gentle romance, Dorian Box has created a potential bestseller." — *Readers' Favorite Award for New Adult Fiction*

"Having read The Girl in Cell 49B (in one evening), I am on a quest to read many more books by this author. Mr. Box places his audience in the moment. He doesn't overdo it with embellishment. Rather, he has mastered the art of show; not tell. Well done!" *Feathered Quill*

"This is how you write a sequel! I completely fell for Emily and Lucas while reading The Hiding Girl ... Like its predecessor, this book packed a hugely satisfying punch. ... I loved witnessing Emily's growth and self-discovery ... Dorian Box has done a masterful job creating a multidimensional character that you can't help but love." — *NetGalley*

"What makes this book such a good read is Box's sympathetic and deeply engaging portrayal of a tough, smart girl determined to beat the odds, even when there doesn't seem to be a ray of hope anywhere. There's plenty of action too. If you're looking for a good thriller with character and substance, this one's for you." — *Andrew Diamond, bestselling author of Gate 76 and Impala*

TARGET: THE GIRL

ISBN 978-1-7346399-1-9

Also by Dorian Box

Psycho-Tropics

The Hiding Girl

The Girl in Cell 49B

For my sister, Robin

Trouble follows me wherever I go.
Thing I'm in is just a sac o'woe.
—Julian Adderley & Jon Hendricks, *Sac O'Woe*

There is no exception to the rule that
every rule has an exception.
—James Thurber

Prologue

"YOU SURE you gonna be alright?" Lucas says.

He's wedged in the driver's seat of his glossy black Mercedes SUV. No matter how big the vehicle, Lucas is always bigger. Stevie Wonder is singing *Living for the City* on the sound system. The empty U-Haul trailer is hooked to the back, ready to be dropped off before he heads home to Memphis.

It's a steamy-hot, late-summer afternoon in St. Augustine, my first time back in Florida since the bloody night in Pensacola ... eight years ago? Seems impossible it's been that long. *I'll be back someday.* That's what I told the beach when I said goodbye.

Now here I am, *all growed up* as my dad would say, if he were alive. Twenty years old and ready to start law school at the First Coast College of Law. I'm standing in front of my new home, the Seaside Apartments. Dated and run down, but so close to the water seagulls patrol the sidewalks.

"I'll be fine!" I say for the third time today.

He doesn't believe me and there's no reason he should. Not the way I've been acting lately. I was doing fine until a few months ago when the PTSD train went off the rails again. Simple stuff, things I loved, turned into triggers. Last week Lucas and I went out for barbecue. Pulling into the parking lot, I freaked. *Turn around, turn around!* The smell flooded me with images of Mom and Becky being cooked in our burning house the day everything ended.

I can never pin down what wakes it from hibernation. Lucas

has a theory: *Today.* Moving seven hundred miles from home to live alone for the first time in my life.

He tried so hard to talk me into staying in Memphis and going to law school there. He's been protecting me—*over*protecting—since I was twelve. I had to earn my undergrad degree online from safe inside his fortress. Too many freaks still around after the *missing Calby girl* was discovered four years ago.

"Lucas," I argued. "I'm twenty, not twelve." Part of him still sees me that way, the traumatized "skinny white girl" he rescued off the streets. In my most honest moments, I see me the same way. I told him, told myself, the time had come to set his little hawk free, see if she can fly on her own.

He asks again if I need anything before he leaves. I pretend to sweep a mosquito from my moist eyelashes, almost saying, *Just you*. I lean in and kiss his cheek. "I'm good. Promise. I'll call every day. Drive safely, and don't speed."

"Listen up," he says. "Somethin' goes wrong, you can always change your mind and come home to Memphis. Ain't no shame in it."

I spread my arms and tilt into the bright Florida sun, filling my lungs with the wet salty air. "What could possibly go wrong in a beautiful place like this?"

1

PROFESSOR Edgar Nemworth squints at a piece of paper and says, "*Calby*. Emily Calby." I can tell his thick glasses need cleaning even from the back row. My first law school class. Contracts. Seventy-five students in my section and I have to be the first person called on. I haven't even opened my book.

No introduction, not even a *Welcome to law school*. The Socratic method. I read all about it. A torture instrument where professors cold-call on students expecting them to give intelligent answers to complex questions they've never thought about before, all in full display of their ultra-competitive peers.

Nemworth is a big deal, or used to be. Taught at an Ivy League school and wrote a legendary treatise on contract law. Rumor says he came to the First Coast College of Law to retire. He's eighty-four according to a Wikipedia page, and looks it, stooped and craggly with rectangular glasses and wiry gray hair. His gruff voice is covered in dust.

"*Hamer v. Sidway*. Please tell us the facts."

I'm flipping pages in my book to find the court's opinion and willing my computer to load faster so I can find the summary I typed up last night, a *case brief* they call it. "Um, just a sec."

If my classmates have figured out who I am, they haven't let on. Most were kids, like me, when everything happened. Even when the news broke that I'd been discovered—on trial in Louisiana for murder—they were just teenagers. But the professors might remember. Did Nemworth call on me on purpose?

"Miss Colby," he barks. "What are you waiting for?"

Guess not. He already forgot my name.

"Almost there." There it is, my brief for *Hamer*, a moldy oldie from New York. Case briefs are supposed to be short. Mine's two single-spaced pages, almost as long as the court's opinion. I wasn't sure what I was looking for, so I wrote down everything.

"Okay, the facts. Well, a man promised his nephew—"

"Louder, Miss Colby. We can't hear you," Nemworth says.

"Actually, sir, it's *Cal*by, but you can just call me Emily." I'm not trying to be a smartass, but someone laughs. Nemworth silences them with a look.

"Miss Calby, this is a professional school. You will be treated and expected to act like the professional you might one day become. The facts. You're wasting everyone's time."

I clear my throat. "As I was saying, a man promised his nephew if he didn't drink, swear or smoke cigarettes until he was twenty-one, the uncle would give him five-thousand dollars. When the nephew turned twenty-one, he told the uncle he had refrained from doing all those things, but the uncle refused to give him the money. So he sued."

"What was the legal issue?"

"Let's see. I have in my brief that the defendant argued the nephew didn't give consideration for the contract."

"And what, Ms. Colby, is *consideration*?"

"I'm not completely sure. I think it's getting something back in exchange for a promise."

"But the uncle didn't get anything in exchange for the nephew's promise, yet the nephew prevailed in the case, which means your definition must be *wrong*."

Not only is it so quiet you could hear a pin drop, I actually hear one. Well, a paperclip. The girl next to me started nervously fiddling with it under the table when I got called on. It bounces off an electrical outlet stuffed with computer cords.

"Um ..." Everyone's looking at me. A fog of anxiety envelopes my brain. After everything I've been through, failure is still my biggest fear.

Dale Olson waves his hand from the front row. I met him at last week's orientation and already predicted he would be the class *gunner*—the annoying student who tries to answer every question. They say every law school class has one.

Nemworth's head is swiveling in his direction. *Get a grip, Calby. You've killed people.* "Professor," I pipe. "I wouldn't say my answer was *wrong*. However, it was incomplete."

The answer's right in front of me, in my case brief. "The court in *Hamer* said consideration can consist of getting something for a promise or giving up something, a *forbearance* of some kind."

I can't read his eyes through the smeared lenses. "Continue," he says.

"So, think about everything the nephew gave up. He couldn't smoke, drink or curse, and, oh yeah, couldn't even play cards or shoot pool. I have no idea why those were on the uncle's list. I can understand the other things, but playing car—"

"Miss Colby, your personal opinions are irrelevant."

"Right. Anyway, while I don't condone all of those activities, it was the nephew's right to do them, assuming they were legal. I don't know what the drinking age was in eighteen ninety-one."

He raises his chin in what could be liberally construed as a nod of affirmation and I feel like I passed some kind of test until, "To be clear, your first answer was *wrong*. Incomplete statements of the law are always wrong."

He moves on to a guy on the other side of the room with long brown hair in a ponytail, wearing a psychedelic band t-shirt. I relax, but get distracted by Brady Chapman, one row in front of me. He's been shopping for Adderall from Canada since class started, violating every professor's rule against computer-multitasking.

Chapman's gorgeous, with dark hair and green eyes, sort of a tall Tom Cruise. But he knows it and I can't stand guys like that. He's also the class party animal. During orientation, while the professors were beating into us how hard law school will be, he organized three happy hours.

I went to one even though I don't drink and can't, not legally. Other than the lying, stealing and killing, I'm still the good girl from Dilfer County, Georgia. At twenty, I'm the youngest person in the one-L class. That's what they call us. 1Ls. I did my online degree in three years. When the waiter asked for my ID, I said, "For coffee?"

"How old are you?" asked a future lawyer of America named Rachel downing her third vodka and tonic.

"Twenty."

"And you don't have a fake ID? You really should get one."

If she only knew. I received my first fake ID, a driver's license, at age twelve, the day I met Lucas, expert document forger. I just smiled.

All people talked about the whole night was law school. Chapman tried to hit on me. I wanted to punch him in the throat, just to see the reaction on his arrogant face. *Of course* I didn't do it, but the fact that I thought about it isn't a good sign. Lucas would not approve.

"Miss *Orly*," Nemworth calls out. "Julie Orly."

A chubby girl with dirty-blonde hair raises her hand ever so slightly. She's wearing a baggy red University of Georgia t-shirt with a bulldog on the front.

"Was the contract in *Hamer* unilateral or bilateral?"

I see the telltale signs of freezing before he even finishes the question. Tensed neck, wide eyes. I probably had the same look a minute ago. Dale Olson already has his hand up.

I think it was unilateral. The uncle said *if* his nephew abstained from the activities, he'd pay him the money, so it was up to the nephew to do it or not. But the forty-page reading assignment only had a couple paragraphs explaining the difference.

"Um."

"Come, come. We don't have all day."

"Bilateral? ... Unilateral?"

"Ms. Orly, did you come to class unprepared? That is unacceptable in this course."

Dale Olson leans forward waving his hand like he's reaching for a foul ball at a baseball game. Other hands start going up.

Can't Nemworth tell she's scared? Leave her alone. "Professor," I blurt. "The reading didn't clearly explain the difference between unilateral and bilateral contracts."

"Did too," Dale Olson retorts like a five-year-old. His hair, spirally and close-cropped, looks like fur. Soft and plump in a brown shirt and pants, he reminds me of the Beanie Baby bear I had as a kid.

"Note fourteen, page twenty-eight," he says. "But you had to actually *read* it."

I've never reacted well to bullying, and it's gotten me in plenty of trouble. *Control yourself.* But I don't. "Actually, it was note twelve," I say. "But you have to actually be able to count. Maybe you're not as smart as you think you are."

"Oh, really. I got a one-sixty-six on the LSAT. How about you?"

My perfect score of one-eighty got me some full-ride scholarship offers from big-name law schools. I would have got more, but most schools don't recognize online undergraduate degrees. Didn't matter. Against everyone's advice, I picked the First Coast College of Law because I always wanted to live on the beach, and thought it might be easier to hide in the shadows at a lesser-known school in a small city.

It's tempting to answer Olson honestly, but the only thing it would prove is I'm no better than him. *Pride goes before destruction, and a haughty spirit before a fall.* Proverbs 16:18. I also don't like people knowing my personal business, a preference that could be described as quaint given that a Google search for Emily Calby turns up about a million results.

"Silence," Nemworth growls. "Both of you. No one speaks in this room unless spoken to—by me. Miss Orly, I would like to see you in my office after class."

Nemworth memorializes the end of our first class by writing an inspirational message across the dry erase board in large letters. *STUDY HARDER*, underlined three times. The second he releases us, the girl next to me flees the room like a fire alarm went off.

Ever vigilant, my eyes track a thin white guy approaching from across the room as I cram the three-inch thick Contracts book into my already bulging backpack. He has short brown hair and a pointy nose that slices his narrow face like a shark fin.

"Hi," he says. "I'm Henley Oliver." He's the definition of clean-cut, with rectangular wire-rimmed glasses and a stiff button-down shirt tucked into his jeans, which have a crease in them. He irons his jeans! Too funny. His cordovan belt matches his polished, tasseled loafers.

"You're Emily Calby, right?"

My head jerks back. "How did you know that?"

"Well, Professor Nemworth called on you."

"Oh, right."

I look different since my face was plastered on news sites across the country. I still have my can't-hide-in-a-crowd blonde hair, but grew into my face and wear glasses, just as I predicted I would need four years ago reading law books in the dim light of Cell 49B at the Pochachant Detention Center for Juveniles in Louisiana.

It's only a matter of time before someone makes the connection. Lucas bugged me to change my name, legally since he's out of the document-forging business. I told him I already lived too much of my life as someone else and couldn't let go of Emily Calby again. I nearly lost her the first time. There are still times when I feel she's on the edge of disappearing.

Henley says, "I was wondering if you'd be interested in joining my study group?"

I like studying on my own, but the prep books say study groups are the way to go in law school.

"Why me?"

"Study groups form fast," he says. "My plan is to invite the smartest people to join before they're snapped up by other groups. You got everything right today."

"Not according to Nemworth."

"Well, I also heard a rumor you crushed the LSAT."

"What? From who?" I didn't breathe a word about it to anyone except Lucas.

"Um, I'm not really sure. Maybe someone in the admissions office when they were recruiting me."

"No friggin' way. That's illegal. Student records are private under federal law." *FERPA*. I researched it in advance, fed up with my private information being handed out like candy to everyone in the world. First it was medical, then judicial. "Someone's in big trouble."

"Hold on. I might be wrong. I honestly don't remember where I heard it. Don't worry, I won't tell a soul. So how about the study group?"

I say I'll think about it. Ticked off by my latest privacy breach, I huff out of the classroom to find the girl in the Georgia t-shirt waiting in the hall.

She sticks out her hand. "Julie Orly," she says.

I shake it. "Emily Calby."

"Thanks, in there," she says.

"No problem. Don't let Olson get to you. He's obviously a total jerk."

Chewing her lip, "The thing is, I did read everything, including that note, but my brain froze up."

"Just explain that to Nemworth. I'm sure it happens all the time. I was half a second away from freezing myself. You want me to go up there with you?"

"That's okay, but thanks."

* * *

Julie and I end up eating lunch together at a picnic table in the breezeway after Torts—the law of personal injuries—taught by

Professor Olivia LeMoy. Petite with short dark hair and larger than life, she reminds me of Rachel Maddow. She talks a hundred miles an hour and stays in constant motion around the horseshoe classroom.

Julie's chin flattens in her hands. In front of her is a meatball sub from the student center.

"I'm doomed," she says. "I'm going to flunk. I just know it. *Bye-bye. Ta-ta.* Hi Mom! Hi Dad! Guess what? Your stupid daughter just flunked out of law school."

"You are not going to flunk. How was your meeting with Nemworth?"

"Short. I apologized and told him I was prepared. I offered to show him my case briefs and marked-up casebook. He wasn't interested. Just said I need to *study harder.*"

"That's not fair," I say. "There wasn't even a clear right or wrong answer to that question. He said so himself."

"No, it's worse. My Legal Writing professor asked me the easiest *Bluebook* question in the history of law school. What does *id.* mean? It sounded like she was talking in a foreign language even though I've known the answer since I was a freshman in college."

"Fear can paralyze anyone. My best friend once gave me some good advice about it. He said whenever you're in a scary situation, it's going to be the same situation whether you're scared or not, so you might as well make the choice to not be afraid. What do you have to lose?"

"Do you think it works?"

"I know it does." I just haven't been following it lately.

"It's so frustrating. They don't give you time to think around this place. Everyone wants an instant answer."

"See how smart you are? In one day you've identified a huge flaw in legal education."

She laughs.

"Oh gawd," I say. "Here comes Olson and Chapman. Have you met Chapman? He's a pig. Thinks he's God's gift to women."

"Well, look what we found," Chapman says. "It's the *Legally Blondes.*"

"Did you bring your Chihuahua?" Olson chimes. He looks especially dumpy standing next to Chapman.

The joke is so lame it makes me wonder whether he lied about his LSAT score. I say, "Do either of you happen to remember how that movie ended?"

Olson laughs. "Oh, I see. You're going to end up the superstar, huh? Do you have any great words of wisdom you can share?"

"Yeah. Stay away from us."

I hear Chapman mutter *Stuck-up bitch* as they walk away.

I shake my head and point to Julie's t-shirt. "Did you go to Georgia?"

"Yeah. That's where I'm from. Born and raised."

"I thought I recognized a Georgia accent. I grew up in Georgia too. Dilfer County, up north. Farm country, not too many people, but nice and peaceful ... most of the time."

"I don't hear a Georgia accent in you."

"Probably because I moved to Memphis when I was twelve."

"Why'd you move?"

Two men broke into our house and raped and murdered my mother and little sister. I ran away.

"Um, just, you know ... reasons."

2

I HURRY home after my last class. My apartment's only five blocks from the law school, one of the main reasons I chose it. I have a dozen mind-tangling judicial opinions to read and brief for tomorrow. I unlock the lobby door and go straight to the wall of mailboxes. A wad of junk mail sinks my spirits.

After the flood of attention when I won my trial at age sixteen for killing a sex predator, I never thought I'd miss mail. I got a thick stack of it every day. Interview requests, job offers, book deals, even a modeling contract.

I had lots of fans. Most of them were sweet as can be. A group of girls called themselves the *Calbies,* like *Swifties.* But some of my admirers were creepy. One guy sent anonymous love letters every week for an entire year, swore we'd be together someday, *one way or another.* His last letter quoted Shakespeare, ending with, *Some Cupid kills with arrows, some with traps.* Then they suddenly stopped.

There were plenty of haters too. Misogynists, conspiracy theorists and once they found out I lived with Lucas, racists. The stuff they wrote was horrible. Most of it was online, but some of the trolls put a stamp on it. I ignored them until a guy sent a recipe for how he planned to cook and eat me for dinner. The dumbass even signed his name. *Roland Romansky.*

I called FBI Special Agent Jeffrey Forster, my captor turned liberator when I was young. They tracked down Romansky and charged him with terroristic threatening. I wonder whatever happened to him.

Yesterday I got a card from Rebecca, my cellmate at Pochachant. She's living with her mom in New Orleans, working as a server and taking art classes at a community college. She and her mom are both still clean. That news made my whole day.

Today it's just garbage.

I pass the elevator and take the stairs, ignoring my sore quads from this morning's five a.m. gym work out. Seaside has four floors. I'm on the top in a corner unit. Apartment 412. Just one-bedroom with a kitchen and bath, but it's all I need.

The straps of my backpack cut into my shoulders. Law books weigh a ton. You could do bicep curls with them. I'm breathing heavy when I reach my floor.

Toby, a fat ginger cat, waits at my door. He belongs to Mrs. Alvarez, a sweet old lady on the other side of the floor. She lets him roam the halls every afternoon, for exercise, she says. I gave him some tuna the first day and he's been back every day since.

I scratch his ears. "Hey, Toby. Whatcha doing? Another tough day on the fourth floor?" He purrs like an electric motor.

I use my shirttails to dust the fronds on my kentia palm, parked next to the door in a bright yellow planter. I bought it with a gift card from Kiona, Lucas's wife. She's still living her dream in Las Vegas working as a boxing trainer. One of these days I'm going to get those two living in the same place.

I kiss my fingers and tap the bleached starfish pinned to my door. I do it for luck every time I come home, like a talisman. I've become superstitious, more so all the time it seems. Dr. Laura, my trauma therapist in Memphis, said it's part of my PTSD, with a dash of OCD thrown in.

Inside, I dump my backpack on a school of fish, my kitchen rug. I went all out on the beach theme in decorating. Lucas paid for everything of course. He always does. I told him I should take out student loans, but he wouldn't hear it. Gave me the same refrain as always, *Money might be the only problem you ain't got.*

How many other young drug dealers would have had the wisdom to invest their proceeds in stocks? One more way I'm a lucky girl for having him in my life. Most of my classmates are in debt up to their eyeballs.

Waiting for a bowl of muesli to heat in the microwave, I grapple to open the sliding glass door—off its salt-corroded track again—to my tiny balcony. I stretch over the railing until I can see a sliver of the Atlantic Ocean. I love it here!

I settle in at the kitchen table with my laptop and Property casebook. The first case, *Pierson v. Post,* is another legal artifact, a lawsuit over who owned a dead fox. The Old English is hard to decode. The plaintiff was a hunter chasing a fox. The fox ran onto the defendant's land and the defendant shot it and kept it for the pelt. Who owned the fox, the hunter or the landowner? ...

My eyelids are heavy by the time I finish. I search for my phone before remembering it's in my backpack with the ringer off. A guy's phone went off in Contracts, sending Nemworth on a tirade about how we're not in undergraduate school anymore.

Oh, jeez. Three texts from Lucas. I forgot to call him.

What happened on your first day?

You alright?

I'm going to bed.

I start writing: *Lucas, I'm SO sorry I forgot to call. They make us turn our phones off in class and I've been studying all night. The first day was good! I'll tell you everything tomorrow. Love and miss you bunches! Em*

I need to go to bed too. I pack up and take a quick shower.

In the middle of my prayers, a knocking sound makes my muscles tense. I'm still getting used to the night sounds of the apartment. Maybe the air conditioner switching on.

No, there it is again. I get out of bed and tiptoe to the front door. Out the peephole I see only my neighbor's door across the hall. I unhitch the chain lock, twist the deadbolt and scan the hallways. Everything is quiet and still.

Disgusted by my paranoia, I slam the door and yank it open

just as fast. My palm tree! It's on the right side. It was on the left side when I came home ... wasn't it?

Hypervigilance: A state of being abnormally alert to potential dangers or threats. I'm a poster child for it, always waiting for another door to open, another phone call with bad news, the other shoe to drop. It's exhausting and time-consuming. As Dr. Laura once explained, "Some of my clients"—meaning me—"believe that if they don't worry about something bad happening, it's more likely it will happen."

I assess the planter. I must be used to seeing it from the opposite side when I come home. The icemaker rumbles behind me. *Duh!* That's what I heard.

I laugh at myself and go back to bed to finish my prayers. I pray for God to take care of my family in heaven and Lucas in Memphis and ... I could have *sworn* that palm tree was on the other side.

3

DAWN IS BREAKING as I rush down the sidewalk to the gym. I overslept. It's almost six. My first class is at eight. At the cross streets, I catch glimpses of the sun's golden petals blooming above the water, radiating hope, a new day, new possibilities. I wish I could stop to enjoy it.

Why do I kill myself by working out two hours a day? Because it's saved my life more than once.

It started when I met Lucas and he agreed to teach me *self-defense*. He persuaded Kiona to help and she punished me for it. It was before they were married and she was not happy—to put it mildly—about him taking in a twelve-year-old white girl off the streets.

She tried to break me to make me give up, but it only made me stronger. Whenever I fell to my knees puking my guts out, I'd picture the red-tailed hawk circling our yard the day the two men came. *Predator, not prey. Never again.*

After I blurred the line between self-defense and murder during my stay at the Pochachant detention center, Lucas made me swear off violence as a path to justice and rely on *The Law*. I even had to surrender my favorite weapon: a neck knife. It hangs on a lanyard around your neck, concealed under your clothes.

Maybe I was always meant for law school because I managed to work in a loophole for self-defense, which meant I got to keep training to fight.

So much for that, I think, entering the Peaceful Moon Gym and Spa, where they play spa music and hold mindfulness classes. I only joined because it's right on my way to school. I already miss Max's, the gritty boxing gym in South Memphis.

"Hi, Emily."

It's Greg, one of the personal trainers. About my height, but built like a tank, a legit bodybuilder. He's been friendly since I signed up. A little too friendly.

"Hi Greg," I say, swiping my card.

"How was your first day at law school?"

Did I tell him that? "Um, good."

"Do you happen to have a professor named Dalbert or Dalrymple, something like that?"

"Nope."

"Just wondered because one of my clients is in law school and mentioned that name."

"Probably an upper-level student. I'm just a first-year."

"So, do you think you're going to like it?"

"We'll see. Good to see you." I hurry away, inserting my earbuds and turning up the music.

He's still talking, but I can't hear it through the Staple Singers singing *I'll Take You There*. I grew up on country music. Then I met Lucas and was deluged with gangsta rap until he reached his mid-thirties and started mellowing. Since then it's been old school R&B.

I race through my workout and hurry to the law school for day two. First up, Property.

* * *

Professor Sarah Owusua, a tall, commanding black woman in a conservative form-fitting suit, is actually making the dead fox case interesting. It was the first case to decide how *personal property* can be legally possessed by a human being. The class is debating between the hunter's and the landowner's rights to the fox.

I raise my hand.

"Ms.?"

"Calby. I was just wondering, what about the fox's rights?"

Up front, a horsey laugh from Olson.

"The fox?" Owusua says.

"Mm-hm. Why should a fox be anyone's personal property? He's a fox, nature's property or God's."

"Intriguing question," she says. "Let me ask you this? Have you ever had a pet?"

"Yes, a dog." Rocky, our black Lab. Like everyone in my family, he died, of kidney disease.

"Did you own that dog?"

"Um, my family did." The trap is obvious. Law professors are *in love* with trapping you. "But he wanted to be with us."

"Oh, did you ask him?" Laughs all around.

Owusua's toying with me, but I don't feel like she's trying to embarrass me, more like playing a game. And it hits me. That's what the Socratic method is. A game. Let go of your fear and just play the game.

"No, because he couldn't talk. But the circumstantial evidence strongly suggested he liked being part of our family."

"What kind evidence?"

"Well, he wagged his tail whenever he saw us. And he licked our faces any chance he got."

A smattering of chuckles, including from Owusua.

"And we definitely didn't shoot him. Just because animals can't talk or reason doesn't mean they can't suffer."

"That sounds familiar. Jeremy Bentham?"

I blush. "Yes, ma'am. I plagiarized him from a philosophy class I took in undergrad."

"It's a valid argument. Scholars have advocated for centuries that animals should have more legal rights, and in some countries they do. But as harsh as it sounds, the common law of the United States is that animals are considered personal property, no different from your laptop or Property casebook."

Henley Oliver raises his hand. "While I appreciate Emily's point, the common law is the correct policy choice. If humans couldn't own and kill animals, we'd all have to be vegetarians. I wouldn't be able to wear these shoes or my belt."

"Would that be so bad?" I say.

This exchange ignites a spirited class debate. Turns out my statement wasn't so ridiculous after all. My favorite part was watching Owusua ignore Dale Olson's waving arm.

* * *

Henley runs me down after class on my way to Legal Writing. "Hey, I wasn't trying to show you up in there when I disagreed," he says.

"No problem. It was totally cool. That's what law school should be like. You helped generate a great discussion. And I confess, I eat chicken and fish."

"Glad you feel that way. So have you thought about the study group? You know, most of the professors recommend them."

"Who's in it?"

"I've talked to a few people." He lists a couple names and hesitates. "I was also thinking about Dale Olson because of his LSAT, but I have a feeling you wouldn't be a big fan of that."

"That's an understatement. I'd flunk out of law school before joining a study group with Olson. He's a tool."

"No problem. If you agree to join, no Olson."

It might not be a bad idea. I have heard a lot about the benefits of study groups. "I'll give it a try, but only if you invite Julie Orly too."

"Orly? I don't think she's up to our level."

"What level is that and how do you even know?"

"I know she gets the answer wrong every time she's called on."

"That's just because she's nervous. I'm not joining without her."

"Alright. But I have to run it by the others. We agreed to do everything by majority vote. I'll try to talk them into it."

* * *

Legal Writing is completely different from the other classes. For one thing, it's divided into small groups, which I like. Fifteen students instead of seventy-five.

But the main thing I like is the professor. Bryce Stafford, a civil rights and criminal defense lawyer with his own law firm who teaches as an adjunct. He's brilliant, funny and super-cute, tall with crisp charcoal-colored hair and sleepy hazel eyes. He was editor-in-chief of the law review as a student here, which apparently is the law school equivalent of being captain of a starship.

I researched all my professors, but spent the most time on him. He's a real lawyer and exactly the kind I want to be. A champion of underdogs. I found an article about how he represented a group of Haitian migrant workers suing a farm conglomerate for labor law violations and won. The article quoted one of the workers saying, *We are forever grateful to Mr. Bryce for letting our voice be heard.*

We spend the first class talking about the *Bluebook,* more than three hundred pages of ridiculously technical citation rules for legal documents. Put a comma in the wrong place and your grade gets lowered. It's dry as dust, but Professor Stafford said attention to detail is a mark of a good lawyer.

After class I head upstairs to Professor Nemworth's office. We each got assigned a *faculty mentor* at orientation. Lucky me, I got Nemworth. The email said it's up to us to go meet them.

The faculty wing is mostly empty. Nemworth's office is at the end of the hall. The door's open. He's at his desk, leaned over a book in the glow of a brass banker's lamp, forehead almost resting on the pages, holding an unlit pipe.

I stand in the doorway waiting for him to notice me. His office is like a museum, full of old books and faded photographs, including Nemworth posing with presidents and Supreme Court justices. A minute passes before I say, "Knock, knock."

He looks up, squinting again. "Yes?"

"Hi, Professor!"

If I had to pick one quality that has helped me the most in life, other than lethality, I'd go with *effervescence*. It works on almost everyone. It's just hard for people to be mean when you switch on that merry state.

"I'm Emily Calby. I popped by to talk with you about being my faculty mentor. Is this a bad time?"

"Your what?"

"Faculty mentor."

"What the hell is that?"

"Oh, well, I'm not really sure, but they assigned me to you. It's right here in the orientation instructions. I can show you." I reach into my backpack.

He sets down the pipe and points to a worn leather guest chair, one of a pair parked in front of his desk.

"Sit."

He scans the orientation printout. "This is obviously another misguided initiative from our new baby dean to make us more *student-centered*. Soon she'll be asking me to read you bedtime stories. What exactly am I supposed to mentor you about?"

I shrug. Realizing my goofy smile while being dressed down is probably making me look like a mental patient, I relax it.

He takes his glasses off and rubs them with a dirty handkerchief that succeeds only in moving the smears around. I'm surprised he can see anything through them.

"I'm really enjoying Contracts," I say to fill the silence.

"Enjoying? Then I'm obviously doing something wrong. You are not here to enjoy, Miss Colby. You are here to learn."

"It's Calby, sir, and with all due respect, I think a person can learn and enjoy at the same time."

"*Hmph.*" He puts his glasses back on. "Calby, you say. Have I called on you?"

"Yes, sir. The first day. *Hamer v. Sidway.*"

On the credenza behind him is a framed photograph of a stately white-haired woman in a black dress with a scoop neckline. She's wearing a silver necklace with a green stone in it. "Is that your wife?"

"My wife? Since when do first-year law students ask professors about their personal lives? I don't think I'll survive the Millennials."

"Good news on that front, sir. You've actually made it through most of the Millenials. I'm part of what they call Generation Z."

"God help me."

"Anyway, I didn't mean to offend you. It's just that you have her picture there and she's very beautiful so I thought you might want people to notice her. Her necklace is so pretty. Is that an emerald?"

He gazes at the picture with sad eyes. "Yes, she is ... was my wife. And yes, that is an emerald."

Someone enters behind me and my hands reflexively move into position to grab my nonexistent neck knife. Old habits.

Even through the dirty lenses, I see Nemworth's eyes widen. "Christina, what are you doing here?"

It's a short woman with alert eyes so dark they almost match her inky black hair. She's wearing yoga tights and a blouson top cinched at the waist. I'd guess mid-to-late thirties.

"So sorry to interrupt, Edgar. I was nearby and thought you'd be alone. I just dropped by to get the ... envelope."

"Envelope? Oh, yes. The envelope. Well, I haven't had time to prepare it." His commanding voice has disappeared, replaced by ... I can't tell exactly what, but definitely different.

"No problem. I'll pick it up tonight." She blows him a kiss and leaves.

"Is that your daughter, professor?" I ask.

"No, no."

"Granddaughter?"

Sputtering, "You want mentoring advice? Stop posing intrusive questions to your professors and devote one-hundred percent of your non-sleep hours to studying."

"Got it."

4

DARK CLOUDS roll in as I make my way home, calculating tonight's workload. I managed to read and brief tomorrow's Torts assignment between classes. That was smart. Need to do it more often.

Henley headed me off on my way out. "Emily. I'm sorry to say the others voted against Orly joining the study group. I tried to persuade them. Would you reconsider joining without her?"

"Nope," I said.

Snobs. I made the mistake of mentioning the study group to Julie and she got all excited. I'm wondering how to break the news when a thundershower lets loose.

I duck under the awning of a hair salon to wait it out. Across the street I notice a man in a white shirt and shorts gyrating behind the glass. *Jeez,* it's Greg. I'm in front of the gym. He's waving. I wave back and decide to brave the rain.

I reach Seaside wet as a fish. Fumbling for my keys in my backpack, the door swings opens, held by a tall guy with dark slicked-back hair, wearing a crisp blue blazer over a white shirt open at the neck.

"Come on in," he says. "Looks like you have your hands full."

"Thanks," I say, entering the foyer, shaking off water like a dog. "But how do you know I live here? I could be breaking in."

He laughs. "You don't look like the dangerous type."

"Looks can be deceiving," I say.

"I'm Matt Jurado."

Going to my mailbox, "Emily."

"I've never seen you before. Lived here long?"

"Not long." Dang, nothing but more junk mail.

"What do you do?" he says.

"The usual stuff."

"No, I mean, what kind of work do you do?"

I knew what he meant. Can't people take a hint? I keep my answers short talking to strangers, like I learned to do on cross-examination.

"Student. How about you?"

"Entrepreneur."

I relock my mailbox, try to. The lock is jammed. I notice other doors ajar. "What's up with these mailboxes? Doesn't anyone complain to the landlord?"

"Crappy maintenance," he says. "That's why the rent's affordable three blocks from the water. So you're in four-twelve. I'm in three twelve, directly below you. Vertical neighbors. Let me know if I ever get too loud."

"Likewise."

He walks to the elevator and holds the door.

"I like to take the stairs. Good exercise. Nice meeting you. Thanks for letting me in."

I jump them two at a time, holding my backpack tight to keep it from walloping my spine.

The fourth floor is quiet. It usually is, one of the things I like about the building. Let's see. I have twenty-three pages to read and brief in Contracts, plus I need to do a research assignment for Legal Writing. So if I—.

What the ... my palm tree is back on the right side of the door!

I knock on the apartment across the hall. No answer so I pound harder. A gangly stoop-shouldered guy answers, cinching a dirty white bathrobe around his waist. He needs a shave and some sunshine on his ghostly skin. His red eyes do not look happy.

"Hi! I'm Emily." Big smile. "I'm your new neighbor across the hall. Right there."

"Don't you know how to knock like a lady? You scared the shit out of me." I catch a whiff of burning pot. Never tried it, but Lucas is a fan.

"Sorry."

"What do you want?"

"I was just wondering if you happened to move my palm tree."

"If I what?"

"Moved my palm tree. Someone moved it to the other side of the door last night, at least I think so, then moved it back today."

"Why would I move your palm tree?"

"I don't know. Maybe it was in your way or something."

"I didn't touch your palm tree."

"Okay, cool ... do you have any idea who might have?"

"No. Here's a better question. Why do you care? I have a suggestion. Move it back to where you want it."

"Um, someone did that today."

He throws up his hands. "Problem solved. Case closed." The door slams in my face.

I take the palm inside and dump my backpack on my purple couch. *Why do you care?* Good question. Because I'm a PTSD-addled freak.

It's a stupid plant! Plant moving is not a threat. Get it together. You are Emily-the-Powerful. Lucas has been making me recite it since I was twelve. I park the palm tree on the balcony.

* * *

"You still there?" Lucas says. I have him on speaker.

"Um, yeah." I got distracted checking the peephole again. Not a soul all night. He's asking about law school. "It's not too bad—yet. The professors have started slow, but everyone says it gets a lot worse."

"You can handle it."

"Yeah. At least it's interesting. Some of the cases we study are crazy."

"They oughta study your case. Talk about crazy. Anything else going on?"

"Not really." I don't want to bore him with law school stuff and I'm definitely not telling him about the palm tree. "I found a gym, but it's pathetic. Get this. They do massages and play spa music."

He snorts, "Should be illegal to call it a gym."

"I agree, but it's convenient. There are a couple of martial arts places I want to check out. I really miss fighting."

A heavy sigh. "You don't need any more fightin'. You startin' a new life."

"You know, just for training. Don't worry, I'm not going to get in any fights."

"Good," he says and changes the subject. "Did it happen yet?"

I know what he's talking about. "I don't think so. Everyone treats me like I'm just another student."

"Get ready. Only a matter of time. Be prepared."

"Maybe I'll get lucky and it won't be until after this semester. I don't need any more stress."

5

HUSTLING DOWN the sidewalk, slurping coffee from my travel cup, I'm running late again. Something's going to have to give on this workout schedule. I'm not getting enough sleep. I enter the Peaceful Moon and see Greg behind the counter. I reach for my earbuds, too late.

"Bright and early, as usual," he chirps. "You are one dedicated gym rat."

"Thanks." I scan my card and hurry away. He follows me.

"Hey, I was wondering if you might be interested in some personal training sessions."

"Can't. I'm on a really tight budget."

"Complimentary," he says.

"I couldn't do that. It wouldn't be fair."

"Don't worry about it. No one else comes in this early anyway."

"I appreciate it, but I like to work out on my own. Get in my zone, you know?"

"Okay. Would you be interested in maybe getting together for a drink some time?"

"Sorry. Don't drink." *Please, please, get it.*

"It doesn't have to be alcohol. Maybe coffee or a protein shake?"

"Law school takes up all my time. Really."

"Fine. I get the picture," he says and turns away.

I don't like being rude, but at least that's settled. I climb on a bike and arrange my Contracts notes on the reading tray. I have the feeling I'm being watched and when I look up, Greg turns away. I cut the workout short. I'm late anyway.

Another steamy-hot day. *I cannot wait* for Saturday. I'm taking my books and hitting the beach. When I reach the law school, I literally run up the promenade. Contracts starts in two minutes. The one time a student came in late, Nemworth ordered him to leave.

The clamor inside tells me I beat Nemworth to class. Law students love to talk. Pulling on the double-doors, it sounds like I'm entering a rowdy bar, until a girl in the front row nudges the guy next to her and points. Law school social life grinds to a halt, replaced by a deafening silence as face after face turns in my direction.

It happened. Just like Lucas predicted. The *missing Calby girl* has been discovered once again: at a law school in Florida. *Be prepared,* he said last night. I'm not.

I take my seat and set up my casebook and laptop. Just another day, I tell myself. Brady Chapman's on the internet. Just another day ... except that instead of shopping for Adderall he's reading a CNN article with a bold headline.

Home Invasion Victim on Trial for Murder in Louisiana

He cranes his neck, incredulous. My curled smile says, *Yep, I've killed people. Better be careful.* Across the room, Julie's biting her nails. I should have told her. Henley Oliver looks at me with tightlipped sympathy.

Nemworth enters and begins his slow descent to the lectern, cane thumping on the gray carpet. Has he heard the news?

He adjusts his glasses, opens his casebook, and says, "Miss Calby."

Well, at least he finally knows it's not *Colby.*

"I believe you have something to tell the class."

"I do?"

"Yes, something of which I was previously unaware and which the entire class may not yet know about."

And to think I was actually starting to like him. I swallow hard to clamp down the anger gurgling in my gut. "Not that it's anyone's business, Professor, but the short version is that two men came to our house when I was twelve years old and slaughtered my family."

A few gasps. I guess not everyone heard the news. "I ran away and went *missing*—the media loved to call it that—for three years. Along the way I had to kill a man in Louisiana in self-defense."

White knuckles gripping the table, "They put me on trial for murder. Fortunately, I was acquitted. Is there anything else you'd like me to tell the class?"

Nemworth pulls a handkerchief from his coat pocket and dabs his face. "Miss Calby, please tell the class about the new faculty mentoring program you were describing to me yesterday."

It takes a couple of seconds before I say "Oops," which brings nervous laughter around the room.

Julie catches me on the way out, puffy cheeks flushing. "I'm so, so sorry. I don't know what to say."

"There's nothing good to say. I knew people would find out. I just hoped it wouldn't happen this soon. Sorry I didn't tell you."

Up ahead, Dean Louise Trapano, *baby dean* as Nemworth calls her, is moving fast in our direction, dodging students with surprising agility.

"Emily," she says buoyantly. "May I speak with you in my office?"

"Right now?"

"If you don't mind."

"I only have a few minutes before Torts."

I follow her, thinking Lucas was right—as usual. I should have changed my name. Why don't I listen to him more? He asks the same question, frequently.

I sit across from the dean in an upholstered floral chair. With her perky personality, heart-shaped face and shiny brown hair in a ponytail, she really does seem young to be running a law school.

Adjusting her hip blue glasses, "Emily, I don't know if you're aware that news of your background has spread through the law school."

"I'm aware."

"I want to assure you we have treated your history as confidential, but we all expected the news would get out eventually. I assume you did too." Her eyes plead with me not to blame her.

I'm tempted to get on her about the admissions office leaking my LSAT score to Henley, but let it go. "I did expect it. I just hoped it would take longer, so people could get to know me as someone more than *the missing Calby girl.*"

"They still can and will. In the meantime, let me know if there's anything I can do to help. We're all thrilled you chose to attend the First Coast College of Law and we support you one-hundred percent. I'm sure that goes for your peers as well."

It was a nice speech and she meant it sincerely, but as soon as I leave, I run into Dale Olson. My supportive peer says, "Is that how you got into law school? With your sad personal story?"

"You're an asshole," I say and keep walking.

I'm in a foul mood entering Torts class. People don't stop talking this time. Worse. They whisper.

The tort of the day is *assault*. The case is another old one. *Western Union v. Hill*, from Alabama in 1933. Professor LeMoy calls on Lyla Barrett to state the case. I like her. A nontraditional student, older with three kids. Western Union was supposed to fix the clock where the plaintiff's wife worked, but didn't do it.

"The plaintiff's wife went to Western Union to complain," Lyla explains. "She asked the man working there, a Mr. Sapp, why he hadn't sent someone to fix her clock. Sapp said, *If you will come back here and let me love and pet you, I will fix your clock.*" Scattered laughs. "Then he reached out and tried to grab her. The court found this to be an assault."

"Who can tell me the most important takeaway from this case?"

I shoot my hand in the air. LeMoy seems surprised.

"Emily?" she says. Most of the professors use surnames. LeMoy and Professor Stafford are the exceptions. She's never called on me, but knew my name without hesitating. Word has spread.

I look directly at Olson, waving his hand as always. "The most important takeaway of the case is that men are assholes."

Some women laugh and some men boo and hiss, although the longhaired guy across the room nods along. He wears a different band t-shirt every day. Today it's Phish.

"Sapp was a typical man, trying to exploit the plaintiff's wife when all she wanted to do was get her clock fixed."

"O-kay," LeMoy says, measuring her words. "How does that support your much broader proposition?"

"The case is representative of the fact that men commit the vast majority of sexual assaults and other violent acts in our country. Think about it. Women make up half the population, but men commit more than ninety-five percent of all homicides. How many female mass shooters can anyone name? Who's led us into war after war after war? *Men*. Always."

She holds up a hand to slow me down, but I can't stop. I seriously need to consider having my mouth sewed shut. "Men have been subjugating women since the beginning of time. Look at this case. The woman was the victim, but Alabama law didn't even let her bring her own lawsuit. Her husband had to bring it."

Olson gives up on waiting to be called on. "Look who's labeling all men as murderers—the killer herself."

Afraid of what I might do, I gather my stuff and leave. Hurrying to the restroom, I lock myself in a stall and rest my head against the wall. All this time, all those hours of trauma therapy, and I'm still a runaway train.

Yes, there were triggers. Being outed and Olson saying what he did right before class. But all we can control are our own actions. Why can't I? I cry in complete silence, a talent I mastered long ago.

* * *

I join Julie for lunch at our picnic table in the breezeway. She's devouring a Big Mac and fries. I just pick at a bowl of quinoa and diced sweet potatoes.

"You okay?" she says.

"Not really," I say, all too aware of the glances and whispers around us. "My big mouth just made me the law school freak-show. You wouldn't believe the trouble it's gotten me into."

"Well, everything you said was true. You probably just should have left out the part about ..."

"Men being assholes?"

"Yeah, that," she says. She laughs and apologizes. "It was pretty funny if you think about it. Definitely one of those 'memorable law school moments' they talk about."

"The thing is, I don't even think that. My best friend in the whole world is a man and he's, like, perfect." If you don't count being a former drug dealer, document forger and occasional ruthless killer.

"Lucas?"

"Yeah."

"You talk about him a lot. Is he your boyfriend?"

"More like a dad. I've only had one boyfriend." A picture of Ben Breyer and his dreamy eyelashes back at the Pochachant detention center resurrects itself. "He dumped me. How about you? What's your situation?"

"I have a girlfriend. Addie. She's a medical student in Atlanta."

"Perfect! Lawyer and doctor. You'll have everything covered."

"If I don't flunk out."

"Hey, that reminds me of something I wanted to ask you. Would you be interested in forming a study group?"

"With who?"

"Me. The Georgia girls."

She slumps. "I take it Henley's group rejected me."

"Who needs them?"

"Are you sure you want to be in a study group with the *dumb girl*?"

"Quit saying stuff like that. Of course I'm sure."

"Well, in that case, yeah!"

6

I TAKE a different route home to avoid the gym. Walking always clears my head. I come to two decisions. First, flip my schedule and work out in the afternoon. I'll get extra sleep and hopefully Greg won't be there. Second, write an apology for my outburst in class. I'm stuck with those people—or they're stuck with me—for an entire year. We all take the same classes.

My first thought entering the dingy Seaside lobby is *palm tree. You moved it inside.* Silly, but one less thing to worry about.

My mailbox door is open. I'm complaining to the landlord in the morning.

Just more junk ... but not so fast. Sandwiched between glossy flyers for timeshare units and cemetery plots is a card from Lucas! Something to smile about. And I do, until I notice something else, resting at the bottom. A chocolate kiss wrapped in red foil sitting on top of a yellow sticky note. In block printing, the note says, *WELCOME TO THE NEIGHBORHOOD!*

Who would leave that? Is it even legal to go into someone's mailbox?

I head up the stairs and take the third-floor exit, tracking down apartment 312.

A whirring from inside, like a coffee grinder or power tool. I knock. The sound stops and restarts. I knock louder. It stops again. The sound of things being moved around before the door cracks open with the chain lock attached. Matt Jurado peeks out.

"Hi Matt," I say. "I'm Emily. We met in the lobby yesterday."

"Sure, I remember. What's up?"

Why is he keeping the chain on? "I have a question. Did you happen to leave a chocolate kiss in my mailbox with a note? I'm just asking because you saw my mailbox and knew the lock was broken."

"Are you accusing me of something?"

"Accusing? No, no." *Yes, yes.* "I just wanted to thank whoever did it because it was such a nice gesture." *It's creepy.*

"Well, it wasn't me. Maybe it was your neighbor across the hall."

"I doubt it. He doesn't seem very friendly. What's his name?"

"Lyle Gabberman. Total prick. Hey, I'm in the middle of something. Gotta go."

He closes the door before I can say goodbye.

Back on my floor, I wonder about Lyle Gabberman. He obviously knows which apartment I live in, but I don't see him leaving welcome notes and chocolate kisses.

Toby is waiting outside my door. "Hey, buddy. I know what you want. Wait here."

He follows me in. I open a pack of tuna and fork some into a bowl before tearing into Lucas's card. *Thinking of You* ... except the words are farts coming out of a unicorn's butt. Only Lucas.

Em — Hope you liking law school. Miss you. Lucas.

Aw, that's the equivalent of a love sonnet coming from him. I attach it to my refrigerator door with a pink flip flop magnet, put Toby outside and head for the shower to wash off the baked sweat from this morning's workout.

With so much homework, there's no time to cook. I make a protein shake, adding a banana and strawberries. The chocolate kiss and sticky note stare at me from the counter. I toss them in the trash.

It's going to be another too-late night. Property tops the list of assignments. The first case is *Armory v. Delamirie,* from 1722.

What is the point of making us read three-hundred-year-old cases? Armory was a chimney sweep who found a ring while cleaning a chimney ...

My attention strays to the trashcan. Where do you even get red-foiled kisses this time of year? The only time I've seen them is at Christmas. Red. Blood. My automatic association. And the note, why didn't the person sign it? Maybe I should save them, just in case.

In case of what? *You are out of your effing mind. Study.*

Four hours later I call it a night, shutting down my computer and picking up my phone to call Lucas before remembering the apology. I get out a pen and legal pad.

> *Good morning. I asked for Professor LeMoy's permission to ...*

I change LeMoy to Owusua. This can't wait until Friday. I want to get it over with. I'll apologize to Professor LeMoy in person.

> *I asked Professor Owusua's permission to address you this morning. I want to apologize for what I said in Torts yesterday. Not the part about women being subjugated by men because that's a fact ...*

Don't be defensive. I cross out the whole thing. I think back to the lessons I learned during my trial. *Be yourself. Connect emotionally. Admit fear.* They worked there. Everything will be more real if I don't read it. I tear up the sheet and call Lucas.

"Lucas! It's me, Emily."

"No shit."

"Haha. I *knew* you'd say that. That's why I said it. How are you?"

"Fine."

For Lucas to send a card saying he misses me means he must be lonely. Time to quit thinking only about myself. All we've talked about since I got here is me. "I got your card today! I *love* it. Thank you!"

"You welcome."

"So how are you? Give me some details. I'm sick of talking about me. What did you do today?"

"Went to the range."

"Shooting range?"

"Golf."

"You're learning golf? Whoa, you really are getting old, no offense. How'd you do?"

"I broke my damn club."

"Really? Wow, you must have really smashed that ball."

"I broke it over my leg 'cause I kept missing the damn ball."

"*Bwah.* Aren't you the person always lecturing me to control myself?"

"Yeah, well."

"What else is new?"

"Kiona's coming to visit this weekend."

"Good! Be sure to buy her flowers or something. And give her a humongous hug and kiss from me. What are you guys going to do?"

"Nothing special. Go to the gym, hang out."

"You should take her somewhere nice, a fancy restaurant, maybe a show at the Orpheum."

"We'll see."

"What else is new?"

"James is coming to town in a couple weeks."

"I wish I could see both of them. How's he doing?" James is a genius computer hacker from the hood who Lucas took under his wing, sort of like he did me. James got tech mentoring and went off to Stanford while Lucas taught me how to kill.

"Real good. My little man is now a cybersecurity analyst in Silicon Valley."

"James went *legal*?"

"Hundred percent. Just started last week. No more high-tech assistance for any of our nefarious activities."

"That's a huge loss, but a good thing. I know you're proud of him."

"Proud of you too."

"Thanks, Lucas." I wonder if he has any idea how important that is to me.

"So what's new with you?"

I'm standing over my trash can staring at the crumpled sticky note and chocolate kiss. *Don't say a word.* "Actually, I do have some news. Bad. I got outed today."

"Don't surprise me."

"I know. I should have been better prepared, like you told me. I guess I just didn't want to think about it."

"How'd you handle it?"

"I'll give you three guesses. One, I reacted calmly and professionally. Two, I—"

"You blew up at someone, didn't you?"

"You're so smart, Lucas! It only took one guess and I didn't even finish giving you the options."

"Don't try to flatter me. Who'd you go off on this time? Lemme guess, since I'm so smart. A student?"

"Worse."

"Teacher?"

"Worse ... my entire class."

7

"GOOD MORNING, everyone. First, I want to thank Professor Owusua for allowing me to address you." I didn't have to explain to her why. Gossip spreads like wildfire in law school.

It sure is a different view from up here. I'm standing at the lectern. Tiered rows of expectant faces surround me in a semicircle. I'm glad I decided to change clothes at the last minute, into a gray suit from my usual double tees and jeans. I also ditched the glasses for contacts. No point in a disguise anymore.

"I want to apologize for what I said yesterday in Torts class and explain why I said it. First, I want to make it clear that I do not think all men are, um, a-holes. Except for my mom, the most important people in my life have been men."

My dad and Lucas.

"And I shouldn't have used profanity in class. So why did I do it? I think it was because having my past outed triggered a lot of bad memories I try hard to shut out."

I omit that five minutes before class, asshole Dale Olson confronted me in the hall and suggested I only got into law school because my family was murdered.

"I'm sure a lot of you have Googled me by now. I don't blame you. I would do the same thing. Let's face it, my life is a juicy story. And I'm not stupid. I knew this would happen ... I–I just wasn't ready for it.

"I wanted to be plain old Emily, a new law student trying to do her best. I know I can come across cold or rude sometimes. It's because I've had to build walls around me, as a coping mechanism, but I'm going to try harder not to be like that. Again, I'm very sorry for my words and for disrupting class."

I thank Professor Owusua and ascend the aisle back to my seat, surprised to hear some people clapping.

* * *

I'm lost in thought on my way to Legal Writing when a loud bass-y voice attacks me from behind. "Welcome to the neighborhood!"

The sticky note. I whirl, tensed for a fight. It's a black guy with a goatee wearing a white dress shirt and red bowtie.

"What did you just say?" Maybe I imagined it.

"Welcome to the neighborhood," he repeats, pointing to a banner draping a folding table. Gold letters over a blue background say, *The Neighborhood Legal Clinic.*

"I'm Thomas Acedyo, president of The Neighorhood Legal Clinic. We're a student organization dedicated to providing civil legal assistance to low-income people. We also sponsor lunchtime presentations on legal issues that disproportionately affect diverse communities."

"That's cool," I say, embarrassed by my initial reaction. "I'm Emily Calby. Sounds like a really good organization. I'm just a one-L though."

"We welcome everyone. Take this brochure and look it over. See if it's something that interests you."

"Okay. Thanks."

We spend Legal Writing learning about case precedent. I got a big head start on it in the hidden law library I discovered at the Pochachant detention center four years ago.

"Remember," Bryce Stafford says. "When you're looking for relevant cases, don't get hung up on trying to find a case with identical facts. That can happen, but usually doesn't. Focus on cases that stand for the same *legal principle* you want to advance."

That exact epiphany was my breakthrough in helping Ben Breyer, my prison boyfriend (for about five seconds, haha) get habeas corpus relief from his illegal confession.

"Looks like our time is up," Stafford says. "Take care and I'll see you all next week."

I'm gathering my stuff when he asks if I have a minute to talk. He waits for the room to clear. "I heard what happened, and that you were pretty upset," he says. "I can't even begin to imagine what that feels like."

"Not great. I can't believe how fast news travels here."

"Law school gossip is worse than high school," he says.

I have to take his word for it. I earned my GED in prison.

"With everyone stuck in the same classes with the same people in the same rooms every day, the world of a law student shrinks to the size of a marble and the marble is solid law school. If it helps, the attention will probably die down quickly. They'll find something new to latch onto."

I puff my cheeks. "I hope so."

"I have a confession. I already knew who you were. I remember reading the New York Times article that dissected how you represented yourself in your trial. I was only a year out of law school. It really inspired me."

I give him a doubting look.

"No joke. You overcame a stacked deck against an unethical prosecutor and won. It re-enforced my belief in the justice system."

"For real? Wow, thanks."

"Any idea what kind of law you want to practice when you graduate? There's no reason you should. Most students don't have a clue. I wasted a year at a stuffy corporate firm before figuring out I wanted to go it alone."

"I know exactly what kind. *Victim Law.*"

"Interesting. I've never heard of that as a specialty. Any particular kind of victim?"

"Almost any kind, I guess. Anyone who's been preyed on but has no power to fight back. You inspired me too. Before I got here I read an article about you representing the exploited Haitian farmworkers. One of them said you gave them a voice. That's what I want to do. That's why I'm here."

He rubs his baby-smooth chin. I couldn't find his age online. From his bio, I'm guessing around thirty.

"Well, you just made my decision easy. I'm looking to hire a law clerk. Ten hours a week, mostly research. The pay is only fifteen bucks an hour, but that's about all I can afford. The bad part about *victim law* is that most victims don't have the money to pay a lawyer."

"You're offering me a job? Seriously?"

"I am. But think about it first. I don't want it to take away from your studies. Grades matter in law school. I don't usually hire one-Ls, but you're an ... unusual case."

Unusual case. Haha, that's me in a nutshell. "Okay, I thought about it. Yes!"

* * *

I'm on cloud nine heading to the gym. The class apology was a good decision, one of my few. Some classmates came up and introduced themselves during the day, including the guy with the ponytail and band t-shirts.

His name is Russell. Today's shirt was Pink Floyd. He agreed with every word I said, even the a-hole remark. Said his mom and three sisters raised him after their dad abandoned the family.

But what really has me floating is my first real legal job. And with Bryce Stafford! I can't wait to tell Lucas.

I peek in the windows of the gym. No sign of Greg. I'm sure he's harmless. I just don't want to deal with it. I jump into intervals, concentrating on plotting out a new schedule that accommodates a ten-hour-a-week job. I need to be more efficient.

I'm grunting through lunges with twenty-five pound dumbbells in my hands, Sam and Dave singing *Hold On, I'm Coming* in my earbuds, when a tap on the shoulder makes me drop the dumbbells, barely missing my feet before they bounce off the blue mat.

It's Greg. I pull out the earbuds.

"Hi, Emily."

"You startled me. Please don't sneak up on me like that."

"I wasn't *sneaking*. I just wanted to apologize for whatever it is I did that's making you try to avoid me."

Good grief. "I'm not trying to avoid you," I lie. "I had to change my workout schedule because of school." Why am I even having to explain?

"Whatever," he says and walks away.

Whatever is right.

* * *

Mopping sweat with my sleeve, I enter the Seaside Apartments, not surprised to find my mailbox lock is still broken. I called the landlord this morning: *Regal Estates Property Management*. I got sent to voicemail where I left a snotty law student message about how *Regal* is going to meet *Legal* if they don't fix my mailbox.

Today, it's empty except for my first electric bill. I guess that makes me an official adult, except not really because I'm still sponging off Lucas.

I reach my apartment thinking about Bryce Stafford. I *knew* my starfish would bring me luck. I kiss my fingers and reach for it, searching for my keys.

I know something's wrong as soon as my fingertips tap wood instead of prickly calcium carbonate spines.

WTF? My starfish is missing two of its limbs! It looks like an inverted Y, like someone chopped the arms off a stick figure. It was fine when I left.

This is getting weird. The palm tree, the chocolate kiss, now this. I start hyperventilating. *Stop. Breathe.* Be logical.

I slammed the door when I ran out this morning. Dried starfish are brittle, too fragile for front doors. The arms broke off and I was in too much of a rush to notice. That's all. I'll find them and glue it back together.

But there are no starfish arms. Not around the door, not down the hall, not anywhere on the fourth floor. I go inside, lock the door and text Lucas.

Need to talk to you!!!

* * *

An hour passes before Lucas's name pops up on my phone. I'm deep into my Contracts assignment, having second thoughts about my text. He's going to think I'm *PTSD'ing* on him. That's what he calls it. I'm thinking the same thing.

"Hi, Lucas," I say cheerily.

"What's going on?" he says. "I just saw your message. I'm at Max's working out."

"Not much. Just studying."

"Not much? You said you needed to talk to me with three exclamation points."

"Well, you know me. I tend to overuse them."

"You're lying. What's happening?"

"No big deal."

"Tell me."

"Okay. Well, *first* I want to emphasize I'm not saying anything as a fact. Just as a possibility, that's all I'm saying."

"You ain't saying nothing. Possibility of what?"

"That I'm being stalked."

"By who?"

"I'm not sure. Again, probably no one ... um, maybe someone in my building."

"I ain't got time for twenty questions. I gotta finish my workout and pick Kiona up at the airport."

I tell him about the palm tree and chocolate kiss and sticky note. "And remember the starfish we bought at the shell shop? I hung it on my front door and when I got home today, two of its arms were missing."

"What else?"

"Um, that's all."

"That's it? Ain't nothin'."

"I know ... I just have a bad feeling."

His voice softens. "Em, you always got that feeling. It's the trauma. You know that. And we know it's been getting worse lately, right?"

"Yeah. You're probably right. I mean, I'm sure you're right. Sorry to bother you with it."

"Ain't no bother. Call whenever you want."

"Thanks, Lucas. Talking to you always calms me down."

"Glad to hear it."

"I have a question though. Could you loan me the money to buy a gun?"

I visualize the half shoulder-roll that goes with his snort. "You already know the answer. We have an agreement. No weapons."

"Just for self-defense."

"You don't need no gun."

"Why not? You have like twenty."

"'Cause you don't live in South Memphis. Your biggest worry is gettin' mugged by a senior citizen. And in case you forgot, the last time you had a gun, you got arrested. Think about it. If someone wanted to stalk you, why go through all the trouble of moving plants and breaking starfishes?"

"Valid point. Okay, no gun."

"Good. See? You're making progress. Being reasonable."

"Thanks. How about just a new neck knife? I miss my old one."

"*No* weapons. Besides, you already a deadly weapon. Pity the poor fool that gets in Emily Calby's way."

"Less and less every day. All I do here is cardio and weights. *Lame-o.*"

"Tell you what, I'll send you a door camera."

He's not going to budge. "Okay. I should get back to studying. I still have a lot for tonight. Wait, I almost forgot! I have good news too. I got a job as a law clerk doing research for one of my professors. He has his own law firm. I'm really excited about it."

"How much it pay?"

"Fifteen dollars an hour."

"That's it? My last lawyer charged three hundred dollars an hour."

I laugh. "Maybe someday. It's only my fourth day of law school."

"Well, congratulations. I gotta run."

"Be sure to do something fun this weekend with Kiona."

"What about you?"

"Studying, what else? But at the beach!"

"Don't forget the sunscreen, *Pinkie*."

My family nickname when I was little because my pale skin fried so easily in the sun. "I never should have told you that."

"Enjoy the beach, and remember. You can change your mind and come home any time."

"You know me better than that. I never run from trouble."

"That's what I'm afraid of. You run straight into it."

8

FRIDAY! FINALLY! I can't believe it's only been one week of law school. Seems like a month. I am *so* excited for the weekend. Turns out Julie is a kindred beach bum. We decided to hold our study group session on the sand.

It's seven-thirty and I'm on my apology tour of the faculty wing. First up, Professor LeMoy. She surprised me by laughing off my outburst in Torts.

"Believe me, I wish we had more passionate dialogue about controversial issues in law school. Unfortunately, we've evolved to the point where most law students are afraid to open their mouths and ..." She turns up her palm.

"Put both feet in it?"

"I was going to say speak their mind. There's so much more to a legal education than rules. Ha, listen to me, only forty and already sounding like Nemworth."

"What's he really like? Is he as mean as he acts?"

"Nah, just old school. He's actually a sweetheart deep down inside. He was one of my strongest advocates when I was up for tenure. Being stern and abrupt are his trademarks, although he's been grumpier since his wife passed away from cancer two years ago. They were married for more than fifty years. I've actually been worried about him ... but I shouldn't be telling you this. Shoo, shoo."

She waves me out and I head to Nemworth's office, finding him in the same position at his desk, bent over a book under the brass lamp, sucking on his unlit pipe.

"Professor Nemworth, do you have a quick minute?"

"Come in," he grunts.

I plop down in the same worn leather chair without waiting to be ordered to sit. "I came to apologize about our last Contracts class."

He looks up. I swear I'm going to find a way to steal his glasses and clean them.

"You need to study harder."

"Um, no, that's not it. I didn't give a wrong answer and I'm already studying very hard."

"Then why are you here?"

"I wanted to apologize for what I said in class on Wednesday when you called on me."

"About what? Who are you?"

Seriously? "Emily. Emily Calby?"

"Ah, yes. Miss Colby."

"*Cal*by."

"Calby. Indeed. I called on you to explain the faculty mentoring program to the students. I was quite rude to you when you came to inquire about it. After giving it some thought, I concluded baby dean might actually have had a decent idea. Better new students get advice from someone who knows what the hell they're talking about than from upper-level nitwits."

"Yes, sir. I thought you were asking about something else and wanted to apologize for catching you by surprise with my answer."

"What was so surprising about your answer?"

"Well, you know, blurting out about ... you know, the attack on my family and all."

"Your family was attacked?"

I'm not sure what to say. "Yes, sir. Remember? I sort of outlined it for the class."

"I can't hear a damn thing in that room. The acoustics are

terrible. If the administration had any sense, we'd sue the architects. What attacked your family?"

"Um, two men."

Nothing.

"The *Calby Murders?* Only survivor? Latest law school news?" None of it seems to register.

"Murder?"

I give up. "Yes, sir. Anyway, sorry I bothered you." I get up to leave.

"Calby Murders," he murmurs. "Dilfer County, Georgia. Years ago. A mother and a young girl were killed in a home invasion. The goddamned media kept it in the news for months."

He's gazing at the ceiling like Lucas. "An older girl got away. I recall she was arrested in Arkansas and extradited to stand trial for murder. A most unusual case."

"So you *did* know."

"My memory comes and goes lately. I believe the girl ended up representing herself in court. Yes, indeed. A most unusual case."

"Yes, sir. It was." His look is far away. "I was that girl. I mean, I *am* that girl."

Awkward seconds tick by before, "You're *that* Emily Calby?"

* * *

Classes went smoothly for a change. No one called on me and I kept my mouth shut. I approached Professor LeMoy after Torts while she was erasing the whiteboard.

"Professor?"

"Hi, Emily."

"I enjoyed class. You always make it interesting and fun. Professor Nemworth said you can't learn law and enjoy class at the same time, but I told him I disagree."

"Good for you."

"Actually, I have a question about him. I went to see him after I talked to you this morning. You said you were worried about him. Is it because his memory isn't too good?"

"Let's just say I wish his wife were still here to look after him."

"Does he have any children?"

"Unfortunately, no."

"Well, at least he has that one friend. She seems to like him a lot."

She looks surprised. "What friend is that?"

"He called her Christina. Short with dark hair. She's young. She came to his office the other day while I was there."

"Probably a student."

"I think she's more than that. She blew him a kiss when she left and said she'd see him later that night."

"Really. That's interesting. I'm obviously out of the loop. I'm going to have to start coming to you for my law school news. Maybe he has relatives I don't know about."

"Maybe," I say.

9

CRISP WHITE sand. Emerald water reflecting the sun, so bright I have to squint even through my sunglasses. Sandpipers racing in and out with the tide. *This* is why I'm here. *Hold onto the moment. Capture the good things.* More advice from Dr. Laura, my therapist.

Julie and I are stationed under the meager shade of two palm trees. We stopped on the way and bought a couple of cheap folding chairs. We've been here three hours.

She looks cute in a ruffled pink bikini that reveals mounds of skin white as snow. On her shoulder is the sweetest tattoo I've ever seen, Tinkerbell tripping across stars.

I, of course, am dressed in a very un-sexy navy blue unitard that reaches my knees, covering the *NO ONE* scar I carved in my thigh when the FBI put me in the hospital at age thirteen. Still legible after all these years.

I'd wear it even without the scar. To say I don't like to feel exposed is an understatement. Who else wears double shirts and long pants year round?

Sipping iced tea, I dig my toes into the warm sand and quiz Julie about what we learned in our first week of Torts. A seagull stands guard a few feet away in case food makes an appearance.

"Battery," I say. "Name the three elements."

"A volitional act, intended to cause a harmful or offensive bodily contact, and such a contact results, either directly or indirectly."

"Perfect!"

"I always thought battery was a crime. Who knew it was also a tort?"

"Who even knew what a tort was until a week ago? It's amazing how much we're learning." I close my computer. "I think that brings us up to date."

"Nemworth would disagree."

"*Study harder,*" we synchronize and bust up.

"Seriously," I say. "We make good study partners. You're plenty smart. Don't let anybody make you doubt it."

"Thanks," Julie says. "I appreciate that. I don't have a lot of confidence."

"Any particular reason?"

"Probably lots of them. I'm fat for one thing."

"You are not fat."

"You don't have to lie. My own parents like my skinny little sister better than me. Her pictures are all over the house. Mine are hidden in the corner."

"Oh, come on."

She ends the discussion, saying, "Lookee yonder. Here come a couple of cute guys for you."

Frat-boy types, weaving along the shoreline, drinking from red plastic cups and laughing too loud. One is a blond surfer-dude. The other guy is darker, with a chest of thick fur.

"Thanks, but *not* my type," I say.

"What is your type?"

"Not *that*."

"Objection, Your Honor. Unresponsive to the question."

I laugh. "Honestly, I'm not sure I have a type." It's true. Maybe having a type requires more relationship experience than a three-week flirtation with a boy locked in a separate prison unit. I've been isolated with Lucas since I was twelve.

"You must have some idea what you like."

"Well, if I *had* to choose I'd say maybe someone like ... Professor Stafford." I reach out and squeeze her arm. "*Don't* repeat that."

"*Woo-ooh. Ms. Calby* is crushing on the teacher."

I cover up my embarrassment with an awkward laugh while staying hyperaware of each step the frat boys take. They've shifted direction, putting them on a collision course with us.

"This is going to be annoying," I mutter as they get close.

"What's up, my lady?" surfer-dude says.

"Not much," I say.

"What-choo studying there?"

"Books." They're both staring at me. Neither of them has glanced at Julie, which irritates me. They don't know she's gay.

He laughs to the furry guy like they just stumbled onto the World's Dumbest Blonde. "We can see that. What kind of books?"

"Thick ones." Empirical studies show that if you act friendly to men, even if you're just trying to be polite, their primordial brains interpret it as interest.

"I'm Colton, this here is Serge. What's your name?"

"Thelma," I say.

"Thelma what?" he says, still acting like Julie doesn't exist.

"Just Thelma. Like Cher or Beyoncé. And this here is ..."

"Louise," Julie chortles.

"Come on, what's your real name?"

"Sorry. National secret. I'm working undercover."

"How about this? If I can guess what state you're from, you tell me your name."

"Alright. One guess. And if you guess wrong, you turn and quickly walk away."

He blurts, "Tennessee."

Startled, "What?"

Julie does a face-palm.

"How did you know that?"

He grins and raises his cup like a trophy. "Because looking around here, you're the only ten I see."

Julie groans. "Dude, that is the world's lamest pick-up line."

He laughs. "What would a whale like you know about pick-up lines? You probably never even heard one."

I spring to my feet. "Leave. Now."

Colton slaps Serge on the back and takes a slurp from his cup. "Uh-oh, I think I insulted her and her supersized friend."

I reach out and snatch his wrist, slipping my other hand under his armpit and twisting his arm out. A classic arm bar that drives him face-first into the sand. Easy, if you've been practicing it since when you should have been in middle school. I did it without thinking.

Without thinking. Of course. Now I'm thinking, too late. With my knee on Colton's spine and his arm locked backward at a ninety-degree angle, I'm thinking about how I just broke my no violence pledge to Lucas. I gave him my word. But I'm in too deep to stop now.

Colton's cursing, "Get the fuck off me."

Serge stands by rocking on his heels, driving them deeper into the sand, eyebrows knitted like mating caterpillars, trying to make a decision. I shake my head and mouth, *Not worth it.*

"So, *Colton,*" I say, eyes scanning around me. At least we picked an empty spot. "You have three seconds to apologize to my friend for being an insulting prick."

"Shove it."

I give a little wrench and he howls.

"Ah, okay. I'm sorry, *bitch.*"

"I don't mean to be picky, but that didn't sound completely sincere. Now you have to apologize to me too." I give another twist and his entire body melts into the sand.

"Alright. I'm sorry, I'm sorry."

"To both of us."

"To both of you."

I let go, stand up and back away. He scrambles to his feet looking like a sand candle. I smile and wave. "Bye, Colton. Have a nice day."

He stumbles away rubbing his shoulder and cursing at Serge for not helping. "She's a girl!" Serge says. "What was I supposed to do?"

"*That* is no girl."

I return to my chair, amped up, trying to contain my trembling. Not only did I break my word to Lucas, the whole scene was eerily reminiscent of the episode at the gas station on my sixteenth birthday, when I unnecessarily escalated a confrontation with a rude biker and ended up in prison fighting for my life.

Julie looks at me and deadpans, "Battery. A volitional act, intended to cause a harmful or offensive bodily contact, and such a contact results."

It's funny and I force a smile, but my insides are churning.

She pats my knee. "Just so you know, you don't need to stand up for me. I can take care of myself."

"I know. It just gets my back up when people insult my friends."

"I appreciate it."

My slowing pulse frees up space in my heart for shame. How am I going to tell Lucas?

"Do you want to grab lunch?" Julie says.

Even with two layers of sunblock, I'm the color of a salmon. *Pinkie*. "Sure."

I drive us in my red Kia to a dive seafood restaurant I heard about. Calo's. A green shack with flaking paint and torn screens over the open windows. Grimy fans churn lazily on the ceiling. Our table is so sticky I'm surprised it doesn't catch the flies that land on it.

"The special is mango tilapia," Julie says, reading from a stained paper menu. "That sounds good."

"It does but I'm allergic to mangoes." When I was little, my family took a beach trip to Panama City. I bit into a mango and almost went into anaphylaxis. I go with a broiled grouper sandwich, the fish so fresh it falls apart in my mouth.

"Julie, can I ask you something? Why didn't you seem shocked when all that happened at the beach?"

"Because I already knew you were a bad-ass. I read all about your case online. Sorry, couldn't resist. Killing a man with a knife? I knew from the start that this girl isn't going to take shit from any *Colton*."

A doleful shake of the head. "I hate that everyone thinks they know me, just from the internet."

"Cheer up," she says. "There are a lot worse things to be known as than a bad-ass. You could be known as a fat-ass."

I open my mouth, but force it shut.

We stay at the restaurant laughing and gabbing for more than an hour. It makes me realize how starved I've been for a friend.

As Julie's second piece of key lime pie disappears, I can't help wonder how much of her self-esteem is tied up in body image. It has such a powerful impact, especially on girls. I've only known her a week and she's already mentioned her weight several times. Maybe she's dysmorphic.

Here I go again. *It's none of your effing business, Emily.*

10

AFTER THREE weeks of much needed normalcy, the craziest thing happened. I can't decide if I'm more embarrassed or relieved. I came home after a long day of school followed by a two-hour workout and wimped out on taking the stairs. In the elevator was a woman with a vacuum cleaner, a bucket of cleaning supplies and a scowl etched in the crevices of her face.

She turned out to be the housekeeper for the Seaside Apartments. I saw an opening and took it, politely asking if she happened to remember moving a palm tree in a yellow ceramic planter on the fourth floor.

"I got to move every damn thing you people leave out there so I can vacuum. I know you," she said, wagging a finger. "Beach girl. Had the starfish on the door."

"Yes! Do you know anything about that? My starfish?"

"I know my aching back had to pick up the pieces when it fell apart. You people need to learn to take care of your own front yards."

So much for my mystery stalker. That left only the chocolate kiss and sticky note, a harmless greeting. Lucas laughed his butt off when I told him about it. "Good thing I didn't let you get that gun," he said. "Might of shot the poor cleaning woman."

Still, I went ahead and installed the door camera he ordered for me. It's made for apartments. Attaches to the peephole. The only alerts I get are Lyle Gabberman coming or going or Toby the cat taking his daily stroll.

I haven't found the right moment to tell Lucas about my fracas on the beach, which is another way of saying I've been too chicken. I've rehearsed trying to frame it as self-defense, but it's impossible to do without lying. I put surfer-dude down because he insulted Julie, pure and simple.

Law school's settled into a routine after a month. Everyone's more comfortable because we know the expectations. Getting called on isn't as terrifying. The professors don't care if you give a wrong answer as long you're not unprepared. Nemworth is the exception. He seems to get crankier by the week.

We took our first test last week, a *Bluebook* quiz in Legal Writing. Julie and I studied really hard for it. Everyone's holding their breath for the results.

One day I was looking for a quiet place to study and accidentally stumbled into a room where Henley Oliver's study group was meeting. All guys, of course.

"Emily," Henley said brightly.

"Excuse me," Dale Olson said. "This room is reserved for asshole men."

Henley frowned and shook his head.

I laughed. "You said it, not me."

Julie and I have bonded, even had a sleepover study night last weekend at my apartment. I made an awesome spinach salad with apples and pears, pecans, goat cheese and vinaigrette dressing. The look on her face when I told her we were having salad for dinner was classic, but she really liked it. Even asked for the recipe.

Ms. Buttinski used that as an opening to extoll the benefits of a healthy diet. Then we made popcorn and watched The Paper Chase, a classic movie about the first year of law school. The ornery Professor Kingsfield reminded me so much of Nemworth. The next morning we took a long walk, me gushing about the value of exercise for reducing stress.

My job with Bryce Stafford hasn't been as spectacular as I imagined because all my work is done at home on my computer.

I was hoping to work side by side with him at his law office. Julie was right. I think I might have a crush on him. Okay, I *know* I have a crush on him.

All the professors know my name now. Even Professor Nemworth gets it right most of the time. I bought a used copy of his famous treatise on contract law and try to read a few pages every night. Almost a thousand pages of pure brilliance.

He did a turnabout on being a faculty mentor, setting aside an hour a week for his group of one-L mentees. The entire group showed up for the first session, but only three of us came to the second. The third session is about to start. I'm the only one here.

"Well, well, Miss Calby," Nemworth says. "Apparently, you're the only one of your classmates who thinks they are in need of mentoring."

"I'm glad to be here, Professor. Thank you for doing it."

Honestly, the mentoring sessions haven't been very helpful. Nemworth spends most of the time complaining about the demise of rigor in legal education. I come out of respect and because I'm getting to really like the guy. His bitching reminds me of an old white version of Lucas. Instinct tells me he has a good heart, even if he keeps it hidden, also like Lucas.

Right now, he's ranting that modern law students are snowflakes. "God forbid a professor hurts their delicate feelings by having the audacity to expect them to work."

I nod along.

"Anyway, enough about that," he says. "Miss Calby, I'm going to ask you a question and want you to feel perfectly free to say no. Do you understand?"

"Um, sure."

He rearranges himself in his chair. "I have to go into the hospital for three days. Would you by any chance be willing to check on my house while I'm gone? All you'd have to do is take in the newspaper and mail and feed my cat. I hate asking a student ..."

His contorted face makes it obvious he really, truly does hate it.

"... but there's no one else available right now. And you seem reliable."

"I'd be happy to help, Professor." And I am, although I'm wondering why his kiss-blowing friend can't do it. "I hope it's not anything serious."

"No, no. Just some tests. Of course, I insist on paying you. Would thirty dollars per day be sufficient? You only need to stop by once a day. Just be sure to leave enough food and water for the damn cat or he'll tear the place apart."

"You don't have to pay me."

He holds up a hand. "Non-negotiable."

"Alright, if you insist. Offer, acceptance and mutual consideration. I guess we have a bilateral contract."

If he thinks my joke is amusing, he doesn't show it.

"What's your cat's name?"

"Sidney. A worthless loafer, but he's been with me a long time."

I take notes as he dictates his address and some instructions. At the end he hands me a key.

"Should you give me your phone number in case I need to reach you?"

"Phone number? I'll be in the *hospital,* Miss Calby. Oh, you mean one of those," he says, pointing to the phone sticking out of my pocket. He says he doesn't own a mobile phone and never will, but gives me the name of the hospital.

"Do you need me to bring you anything while you're there?"

"No," he says curtly.

"Do you want my phone number?"

"That's not necessary."

"Okay. Well, good luck in the hospital, and don't worry about your house or Sidney. I'll take good care of them."

11

I PILOT my Kia through a pretty neighborhood of distinguished old homes and quiet tree-lined streets, stopping in front of a Spanish-style two-story with yellow stucco walls and a clay roof. I double-check the address. This is it. I figured Nemworth would live in a nice house, but the place is definitely lagging on maintenance.

The paint is blotchy and faded. Broken tiles blackened by mold lie in disarray on the roof. A natural stone walkway to the front door would be pretty except weeds have displaced most of the mortar.

I start by looking for the newspaper. The grass must be six inches high. I plow through it for ten minutes before giving up, grabbing the mail from a salt-corroded box and letting myself in. Excitement fills me as I turn the lock. Me, all alone in the brilliant Professor Edgar Nemworth's home. Little ol' Emily Calby. What will it be like?

Two steps in, I do an about face and retreat to the porch, gagging from an ammonia stench that burns my nostrils. *Gross.* Filthy cat litter.

It's dark inside. I can barely see the furniture. I hold my breath and run in, pulling back the curtains and opening windows, sneezing in a cloud of dust and cat hair.

Holding my shirts over my mouth and nose, I find the kitchen and turn on a light. Good grief. Dirty dishes fill the sink. Kitty litter and kibble are spread across the floor. The place is a complete mess.

How can the professor be living like this? I check the time. I set aside the afternoon to start my course outlines, but I can't leave his kitchen like this.

I set about cleaning. I'm scraping the biohazardous cat litter into a garbage bag when the front door opens. The last time a surprise door opened, my family was dead in an hour. I gingerly lower the garbage bag and slide a carving knife from a butcher block.

Footsteps clack across the foyer tiles. I peek and see the woman Nemworth called Christina, the kiss-blower, dressed in too-tight jeans and yellow high-heel ankle boots. I set the knife on the counter and slide into the doorway.

"Hi!"

She spins, dark eyes flashing. "Who are you?" Her thick black hair looks blown out. Glossy yellow nail polish matches her boots.

Fake smile locked in, "So sorry to startle you! I'm Emily, one of Professor Nemworth's students. You're Christina, right? I was in his office a few weeks ago when you stopped by."

"What are you doing here?"

"The professor asked me to take care of his house while he's in the hospital."

"I see. That's kind of you." She doesn't mean it. Her annoyance is obvious. "I'm a close friend of Edgar's. I stopped by to pick up something I left here."

Close friend? Effing really? Then why does he have to pay a student to look after his house when he's in the hospital?

"Then you probably knew his wife," I say. "I heard she was a wonderful woman."

"No, unfortunately. We met after she died."

"Oh, really? How did you guys meet?"

A scowl. "Edgar does not share private information with his students. Frankly, I'm very surprised he let one in his house."

"Me too. He said he couldn't find anyone else to help him."

I say it nicely but she gets the point, breaking away without a response and heading for the stairs. "Hey, since you know the professor so well, can you tell me where Sidney likes to hang out?"

"Sidney?"

"Uh, yeah. The professor's cat. I haven't seen him since I got here."

"He's around somewhere. He always is."

I fall in behind her going up the stairs. She stops. "Where the fu—. Where do you think you're going?"

"To look for Sidney. The only place I haven't looked is upstairs. The professor hired me to check on him."

We head in opposite directions on the landing. The house is huge, way too big for just Professor Nemworth. I find Sidney in a room at the end of the hall, sprawled like a manatee in the middle of a bed on a thick mat of fur. He's a big fat Persian, no wonder there's so much cat hair everywhere.

I scratch his ears. "Hi, Sidney. Guess I know where to find you now. Let's go, big boy."

Down the hall, I hear Christina going from room to room, banging doors and drawers.

Then her heels click rapidly down the stairs and the front door slams. I watch out the window as she climbs into the passenger side of a white Nissan in the driveway. A man's behind the wheel, but I can't make him out.

With two-ton Sidney draped over my arms, I return to the kitchen, sneezing again. It can't be healthy for the professor to live and breathe in here.

Need to get home and start my outlines or I'm going to be up all night, but I can at least air things out and vacuum. I'll stick to the first floor. Nemworth wouldn't want me upstairs anyway.

Sidney's happy to see a full bowl of food, until the roar of an old-fashioned canister vacuum I found in the pantry sends him waddling for dear life back up the stairs.

By the time I reach the other end of the house, my arms feel like spaghetti from going over and over the thick cat hair. Just one room left. The professor's office. He'd probably call it a study. The walls are lined with books. Aristotle, Proust, Kant. No breezy reading here.

I shut down the vacuum and plant myself in his beat-up desk chair. Probably a million great thoughts have happened right here. I imagine myself as a law professor, stalking the classroom, uttering brilliant words that students race to write down.

Perched on the corner of the desk is the same photograph of his wife he keeps at the law school, wearing the black dress and emerald necklace. The only thing in the house that's not covered in dust. The rest of the desk is a total mess. I start straightening, gathering paper clips in a pile, sweeping pipe tobacco into a waste basket.

Beneath the clutter is a large calendar pad. Today's date peeks out. Scribbled in the box is *Hospital*. More calendar boxes appear as I work. *Sidney vet. Termite inspection*. When I see *Mentor students* it strikes me that Nemworth would want to hang me for touching his desk and violating his privacy.

I start to re-messy everything the way it was when my eyes land on a calendar square from two weeks ago: *Write check for cancer treatment, $15,000.*

Cancer? He said he was going in for tests! I pick up the pace, dropping papers anywhere there's a gap.

I plunk down a greeting card. Cursive script over a bouquet of roses says, *So Glad We Met*. Already feeling guilty for invading the professor's private world, I force myself to tuck the card unopened beneath a faculty memo from Dean Trapano proposing a faculty-student picnic.

I return the vacuum cleaner to the pantry and trudge upstairs to say goodbye to Sidney. "See you tomorrow," I say. He yawns.

Out front, I search one more time for the newspaper. Still can't find it.

* * *

I spend what's left of the afternoon laboring over my Civil Procedure outline, my hardest and least favorite class. It's slow going. The material is dull and the instructor, Professor Galen Cricks, talks like he's half asleep.

Slowing me down more is the worry that Professor Nemworth has cancer ... along with a nagging question. *Who the heck is Christina?*

Something's *off*. They're close enough for her to blow kisses at him and randomly drop by his house when he's not home, but she barely remembered his cat's name and lets him live in a pigsty. Worst of all, she's apparently too busy hanging out with some man to help him while he's in the freaking hospital!

So Glad We Met. Screw privacy. I'm looking at that card tomorrow. I have a bad feeling.

Should I call the professor? He gave me the name of the hospital. He'll probably be like *Emily who?* But he did entrust his house to me and I let someone inside without permission. *Think first, act later*. I go take a shower.

Pounding on the front door brings me out grabbing for a towel. The camera app is lighting up my phone. It's Gabberman in another bathrobe, this one brown terry cloth. He must have a whole collection. I put on my own robe and wrap it tight.

Chain lock attached, I crack open the door. "Can I help you?"

"Yeah, you can help me." He stabs my door with a finger. "Get rid of that camera, or I will."

Prick, like Jurado said. "I would advise against that. Destroying personal property is both a crime and a tort."

"How about this then? I'll buy my own camera and point it at your door so I can watch your every move twenty-four seven. Would you like that?"

I'd smash it with a hammer. "No," I admit. "Look, it's nothing personal. I only got the camera because some weird things have happened to me."

"Oh, I know all about that. The crime victim of the century," he says dramatically.

"How did you know about—"

"Victim of the mysterious St. Augustine palm tree mover. He terrified the citizenry for years. They never found him."

I can't help but laugh because it's funny. "Lyle, is that what I should call you? I'm sorry. The camera has privacy zone settings. I'll figure them out and block out your door. I promise."

"You'd better," he says, and huffs back into his apartment.

I make teriyaki tofu stir fry for dinner with enough leftovers to give me extra meals during the week. They neglected to build cooking and sleeping time into the law school curriculum.

My phone beckons from the table as I eat. I can't stop picturing Professor Nemworth alone in a hospital room—with cancer. I find the number he gave me.

"Mercy Hospital. How may I direct your call?"

I ask her to connect me to the room of Edgar Nemworth. It rings eight times before he picks up.

"What is it?" he says, already annoyed.

"Hi, Professor. It's Emily!" Silence. "Emily Calby."

"Is there something wrong at the house?"

"No, sir. Everything's fine. I called because I wanted to know if you have ... um, a lawnmower."

"Lawnmower?"

"Yes, sir. Your grass is really tall. I couldn't even find the newspaper today. I thought I'd go ahead and mow it."

I expect an outburst, but he says gently, "That is far beyond the scope of your job duties, Miss Calby."

"I don't mind. It's good exercise."

"That's quite alright. I have other people who help me take care of things."

That's an opening if I ever heard one. "That reminds me, your friend Christina stopped by today while I was at your house."

"Oh?"

"She said she left something upstairs. I never would have let her in except she said you two are close friends."

"That is correct."

"She was with a man," I blurt. "He was driving the car."

"Not that it's any of your concern, but that is her brother. They live together. Is that all?"

"Yes, sir. I hope your tests are going okay."

"Fine, fine. Well, good night."

"Professor, I have one more question. Do you have ..." I choke on the word *cancer.*

"What? Do I have what?"

"Any extra food for Sidney? His bag is almost empty."

"Damn, I forgot to buy it."

"No problem. I can do it."

"I'll reimburse you, of course. And Miss Calby?"

"Yes?"

"Thank you."

12

PROFESSOR NEMWORTH is back in class on Monday, lecturing about *promissory estoppel.* After spending a month studying the essential elements of a valid contract, I'm not surprised to find out they're not always required. As I learned during my murder trial, the most reliable legal rule is that there's an exception to every rule, one reason *It depends* is the answer to most legal questions.

I can't help but look at him differently. When I got to his house Saturday, I headed straight for his study and opened the *So Glad We Met* card. The inside was even worse than I thought. *Edgar, my love for you grows deeper every day. I don't know what I would do without you.* Signed *Christina* with a big heart.

Something's fishy. Nemworth's amazing, but he's also eighty-four. Why would a woman less than half his age be interested in such an old man? It doesn't make sense.

I went by his office before class to ask about his test results, hoping he'd reveal something about his cancer, but he brushed off the question and asked if he could pay me with a check. I said that was fine and he dug a checkbook out of his top desk drawer. In shaky handwriting, he made it out to *Emily Colby,* adding thirty dollars for my cleaning and ten bucks for the cat food.

After class, I'm at my locker exchanging my Contracts book for Torts when Henley strolls up wearing his usual uniform of pressed jeans and an overly starched button-down shirt. Today's is white with red pinstripes. He looks like a candy cane.

"Hi Emily. How's it going?"

"Hey, Henley. Same as everyone, I guess. Just grinding away."

"You gave a good answer in Contracts today."

"Thanks." I volunteered when Nemworth asked a question and no one raised their hand, not even Olson.

"I've been meaning to tell you I feel really bad about the whole study group thing."

"No problem. It worked out fine. Julie and I make a great team."

"That's good. Hey, maybe you and I could get together and compare outlines sometime."

The more he expresses his determination to study with me, the madder I get at whoever told him my LSAT score. I thought I was competitive, but in law school, I've met my match.

"Isn't that what our study groups are for? I gotta run to the restroom. See you in class."

We pass a minor one-L milestone in Torts, finishing the intentional torts and shifting to negligence law. Julie and I claim our usual lunch table in the breezeway after class.

"What was Nemworth's house like?" she asks, eating a salad with grilled chicken. It's loaded with cheese, creamy dressing and croutons, but it beats a Big Mac and fries. Baby steps.

"Kind of messy, but nice."

When she presses for details, I change the subject out of respect for Nemworth. "Hey, this afternoon I'm going to a meeting of The Neighborhood Legal Clinic. Have you heard of it? It's a student organization that helps low-income people with legal problems. I think I'm going to join. Want to come?"

"I'm barely surviving as it is. Are you sure you want to take that on, especially since you're already working ten hours a week for Stafford?"

"It is a lot, but it's why I came to law school. Did you know Professor Stafford founded the organization when he was a student?"

She snickers. "Ah, that's the real reason you're joining."

I laugh with her. "*No-oo.* I really wanted to join ... but I admit that didn't hurt."

Her face pinches. "Look, I don't know how to put this delicately. Have you heard the rumor about you and him?"

"Oh, gawd. I can guess. That I'm working for him to get a good grade. But grading's anonymous. Everyone knows that." We use random assigned numbers for all our work.

"Well, that's part it." She pauses to crack her knuckles. "The other part is you two are supposedly doing it."

"Doing what? ... Omigod, that's crazy! Who's spreading that?"

"Um, everyone? Don't worry. It's just more law school gossip. It'll go away."

"But why that? Of all rumors. He's probably ten years older than me and he's my professor. What is wrong with these people?"

"Sorry to be the one to break the news. I thought you should know and didn't realize you'd get this upset."

A drawn-out leaky breath. "Can I can tell you something private?"

"Sure. I've told you everything about me."

She has, from her father's affair to her having genital warts. I've told her almost nothing about me. Same old fortress mentality.

"Okay, but this is absolutely, one-hundred percent in the vault. You want to know why it makes me so upset? ... Because I've thought about it."

"So what? No need to blush. I'm sure you're not the only one. He's cute. So, personal question. Have you ever had sex?"

The answer is no, but not for any moral or religious reason. It's because sex and violence became the same thing to me the day the two men came. I dated a guy in Memphis a few times and we made out, but I slammed on the brakes when he tried to go beyond that.

"I hereby invoke my Fifth Amendment right not to incriminate myself by sounding like a Mrs. Grundy."

"I didn't think so. There's nothing wrong with it. Hey, if I saved myself for Addie, I wouldn't have genital warts."

She rubs my shoulder. Such a good friend.

* * *

Thomas Acedyo, president of The Neighborhood Legal Clinic, stands at the front of the classroom, hands clasped, wearing what I've come to know is his standard attire of black pants with a white shirt and bow tie. It's the organization's first meeting of the school year. He just finished welcoming everyone, including the new members, a handful of one-Ls.

He says, "As you know, our mission is to expand access to civil justice for the poor." We do this, he explains, by interviewing prospective legal-aid clients and writing up summaries of their legal problems, freeing time for the legal-aid lawyers to accept more cases.

"Engraved on the Supreme Court building is *Equal Justice Under Law*, but we all know there's no equal justice in this country without a lawyer. Even the one-Ls have figured that out. No offense," he says and we all laugh.

"Legal-aid provides life support to real people with real problems that often involve the basic necessities of life." He lists healthcare, housing and employment as examples, citing a statistic that fifty percent of people seeking legal aid get turned away because there aren't enough resources.

"Think about that. Fifty percent. Even if they have strong cases."

Thomas is a good leader. He makes me want to follow.

"Which brings me to my first point. The legal-aid folks appreciate our help, but the main thing they need is money. Every dollar donated helps. As your new president, I have an idea."

He explains he wants to turn the organization's speaker series into fundraising events. "For that to work, we need topics and speakers that will attract an outside crowd, not just law students. Our first event is next month."

He asks for ideas, making a list on the whiteboard. *Climate change. Voting barriers. Educational inequality. Access to healthcare.*

A woman with a spikey haircut and nose ring says, "For what it's worth, I was a journalism student in undergrad. One of the first rules we learned was, *If it bleeds, it leads*. Sounds bad, but if we want a good crowd, just saying."

"Ah, very interesting," Thomas says. "Because one of my ideas was gun violence."

A guy across the room says, "Especially with all the attention given to mass shootings."

I raise my hand.

"Emily, you don't have to raise your hand here," Thomas says. Chuckles all around. Good-natured, not mocking.

"Mass shootings do get a lot of attention," I say. "But most gun violence happens in poor minority neighborhoods. In South Memphis, where I'm from, people get shot every night and it barely makes the news." Plagiarizing Lucas, "If they were white people, we'd call out the National Guard."

He tugs his goatee like a professor, which I could totally see him as. "*And* urban gun violence aligns with both our constituency and mission. I like it. If we go that route, we'll need to find a legal scholar on gun violence, someone interesting, someone who can inspire people to donate money. "

"Maybe we'd be better off with a regular person, instead of a scholar," I say. "Someone who's actually lived with gun violence, not just read about it in books and law journals."

"Sounds like you have someone in mind."

"I do. I know the perfect person." I describe a certain former gang leader in South Memphis who lost his brother and sister in a drive-by. "He's also been shot, more than once." I leave out he's also been a practitioner in the area.

"Is he an expert?"

"Totally." In gun-trafficking, up-close shooting strategies, obliterating serial numbers on stolen guns ...

"Is he a good speaker?"

"Well ..." Lucas doesn't talk like a legal scholar, that's for sure. He was born and raised in South Memphis and dropped out of high school in the tenth grade.

"He's an excellent motivational speaker." *Raise the knife like you fuckin' Jason and stab that piece of shit. Once you start, don't stop.*

"Do you know him well? Do you think he'd do it?"

"I know him very well. I'll bet I can talk him into it." We'll see.

* * *

"*Loo*-cus, I have a little favor to ask." I'm stretched out on my couch reading Property, computer balanced on my stomach.

He groans. "Seems like every time you need a *little favor,* blood gets spilled. If you're callin' to say you need me to pick up another body, I'm hanging up. Fair warning."

"Of course not. It's nothing like that. It's a good thing! But before I say what it is, let me tell you about all the benefits involved. First, you'll get to educate people, mostly white people, about a real-world problem they know little about. And we know what a *grayyy-ate* teacher you are."

"Don't try to butter me up."

"Second, you'll be helping low-income people get legal help, and you know how important that is."

"Spill it."

"Wait, wait. Third and best of all, we'll get to see each other!"

"Just fuckin' tell me."

I explain my grand idea to have him come to St. Augustine to make a presentation on gun violence to support The Neighborhood Legal Clinic.

"Get real. No one's gonna wanna hear a speech from a high school dropout, especially a bunch of law students."

"It's not just law students. The event's open to the community. And yes, I absolutely think people will want to hear from you, someone who's actually lived with gun violence."

"How many people we talking about?"

"Well, we're hoping for a big turnout."

"How big?"

"The auditorium holds two hundred."

"Two hundred? How much they paying me?"

"Nothing. We don't have any money. That's why we're holding the event as a fundraiser."

Pause. "I'd like to help you, but you need to get some egghead to talk."

I hear a note of self-consciousness, a slight catch in the throat. From Lucas Jackson, the strongest of the brave and the bravest of the strong. Not afraid of anything. Not death, nothing.

I've wondered about it before. Constantly pushing my education, even when we lived on the bus, making me take online courses in math and hard science. Always bragging about his *little man* James when he was at Stanford.

"Lucas, you're as smart as any egghead, and no one knows more about real-life gun violence than you. You'd really be helping a good cause. And remember, we'd get to see each other!"

He says he'll think about it, but don't get my hopes up.

13

DEAR DIARY: *All is right with my world.*

I had a diary once. It burned in the fire with everything else when the two men blew up our house. If I had one now, that's what I'd write. I'm at Bryce Stafford's law office for the first time.

It's not exactly what I expected, sandwiched in a strip mall between a tattoo parlor and bail-bond business. Not much to it. The front is a sparsely furnished reception area with no receptionist, then you go down a hall past a small conference room on the left and unisex bathroom on the right to reach two offices at the back.

We're sitting in his office, me on one of two mismatched guest chairs in front of his desk. It's the anti-Nemworth office. Instead of pictures of presidents and Supreme Court justices, the dominant decoration is a poster for Widespread Panic hanging behind him. I'm pretty sure it's a band.

"Thanks for coming," he says. His eyebrows have little arches in the middle that make him look like a mischievous prince. "I know the work I've been giving you so far has been somewhat less than scintillating."

Yay! This must be the prelude to something exciting.

"Now it gets worse," he says.

He points to four towers of boxes. "These are documents I received in response to discovery requests in a lawsuit against a property management company, for negligent security at a local apartment complex. I need you to go through them."

Sounds boring, but I don't care. I get to work next to Bryce Stafford. I'd sweep the floors if he asked me. "Sure!"

"It's a sad case," he explains as we haul the boxes to the extra office, already piled high with other boxes, case names and numbers written on them with a marker. The only furnishings are two fiberglass folding tables and four plastic bucket chairs.

"Our client is an elderly man named Artiel Jones. He lived in a nearby apartment complex called Bantam Roost. Two men got access to the building and ... Emily, before I go on, and I hope this doesn't sound presumptuous, I'm worried it could be a trigger for you."

"Thanks. I can take it. Please don't think you can't say things around me. I'm a normal person." Well, that's a bit of an exaggeration, but I hate pity.

He nods. "Two assailants robbed and beat Mr. Jones in the stairwell, almost to death. He's still in the hospital. The police haven't found a suspect and the property manager claims to lack any knowledge as to how they entered the locked building. Do you know much about negligence law?"

I wish I could lie. "Um, not a lot. Well, honestly, nothing. We're just starting it in Torts. The only thing I know is that negligence is a failure to exercise reasonable care in a way that causes injury to someone."

"Actually, that's about all you need to know to get started. We're looking for any information showing the defendant followed unreasonable security procedures to protect tenants from criminals."

"Okay."

"We also need to establish the attack was *foreseeable*—that's an important legal concept here—so anything showing the defendant had notice of prior dangerous incidents or conditions at the properties they manage would be extremely helpful. They manage several in the area, so we're not limited to Bantam Roost."

I like the way he says *we*. "Got it."

He explains how I need to extract and number any relevant page with something called a Bates stamp—it's like a postage stamper—and attach a sticky note explaining why I think it could be useful.

"I know it's grunt work," he says, "but document review is part and parcel of litigation. Big firms use AI software and warehouses full of lawyers to review documents, but as you can see"—he waves at the surroundings—"this is not a big firm."

"No problem at all, Professor. I'll get right on it."

A slight twinge. "Emily, would you mind just calling me Bryce outside of the law school? *Professor* still sounds ridiculous to me, especially coming from someone I'll be working with."

"Sure."

"I'm going to make a pot of coffee. Do you drink coffee?"

"I live on it, Prof—, um, Bryce." I get a tingle as I say it. "Do you want me to make it?"

"Hell no. You're not a receptionist. In fact ..." He picks up a Sharpie and writes on a sheet of paper. "This makes it official." He sticks the note to the door with a piece of tape.

EMILY CALBY
Student Law Clerk

"Your new office," he says. His eyebrows arch even more when he smiles. He's so adorable.

He leaves me with the stacks of boxes. I arrange the stamper, sticky notes and pens in a row and set the first box on the table. I remove the lid and pull out a manila folder.

Rental Agreements. That sounds thrilling. I open the folder and *hol-ee!* The defendant is *Regal Estates,* my landlord. It doesn't surprise me. I march into Bryce's office, brimming with excitement.

"Excuse me. Bryce?" I freaking *love* saying his name. "I think I might already have something."

"Already? It hasn't even been a minute."

"The defendant is my landlord and I have firsthand knowledge of their negligent security."

"Really?"

Standing next to him, I can smell his deodorant. Just like him, subtle and fresh. If I knew what kind it was, I'd buy some and sniff it at home. Haha.

"Yep. Seaside Apartments, unit four-twelve, corner unit on the top floor," like I'm inviting him to dinner. "The lock on my mailbox has been broken since I moved in a month ago. I reported it, so they have notice, but they still haven't fixed it."

"O-kay. Well, that's something, but we're looking for incidents that are a bit more, um, severe."

"Right." I head back to my office and return to the box. Duh. What was I thinking? *My mailbox is broken.* And I have low water pressure. Cracked the case wide open. I'm an idiot.

The files in the first box are for an apartment complex in Jacksonville. My eyes go glassy after an hour. Everything is unorganized or incomplete. In the middle of a folder of eviction letters—the thickest folder in the box—I find a recipe for key lime pie.

But then *Eureka!* Misfiled in the same folder is a report of a car burglary in the parking garage. I stamp it with the Bates stamp and race to Bryce's office.

"I found something good, I think." I hand it to him.

"So you like Widespread Panic?" I ask while he examines it.

"Yeah, I'm a big fan of jam bands."

"Did you know they got their name because their lead guitar player suffered from panic attacks?"

"I did know that. So you must be a big fan too."

"Well, not as big as you." I read their Wikipedia page five minutes ago between files. "I need to listen to them more." I'll start as soon as I get home.

"What kind of music do you like?"

"My dad raised me on country, but lately I've been listening to a lot of old-school soul and gospel music. Otis Redding, Staple Singers, stuff like that."

"That is *great* music. I doubt most people your age have even heard of those artists. Probably even most people my age."

Might as well go for it. "So how old are you?" I say. His silence makes me quickly append, "Sorry, that's none of my business."

He laughs. "No problem. Actually, I paused to confront my mortality. Next month I turn the big three-oh. How about you?"

"Early twenties," I say. No way am I admitting I just turned twenty and am the youngest student at the law school.

"You seem very mature for your age."

"Oh, I am. My mom always said I was an old soul and I usually hang out with much older people." Lucas. Not to mention that my life experiences starting at twelve probably aged me fifty years.

He hands the document back. "This is good. Keep it in a separate folder. You're on the right track. But what we really need is evidence showing Regal had advance notice of other *physical* attacks on tenants or dangerous conditions that could lead to one."

"If it's in one of those boxes, I'll find it." I keep glancing at the wall clock. Each minute that ticks by puts me one more minute behind preparing for tomorrow's classes. "Um, Bryce, I need to go home and study if that's okay. I could come back later tonight."

"No, no. School comes first with this job. Are you free to work on Saturday afternoons?"

"Definitely!"

14

MY VIBRATING phone interrupts my concentration. Professor Owusua is explaining the Rule Against Perpetuities, trying to. It's an inheritance rule so complicated the California Supreme Court held a lawyer who screwed up his client's will because he didn't understand the rule wasn't guilty of malpractice because no one understands it.

I check the phone as I leave class. Just another alert from the door camera. They happen all the time. I used the privacy feature to block out Gabberman's door but the motion sensor still goes off when he comes or goes.

"Something important, Emily?"

"Huh? Oh, hi Henley. No."

"How'd you do on the *Bluebook* quiz?"

The law school buzz of the day. We got our grades back, first ones since we started. I got a *B*, docked ten points for not italicizing one freaking word. Julie got a *C*. We were both disappointed.

"Not as good as I hoped. How about you?"

"Not bad. How'd your study partner do?"

"Julie? Why is that of concern to you?"

"Just curious. I was wondering if you'd like to get together and go over the *Bluebook* sometime?"

"Henley, you should spend less time worrying about grades and more time finding joy in the world around you." Like I do, LOL.

"As a wise philosopher once said, *Only through worry can one find the true joy of ranking at the top of one's law school class,*" he says.

"What wise philosopher said that?"

"Probably Nemworth," he says and I laugh.

* * *

Greg's at the gym. He not only gave up trying to talk to me, he ignores me completely. I was probably too brusque, but don't want to risk reigniting him by saying anything about it.

Struggling to finish a set of reps on a bench-press machine with a hundred pounds on it, it occurs to me my appetite for obsessively working out is shrinking. Law school has something to do with it. It takes so much time. But there's a deeper reason. For the first time in eight years, my training has no purpose.

When I started at twelve I had the motivation of the two men. Getting justice. Locked up at Pochachant, it was a matter of survival. Even after that, threats lurked, the crazy letters and everyday dangers of living in South Memphis.

Now? In sleepy St. Augustine, my biggest danger is, what did Lucas say? Getting mugged by a senior citizen?

I call him when I get home. Last week he caved and agreed to do the gun violence presentation, probably to shut me up. Nagging is one of my most powerful abilities. We're going over the details. It's in two weeks.

He balked at talking for an hour so I suggested thirty minutes and then take questions. "I can be the moderator."

"How am I supposed to fill thirty minutes?"

"Just talk about the impact gun violence has in a place like Memphis."

"Impact? People stop breathing. What else?"

"Tell them about the death bears." Stuffed teddy bears, memorials where people got shot. They hang from utility poles all over South Memphis.

"Twenty-five minutes left, being generous."

"You could talk about Jarrett and Shondra." His little brother and sister, killed in a drive-by shooting. "I mean, if you felt comfortable. I think that would be really powerful. Just be sure to leave out the retaliation part. Don't say anything incriminating."

"Really, Thurgood? I never would have thought of that. Don't go gettin' the big head just because you're in law school."

"Sorry. Just being careful. Law school makes us that way."

A pause. "Look, Em. I'm gonna ask one more time. You sure you don't want someone more qualified? It won't hurt my feelings. I don't wanna embarrass you."

"Aw, don't think like that. You never embarrass me. Just the opposite. I'm the proudest girl in the world to have you as my best friend or dad or mentor or whatever we are." We've never been able to nail down the exact term. He's all of them.

"You'll be awesome. Just be yourself, except you realize you can't cuss, right?"

"Why the fuck not? Just kiddin'."

I offer to let him stay at my apartment, but he says it's too small. He booked a suite at a posh hotel—the Franklin—a couple blocks away.

I'm just getting into my Torts assignment when the door camera sends a motion alert. I don't bother to open it, just wait to hear the door slam across the hall. But there's no sound.

I open the app and see an empty hallway with a black rectangle in the center where I blocked out Gabberman's door like I promised. Unfortunately, it also blocks out exactly where an ax murderer would be standing if he were at my door.

I go to the peephole. No one there. Probably Toby out for a stroll. Of course, being me, I have to check.

Nothing. Not even a cat. The camera's more trouble than it's worth. I'm going to see if it's too late for Lucas to get his money back.

I turn to go back inside and stumble. Glass breaks at my feet. I look down to see a fractured blue vase spilling water and a long-stemmed red rose onto the worn carpet, soaking a white envelope.

A clank resounds from down the hall. The metal fire door leading to the stairs. I hop over the glass and sprint to the stairwell in bare feet. Steps echo from below and another door clangs. The ground floor?

I stub my big toe flying down the stairs and hop into the lobby squeezing my foot. Empty. The only sound is heavy rain lashing the front door.

What if I misjudged the exit floor and the person circled back to my apartment? I'm about to retreat when a wide shadow appears outside. A man. He enters the foyer, head down, shaking water from his hair. When he looks up, my jaw falls open.

"What are you doing here?" It's Greg, the trainer from the gym, completely drenched.

"I live here. Is that okay with you?"

"Yeah, I mean, sorry. I'm just surprised I haven't run into you before."

"From the look on your face, it's obvious you're sorry you just did."

"It's not that, it's just ... did you just get here?"

"What does it look like?"

It looks like he just got here, unless he ran into the rain to escape. "Did you happen to see anyone run out of the building when you were coming in?"

"I was staring at my feet so I wouldn't step in a lake." He turns his back to check his mailbox, body blocking the number. I evaluate the oddity of him living here and conclude it's a coincidence. Seaside's only a block from the gym. Makes sense to live here.

If not Greg, who? I picture my open door. "Welp, better get going. Bye!"

Everything's in the same place when I return. I pluck the soggy envelope from the floor and take it inside, slitting it with a butter knife. The wet paper tears like tissue. Inside is a single sheet of white copy paper. Typed in the center in Times New Roman font:

Roses are red
My feelings are blue
God made you smart
I know your sweet too

Unsigned.

I resist an urge to call Lucas after cleaning up the glass. The more crazy things I tell him, the more he's going to insist I come back to Memphis. I sit on the kitchen floor and force myself to think like a rational adult, instead of the scared child I am right now.

I have a secret admirer, maybe the same person who left the chocolate kiss, someone who doesn't know the difference between *your* and *you're*.

My first thought is Greg, of course. He doesn't strike me as a grammarian. But why would he have run all the way out of the building into the rain? He really did look like someone just getting home.

The more important question is the same one Gabberman asked about my palm tree. Why do I care? It's a silly love note. It says God made me smart, not *I'm coming to cut you into pieces.* That's what stocky man shouted after I climbed out the bathroom window and ran into the woods on the day everything ended.

I try to will myself back into Torts, but it's no use. My head is spinning like a centrifuge. I skim the cases and type up some crappy briefs. In the karma of law school, LeMoy will probably call on me tomorrow.

In bed I think about the secret admirer I had in elementary school. He left a crayon-colored heart on my desk. *You are a very nice girl and I like you,* with *Xs* and *Os* across the bottom. I was so excited I could hardly sleep that night.

Tossing and turning, I can't sleep tonight either.

15

MORNING FINDS me digging through the boxes stacked in my closet searching for my bottle of Xanax. I woke up in an awful mood. The little sleep I got included a nightmare where a tsunami swept over the Seaside Apartments and washed me out to sea. I treaded water in the blackness, nothing around me but rising swells and menacing clouds. I pulled the covers over my head with just one thought repeating itself. *A storm is coming. A storm is coming.*

I find the pills. A doctor prescribed them after I got out of Pochachant and was having panic attacks about correctional officer Twiggs coming back to life and gouging my eyes out. I never took any but kept the bottle as an insurance blanket. They expired three years ago.

What's happening to me? When did Emily-the-Powerful become such a scaredy-cat? *You do not need pills.* I start to toss them, but stop and stash the vial in my medicine cabinet.

I pour down a cup of coffee and throw on a pair of smelly tees and jeans with a soy sauce stain on the front. I haven't done laundry in two weeks, and not just because of law school. Two of the four washers in the basement laundry room are broken. Of course they are. Every time I go down there, the two working ones are being used.

Smoldering heat smacks me in the face when I step out of the lobby. Late October and the humidity is still thick enough to cut with a knife. Sensors on high alert, a fast-moving reflection in a store window triggers my fight or flight response. As usual, I choose to fight, turning and setting my feet.

It's just a jogger. I wait and let him pass.

* * *

Julie and I eat salads from the student center for lunch while she bemoans her C on the *Bluebook* quiz and how she's going to flunk out. I'm only partially listening. I've heard it a hundred times and my dark mood followed me like the storm clouds in my dream. I can't shake the weird rhyme and rose.

With forced patience, "We just have to keep doing our best and trust everything will work out."

"I'm sorry to be such a whiner. I'm just feeling blue. My parents are going to be so disappointed."

My feelings are blue.

"*Blue?*" I say. "That's a strange word to use."

"Why is it strange? It means sad. My mom says it all the time."

Down girl. "I just mean you don't hear it used that much anymore like, you know, in that way. Hey, everything's going to be okay. And a C is *not* flunking."

A long fluttery breath. "I wish I could be as smart as you. My parents would adopt you in a minute."

God made you smart.

"Stop it. You're smart too."

"Thanks for the support, and for putting up with me. No matter what anyone else around here says, I know you're sweet."

I know your sweet too.

She pats my hand and I jerk away. "Hey, I have a question on a totally different subject. I'm writing a thank you note to Professor Nemworth for being my faculty mentor. I'm trying to say, *You're the best professor,* or something like that. For some reason, I always mix up *your*—y-o-u-r—and *you're,* as in you are. How do you keep them straight?"

She ratchets upright. "Are you making fun of me? Is this a test for the *dumb girl*?"

"Of course not. I was just asking."

"Give me a break. You're the frigging grammar queen. You know the answer. This is because of the *Bluebook* quiz, isn't it? You only got a *B*. It's not like you're perfect."

"That's not what I was thinking at all."

I spot Brady Chapman and Dale Olson watching us from the other side of the breezeway.

"Then what are you thinking?"

I squeeze my head with both hands. "Obviously, my thinking is not right today. I'm sorry."

"I just don't understand why you would make fun of me for my grade."

"I wasn't. I swear."

She wipes her eyes.

"Okay, here's the truth. It's going to sound silly, I warn you. Maybe even crazy, but can I ask you a question? You didn't by any chance happen to come to my apartment building last night, did you?"

It was apparent before I finished explaining about the rose and note that she opted for *crazy* over *silly*, standing and gathering her things.

"You think I left you a love letter?"

"No, I was just asking because ... because ..." Because I'm a hyperaroused hazard of a human being.

"That's what you think of lesbians? That we fall in love with every woman we meet? Or maybe it's because you think the famous Emily Calby is so special that no person—man or woman—could possibly resist her. Have you ever had a *friend*, just a regular friend? I'll tell you what's crazy. *You*."

She hoisted her backpack and said, "Stay away from me," stomping off with everyone watching.

Have you ever had a friend, just a regular friend? The answer is just barely. Meggie Tribet, back in Georgia, was from another lifetime, and we were only kids. After everything happened, I never had a chance to make a regular friend, or learn how to be one. I was living on a bus with Lucas or secluded in his building. The closest I ever came was Rebecca, my cellmate at Pochachant. I suddenly miss her terribly.

The day kept rolling downhill. Skulking through the halls, it was impossible not to notice the side glances. My latest PTSD freakout had the law school gossip mill operating at peak efficiency. On top of losing Julie, now people think I'm homophobic.

I never thought I'd see Nemworth's office as a sanctuary, but it feels good to arrive for our weekly mentoring session.

"Hi, Professor."

"Good afternoon," he says, waving to my usual chair with his pipe. "How are you today?"

"Fine," I say dully.

"What topic would you like to discuss?"

Last week we talked about the qualities that make up a good lawyer. His top three were *preparation, preparation, preparation.*

"Um, I don't care. Anything is fine."

"Miss Calby, you don't seem like your usual self today."

I squish my cheeks. "Sorry."

"You look pale. Are you ill?"

"No, sir. Just tired. I've been studying really hard."

He takes off his glasses and leans forward, first time I've seen him without them. His grayish-blue eyes are webbed with a roadmap of tiny red veins.

"Miss Calby," he says in a soft voice I've never heard from him. "Diligent studying is essential to law school success, but you also have to take care of your health. Nothing is more important than health. Nothing. Let's make that your mentoring lesson for the day."

"Okay," I say dully.

He picks up the framed picture from the credenza. "You once inquired about this picture of my wife. This is Claire."

"Claire's a nice name. She looks like a Claire."

"She lost her battle with cancer two years ago. It was a long, painful journey, the most terrible thing I've ever witnessed.

"This necklace you asked about is very special. It was the only earthly possession that mattered to Claire. Her father gave it to her as a young girl, before he went off to war, in case he never came back. He never did."

For once in my life, I have the good sense to keep my mouth shut and listen.

"The insurance company wanted us to keep the necklace in a safe deposit box, but Claire was having none of that. She wore it everywhere ... even in hospice."

I feel the pain of deep longing in his voice, imagine what they must have looked like together a half a century ago, when all of life was an adventure waiting to unfold. It hits me for the first time how sad and empty it must feel to be old and alone.

He dips his eyes, "She was wearing it when she drew her last breath. I promised her I would take care of it and, damn me, I somehow lost it. One day it just disappeared. I failed her."

He probably just misplaced it. I'm dying to reassure him it's still in the house somewhere, offer to help look for it, but the timing doesn't seem right.

Obviously embarrassed by his self-disclosure, he chastises himself with a *Hmph.* "Please forgive my reminiscence, but remember the message. Nothing is more important than health. Why don't you go home and get some rest? We'll save this mentoring session for another day."

"Yes, sir. Thank you." I gather my backpack as Professor Cricks pokes his head in.

"Sorry to interrupt, Edgar. Could I speak with you briefly? The dean just told the curriculum committee about her new plan for—" He looks at me. "A new plan I'd like to get your thoughts on."

"Another one? I'm quite certain I will despise it." He sets his pipe down and pushes himself up with his cane. Skirting my chair, he heads out the door.

Nothing is more important than health. Was he talking only about his wife, or also thinking about his own cancer? How bad is it? How long has it been going on? The image of his desktop calendar burns my brain. September 5th. *Write check for cancer treatment, $15,000.*

His checkbook might contain answers. He keeps it in his top desk drawer, at least that's where it was when he paid me for housesitting. I glance behind me, lean across the desk and slide the drawer open.

It's on top, blue plastic cover peeling at the edges. I could get kicked out of school for this. Listening for sounds, I snatch the checkbook and flip pages in the register. Footsteps in the hall. I drop it back in place and pull the drawer shut just as Nemworth returns.

"You're still here," he says, surprised.

"I just wanted to wish you a good weekend," I say and vanish into the hallway.

I run from the law school, a confused, conflicted ball of relief and fury. The entry in the check register on September 5th for check #2109, said:

Christina Smith, $15,000.00
For cancer treatment

My instant reactions, in order, were:

—Yay, the professor doesn't have cancer!

—Aw, I knew he had a good heart.

—Poor Christina.

I don't like her, but I wouldn't wish cancer on anyone. Mom's sister died of breast cancer at an early age.

That reaction lasted about a billionth of a second, just long enough for my eyes to drift down the check register to the lines below. Over and over: *Christina Smith, Christina Smith ... Cancer, Cancer ...* Each check for thousands of dollars.

I'm sailing through the courtyard when Henley trots up.

"Emily," he says breathlessly. "I heard what happened with you and Julie. Would you like to talk about it?"

I give him an *Are you out of your mind?* look and speed up.

From behind, "Let me know if you change your mind. If you need a friend, I'm around. Have a good night."

* * *

Preying on the Graying: The Hurdles to Prosecuting Elder Financial Exploitation. The title of a sixty-page law journal article I'm reading on my laptop, wedged onto my narrow balcony eating an apple as the late afternoon sky turns from orange to purple.

> *Elder financial exploitation cases do not involve situations where perpetrators conk their victims on the head and steal their wallets. They would be much easier to prosecute if they did.*
>
> *Rather, victims are tricked into "voluntarily" parting with their assets. To outsiders, the transfers can look like gifts or loans, when in fact they are the result of undue influence, psychological manipulation, and misrepresentation.*
>
> *A particularly cruel form of elder financial exploitation is known as a "Sweetheart Scam" ...*

Sweetheart Scam. Everything after that reads like it was written about the professor and Christina. A much younger predator seeks out a vulnerable elder and establishes a counterfeit relationship with him or her, after which the exploiter begins making requests for money, claiming to need it for things like rent or medical care.

Medical care. I'll bet anything she doesn't have cancer.

The list of risk factors reads like a biography of the professor's life. He lives alone, suffers declining memory and lost his longtime wife to cancer. The most terrible thing he'd ever witnessed, he said.

> *The term "sweetheart scam" is somewhat of a misnomer. Exploiters intentionally go after the oldest of the old. Victims of these schemes aren't looking for romance or sexual contact, but rather companionship to alleviate loneliness and in many cases depression. The exploiters prey on this need by feigning love and affection.*

Successful prosecutions are rare because of *the dirty word of CONSENT.* That's what one investigator called it. *It's not a crime to give your money away.* That's what some tone-deaf cops tell people who report it.

It's dark by the time I finish reading and snap the computer shut, blood roiling.

* * *

"A man's entitled to give his money away," Lucas says.

"That's exactly what the cops say! They're not gifts. They're cons."

"Maybe she really likes the man."

"Come on. She's not even half his age. He's eighty-four."

"Hey, when I'm eighty-four, them young women gonna be lining up for me."

He makes me laugh even when I don't want to. "Good luck with that."

"If the woman has cancer, he's doing a good deed."

"That's just it. I don't think she has cancer. I think it's a scam. The article specifically said the predators look for a vulnerability in the old person and target it. Nemworth's wife died of cancer. Professor LeMoy said they were married for more than fifty years. I need to do something about it."

His groan overloads the speaker. "Look," he says. "I agree it sounds sketchy, but here we go again. Why are these things always your problem?"

"Because he doesn't have anybody else, Lucas. He's all alone."

"And what exactly do you plan to do about it?"

"I'm not sure. Don't worry. I don't plan on killing anyone."

I meant it as a joke but he didn't laugh, just changed the subject to his weekend with Kiona. He followed my advice and took her out for a nice dinner, then to a Grizzlies game.

I hung up without mentioning the rose or note—or Julie. The first ones sound like more paranoia and losing Julie is too sad to think about. One friend. Just one. And I couldn't hold onto her without messing up.

16

ANOTHER LONELY weekend. Sunday night and I'm updating my course outline for Contracts and listening to an Aretha Franklin playlist on Spotify. The Queen of Soul was born in South Memphis, just a few blocks from where Lucas grew up. The power and pain in her voice are things you feel as much as hear.

The only bright spot was spending Saturday afternoon at Bryce's. I was stuck in my office most of the day going through documents, but we got to talk a little.

He asked how I ended up in Memphis and I told him about Lucas, making it clear he's like a dad, not a boyfriend. I wanted to ask about his situation, but didn't dare. I haven't seen any clues he's in a relationship. No wedding band, no pictures in his office.

I check the time. Oy, already ten and I haven't even started my laundry. I vowed to do it tonight because I have no choice. I'm completely out of clothes. For the first time ever, today I wore the lacy pink bra and underwear Kiona bought me last year after seeing my collection of the world's most basic undergarments.

"Sweetheart, you need to up your game," she said. "We had nicer underwear than this in Afghanistan." She was in the Army, like Lucas. That's where she took up boxing.

I dig quarters from my change jar and wedge the detergent bottle into the already overflowing laundry basket. The pink bra pokes out and I bury it under a towel. I take the creaky elevator to the basement, starting to sweat as soon as the doors close. I don't like elevators. Nowhere to run.

The laundry room is empty. The broken washers still have *Out of Order* signs taped over the coin slots. Regal Estates sucks, plain and simple.

I fill both of the working washers. I'm pouring detergent when a clank makes me freeze. *Relax*. Only the plumbing. Working on the Artiel Jones case, I've learned a lot about apartment building security. This room would be a perfect place to attack someone. Isolated, poor lighting.

It's almost midnight when I lug my dry clothes upstairs. Too tired to fold them, I drop the basket next to the door and head to bed.

* * *

A front passed through overnight and lowered the temperature by ten degrees. I had to go back inside to get my hoodie. It feels like fall, a nice change.

The law school campus is iridescent as I approach, almost like a photo effect. First Coast may not be the highest-ranked law school, but it has to be one of the prettiest, so lush it feels cut out of a rain forest. A heron sits on the fountain in the center of the promenade, poking the water with its needle beak.

The postcard picture helps me decide I'm not going to let these people bring me down anymore. So what if I'm alone? What else is new? I don't need anyone else.

Last week I caught up with Julie leaving Property. I told her I was sorry, but as bad as I felt, couldn't bring myself to explain. To admit weakness, my mental illness, that I'm suspicious of everyone and everything. "I'm just really sorry." She kept walking. The next day I approached her from behind for another try, but heard her telling another girl, "Then she had the nerve to fat-shame me, tried to put me on a diet. Do you believe that?"

Now I eat lunch alone.

My phone rings as I enter the building. Thomas Acedyo. "Hi, Thomas. What's up?"

"Quite a bit actually. I have some good news and bad news about the gun violence presentation."

Here we go. Good news, bad news. Never just good news. Story of my life.

"Have you seen the Jacksonville newspaper this morning?"

"No, why?"

He explains that to drum up attendance, he contacted the paper and asked if they could run a little article about the presentation.

"Great idea," I say.

"Well, yes and no. They ran the article this morning, but it's not little and it's mostly about you. I didn't tell them who you are, I mean, about your past or anything ..."

I've already gone numb.

"... but the flyer I emailed to the reporter listed you as moderator. She must have looked you up."

Or she's old enough to remember the *Calby Murders*. They probably got a lot of news coverage down here. We used to call Jacksonville *South Georgia*. "What's the good news?" I say weakly.

"From the calls I've been getting, it's going to be a packed house."

In Torts, I become Brady Chapman, first time I've broken the rules against misusing computers in class.

Home Invasion Survivor
Now a Law Student in St. Augustine

A small subhead says, *Will Be Moderating Upcoming Presentation on Gun Violence.*

> *Emily Calby, the only survivor of the brutal 'Calby Murders' eight years ago in North Georgia, is now a first-year law student at the First Coast College of Law in St. Augustine.*

> *Perhaps it was her destiny. At age 16, she successfully defended herself of a murder charge in ...*

The article describes the home invasion, my disappearance and reappearance, my trial for killing Scott Brooker, the whole shebang. Even has the picture of me giving two thumbs up walking out of the St. Landry Parish courthouse. The presentation gets a lonely paragraph at the end.

> *... The organization is holding a fundraising event devoted to urban gun violence. The guest speaker is Mr. Lucas Jackson of Memphis. Ms. Calby will serve as moderator. The event is open to the public.*
>
> *Attempts to contact Ms. Calby for this article were unsuccessful.*

What attempts? Liar.

Professor Lemoy is in the middle of explaining that at common law married women lost all their legal rights. *Nice!*

"In legal effect," she says, "a married woman became the husband's chattel." She looks to me with an invitation to speak up. Normally I would, but I shake my head and go back to staring at the computer screen.

Now the whole world knows where I am.

* * *

Okay, I lied. I *do* need someone. Maybe Thomas Acedyo could use an extra friend. He seems nice. How does that work? Do you just walk up and ask someone if they want to be your friend? My social growth got stunted at twelve.

I'm eating chicken and broccoli from a plastic bowl in the shade of a banyan tree in the courtyard. It only took a couple days eating alone before I vacated my table in the breezeway. I'm trying to get a head start on tomorrow's Civ Pro assignment. More personal jurisdiction. Professor Cricks is obsessed with it.

Knots of students move up and down the promenade. Here

come Dale Olson and Brady Chapman. You absolutely cannot escape people in law school. Looking my way, Olson says something and Chapman laughs.

Professor Nemworth exits the front doors, shielding his eyes from the sun and laboring down the steps on his cane. It takes him forever just to make it to the fountain. Where could he be headed? It's a long way to ... oh, brother.

There she is, waving from her white Nissan at the curb. Christina, wearing sunglasses.

I drop my casebook on the grass and lope toward Nemworth, fumbling to open the camera on my phone. We meet up just as he reaches the sidewalk.

"Hi, Professor Nemworth! I didn't expect to see you out here."

"Hello, Miss Calby. Goodbye, Miss Calby. I don't have time to talk."

"Just wanted to say hi. Hi, Christina! You look nice today. Remember me?"

She doesn't even pretend to smile.

"I have an idea. How about I get a picture of you two? Wouldn't you like to have one?"

"Edgar," Christina says sharply and climbs into the car, hiding behind the tinted windows.

"No," Nemworth says flatly.

"Okay. Just a thought. Well, have a good day, Professor!"

Christina pushes open the passenger door. "Edgar. Hurry."

He's eighty-four and has a freaking cane. How's he supposed to hurry? She guns the motor the second his door closes. If she's looking in the rearview mirror, she sees me standing in the road taking a picture of her license plate.

I return to my picnic spot as Henley strolls up.

"Hi, Emily. See you're prepping for Civ Pro. I don't know about you, but I'm finding personal jurisdiction to be quite challenging. Would you be interested in going over it together?"

"No."

His thin face behind his wire-rim glasses is as unflappable as always. Henley's the complete opposite of Greg from the gym. Greg looked like a wounded puppy when I brushed him off. Henley smiles as if I said, *Love to! How about tonight?*

He's not so bad. I'm not sure why I've been so snappy with him. He's smart, and calm. He reminds me of Ben that way, my short-lived boyfriend at Pochachant. They're different though. Ben was chill through his core. I sense an inner-intensity pulsating from Henley.

Softer, I add, "Maybe some other time."

"Sure, some other time. Hey, can I ask you something personal?"

I doubt it. "What?"

"I saw that article about you in the newspaper today. It must be hard being you sometimes. I guess that's my question. Are you okay?"

The question lands in a deep dark place I don't want to go, certainly not with him. I open my mouth to tell him I don't need his sympathy, but the sincerity in his eyes makes me stop. "Yeah, sometimes it is hard," I say. "I'm okay. Thanks for asking."

After lunch, I'm headed to the law library when my phone pings. An email from Dean Trapano with the subject line, *Urgent We Meet*. I make my way to the administrative wing. Her assistant stands and waves me in like I'm rounding third base.

The dean sits behind her spacious modular desk tapping her fingers together. Dressed in a luminous shocking-pink suit, she looks like a flamingo. "Emily, so good to see you again. How is your law school experience going so far?"

"It's going."

"Sorry to interrupt your day, but did you happen to see the article about the Neighborhood Legal Clinic presentation in the Jacksonville newspaper today?"

"Yep."

"I just learned the reporter has been calling here wanting your contact information, which of course we did not give her."

Again, the memory of the admissions office bragging about

my LSAT score to Henley makes me bristle, but I keep my lips buttoned.

She leans forward like she's sharing a secret. "Emily, have you experienced any security issues because of your notoriety?"

"Just some crank mail and online trolls. When the news of my trial broke, people either loved me or hated me."

"I was thinking maybe we should cancel the presentation, out of precaution."

"No, please don't do that. We're hoping to raise a lot of money. It's an important cause. I'm sure there's nothing to worry about."

"Well, if you're sure."

* * *

Of course, I'm anything but sure. Pacing my living room, twirling my hair, I call Lucas to tell him the news. He's not going to like it. I can already hear him. *I told you to change your fucking name.*

"Yeah?"

"Lucas! How are you?!"

"Uh-oh, here we go. Extra exclamation points. Never a good sign. Why you calling so early?"

"What, don't you trust me?"

"Hell no. I *know* you. What happened now?"

"It's not that bad. ... Okay, it's pretty bad." I explain about the newspaper article, leaving out that it mentions him too.

"I told you ten times to change your name."

"I know. And I admit you were right, if that makes you feel any better."

"Any fallout yet?"

"Not that I know of."

"Well, I'm sittin' here looking at my computer for Emily Calby news and guess what? That article has already been picked by at least ten news sites."

I figured that would happen. He joins Dean Trapano in suggesting we cancel the presentation.

"Oh, no. You're not getting out of it that easy. Besides, I couldn't be any safer than when you're here."

"You be careful 'til then. Keep me up to date on anything that happens."

I still haven't told him about the rose and note. I change the subject to getting the picture of Christina's license plate. "I researched it. Florida has a broad public records law, but vehicle registrations are private. Do you think you could possibly hack into the motor vehicle bureau?"

"Why?"

"So I can investigate her."

"I ain't gonna try to hack into a government computer system so you can play Nancy fucking Drew. It's hard, and dangerous. I left that world behind."

"Maybe James could help."

He reminds me James has gone legal in Silicon Valley, but says unenthusiastically he'll do some poking around on the web to see what he can find.

For dinner, I eat more chicken and broccoli. I made enough to last the week. My casebooks taunt me from the kitchen table. At least I already prepped for Civ Pro.

I decide to shower before tackling Property, worried I'll be too tired to do it later. I stink from an intense workout I squeezed in to release some of the stress of knowing that any freak with a phone or computer can track me down.

Stepping out of the tub, I reach for a towel that's not there. D'oh, my laundry. It's still parked next to the front door from last night.

I grab my robe and retrieve the basket, dumping it on the bed. What a mess. My clothes are wrinkled beyond belief. I smooth them best I can and stash everything that doesn't need ironing in my dresser. I put the rest on hangers and go back to Property.

The hot shower has me yawning. I could use a cup of coffee, but have been having enough problems sleeping.

The assignment is about what kinds of intangible things can be property under the law. The first case involves an insulation company suing to claim a trademark in the color pink. The court ruled in the company's favor. Seriously? I type up a brief and flip to the next case.

A trademark on the color pink. That's crazy. How can you own a color? Maybe I'll trademark purple, my favorite.

Pink.

I leap up and run to the bedroom, pulling out my underwear drawer and emptying it on the bed. Not here. I go through every drawer, then check the laundry basket. Nothing.

If it was just one of them, I might be able to let it go. Could have left it behind in the washer or dryer or dropped it on the way back up to my apartment. But not both.

Someone stole the fancy pink bra and underwear Kiona bought me.

17

AS PROFESSOR Lemoy writes *The Reasonable Person* on the whiteboard, I notice for the first time she's left-handed, like me and Lucas.

"As complicated as it can get, the entire world of negligence law boils down to one thing. The hypothetical reasonable person. What would a *reasonable person* have done under the same circumstances?"

I raise my hand. "How come all of the cases in the book call this person the *reasonable man*?" I say serenely.

I started getting panicky again last night and actually took a Xanax when I woke up. A rose and love note are one thing, but stealing my underwear feels like a direct assault. Then as soon as I swallowed it, I felt like a weakling and flushed the rest down the toilet.

Maybe it took being disgusted with myself to reach my next decision, to quit being afraid and get mad instead. *Rage beats fear.* One of the best survival lessons Lucas ever taught me. *I am Emily-the-Powerful.* On the other hand, the Xanax had kicked in, so it might have been easier said than done.

"That's an interesting question, Emily," she says.

Dale Olson butts in without raising his hand. "Maybe because women are incapable of acting reasonably."

This brings mixed laughs and boos. I say, "That is so hilarious, Dale, but I would argue it's a product of the same patriarchy that permeates the entire legal system."

"Here we go again," Olson says, sticking two fingers down his throat.

"Do you disagree with her proposition?" It's Henley, from the other side of the room.

"What?" Olson says.

"I asked if you disagree with her proposition."

A sniffy laugh to go with his confused look. "Of course I disagree with her proposition. Don't you? That everything's *our* fault? Just because we're men? Don't tell me you're on her side."

"I'm not on anyone's side. We're having a legal discussion. Emily made a legitimate policy point and I think we would all prefer to hear a response on the merits rather than a lame joke and vomiting gesture."

Surprised looks all around. Henley never takes a position on anything, always careful to stay perfectly balanced. Olson's even in his study group.

Professor LeMoy intervenes. "Dale, would you like to respond to Emily's question on the merits?"

Would he like? Don't give him a choice. Make him answer.

Olson huffs and waves her off.

LeMoy takes over the discussion and it turns out that not only did my question have merit, feminist legal scholars have written entire law journal articles about it.

I find Henley in the hall after class. "Hey, thanks for the assist in there."

"No problem. You were right when you called Olson a tool."

"Why'd you do it? Seemed out of character for you to jump into the fray."

"I'm tired of his personal attacks and wasting class time on garbage like that. I'm here to learn. Second, okay, maybe first, I suppose it's already obvious. I like you."

"You do? Seriously?"

He laughs as if I just asked if the earth is really round. "Maybe you're not as smart I give you credit for," he says. "You haven't noticed all the times I've asked you to study together?"

"I thought you were trying to get a competitive edge because of my LSAT score."

"No offense, but I'm doing fine on my own."

He starts to walk away. "Henley, would you like to get together sometime?"

* * *

Late afternoon finds me at the Sunny Beaches Gun and Pawn Shop. I parked next to a pickup truck with mud tires and a bumper sticker that said, *If Jesus Had a Gun, He'd Still Be Alive.*

I'm evaluating a collection of knives through a smeared glass display top. A burly guy in a Motörhead t-shirt saunters over. A tattoo of an AR-15 runs down his bicep. Lucas has one. We used to take it into the woods and blast pumpkins I drew faces on. It was fun, a good bonding experience.

"Help you?" the man says. Stubble helps hide a scar on his cheek.

"I'm looking for a neck knife but don't see any."

"What's a nice girl like you need a neck knife for? How about some keychain mace?"

"Ooh, does it come in pink?" I say innocently.

"Sure does."

"Just kidding. I don't want mace. I want a neck knife. Got any?"

"Nope. If you leave your number, I can call you when we do."

"No thanks."

A pump-action shotgun hangs on a pegboard above his head. Federal law prohibits handgun sales to people under twenty-one, but you can buy a shotgun in Florida at eighteen. I researched it. Unfortunately, you have to be a resident. My driver's license still says Tennessee.

Of course, I'd also have to convince Lucas I need one and have severe doubts that my latest obsessions—the rose and note and Great Underwear Robbery—would be sufficient evidence. He'll probably laugh when I tell him.

On the way home I stopped by the martial arts places I found online. When I told them I was only interested in honing my lethal street-fighting skills—not taking classes or finding a Zen state of mind—they sent me away.

18

"IT PROBABLY sounds like a dumb reason to pick a law school," I say. I stop to ward off a squawking seagull trying to steal the fried conch strip I'm dipping into pineapple sauce. "But I just always wanted to live on the beach."

Saturday and I'm eating lunch with Henley at the Conch House, a restaurant built over the water on a dock. We're sitting outside under a thatched umbrella. Boats, mostly cabin cruisers, line the finger piers of the marina around us. Henley just asked why I decided to attend First Coast. I left out the bigger reason, my irrational belief I could hide here.

"Seems like you could have got into a lot of high-ranked schools with your LSAT score."

Up close, Henley's too-narrow face and sharp nose stand out, but his teeth are nice. I have a thing for nice teeth. And there's depth behind his wire-rimmed glasses in the concentric darkening of his mahogany eyes. If he let his hair grow out a little and got some cooler glasses, some people might think he's cute.

He's wearing a blue Oxford shirt and jeans, un-ironed, his concession to beach life. That and a pair of canvas sneakers. I'm dressed like a complete slob, in gray sweatpants and double tees still wrinkled from being stuffed in my laundry basket overnight. No wonder I don't have boyfriends. I need to up my game, like Kiona said.

"I got admitted to some," I say. "Most don't accept online

undergrad degrees. But honestly, so what? We all get the same license to practice law."

I tear another bite from the conch strip. Not exactly the world's most tender seafood. "What about you?" Not hiding my sarcasm, "The admissions people didn't tell me your LSAT score, but I figure you must have done pretty well. Why'd you come here?"

His eyes flit to a pelican perched like a sentinel on a nearby dock piling with a Tiki face carved in it. "Well, they gave me a full-ride scholarship. And I really like the beach too."

"Really?" I picture Henley at the beach in his long-sleeves and jeans wearing one of those dorky umbrella hats.

"And First Coast does have a good faculty."

"I agree. Especially Nemworth. He's famous."

"A little past his prime though. Seems like his memory is slipping. Have you noticed that?"

"I have," I say with a sigh. "So where are you from?"

He reacts like he bit into a piece of crab shell. "Sore subject. My parents got divorced when I was young and bounced me back and forth from place to place. Brings back painful memories. Sorry. That sounded whiny. I'm sure they're nothing compared to your bad memories."

"That's okay. It didn't sound whiny. I'm sorry it happened. What was your undergrad major?"

"I had a double major. Computer Science and English Lit."

"That's an interesting combination."

"It was. Bytes and books. I learned to code while reading the complete works of the *dead white male poets,* as you would probably call them. Shelley, Keats, Shakespeare, et cetera."

"Come on, I'm not that bad. Am I? I'm a fan of some dead white male poets."

"Name one."

"I like ..."

He laughs. "I'm just messing with you. Analytically, it's an accurate description. They're white, male and dead."

My first impression of Henley was off. I thought he took himself too seriously. He really doesn't.

"What about you?"

"Women's Studies."

"Ah, now it's all making sense. Where do you live in St. Augustine?"

"Not far from the law school. I wanted to be able to walk."

He doesn't press for specifics, which I appreciate. Just says, "Same here."

The server asks if we want dessert. I check the time on my phone. "Sorry, I have to run. I work for Bry— Professor Stafford as a law clerk and put in most of my hours on Saturdays. I have to go home and get ready."

"I heard about that job. Pretty cool. What kind of work does he have you doing?"

"Pouring over boxes of documents. That's my legal specialty."

"*It's good for you,*" he says, perfectly imitating Nemworth's gruff voice. "*You snowflakes need to learn about the real world.*"

I laugh so hard my stomach hurts. "I really enjoyed this," I say at the end. Surprisingly, I did.

He offered to pay for lunch and I declined, didn't want him thinking it's a date.

* * *

Need to up my game. Kiona's words return as I get dressed for work. I'm holding up my one and only dress, a lavender flared sundress with white polka-dots and a keyhole neckline. Way sexier than anything I've ever worn in my entire life.

Still has the tags attached. Lucas of all people made me buy it when we were shopping for apartment stuff. *Em, like it or not, you a lady. Sometimes you got to act like one.*

I try to step into it before figuring out I have to pull it over my head. Good grief, my arms are completely bare. It's short too, barely hides the *NO ONE* scar.

Applying makeup, I stare at the woman in the mirror. Maybe this is why I don't dress up more. I look exactly like Mom. "I hope you're still proud of me, Mom," I say.

Is that even possible, after everything I've done?

* * *

I'm hammering on the door of Bryce Stafford, Attorney at Law. I tapped politely three times with no answer. His car's out front, a beat-up Audi with an ACLU sticker on the rear bumper. I'm Googling the law firm number when the door swings open.

"Emily," he says. "Sorry to keep you waiting. I forgot to unlock—wow." He stops cold. "You look so, so ..."

"Dressed up?"

"I was going to say dazzling. What's the occasion? Hot date tonight?"

Even my bare arms are blushing. I erupt in laughter at his comment, overdoing it, just to make sure he knows it's a preposterous thought. "No, nothing like that."

"Come on in. Were you out there long? I had the music cranked up in back."

"Widespread Panic?"

"No, actually I was in the middle of a playlist of Stax classics, from your stomping grounds."

Johnnie Taylor sings *Who's Making Love* as I stroll happily alongside Bryce down the hallway toward the offices at the back.

"Did you ever go to the Stax museum when you lived in Memphis?"

"Oh yeah." Lucas made me go three times. Parts were interesting, but Lucas loves to lecture and turned each trip into a way-too-long history presentation. Example: I thought it was cool that Booker T. and the M.G.s were one of the first interracial soul groups, but I could have lived without the dissertation on whether the name *M.G.s* came from a sport car or stood for *Memphis Group*.

Bryce says, "Let's make sure you don't get stuck out there again." He pulls a key off a hook and hands it to me. "And let me give you my cell number."

"Um, okay." My own key and Bryce Stafford's cell number!

We get right to work, him in his office, me in mine. I've soldiered diligently through eight of the twenty-four document boxes, but the only report of a direct crime against a person I've found was a grocery bag snatched from a tenant as she entered a Regal Estates building.

Clients come and go in the hallway as I work. Mostly men who look down and out. As a solo practitioner close to the courthouse and next to a bail-bond business, Bryce gets a lot of business from criminal defendants.

Five hours of fruitless searching later, he comes into my office. "Anything?"

"Nope. I'm a complete failure as a lawyer."

"You can only find what's in there. It's getting dark. Let's call it quits." He hands me a check. "This is for your hours this week."

I say thanks and tuck it in my purse. The last time I carried a purse was playing dress-up with Mom's stuff when I was a little girl. If I had worn heels, I really would look like Elle Woods.

He says, "So you must have some big plan for tonight. I've never seen you so dressed up."

"Unfortunately, my only plan is to go home and work on my thrilling Civil Procedure outline. I'm hoping personal jurisdiction will have a surprise ending."

He laughs. "Don't get your hopes up. Are you hungry? The least I can give you as a bonus for your meager pay is dinner."

"Dinner? Sure!"

* * *

We're at a round two-top covered by a white tablecloth, an Italian restaurant close to Bryce's office, dark and cozy. A candle in the center paints dancing shadows on Bryce's face, not three feet away. Smooth jazz wafts from speakers in the ceiling.

This is the moment I expect a camera crew to burst in and expose the whole thing as a practical joke. It's too good to be true. A romantic dinner with Bryce Stafford. At least it feels romantic.

The server approaches, a pretty Asian woman. "Welcome to Little Italy. I'm Terese. I'll be taking care of you tonight. Can I get you started with something to drink?"

"Sure," Bryce says. "I'll have a glass of the house Merlot. How about you, Emily?"

"I'll have the same." I can count on one hand the number of times I've consumed alcohol.

"Can I see your ID?" she says.

I drop my eyes to hide my embarrassment, pretending to rummage through my purse. "Shoot. I must have left it at home in the pants I wore to the beach this morning. Never mind. I'll just have water."

She looks at Bryce, then back to me. "I'll let it go this time."

She returns with two bulbous glasses of red wine.

"Cheers," Bryce says. "Here's to justice."

"Always comes too late, but it's still justice," I say, clinking glasses. The wine is tasty, not that I have much to compare it to.

"That is a great saying," he says. "Did you just make it up?"

"No, my friend did." Lucas, the first night we met. It became my raison d'être.

Bryce asks if I want to share a Caprese salad. Share? Does that mean it's a date? I wish I knew more about how these things work. He orders pasta primavera with shrimp.

"That sounds good. I'll have the same."

I proceed to have one of the funnest nights of my life, even managing to let go of my nagging anxieties. The wine probably helps. At one point Bryce's knee bumps mine and I almost jump out of my seat.

"Sorry," he says.

Gulping more wine, "Oh, that's alright."

It ends when Terese clears our plates and brings the check. But I don't want it to end.

Don't think. Attack. Seize the advantage while the other motherfucker's thinkin'. Lucas's advice for knife-fighting has had far broader application in my life. I was always meant to be with an older man. Not only did Mom call me an old soul, Lucas once joked I'd eat anyone my own age alive.

"Bryce," I say, hung up on the lump in my throat. "Hold on a sec." I take the last swig of Merlot. "Would you like to go for a walk on the beach?"

I blew it. I know right away from the pitched arch in his eyebrows. Major surprise.

"Of course, I didn't mean like right now." Of course I did. I had a perfect picture of us strolling in the moonlight along the water's edge, waves lapping our bare feet. "I was just thinking that maybe sometime ... I sure do love the beach," I say nonsensically. "That's why I moved here. We could talk about our case, I mean, your case."

Word vomit. Cease and desist.

His pinging phone saves me. He looks at the screen. "This is one of the problems with being a solo practitioner. Your clients are always getting into trouble on the weekend. I have to run you back to the office and go meet a new client at the jail."

"Do you need any help, like any research or anything?"

"No, but thanks."

I keep my mouth sealed on the way back. I *can't believe* I asked him that. On the other hand, he never actually said he *didn't* want to go for a walk on the beach. Surprised for sure, but maybe it was a pleasant surprise.

"You sure you're good to drive?" he asks for the third time when we pull alongside my Kia.

"Fit as a fiddle."

"Wait, I just remembered you forgot your driver's license. Let me call you an Uber."

"You know, I'm such a scatterbrain sometimes. I found it when I went to the restroom."

I say good-bye and try to slide out of the car all ladylike, not used to wearing a dress.

"Thanks for all your good work and the privilege of being my dinner companion for the evening." His eyes reflect the green neon of the tattoo parlor next door.

"Anytime!"

19

THURSDAY MORNING and I'm driving to the police station on a law enforcement mission. Professor Owusua canceled Property class. My phone chimes from the passenger seat. A text from Henley. *Meet at the study carrels after Civ Pro?*

The shifting sands of life and law school. Crazy how much can change in a week. Henley and I formed a study group. He quit his after the blowup in Torts with Dale Olson.

I miss Julie, but Henley and I make good partners. We both pay attention to detail and like to get down to business without wasting time. Friday is our first exam, a midterm in Torts, so it's good timing for a study buddy.

This union, of course, ignited a rumor we're sleeping together. I am without a doubt the sluttiest virgin in the law school. At first I worried I might be using him out of desperation for a friend, but the more I know him, the more I see to like. Not *like-like,* of course. My heart belongs to Bryce. Haha.

I came up with an idea for his big 3-0 birthday, unpacking my art supplies last night for the first time since moving here. Other than lethal training, art has been my main hobby since elementary school. I've been mad at myself for letting law school force it aside. Bryce liked Lucas's words about justice so I decided to turn them into a piece of artwork for his office.

I started sketching in august Palatino font, thought about his Widespread Panic poster and switched to paint. In bold black letters over a gradated psychedelic background of yellows and oranges: *Justice. Always comes too late, but it's still justice.* I wanted to add Lucas's name for attribution, but didn't think he would appreciate that.

I pull into the police station, a long rectangle with a facade like a courthouse. Dressed in my go-to gray suit and white blouse, I sling my backpack over my shoulder and enter through the double doors.

"Good morning," I say authoritatively to a dusty-haired cop standing behind a counter eating a croissant. "My name's Emily Calby. I'm here investigating a possible elder financial exploitation case."

"You a lawyer?" he says dubiously.

"I'm a law student employed by attorney Bryce Stafford." I hope he wouldn't mind me saying that. "I'm looking to obtain copies of any criminal complaints filed against a woman named *Christina Smith*."

The research says the pro exploiters are repeat offenders. They clean out one victim and move on to the next. Christina definitely strikes me as a pro.

The cop takes another bite from the croissant, smacking crumbs from his lips.

I say, "According to an Attorney General Advisory Opinion that I have a copy of right here in my backpack, criminal complaints are public records under section—"

"Relax, counselor. We're familiar with Florida's Sunshine Laws." He walks over to a computer. "What's the name again?"

"Christina Smith."

"With or without an h?"

Nemworth's messy handwriting in the check register was hard to make out, but it looked like there was an *h*. I've searched for her on the internet both ways. Unfortunately, Smith is the most common surname in the country. Probably an alias. That's another pro trick. Use aliases and pick common last names that are hard to trace. "I think it has an *h*, but can you check for both?"

He types, studies the monitor, types some more and stops. "No criminal complaints against a Christina Smith in St. Augustine, *h* or no *h*."

Dang.

"But hold on." He clicks more keys. "I do see a criminal complaint filed by a Christina—with an *h*—Smith."

"For what?"

"Domestic violence. Last year, against a man named Cyprus Keane. Her husband. It was dismissed for lack of prosecution."

"Husband? Are you sure?"

"Says right here in her own handwriting, *My husband and I were having an argument ...*"

She told Nemworth she lived with her brother. I thought that sounded suspicious. What grown woman lives with her brother?

Cyprus Keane. Must be the man who was driving the Nissan the day she dropped by the professor's house. That's assuming it's the same Christina Smith. I ask how to get a copy and he sends me to a woman at a desk.

I get into my Kia studying the complaint. Not much to it. In a few scribbled sentences she says she was having an argument with *my husband* and he hit her in the face. The complaint was dismissed after she refused to cooperate.

It gives an address. I search the county property records on my phone. Owned by a corporation. Must be a rental. I map it. Not far. Should I? *No.* Do I? *Of course!* I peel out of the parking lot.

The house is typical old Florida, a small rectangle of cinderblocks, white with rusty blue hurricane shutters yawning above jalousie windows. Everything needs painting. The lawn has more rocks and dirt than grass.

It's the right Christina Smith. The white Nissan is in the driveway. Making my way up the crumbly asphalt, I'm having second thoughts. A voice in my head is saying, *Reckless and impulsive. This is exactly how you get in trouble.*

How would I possibly explain this to Professor Nemworth?

Miss Calby, is it true you've been harassing my friend Christina? It's not until I'm standing at the front door staring at a *No Solicitors* sign that I change my mind. I spin and quick-step back to the car.

"Hey!"

A man's voice. I keep walking.

"Hey, I'm talking to you."

I don't stop until I reach the sidewalk. Landowners have a right to forcibly eject people from their property. We learned it in Torts. The man has a squished-up forehead and flat nose with large nostrils, like a pig. A lime-green polo shirt strains to cover his gut.

"Oh, hi there!" I say with a big blonde smile that fails to disarm him.

"What you doing on my porch?" I can't place his accent. Something European, maybe Slavic.

"You're Christina's husband, right?"

"Who want to know?"

"I'm a friend of hers. Well, not really a friend, more like an acquaintance, a friend of a friend. But it looks like she's not here so I'll be going."

At which point she slides into view, whispering something to the man. They argue back and forth in a foreign language before the man goes inside scowling.

"What are you doing here?" she says.

"Hi, Christina! Well, the honest truth is I overheard Professor Nemworth tell someone you had cancer." Anything that's the *honest* truth is guaranteed to be a lie. "I just wanted to tell you how sorry I am. My mom died of cancer so it's something close to my heart." The forensic report said Mom died from a gunshot to the head, not the fire.

Skeptically, "You came here to tell me that."

"No, no. Not just that. Since the professor thinks the world of you and I think the world of the professor, I wanted to offer my help."

"Help? Are you a doctor?"

"That's funny. No, but I could help with other stuff, like giving you rides to the doctor, assuming it's not too far. Where do you get your medical care?" If I'm wrong about this, if she really has cancer, God's circling the checkmark next to my name on the *Send to Hell* list.

"Look, you little bitch. I don't know what your game is. Leave right now or I'll call the police and have you arrested for trespassing."

So much for the nice approach. "Call the police? Wow, that seems extreme. On the other hand, it does kind of make sense."

Making people wonder if you're crazy is a *way*-underrated altercation strategy. Gets them second-guessing their reactions. I see it now in Christina's eyes, a mix of fury and wariness.

"Make sense?" she says.

"Yeah. You know, in terms of efficiency. You could explain how I walked up your driveway and stood on your porch for a couple of seconds and I could explain how you're a predator who's financially exploiting Professor Nemworth."

There I go again, jumping out of the airplane without a parachute. Puzzlement would be a normal reaction for an innocent person, but her eyes blaze with malevolence of the purest kind.

"You'd better believe Edgar is going to hear all about your little visit."

I was afraid of that.

"I hope he flunks your ass out of law school."

That too. But I keep up the happy front, smiling and waving while my gut cramps. "Bye! And say goodbye to your *husband* for me."

She closes the door with a bang. It reopens and Cyprus Keane steps out, punching his palm. "Trespass on my property again, you be leaving in da ambulance."

Driving away, I crank up the music to drown out the noise in my head. Marvin Gaye is singing he heard it on the grapevine.

20

THE TORTS midterm is in the morning. I've been studying my brains out at the kitchen table for four hours, laser-focused. I even managed to shut out the episode with Christina. But I can't concentrate now because a racket is going on in the apartment below me. Shouting, pounding.

I'm in three-twelve, directly below you. Matt Jurado. I forgot he was that close. I've never heard a peep from down there. I put my ear to the floor. I can't make out the words, but it's definitely some kind of fight. Then all hell breaks loose. Smashing, crashing, like a gorilla is ripping the place apart.

Does Jurado need help? Should I call 911? I grab my keys and a shish-kabob skewer from the kitchen drawer and run down the hall. When I reach the third floor, someone's backing out of Jurado's apartment. I stay in the stairwell and watch through the little window. It's a lanky man with slouched shoulders, yelling, "You're going to pay for this."

He turns my way and I pull back. Gabberman? Why would he be in Jurado's apartment. Jurado said he was a prick. I look again. It's definitely him, limping in my direction cupping his left eye.

I'm about to scoot when someone else exits the apartment. If Jurado's coming after him maybe it is time to call 911. But the second man isn't Matt Jurado. I'd recognize him just from his body, wide and solid as a truck. It's Greg the trainer, with fists balled like sledgehammers and rage in his eyes.

Gabberman sees him and speeds for the stairwell. I break away and sprint back home, hurrying to get my key in the door. I have enough problems. I don't need any part of theirs.

I watch through the peephole as Gabberman hobbles into view wiping blood from his cheek. He enters his unit and slams the door.

Bizarre. I know a total of three people in this whole building: Matt Jurado, Lyle Gabberman and Greg the trainer. And for some reason, all three of them were gathered in Jurado's apartment, brawling.

And I thought life in St. Augustine would be boring. I was actually looking forward to boring for a change. I insert my foam earplugs, fill another cup of coffee and go back to Torts.

* * *

I pass Julie on my way into the Torts exam. "Good luck," I say. I mean it sincerely, but judging from her scowl she apparently misinterprets it as another insult, as if I added at the end, *You're going to need it.*

The midterm counts for twenty percent of our final grade. It's a single one-hour essay question covering the intentional torts. Torts questions have the wildest fact patterns. They're like Rube Goldberg contraptions put to words. *A* does something to *B* and ends up hurting *C*, who attempts to defend herself and injures *D*, et cetera. This one's no different. I spot six issues and start speed-typing.

"Time's up," Lemoy says after what feels like ten minutes.

I hit *Submit* on the exam-security software and pack up my stuff. The emotions on my classmates' faces as they do the same run from relief to sorrow to blankness.

"What did you think?" Henley says as we walk out.

"*Phew,* lot of issues for one hour. Hope I didn't miss any."

He starts to talk about them and I cut him off. "You know what the professors say. Never do an exam autopsy. It'll only make you feel worse. Move on."

"They also say if you're well-prepared, you should be fine, and we were definitely well-prepared." He fist-bumps me, the scintillating extent of the physical relationship that has our classmates abuzz.

"We'll see."

He asks if I want to grab lunch. I tell him I have to go talk to Nemworth about something. He didn't even look at me during Contracts this morning. How in the world am I going to explain going to Christina's house?

His office door is open, but he's not inside. I'm dying to sneak in and do a deeper dive through his checkbook to learn more about Christina, but I'm in enough trouble. I lean against the wall and wait. Fifteen minutes pass before Nemworth rounds the corner on his cane.

He disappears into his office without acknowledging me. Not a good sign. I wait long enough for him to get situated, take a deep breath and knock on the door frame.

"Hi, Professor," I say. "Do you have a minute?"

He looks up wordlessly and points to my regular chair.

My grand opening is a nervous cough. "I just wanted to talk to you about ... you know. I don't even know where to start except to say I'm sorry. I'm so, so sorry."

He frowns. "Halt. Is today our mentoring session?"

"Um, no, sir."

"Then what are you doing here?"

"Well, like I was trying to say, I just came to apologize."

"Did I call on you today?"

"No, sir. It's about ..." And it sinks in that Christina didn't tell him about my pop-in. "I just wanted to say I'm sorry that *had* you called on me, I didn't fully understand why the Statute of Frauds didn't apply in the *Hoke* case."

"I would suggest studying harder."

"Excellent idea and I will definitely do that. Thanks for the advice, Professor!"

I speed down the hall, eyes up, giving thanks to the acoustical tiles, when I practically run over Professor LeMoy.

"Sorry, Professor. I had my head in the clouds. Great exam today. Really enjoyed it!"

"Never heard that one before," she says with a laugh. "Glad I could brighten your day."

I take a long route home to avoid passing the gym. No way am I going back to that place after last night. I'm calling to terminate my membership today. Hopefully Greg won't answer. Why did he punch Gabberman and what were they doing in Jurado's apartment?

As for Christina, there's only one logical explanation why she didn't rat me out to Nemworth. She's guilty as sin and I'm dangerous to her. If nothing else I know Cyprus Keane is her husband—not brother. I have it in her own handwriting. But I need more evidence of exploitation. How do I prove she doesn't have cancer?

No clue. This is a job for the cops. I hear Lucas's voice. *Why are these things always your problem?*

I reach the front door and fish for my keys. Augh, they're in my backpack. What a pain. A dark-haired man in the lobby is checking his mail with his back to me. I knock on the glass. He doesn't turn around. I knock louder. He ignores me.

Jerk! I remember the day I met Matt Jurado, when I was drenched from the rain and he opened the door for me. What happened to simple courtesy? I wrestle the heavy backpack off my shoulders, hoping the a-hole in the lobby will turn in time to see me glaring.

He finally does and *hol-ee!* It's Jurado, arm in a sling and a face that looks like it's been hammered with a meat pulverizer. He pretends not to see me and hurries to the elevator.

21

"DETECTIVE ROBERSON," the man says, sitting behind a metal desk at the county sheriff's office. Shiny-dome bald in a yellow shirt and brown suit. A sign on the glass wall outside says *Financial Crimes Unit.*

I extend a hand and he shakes it. "Emily Calby."

"Have a seat," he says. "I understand you want to file an elder exploitation complaint."

"Well, yes and no. I don't have enough evidence to file a complaint, but I do want to report it. It's a sweetheart scam between an eighty-four-year-old man and a woman who's probably still in her thirties."

"What's your relation to the elder? Granddaughter?"

"Um, no. I'm his student. He's a professor at the First Coast College of Law."

The tilt of his head says, *Come again?*

"I researched it and you don't have to be a relative to report abuse of a vulnerable adult."

"True, although these matters do usually come to us by way of family members."

"That's part of the problem. He doesn't have any family."

"What's the basis for your suspicion?"

"Okay, so first this has to be confidential because he's a famous professor and would kill me if he knew I was here."

"You haven't talked to him about it?"

I shake my head.

"You're acting completely on your own?"

"I guess you could say that."

He leans his chair back. "Go ahead. Fill me in."

I tell him everything I know. About the romantic card from Christina, the cancer story and that Nemworth's wife of more than fifty years died of cancer.

"And look at this." I hand him a copy of the domestic violence complaint. "She told the professor the man she lives with is her brother. He's her husband. Says so right here."

He looks it over and hands it back to me. "That it?" he says.

"So far."

"You realize that's not much to go on."

"I know. That's why I'm here."

"What do you expect us to do about it?"

"What do I expect? Investigate it. That's your job, isn't it?" *Whoa, down girl.* "I mean, I was hoping you could subpoena her medical records to show she doesn't have cancer."

"How do you know she doesn't?"

"I just, you know, know."

"Come on, you're a law student. Gut feelings don't cut it in law. You need proof. We can't go around subpoenaing people's medical records without evidence."

"One more thing. I went to her house and accused her of exploiting the professor and she threatened to tell him I came there—but didn't. To me, that shows—"

"Back up. You went to her house? You can't be doing things like that. It's dangerous in more ways than one. She could end up filing a complaint against you. The best thing would be for you to persuade the alleged victim to file a complaint."

"From what I read, they rarely do."

"Look, I'll be straight with you. These cases are common, way too common, especially in Florida because we have so many single elders. They're one of the hardest crimes to prove, almost impossible in many cases. That's why you get repeat offenders. Relatively speaking, it's a high-profit, low-risk criminal enterprise."

"What exactly makes them so hard?"

"The predators are smart. They select elders who live alone and work on them in secret. The victims often make poor witnesses due to the same cognitive impairments that contributed to their being exploited in the first place. Brain studies show neurological changes caused by aging make elders more trusting. Impaired memory makes them subject to what's called misinformation effect."

"What's that?"

"I'm no gerontologist, but the gist of it you can sometimes alter an elder's accurate memory simply by imparting false information after the fact. And this is all assuming the victim is willing to testify. As often as not, they refuse."

"That's the part I don't get. Why would someone not cooperate against a criminal who defrauded them of all their money?"

"Again, there are often cognitive issues involved, but also psychological factors. Victims have a hard time admitting they've been duped. They're embarrassed. In sweetheart scams, they become emotionally dependent on the exploiter. Trust me. If what you believe is true, that woman has a lot more juice with your professor than you or me."

"And then there's *the dirty word of consent,*" I say. "That's what one expert called it."

"You got it. It's not a crime to give your money away."

"But you *know* they're not gifts. They're the result of lies and psychological manipulation."

He nods. "Even when we know it, it's hard to prove."

22

I PUSH MY Kia north on I-95 in a race to arrive at the JAX airport before Lucas's plane, emotions a stew of excitement and trepidation. I can't wait to see Lucas, but tomorrow's gun violence presentation makes me nervous. He's given me no clue about what he plans to say to two hundred people.

I make it to the waiting area just in time to see him strolling down the corridor, dwarfing the travelers around him. I jump up and down waving.

He breaks into a smile. I love that smile. It takes me back to the night we met, when he was making gumbo while he sang and danced in his *Mr. Good Lookin' is Cookin'* apron. I spot a new goatee as he gets close.

The second he passes security I squeeze him in a bear hug, try to. My long arms barely reach around his barrel chest.

All I can say is, "*Aww.*"

He pats my back. "Good to see you, Em."

I hold his arm as we walk, drawing looks, per usual.

"I love the goatee. What made you decide to grow that?"

"'Cause I'm losing the hair on my head."

"You're not. Are you?"

He leans forward.

"Wow, you really are!"

"You ain't supposed to say that. That's like agreeing with a woman who says she's overweight. Puts your life at risk. Happened with Kiona."

"Well, the good news is you're so tall no one will ever see it. Do you have any luggage?"

"Just this." He nods to his carry-on. "Ready to roll."

When we reach the parking garage, he complains that he should have got a rental. He barely fits inside my Kia. Bless his heart, he has to keep his neck bent because his head hits the roof.

Back on the interstate, I say, "Look in the backseat. I got you a present."

"I can't fuckin' move."

I stretch between the seats and snag a package wrapped in turquoise paper covered with seashells. "Open it."

He tears off the paper and holds up a blue and gold t-shirt with First Coast College of Law across the front.

"It's an XXX-Large. That's the biggest they make. I hope it fits. I bought it with the money I made working for my professor."

"I will wear it proudly," he says. "Thank you."

I drop him off at the swank Franklin Hotel a couple blocks from my apartment and rush to Civil Procedure class. I invited him to come see what a law school class is like. He asked if it would be interesting. Professor Cricks never is and today we're covering venue, another dry topic.

"Honestly, no," I said. "Most of the other classes are, but not this one."

He passed and we agreed to meet at his hotel at six for dinner. I made reservations at a seafood restaurant right on the ocean.

Sitting in class, I'm glad Lucas didn't come. Cricks is even more boring than usual. Henley walks me to my car when it ends. First time I've driven to school.

"I'm looking forward to your friend's presentation tomorrow," he says. "He sounds pretty special from what you've told me."

"He is."

I run home to cram in some studying before dinner. Lucas is staying three days and I can't afford to fall behind.

* * *

We're on an outside deck. Over my shoulder, the sun washes the sky in swirls of orange and red. In front of me, the ocean stretches forever, big enough to swallow even my problems.

Lucas is licking salt from the rim of a margarita, constrained by his new First Coast College of Law shirt, stretched tight as latex. His biceps are thicker than my thigh. I'm wearing a purple hoodie over white yoga pants, sipping water.

"Isn't it beautiful here?" I say.

"It's nice. Gotta admit. Peaceful." He pauses and sips his drink. "Unlike your life seems to be these days."

I get the message. "I know. I wish I could be at peace. I'm beginning to think I never will be."

"That's why I wanted you to stay in Memphis."

"I wasn't really at peace there either. It just was easier to hide it because I felt safe with you."

"Look me in the eyes. Is there anything you ain't told me?"

He already knows the answer. "Yes. A few things. You ready?"

I start with the rose and love poem left outside my door, explaining how I chased someone down the stairs only to find Greg the trainer entering from outside in the rain.

"This guy is huge, Lucas. He's short, but his muscles are almost as big as yours. He tried to flirt with me at the gym, even asked me out, until I brushed him off. I had no idea he lived in my building."

"So you think it was him?"

"He seems like the most likely suspect."

"Didn't the door camera pick it up?"

"The motion detector alerted, but the camera doesn't reach that low. This is the really embarrassing part. I started obsessing about the stupid love note to the point where I basically accused my best friend Julie at the law school of leaving it." I add dismally, "Ex-friend. She won't even talk to me now."

He's shaking his head. "Why didn't you tell me this? I told you not to hold back on me."

"Because I was acting weak and never want to be weak around you. You taught me strength."

The server brings appetizers of fried alligator bites and a veggie tray.

Lucas waits until he leaves and says, "Listen." His hand stretches out as if he's going to grab my cheeks to hold my attention, like he used to do when I was twelve. He drops it and picks up a celery stalk. "Ain't no stronger woman in this world than Emily Blair Calby. And you didn't get it from me. It was already there when we met."

"Thanks, but it's all a front. I'm a complete mess inside. Sometimes I feel like an anxiety bomb ready to explode. My hypervigilance has been through the roof."

"It ain't weak to be scared or alert. Smart, after everything you been through. It's a miracle you turned out as normal as you did, almost makes me believe in that god of yours. I wouldn't worry about the note. Just means you got an admirer."

"Well, there's more. Someone stole my underwear from the laundry room. The pretty set Kiona gave me. That freaked me out so much I took a Xanax. Do you believe that?"

"So fuckin' what? No shame in it. You start taking twenty a day, get back to me. The underwear probably got lost. Happens all the time."

"I don't think so. It was the complete set."

Our order comes. I got grilled shrimp on a skewer. Lucas got steak. He orders another margarita and kicks at two seagulls cawing for a handout at his feet. "These birds are annoying little beggars. Alright, we got a rose and a note and some missing underwear. Anything else?"

"Yes. I went to a pawn shop to buy a neck knife, but they didn't have any. Lucas, I think I would feel better, more *peaceful*, if I had a weapon."

He saws off a fat wedge of filet mignon and sticks it in his mouth. There's no ceiling to look at, so he studies the sky.

"You know how old I am?" he says.

"That's random. Of course. Thirty-nine. Kiona and I are already plotting your fortieth birthday."

"You two plottin' together? That's scary. Any event, years change a person, make you look at life different. I got some news for you. Been doing major housecleaning. Guess what I did?"

"Mm, I don't know. Took the boards off the windows?"

"I said cleaning, not remodeling. Got rid of my firearms."

My mouth falls open. Lucas's building was an armory. "No way. All of them? Even the BMG?" The BMG is a fifty-caliber sniper rifle, the most powerful legal weapon in America. It helped us out of a jam one distant night.

"Everything except one handgun."

"Why'd you do it?"

"This presentation got me thinking. I've been part of the gun violence problem since I was a kid and stole my first nine out of a car. Sold it for fifty dollars to a man who ended up using it to shoot three men at a card game. Wasn't long after that I was shootin' people myself."

I glance around to make sure no one's overhearing. The night is turning cool. The only people on the deck are a middle-age couple twenty feet away. Still, I whisper. "Lucas. The people you shot, at least the ones I know about, all deserved to die."

He takes another drink and smacks his lips. "I guess this is confession night all around. You see, what you just said, that's the part I've been strugglin' with since we met. When you came to me, you was runnin' from a violent world, and I brought you straight into another one."

"And thank you for that. It saved my life. *You* saved my life. Don't ever feel bad about it."

He holds up a hand. "Lemme finish. We both know the truth. If you hadn't come to South Memphis and met ol' Lucas you wouldn't be a killer. All through your training, I was talking self-defense, but I knew I was teaching you how to kill. Not just physically, but psychologically. The second part bothers me most."

I picture myself hiding behind the riot shield while he beat it with a bat. *Desensitization is at the heart of every successful killer. People got to be conditioned to fight and kill. Only psychopaths are natural born killers. The rest of us got to get our brains rewired.*

"You think you rewired my brain to be violent?"

"I think your brain got rewired the day the two men came and murdered your mama and sister. But yeah. When it gets down to killin', I think I did. I taught you not to have a conscience about it."

He took me to a hog farm when I was twelve to kill a pig. *You got to be able to kill when the time comes without stoppin' for a moral conversation with you-self. You don't wanna figure out you can't do it when your life depends on it, do you?*

"Lucas, if you didn't teach me that, I'd be dead. I'd rather be alive and a little effed-up."

"A little? Em, in case you wonderin', it ain't normal for a teenage girl to be able to kill people without giving it a second thought."

"Not just any people. People who deserved to die. And I give it lots of thought."

"I'm talkin' about *before* you do it, not dwellin' on it later."

Fair point. "I was never going to be normal after what happened to Mom and Becky. I have a conscience, a strong one, but it's ... compartmentalized. So, can I get a weapon?"

"I ain't finished. Four years ago, you gave me your word. No more violence."

I raise my water glass so he can't see me cringing about surfer-dude, which I conveniently omitted from my news update.

"Meanwhile, there I was sittin' at home with an arsenal big enough to start my own militia."

"I get it. It's ironic. What's the point?"

His neck muscles twerk. "I'm gettin' to the point if you just quit interrupting. Bottom line is weapons ain't the answer. You gonna be a lawyer. Use the law as your weapon. It's more powerful. You proved it in your trial."

"What about self-defense?"

"Love notes and missing underwear don't justify lethal force, and as you know from experience, weapons can lead to more bad than good."

He's thinking about my sixteenth birthday, when I stupidly pulled my illegal handgun on the biker and ended up in prison.

After dinner, I suggested we take a walk on the beach and was surprised when he said yes. He seems to like it here. Maybe I can talk him into moving to Florida.

He looks so cute with his pants legs rolled up and daintily carrying his size fifteen shoes. His footprints in the sand are twice as big as mine.

Stars stitch the sky and gentle waves rap the shore. The gibbous moon reflects the water like a giant flashlight. Such a nice night. I hate to ruin it, but nothing blows up my compartmentalized conscience more than being untrue with Lucas.

"Lucas, there's something else I need to tell you and I won't dance around it. I broke my word to you. I–I've never done it before. I swear."

We keep walking. He doesn't say anything, waiting for me. "I was at the beach with my friend, Julie—former friend—when two drunk guys ..." He stays silent as I unpack the whole story.

"I've thought about all kinds of explanations, but the only honest one is simple. I thought he deserved it for calling my friend fat. I acted instinctively, without thinking. It was stupid. I've been afraid to tell you. I don't know why I reacted that way."

I can't see his face. I steel myself for a profanity-laced lecture, but he says, "So two men walked up to you?"

"Yeah."

"Strangers."

"Um-hm."

"Started talking all friendly."

I nod, biting my lip. "But then they insulted Julie."

"Hold on. Two strange men approached you talking all friendly. Remind you of anything?"

The two men. Maybe it did have something to do with that. Not an excuse, but a clearer trigger and explanation.

"Least you didn't cause no permanent damage this time. Don't do it again. He probably could have had you arrested."

She could end up filing a complaint against you. Detective Roberson. "Oh, that reminds me of one other thing." I pause to gnash my teeth before telling him about going to Christina's house. "I was just trying to help my professor ... that's no excuse though."

"How many times we got to go through this? You can't fix everybody else's problems. When do you find time to study? Stay away from that woman."

"I will."

* * *

I drive him back to my apartment so he can see it all fixed up. Approaching my building reminds of the crazy incident in Matt Jurado's apartment.

"Oh, here's some more excitement," I say.

He groans.

"Don't worry. I didn't have anything to do with it. I told you about Greg, the trainer. Well, there are two other guys in my building ..." I give him a rundown on Lyle Gabberman and Matt Jurado.

"The other night I'm studying, minding my own business, when I hear a fight break out right below me, in this Jurado guy's apartment. It sounded like a demolition was going on down there. So I went downstairs and—"

"Stop. Why?"

"Just to see what was happening and if Jurado needed help. I know, it wasn't my problem, but I didn't get involved. So don't worry."

I explain how Gabberman came out holding his eye and then Greg stomped out with clenched fists, looking mad.

"Then it gets even weirder. The next day I see Jurado, the one who lives in the apartment, and he's wearing a sling and his face was beat to a pulp. I figure Greg must have gone crazy on both of them."

"And this is the man with the crush on you?"

I nod.

"That's some weird shit. Didn't know St. Augustine was such an excitin' place."

"Seriously, right?"

We reach the door and I grab his arm. "Omigod, that's him. Inside. Greg." He's checking his mail, in his white shirt and shorts from the gym. "Let's wait until he's gone."

"Fuck no. Open the door."

I do, entering with Lucas close behind.

"Hi, Greg," I say.

He turns around, but doesn't smile or speak.

Lucas steps around me and walks up to him. At six-six, Lucas is almost a foot taller.

"You Greg?"

Looking up, "Yeah. Who are you?" I see Greg's muscles tightening.

"Name's Lucas. Friend of Emily's. You lookin' full, bruh. Them boulders are impressive."

Caught off-guard by Lucas's compliment and friendly tone, "Uh, thanks, man."

"So I hear you like Emily."

"What does that mean?"

"Just what the words say. Don't blame you. She's a helluva woman. I like her too, so much I'd do anything in this world to protect her, and I mean anything. Not that she really needs my help."

"Is that some kind of threat?"

Lucas laughs. "Course not. Why would I threaten you? You have a good night."

Greg gets in the elevator. "Let's take the stairs," I whisper.

On the way up, Lucas says, "Hundred dollars says that man's juicing."

"Steroids? How can you tell?"

"Ain't many people with them kind of cartoon muscles up top, especially white dudes. Roids have the biggest effect there. Traps, pecs, delts."

"You think he might have had roid rage the night he went off on Gabberman and Jurado?"

"Possible."

Toby's waiting by my door when we arrive. I pick him up and stroke his neck, "My wittle Toby-wobie. *Mmm, mmm, mmm.* Toby, this is my best friend Lucas." I hold him out. "Do you want to pet him?"

He waves me away.

"He's the sweetest cat. Look at his cute ID medallion. It says, *My name is Toby. If I'm lost, call my mami.* That's Mrs. Alvarez. She lives on the other side of the floor."

I give him a tour of my apartment, which takes about a minute because it's so small. He says he likes it. In the kitchen he spots the painting I made for Bryce's birthday and picks it up.

"You always did like them words. You made this for me?"

"Um, no. I actually made it for someone else." The words pour out like yet another confession. "It's for the professor I work for. He's passionate about justice, legal justice, and when I quoted your saying he loved it. I didn't take credit for it. I can add your name if you want. I didn't think you'd want me to."

"You ain't got to explain. I'm glad I said something profound enough to be in a work of art. Just don't let him steal my intellectual property and make it into a law firm slogan or some shit like that."

I snort a laugh. "Don't worry. I won't. I can make you one too. Do you want anything to drink?"

"You got any good bourbon?"

I yank open the fridge. "I have almond milk and Gatorade."

"Just kiddin'. I gotta get back to the hotel to work on my presentation."

"Um, you've already worked on it, right? I mean, you're not just starting it tonight, are you?"

"That cuts me deep, Em. You worry too much, but we already know that. Course I already worked on it."

23

"THANK YOU, Thomas," I say into a cable mic snaking from the lectern. Thomas Acedyo started us out, explaining the Neighborhood Legal Clinic's mission and encouraging people to support us financially using the envelopes being handed out. So many people! Every seat is filled and people standing line the walls.

I clear my throat. "My name is Emily Calby and—"

Cheers and applause. *Ugh.* I forge a smile, waving with both hands to shut them up.

"I'm a first-year law student and member of the Neighborhood Legal Clinic and will be moderating today's presentation by Mr. Lucas Ellington Jackson, of Memphis, Tennessee."

As a twelve-year-old, I busted out laughing when the Big EZ, as Lucas was known in gangland, told me his middle name. He said his grandfather named him after jazz band leader Duke Ellington.

"Mr. Jackson is an amazing person and a giant of a man, as you can see," I say, tipping my palms to him and pausing for a well-timed laugh. "In more ways than one."

He looks so handsome in a tailored blue suit that must have cost a bundle. The only other time I saw him in a suit was when he came to visit me at the Pochachant detention center posing as an FBI agent.

"He's my best friend and mentor and has taught me more than you could ever imagine."

Lucas coughs.

"Mr. Jackson served in the U.S. Army and was deployed to Iraq, where he worked in the complex area of signal intelligence. He's a computer expert in addition to a long list of other talents."

He coughs again.

"Our topic today is an important one. Urban gun violence. More than twenty thousand people were killed in shootings last year, the most in twenty-five years, and that doesn't include suicides. Although mass shootings get a lot of media attention, they account for only a tiny percentage of gun deaths.

"Most gun violence occurs in low-income urban neighborhoods like the one where Mr. Jackson grew up. South Memphis. Mr. Jackson isn't a professor. He's not someone who can just talk the talk about gun violence. He's lived with it his entire life. It is my great honor and privilege to introduce Lucas Ellington Jackson."

Hearty applause as I step aside. He takes my spot and I turn on the lavalier mic clipped to the lapel of my gray suit. I'm sweating under it even though the auditorium is cool. My nerves are on edge. What's he going to say?

He removes a single sheet of paper from his pocket and smooths it on the lectern, pausing for a sip of water as I catch myself crossing my fingers.

"Good afternoon," he says. "Nice to be here in sunny Florida. Thank you for that introduction Emily and thank you to the Neighborhood Legal Clinic for inviting me. I know most of you probably came here to see Emily and I don't blame you. She is one special lady. Like Emily said, I'm from Memphis. Memphis is a lot different from St. Augustine."

I know what he's thinking, but hope he doesn't say it. Memphis is more than sixty percent black, St. Augustine less than ten percent. Almost every face in the audience is white.

"No beach for one thing," he says. "We have a lot of other good things though. Great barbecue, some of the best music ever made, the National Civil Rights Museum. I could go on and on. But we also have too many damn guns floodin' our streets. Look up the most violent cities in America and you're going to see Memphis on the list.

"You're probably wondering, what qualifies this man to be here talking to me today? It's a good question. I asked Emily the same thing when she invited me."

I watch and listen with fascination. I've lived with Lucas eight years and never knew he could or would codeswitch like this, from Black English—technically African American Vernacular English—to Standard (i.e., White) English.

"Let me start by telling you I don't have any college degrees, just a GED certificate I got in the Army. I dropped out of high school in the tenth grade."

"But he's a genius," I interject.

Everyone laughs, including Lucas. "Nice to have a friendly moderator," he says to more laughs. "Seriously, this girl has more loyalty in her little finger than most people got in their entire soul. No better quality in a human being in my opinion. If you're ever looking for a loyal friend, you'd be lucky to make one in Emily."

I dab my eyes with my sleeve, trying not to smear my mascara.

"So what are my credentials to be preaching about urban gun violence? Well, I've got six bullet holes in me. Maybe that counts for something. They say experience is the best teacher."

I close my eyes amid muted gasps. I'm responsible for four of them. I didn't even know about the other two.

"I also have a dead little brother and sister, shot in a drive-by. My sister Shondra was only twelve years old. She was on her bed doing homework, just being a regular kid. Bullets went right through the walls."

The only sound I hear is my own breathing. All eyes are riveted on him. Of all people, I should have known better than to underestimate Lucas.

"I also have too many friends and enemies servin' long stretches in prison for gun crimes. Some of them have been there since they were teenagers. Today, they're old men like me.

"Gun violence is a way of life in a lot of low-income communities, including black neighborhoods, most of it because of gangs. The homicide rate for black men in Tennessee is ten times the rate for white men. In Memphis, it's not unusual for five people to get shot in a single night. Barely makes the news.

"You've seen the headlines. Fifty people shot this weekend in Chicago. What do we do? Nothing. What would be your reaction if it was your backyard? We need to get people caring about gun violence even when it doesn't directly affect them."

I see a lot of nods, including from my favorite professors: LeMoy, Owusua and Bryce, sitting together in front. No Nemworth, but I didn't expect it. Dean Trapano's here, looking enraptured, probably by the size of the crowd we brought in. Henley catches my eyes and flashes a thumbs up.

Then a voice that grates on me from the very first word erupts. "Isn't it a fact that most gun homicides are black on black crime?"

Dale Olson, four rows back, next to Brady Chapman.

I step forward. "As Thomas announced at the beginning, there will be a question and answer portion to the program after Mr. Jackson finishes speaking. Please show some respect."

Lucas smiles. "See what I told you about loyalty? I got this, Em, but thank you. You're right," he says to Olson.

I have no idea how he's staying so cool, another surprise.

"A lot of killing is black on black, most of it gang related, like I just said."

Olson says, "So why do so many black people join gangs?"

It would be a legit question except for his tone. I butt in again. "Excuse me. As I just said, this isn't the question and answer period."

Lucas just chuckles. Maybe *he* took a Xanax. "First off, bruh, there are all kinds of gangs. Latinos, Asians. And you might have heard of white supremacists. One of the oldest gangs in America is probably the Ku Klux Klan."

Applause shuts up Olson.

"In answer to your question, some kids join gangs for protection, some to find a sense of belonging they can't find in their homes. Some do it because of intimidation.

"To a lot of kids, being in a gang is a way to feel like they got some power, some status. They can't picture gettin' it in the regular ways, by education or a good job. That's the saddest problem of all. The biggest cause of gangs is probably lack of hope. If you have nothin' to dream about, no hope, you got no chance."

I nod along like a bobblehead doll. *So true.* A long time ago, FBI Special Agent Jeffrey Forster asked Lucas why he thought I wanted to be with him. He said he gave me hope and no one can be happy without it.

The minutes fly by before Lucas says, "That's about all I have to say in this short time. I'll turn things over to our moderator and be happy to take some questions."

Dale Olson shoots his arm up like he's gunning in class. *Bwah.* Like I'd call on you, *prick*. Next to him, Brady Chapman is looking at his phone. *Rude!*

I point to a man near the front, wearing a plaid sport coat and taking notes on a pad. "Rick Jensen, WRKG News. Emily, your personal story is extraordinary. Could you tell us how you ended up here in St. Augustine for law school?"

I frown. "This presentation isn't about me. It's about urban gun violence and all questions should be directed to our speaker. Thank you." I point to a thirtyish woman with shiny dark hair.

"Good afternoon, Mr. Jackson. My name is Alicia Vega. I'm a school teacher in Jacksonville. Just curious, are you in a gang?"

He laughs. "Too old for that, but I surely used to be. Got initiated when I was thirteen."

"How does that work, gang initiation? I teach inner-city kids and have heard some scary stories. I've wondered if they're true."

"Probably. They usually either make you commit a terrible crime or gather around and try to beat the hell out of you to see how tough you are. In my case they made a bad choice and picked option number two. I was a big boy even then. Three of 'em went to the hospital and I got an invitation."

The roar of laughter is like something from a Jimmy Kimmel crowd. I begin walking the aisles like *I'm* a talk-show host. A white-haired woman near the back raises her hand.

"Yes, ma'am," I say.

"Mr. Jackson, all this talk about your gang experience makes me wonder, have you ever shot anyone?"

I'm about to intervene when my phone vibrates against my leg. It distracts me for the second it takes Lucas to start talking.

"On the advice of my future lawyer, I'd rather not answer that question. Let me ask y'all a question. What do you think are the best solutions to urban gun violence?"

"Stronger gun laws," someone blurts. A woman with frizzy red hair. I recognize her as an upper-level law student.

"Some laws could help, simple things like making it a crime to leave unsecured guns in cars. Stolen guns fuel the illegal gun market. They're untraceable, making them appealing to criminals. Easy to sell. Breaking into cars as a teenager, guns were the first thing I looked for."

He pauses to look at me. "Was that okay to say, Counselor Calby?"

"Um, I think so. The statute of limitations must have run by now. That was like a million years ago. But I haven't taken Criminal Law yet."

Another good crowd laugh. We have them going.

"But all the laws in the world won't fix the problem. We already have four hundred million guns floatin' around in this country. Think about that. More guns than people. No other country even comes close."

I point to a wizened old guy wearing an NRA cap. "Yes, sir," I say.

In a raspy voice, "Guns aren't the problem. They protect us from the gang members you're talking about. Lock up the criminals and throw away the key. That's the solution."

Scattered applause.

Lucas says, "I understand that point of view, sir, but we've been trying that for quite a while now. It's called mass incarceration. This country has less than five percent of the world's population, but more than twenty percent of its prisoners. See, here's the thing, with all due respect."

With all due respect. I learned that in court and he learned it from me. A polite way of telling people you disagree.

"Say you put a man in prison who's making a thousand dollars a day selling drugs and eating steak, but don't do anything to rehabilitate him while he's there. Then he gets out and can't even find a minimum-wage job because now he's a convicted felon. Bad news. That man ain't gonna end up toppin' the list of outstanding citizens."

Feeling like Oprah, "What do you think is the answer, Mr. Jackson?"

"It's about a whole lot of things. It's about repairing relationships with the police. It's about poverty, education. I don't want to sound like a politician, but nothing stops a bullet like a job.

"And everyone needs to feel like they got skin in the game. I see all the white folk posting on Facebook and tweeting that Black Lives Matter and such. I see the yard signs in the pretty neighborhoods saying the same things. You know what you can do with all those nice sentiments?"

I stiffen. *Please please please* don't let him say *Shove 'em up your asses.*

"Keep up the good work." He winks at me. "It's important to keep spreading the word. But we got to do more. The best way to save a black life is to give a young black man a better choice than a life of street crime. We all got a responsibility. Black folk, white folk, every one of us."

I point to the clock.

"Looks like my time's up and I know from talking to Emily that these law professors have been known to bite people's heads off for coming to class late."

Lemoy and Owusua tap elbows with a laugh.

"Thank you for having me. I hope I didn't waste your time. I know Thomas and Emily and everyone in the Neighborhood Legal Clinic would appreciate any financial support you can give them."

I wave the donation envelope. "You should have one of these envelopes," I say. "You can either write a check or go to the website printed on the back and make a donation online."

Lucas says, "One last thing. If you ever need a persuasive advocate, hire this young woman right here. I guarantee you only Emily Calby could talk Lucas Jackson into giving a speech to two hundred people. Take care now."

People starting clapping. Then a woman rises in the back. It's Julie! I didn't notice her. She starts a chain reaction until everyone's on their feet giving Lucas a standing ovation. I can tell by his tight smile he's blushing, even if it's hidden by his dark skin.

"Mr. Jackson," I say, extending my hand. "Thank you so much for coming today and sharing your valuable knowledge and experience."

He grips it tightly. "Thank you for having me, Ms. Calby. It was my great pleasure."

I turn off the lavalier mic. "*Aww.* You were so great."

He whispers, "You got a visitor behind you."

I turn to find Bryce standing a few feet away. "Oh hi, Bry—Professor," I say, flustered. "Um, Lucas, this is my Legal Writing professor, Bryce Stafford. He's the one I work for as a law clerk. Professor, this is, well, you already know. Lucas Jackson."

"It's an honor to meet you, sir," Bryce says. "Great presentation. So much power and truth in it. I'll be thinking about it for a long time."

"Thank you," Lucas says humbly.

"Sorry to interrupt. I just wanted to tell Emily to not worry if she's late for class."

"Thanks, Prof! I'll be there in a few minutes." He hurries off.

I turn back to Lucas. "That was incredible. You didn't even seem nervous."

"Believe me, I was. Would have rather been in a gunfight."

"I didn't know you could talk like that."

"Like what?"

"You know, like *white*. I never heard you do it."

"Called codeswitching."

"I know what it's called. You're the one who made me take the undergrad course in American dialects. Why did you do it?"

"Because a lot of white people think African American Vernacular English shows a lack of intelligence, even though they steal from it every day. *That sushi last night was lit, bae*."

I laugh. "You would have been awesome either way."

He catches me glancing at the clock and shoos me with a wave of his hand, so large I feel a breeze. "Go on. Don't want goody two-shoes being late for class."

"Do you want to come with me?"

"I'm going back to the hotel and bask in my success as an expert legal commentator, poolside with a cocktail."

"You deserve it. And it sounds a lot more fun than Legal Writing. Can I join you after I get out of class?"

"I'll save you a seat."

"Thanks again for doing it. And now we have the whole weekend together!"

"Go, go."

24

SPRINTING TO Legal Writing, I nearly run into a heavy-set kid standing outside the auditorium, dressed too warm for the weather in a camouflage coat. He's blocking the sidewalk. A fringe of straight-cut black bangs with a cowlick in the center frame his baby-round face.

"Excuse me," I say.

He doesn't move. "I know you."

With a bulky backpack slung over one shoulder, I assumed he was a law student, but studying him, he looks too young.

"I don't think so."

"You're Stacy."

"Um, no." Guess he missed the presentation.

"Oh, yes you are."

"Sorry, nope." I leave him standing there, making it to Legal Writing five minutes late and quietly slipping into the back.

Bryce is dissecting our first big writing assignment with PowerPoint slides. Sounds like I captured the major points, but I've already learned not to be overconfident in law school. *Law school is where smart people go to feel dumb.* Someone wrote it with a marker on one of the bathroom stalls. He says he'll be done grading them by next week.

I approach him after class. "Professor, would it be okay if I miss work this Saturday? Lucas is here for the weekend. I can work double hours next Saturday."

"Of course. He sure was impressive today. So much more impactful than your usual talking-head legal scholar. He has a commanding presence."

"He really does. Very commanding. Hey, didn't you say you're turning thirty this month?"

"Good memory. Now that you mention it, my birthday is ... oh boy, next Saturday." He laughs.

"Do you need to cancel?"

"No, no. I'm just surprised I forgot it."

No way! I get to spend his birthday with him. I'll make a cake and a card, and I need to get my painting to the frame shop.

But right now it's pool time with Lucas. What could be better than that? I hurry out, surprised to find Julie standing alone in the hall.

"Hi," she says. "Do you have a minute?"

"I'm in a kind of a rush to get home to meet Lucas. Do you mind walking with me?"

"Sure. It will be good exercise."

I glance sideways, unsure if her comment was intended as sarcasm. I've felt horrible ever since I overheard her accusing me of fat-shaming. We walk in silence until we exit the law school and clear the front steps.

She says, "I've been thinking about what a total bitch I've been to you. What Lucas said today—he's awesome, by the way—what he said about your loyalty really got to me. It's true. You invited me to be your study partner when Henley's group didn't want me and then stood up for me at the beach, and I abandoned you. I'm sorry."

Glumly, "I'm sorry too. I did feel abandoned, but I caused it. I did a terrible job of explaining—of not explaining—why I went all freaky on you about the stupid note. You were always open with me about your life, but like always, I kept everything about me locked up."

I pause to let some other students pass.

"The truth, which I should have told you before, is I'm basically a mental wreck. I shine it on like I have it all together, but it's a fraud. I have a hard time admitting weakness, even to myself. I worry that if I show it at all, it might take me over, consume me."

If I ever said something so nakedly honest to Dr. Laura, she'd declare a breakthrough. I swallow and keep going. "I have PTSD, ever since, you know, everything happened." I leave out the long list of dissociative disorders that went with it, so many that the shrinks condensed my diagnosis to *post-traumatic stress disorder with dissociative symptoms.* "The symptoms come and go, but since I moved here, they've been worse."

Julie nods sympathetically. "Just to help me understand, what was going on inside you about that rose and note?"

"The whole time I've been here, I've had this feeling someone's been stalking me, even though there's no evidence except silly things like that."

We stop for a light. An old man and woman on canary-yellow beach cruisers pass by, sunbaked skin like leather. A Shih Tzu wearing sunglasses sits in a basket on the woman's bike.

"I used to hide things," Julie said. "I hid my sexual identity most of my life. Didn't come out until college. My parents are conservative Baptists and gave me a hard time about it, tried to save me. People have so many misconceptions about gays and lesbians. I guess I'm sensitive about what people think."

"I get that."

"And my worst insecurity of all, as you know, is feeling dumb, so the whole *your* versus *you're* thing fed into that."

"Again, I'm sorry. The craziest part about the whole mix-up is I wouldn't have minded one bit if the note was from you. It would have been a huge relief. I still don't know who left it."

We reach my building and stop. "I'd ask you up, but I'm supposed to go meet Lucas at his hotel."

"That's okay. I have to run too. Addie, my girlfriend, is coming down this weekend from Atlanta."

"Cool. I'd like to meet her sometime. One more thing. I overheard you telling someone I fat-shamed you. I swear I didn't do it on purpose. I have a bad habit of butting into other people's business. It was just that from all your comments ..."

"You don't have to explain. I shouldn't have said it, didn't even mean it. I was just acting out from hurt feelings. I do talk about my weight a lot and Addie is always on me to eat better. Notice anything different?"

"Um ..."

"I lost six pounds."

"Oh" is all I say. Before I would have said, *Freaking fantastic!*

"Most of it from law school stress," she laughs. "I guess it's good for something. I'm glad we talked."

"Me too. Hey, if you ever need study partners, you're welcome to join me and Henley."

"That's okay. Russell and I teamed up. We work well together. Nothing like a Deadhead for chillness."

"I like Russell," I say. "He supported me when I made my *all men are a-holes* remark in Torts."

"Yeah, he's a good guy. Well, see ya."

"Yeah, see ya."

We hug and I watch her walk away.

Entering my apartment, my mood is lighter than it's been in a long time. Lucas is here and did an incredible job. Then Julie comes out of nowhere and we make up.

I shed my backpack and go change for the pool. I love pools. The Seaside Apartments has one on the roof, but it's been closed since I got here, half-filled with mucky green slime and surrounded by barricades.

I pull shorts and a tee on over my bathing suit and fetch my canvas beach bag from the closet. A silkscreened ocean image on the front says, *I'm Just a Beachy Kind of Girl.*

Grabbing my phone, I remember it vibrating in the middle of Lucas's presentation. There's a text notification from a number I don't recognize.

I open it. Two images above a message. Thought you might enjoy these pictures. The top picture is me in my suit at the front of the auditorium, fuzzy, like it was zoomed in and cropped. The bottom image is Lucas. Same thing, zoomed in and cropped.

Who even has my number? The pictures have captions too, but the letters are too small to read. I don't open them. Phishing expert Lucas taught me more than I ever need to know about the subject. I'm reaching for the off button when I notice something on the thumbnail of Lucas.

Around his head, a red circle.

I hold the phone up close and drop it. It bounces off the refrigerator as a cry like a wounded dove escapes my throat. I snatch it off the floor, grab my bag and blaze out the door.

The circle around Lucas's head was bisected with vertical and horizontal lines ... like the crosshairs of a rifle scope.

25

RUN-WALKING to Lucas's hotel, eyes scanning in every direction, my phone vibrates again. I'm afraid to look at it, but it's only Lucas, saying to text him when I get there because you need a keycard to enter the pool area.

He's smiling when he opens the pool gate, sculpted muscles glistening with sweat. Usually that smile, with his big bright teeth, melts my heart. Today it makes me feel worse. I hate to ruin his big day. I force a smile back.

"Welcome, Em. Come join me at my cabana. Order you something to drink?"

"Water will be fine."

"Fuck water. This is my vacation. How 'bout a daiquiri?"

"Okay, but no alcohol."

We go to the poolside bar. The bartender is an attractive black woman wearing a white shirt and shorts not unlike Greg's uniform at the gym. "Danisha, this here is my friend Emily, the one I'm visiting. She's a law student. She'll have a virgin daiquiri. Emily, I was telling Danisha here she has the prettiest eyes on the East Coast."

Normally, I'd give him a stern look for flirting, maybe even say, *Not as pretty as your wife's.* I look out for Kiona in her absence.

"Nice to meet you," Danisha says. "What flavor daiquiri would you like?" She points to a list written in pink on a whiteboard.

"Any kind is fine. You pick."

"Alright. You guys go sit down and enjoy. I'll bring it over. How about you, Mr. Jackson? Another G and T with extra lime?"

"You bet."

Lucas leads me to a pair of cushioned lounge chairs shaded by an umbrella. Only a few other people are on the patio, including a pasty young couple across the pool with lobster flesh from the sun.

The cushions on Lucas's chair wheeze as he settles in, picks up his glass and swirls the melting ice. "You know what? I could see me living a tropical life. Got its advantages."

"Uh-huh." I roll my shoulders to squeeze out the cramp but it doesn't work.

"Where's your bathing suit?"

Listlessly, "Under my clothes."

"Alright, what's wrong? You know I can tell."

Tears fill my eyes and I'm glad I'm wearing sunglasses. "Well ..."

Danisha sashays over and sets our drinks on a small rattan table, saying she picked strawberry for my daiquiri. I thank her. Lucas waits until she leaves. "You was saying?"

"Lucas, someone's stalking us."

He groans and looks to the sky. "Em, don't let your fears ruin this beautiful day. Ain't no one stalking you and even if they was, I'm here. You're safe with me."

I choke up. "I don't think you're safe with me."

"The fuck you talkin' about?"

"Someone sent me a text and it has pictures and—"

He holds up his hand. "Okay, first thing. Take some breaths and slow down."

"Someone from an unknown number sent me two pictures taken at the presentation, one of me and one of you."

"Message?"

I retrieve my phone. "Thought you might enjoy these pictures."

"See, here's where you worry too much. Probably just one of

your classmates thinking you'd like a couple pictures to commemorate your big event."

I shake my head. "That's not it."

"How do you know?"

"Because ... because ..." I pause and swallow hard. "You should probably just look at them."

"Gimme," he says and I hand him the phone.

He shades his eyes, studies the screen and says, "Let's go upstairs."

* * *

His hotel suite is bigger than my apartment, with separate sleeping, living and work areas. Lucas travels in style these days, maybe because of those years we spent crammed into the bus.

I sit opposite from him at a round cafe table as he studies the photographs.

"I'm sorry," he says.

"For what?"

"Doubtin' you. Apparently, you—or we—do have a stalker. Did you see the captions at the bottom?"

"No, I didn't open the pictures. I worried it might be a phishing message. What do they say? Let me see."

I reach and he pulls away. "For starters, your admirer don't like black men. The caption on mine says death is too good for me, *black man*. 'Cept the sender didn't use that terminology."

I clasp my heart. "Don't tell me it ..."

"With a nice big capital N."

"That's hideous. How bad is mine?"

He scratches his cheek. "Not sure what to make of it. Beats mine though." He hands me the phone.

Even full screen, the tiny words strung across the bottom are hard to see. I stretch out the image and read out loud. "*And your very flesh shall be a great poem*. Creepy. Wonder what it means."

Lucas says, "Sounds almost like a compliment."

"Hold on a sec." I Google the words. "Strange. They're from a poem by Walt Whitman. He was an American poet who died in eighteen ninety-two."

"Any idea who sent 'em?"

"Maybe someone from my apartment building. What if everything's connected? The rose and stolen underwear, even the chocolate kiss. Maybe not though. I could see Dale Olson and Brady Chapman doing something like this as a sick prank."

"Who's that?"

"Classmates, two total jerks who hate me. Olson's the one who kept interrupting your presentation. Wouldn't surprise me if he's a racist on top of everything else. What should we do?"

"One option would be to figure out who sent these and cruelly end their miserable life."

I raise my hand. "Has my vote. I cannot *believe* someone sent that picture of you with rifle crosshairs and saying ... ugh, I can't even think it. Totally deserves to die."

"*However*, as you recall, we swore off violence as a solution to our problems four years ago in favor of the law."

"Every rule has exceptions. One of the first things they teach in law school."

Shaking his head, "We ain't going there. On the other hand, I ain't thrilled about turnin' our lives over to the local police. Lose control of the situation while they're out writing parking tickets."

My eyes keep coming back to the Whitman quote. "My *very flesh* ... *Omigod*, Roland Romansky! Remember him? The crazy cannibal guy who sent the recipe for cooking me?"

"I remember. Didn't your Agent Forster prosecute that man?"

"For terroristic threatening. But I don't know what happened with it. *Blech*, the recipe kept talking about my tender flesh and how good it would taste. I have an idea. How about we contact Agent Forster? You trust him, don't you? If it wasn't for him, we wouldn't even be together."

"Forster's a good man. And the FBI has a lot more resources than we do. Call 'im. But first call the number these came from."

I do, putting it on speaker.

"*Tina's*. This is Tina," says a woman.

"Hi, I got a text from this number and I'm trying to find out who sent it. Did you happen to be at the First Coast College of Law today?"

"The where?"

I repeat it. "It's a law school in St. Augustine."

She laughs. "I'm a hair stylist in Alabama, so no."

"Okay, thanks. Sorry to bother you."

"Spoofed number," Lucas says. "May be impossible to trace, even by the FBI. Who in that audience has your phone number?"

"Just a few classmates. Oh, and Bryce. I mean, Professor Stafford." I may need to stay perpetually sunburned just so people can't tell when my face turns red. "I only call him Bryce at work. Anyway, none of them would do this. Besides, they're all in my contacts, so their name would show up. How hard is it to get someone's cell number?"

"Easy. You get many spam calls and text messages?"

"Practically every day. A lot of them use my name."

"There you go. You see anybody from your apartment building at the presentation?"

"Not that I noticed, but the place was packed. I could have missed them. Hold on." I open my phone and search Recents for Thomas Acedyo.

"Emily," he says. "Glad you called. I had to run to class and never got a chance to say goodbye to Mr. Jackson. The presentation was a phenomenal success. We've received quite a few checks and are already getting donations online."

"That's great. Do we happen to have a list of the people who attended?"

"I wish. I wanted to have a sign-in sheet so we could start a mailing list, but the people in the university development office guard their fundraising territory like pit bulls. Looking for anyone in particular?"

"Yeah, actually. A lawyer from Orlando came up at the end and said he wanted to talk to me about a summer job, but with everything such a whirl, I already lost his card. I thought seeing a list of names might jog my memory."

Lucas rolls his eyes.

"Maybe he'll make a donation. I can show you that list once we get everything compiled."

"That'd be great. One more thing. Did you happen to take a picture of the crowd from the front of the room? I thought a framed photograph of a packed house would be a nice memento for Lucas."

"No, but someone else might have. I'll ask around."

"Okay, thanks." I say goodbye and put the phone down. "Did you hear all that?"

"Most of it. Glad to see law school ain't ruined your ability to lie your ass off. But that's what lawyers do for a living anyway, so maybe they teach you that."

"It's not like that."

He pushes his chair back. "Let's get back to the pool before the sun disappears. I ain't lettin' some racist motherfucker ruin my vacation."

"Are you sure? I'm more worried about you than me."

"If the man who sent them pictures is stupid enough to come in our vicinity, worry about him."

26

ANOTHER LONG day at the end of another long week and I'm in the middle of another long, boring judicial opinion. I stop to yawn and stretch. It's late, almost midnight.

Lucas is home in Memphis. Getting him to leave was next to impossible. He said he wasn't going without me and I said I wasn't quitting law school. To break the stalemate he decided to stay in St. Augustine. I said no to that too.

"Don't you feel safer with me here?" he said.

"I'm not worried about me," I lie. "You had rifle crosshairs on your head. I only have poetic flesh."

"A week ago you was scared of a rose. Now you ain't bothered?"

Of course I was bothered, but in just the few days he was here, I was already falling behind in my classes, the academic kiss of death in law school. There's just no time to catch up.

I finally confessed. "Okay, I'll be honest. I need to get back to focusing on school. I'm behind and finals are getting close."

"Ain't got time for me, eh."

"Come on, don't say it like that. I already feel bad enough."

He finally capitulated, but only on the condition I check in every day and quit hiding things.

I left a voicemail for Agent Forster the day the photos arrived. He called back right away. His voice sent me spiraling back in time to a Mexican restaurant in Atlanta, where he took a traumatized thirteen-year-old into custody and hospitalized her against her will. The disturbed girl who kept insisting she was fine before shattering. Crazy how time flies.

I sent him the pictures and phone number. He wants to help, but said the FBI can't do much without a suspect. I asked what happened to Roland Romansky. Forster said he pleaded guilty to terroristic threatening using an instrument of interstate communication in return for probation. His last known residence was in southern Illinois. Forster offered to contact a local field agent to try to track him down for an interview. He also said he'd ask someone in forensics to examine the photos.

"Thanks, Agent Forster. It's good to talk to you. Sorry to always be calling about something bad."

"No problem. Don't hesitate to contact me if anything else happens. I'm always here for you, Emily."

You could look at my life and say I'm cursed or you could flip it over and say I'm blessed, by the guardian angels who helped me make it this far without my family. Agent Forster is definitely one of them.

I didn't tell anyone at the law school about the pictures. Thomas sent me the list of people who made donations. Forty-four names, none that I recognized. I doubt the person who sent the photos made a donation. If you're smart enough to spoof a phone number, you're smart enough not to leave your name behind at the scene of the crime.

We asked around for pictures, but only got a few of Lucas and me up front and the backs of people's heads.

Just before he left town, Lucas gave in on letting me get a weapon. No gun, but I ordered a neck knife that arrived yesterday. Pulling it in and out of the Kydex sheath, which Lucas made me do one hundred times a day when I was twelve, I realized how rusty I am. Have to be careful pulling out a neck knife or you'll slice your guts open. I committed myself to practicing, one more assignment I don't have time for.

I work until one a.m. before shutting down. I not only needed to catch up, but get ahead. I'm working for Bryce tomorrow on his birthday! Even in the chaos, I found time to get the *Justice* painting framed and wrapped. I baked a chocolate cake while memorizing the difference between remainders and reversions in property law.

I make it to my bedroom just as the camera app chimes. It's only Gabberman coming home. I still wonder what happened that night in Jurado's apartment.

I haven't seen Greg since Lucas confronted him in the lobby. I joined a different gym, another thing I'm behind on: working out. It's a long drive, another time-suck, but at least it's a real gym. They even have punching bags, my favorite.

Melting into the mattress, I adjust the neck knife. I've been wearing it when I sleep. It makes me feel safer, but can't protect me from the nightmares. Last night I was tied to a stake next to an open fire in front of an audience dressed in tuxedoes and gowns shouting questions to a blank-faced presenter. *How do you keep the flesh tender? Do you recommend basting?*

I start my prayers with, *Lord, please don't let me dream tonight.*

* * *

I don a short-sleeve white cotton blouse and khaki capri pants. I overdid it with the dress last time. I weave my hair in a French braid, deciding after a half hour of switching styles that it's a good balance between casual and cute. I skip makeup and assess myself in the mirror.

I look like something out of an Ann Taylor catalog, the opposite of *dazzling*. I unbutton the second button on my blouse, but refasten it. Too easy to see the neck knife tucked behind my bra.

On my way out, I almost trip over Toby, waiting for lunch. "Sorry, Toby-kins, I'm already late."

Parking next to Bryce, I leave everything in the trunk. I want it to be a surprise. Clouds blot the sun, so the cake should be okay. I still feel weird barging in without notice, so I knock.

Bryce answers, reminding me I have a key and don't have to knock. He looks even cuter today than usual, but maybe that's just because I'm excited to see him. He's wearing a Widespread Panic shirt! Must be destiny.

We make small talk before getting to work. Neither of us mention his birthday. In my office, I arrange my sticky pads, pens and trusty Bates stamp and steel myself for more document review. Five boxes left.

Two boxes later, I watch my phone tick down to noon. *Ding ding ding.* Time!

I peek into the hall. Bryce's door is closed. Excellent. I sneak outside and bring the painting and cake to my office, inserting and double-counting thirty candles carefully spaced around an inscription of red-sparkle icing.

Don't Panic, You're Widespread Perfect

The painting makes a good serving tray. I light the candles and hurry across the hall, knocking on Bryce's door with my foot.

"Come in."

I manage to twist the knob without dropping everything and push the door open with my hard head.

"Surprise! *Happy birthday to you, happy birthday to you, happy birthday dear Bry-ice, happy birthday to you.* And you're not getting too old. You're exactly the right age."

I expected his mischievous prince eyebrows to peak in surprise, which they're doing, but his eyes keep flitting to my left, focused behind me. I turn and see a dark-haired woman on the couch wearing a loose dress with her legs crossed. She's pretty, with puffy snowy skin. Next to her is a baby carrier.

"Oh, I'm sorry. I didn't know you had a client in here. I'll come back."

"Emily," he says. "I'd like to introduce you to my wife, Suzanne, and our baby, Marigold."

I feel my face go ashen. I open my mouth, but no words come out. His wife—*WIFE!*—stands and moves toward me. "Emily, it is so lovely to finally meet you. Bryce has told me so much about you."

"He has? I mean, um, nice to meet you."

"Those look heavy. Let me help." She picks up the cake pan. "Look at this wonderful cake. What a clever inscription. Bryce, clear some space on your desk."

She sets the cake down and waits for me to say something, but I'm dumbstruck.

"Bryce," she says. "The candles are melting. Make a wish and blow them out."

He does. Suzanne claps and I join her, feeling like I'm going to puke.

"Well, I better get back to work," I say. "Here." I hold out the painting.

When Bryce is slow to react, Suzanne steps in and takes it from my hands. "Look at this wrapping paper. Gavels and stacks of books. How cute. Emily, surely Bryce isn't that much of a taskmaster. Stay and have some cake. Can he open your gift?"

"If he wants."

"Open it, Bryce."

He pulls the wrapping paper off and holds up the painting. "Wow," he says.

"Let me see," Suzanne says. "Oh, this is fabulous. *Justice. Always comes too late, but it's still Justice.* What a perfect sentiment for a lawyer like Bryce. Did you make that up?"

"Uh, no," I murmur. "I borrowed it from a friend."

"I love the lettering and gradated background. I was an art major in college and know that takes real skill. Isn't it terrific, Bryce?"

"It is," he says. "It's amazing, Emily. Thank you so much."

Silence falls over the room. Probably only a couple seconds, but it passes like a long night.

I put my hand on my stomach. "Bry— Professor, I think I ate something bad for breakfast. I'm not feeling well. I–I need to go. I could come back tomorrow and try to finish the documents."

Suzanne says, "Oh, that's too bad. Do you need me to drive you home?"

"No, no. I'm good."

"Let me cut some cake to take with you."

"No, thanks. I really have to go." I look her in the eyes. "I'm so sorry."

I dash for my office, grab my backpack and trot down the hall. As the front door shuts behind me, I hear Suzanne, voice raised, *Couldn't you see that girl's in love with you?*

* * *

It's only two in the afternoon, but I'm back in my pajamas, trying without success to concentrate on my Property outline, watching rain stream down the window like a waterfall of tears.

My feelings seesaw between sadness and anger. Anger at myself for another blown attempt at romance. 0 for 2. First Ben at Pochachant, now Bryce. *This* is why I shut people out. Don't let people in and they can't hurt you.

I'm also mad at Bryce. He led me on! Didn't he? Called me dazzling and took me to a candlelit dinner with wine. Never once mentioned he had a wife and baby. No wedding ring, no pictures in his office. What's up with that?

Another freaking door camera alert. Sometimes I'm tempted to save Gabberman the trouble and smash the camera to bits. I ignore it, but a second later, there's a knock. I slip my neck knife over my head, dropping the sheath inside my pajama top.

Rap rap rap. Whoever it is isn't giving up. I go to the peephole.

Holy crap, it's Bryce's wife! What's she doing here? Maybe she came to kill me, the woman who tried to steal her husband. Probably happens every day. Can't see if she's holding a gun.

I twist the deadbolt and crack the door, keeping the chain-lock on.

"Hello," I say.

"Hi, Emily." Her tone and soft eyes are about as far from threatening as possible. "Could I possibly come in for a minute?"

"How did you get up here?"

"I was about to buzz your unit but a man in the lobby let me in."

Typical crack security. "Where's your baby?"

"In the car, with Bryce."

"Oh, Bry— he's here too?"

Biting her bottom lip, "I can explain everything, at least try to, if you'd be willing to let me in."

I unfasten the chain-lock. "Come on in. Sorry to be rude."

I motion her to the sofa and roll my study chair over, wheels clacking across the uneven floor boards. I park in front of her, coffee table providing a barrier. I'm not afraid of her. I'm afraid of me, can't even begin to process the emotions coursing through me right now. I can see the headline: *Home Invasion Survivor Stabs Professor's Wife, Claims Insanity This Time.*

"I love your apartment," she says. "You've definitely captured the beach vibe."

"Thanks."

"You're probably wondering why I'm here. Bryce wanted to come himself, but I told him that would be inappropriate after what happened."

I hang my head. "I don't even know what happened."

"I know. And we're both very sorry about it."

"He never told me he was married or had a baby. He didn't even have a wedding ring or any pictures of you in his office."

"I don't know how familiar you are with Bryce's work, but he does a lot of criminal defense. Criminal clients have a habit of blaming their lawyers when their cases don't end well, no matter what the evidence is.

"Last year a convicted client threatened to hurt Bryce and his family. That's when he stopped wearing a wedding band and why there are no pictures of me or Marigold in his office. But don't get me wrong. I'm not defending him. He shouldn't have been so clueless that ..."

"I was in love with him?"

It's a day for tears all around as her eyes well up. Maybe it's because she just had a baby, but her empathy reminds me so much of Mom. I feel it.

"I've known Bryce a long time. We started dating in college. I've never seen the slightest hint of deviousness in him. He's brilliant, but he can be a total space cadet when it comes to absorbing the world around him."

"Did he tell you he took me to dinner, and we drank wine?"

"Yes, he told me about it when he got home. I was furious he let you drive after drinking."

I almost start to defend Bryce, explain that he asked three times if I was good to drive. How did I get everything so wrong? The dinner *seemed* romantic. The candle, the music ... but those came from the restaurant. Bryce was a perfect gentleman the whole time.

On the other hand, he's smart enough to know something's up when a woman asks if he wants to take a walk on the beach after a candlelit dinner with wine. On the *other* other hand, he never replied when I raised the idea.

Maybe he was trying to spare me the embarrassment. I would have been mortified if he chose that moment to blurt, *How could you possibly ask me that, Emily? I'm a married man with a brand new baby named Marigold.* But not as mortified as I feel right now.

Suzanne reaches across the coffee table and touches my knee. She wears a wedding ring.

"Bryce would like to talk to you in person. He's waiting outside in the car with Marigold. Would it be okay if he came up for a minute? Don't feel pressured to say yes. I won't even tell him I asked you. I swear."

"I guess it's okay. Don't you want to stay?"

"I trust you and I trust him."

"You're not mad at me?"

"Just the opposite. I'm glad I finally got to meet you and hope very much it won't be the last time. I'll go get him."

"Give me time to change out of my pajamas."

I rock back and forth on my study chair in a loose Memphis Redbirds tee and jeans, sans neck knife, waiting. It's been fifteen minutes. They probably want to make sure I've had time to change, which took about thirty seconds. Finally there's a knock. I go to the door.

"Hi, Prof—" It's Gabberman, wearing the same dirty white bathrobe as when I met him.

"Hey," he says.

"Uh, hey. What do you want?"

His left eye is still bruised. "I just wanted to tell you ..."

The elevator rumbles to a stop at the end of the hall. He twists away, alarmed. "Be careful."

"About what?"

But he's already closeted back in his apartment as Bryce comes shuffling down the hall, hands in his pockets.

"Hi, Emily," he says.

"Hi, Professor."

"Suzanne said it was okay for me to come up."

I usher him in and point to the same place his wife sat. He looks around. "Great place."

I don't respond.

"I'll get to the point. I came to apologize if I misled you. Suzanne had to knock it into my head, but I can totally see it in hindsight. I didn't do it intentionally, at least not consciously."

"You told me I was *dazzling*. You gave me your cell number and the key to your office. You told me to call you Bryce and took me to dinner."

"You did look dazzling and I would have said the same thing if Suzanne had been there. She would have said it first because it was true. I always give my cell number and the key to people who work in my office. And I truly do hate being called Professor."

"You never told me you were married, and even have a baby." My shoulders droop. I still can't believe it. I dreamed of having Bryce in my apartment. Didn't quite picture it like this.

"Suzanne said she told you about the former client. He threatened to kill Suzanne, who was pregnant with Marigold. I made it a habit after that to not broadcast I have a family."

"But you had to know I liked you, no matter how much of a *space cadet* you are. Sorry, I didn't mean ..."

He smiles. "Sounds like you had a good talk with Suzanne. It's true. I can be oblivious sometimes. I live inside my head and miss a lot of external clues in life. But if I'm honest with myself, I think I was also flattered by your attention."

"Because you're getting old?"

"Not that."

"Did you like me because I'm a 'celebrity'?" With air quotes.

"I liked you—like you—because of who you are. Let me put it this way. When I made my wish before blowing out the candles, I wished that Marigold could grow up to be someone smart and strong like you."

I don't know why everyone keeps thinking I'm so strong when I feel like melted butter inside.

"So what does this all mean?" I say. "For us." I almost laugh because the words sound like something out of a cheesy soap opera. *Laugh or cry, cry and die.* My motto from Pochachant, the tattoo I might get someday.

"It's up to you, of course, but I sure hope you'll keep working with me."

"What about your wife?"

"Suzanne thinks you're terrific. The last thing she said when we exchanged places in the car was that if I return without getting a commitment from you to come to our house for dinner, I'm sleeping on the couch for a month."

"Good! You deserve it. Just kidding. I like her. I'm sorry too, for making assumptions without enough facts. Isn't that what you keep telling us in law school? *It's the facts, facts, always the facts.* I have a few more boxes of documents to review in the Regal Estates case. Could I do them next weekend? I got behind at school when Lucas was here."

"Of course. But do I have that dinner commitment? I don't want to go downstairs and face Suzanne without it. She may seem sweet, but she can be a terror."

I laugh. "Okay."

27

IT'S BEEN a week since the Bryce disaster. I can't say I'm glad it happened, but it discharged some of my pent-up stress, or at least shuffled it around. Now I have more headspace to obsess about other things—like Christina. I dreamed about her last night. She was wearing Mrs. Nemworth's emerald necklace and saying Nemworth had proposed to her.

I wonder how much money she's conned out of him since I saw the checkbook. All those checks were dated close together and it was only one page! Lord knows how many more there are. Rage bubbles through my pores every time I think about it. Including right now, sitting in Contracts listening to Nemworth grill a student about the defense of impossibility to a breach of contract.

The best thing would be for you to persuade the alleged victim to file a complaint. Detective Roberson, Financial Crimes Unit. Maybe it was the dream, but I decide it's time to force the issue—without getting myself in trouble. That's always been the tricky part in my life. As if he's reading my mind, Nemworth rotates in my direction and says, "Miss Calby."

He hasn't called on me in ages. Coincidence or a sign?

"Please give the class an example of a situation where impossibility of performance would be valid grounds for breaching a contract."

Here goes. "Well, suppose A agreed to pay B's medical expenses for cancer treatment. But it turned out B didn't really have cancer, that she lied to get the money. That would make it impossible for A to perform the contract, which would be a valid defense to a claim for nonperformance."

"*No no no.*" His face looks like he just bit into a rotten apple and noticed half a worm missing. "You missed the point completely. What you described would be *fraud,* not impossibility of contract performance. This is Contracts, Miss Calby. Not Criminal Law."

"Sorry."

"Mr. Olson," he says.

Henley gives me a baffled look as Olson expounds on the flaws in my answer. Fine. If it planted a seed, it was worth looking stupid.

Lunch hour arrives like a gift. The first day of November and the weather is clear and crisp, invigorating, the kind of fall day that brings back good memories of throwing the football around in the yard with my dad. I take my lunch to the courtyard and stake out a patch of grass in the sun. I'm opening a bowl of red lentil pasta when Henley ambles over.

"Mind if I join you?"

"Have a seat."

He bends down and sweeps the grass clean before sitting cross-legged and retrieving a peanut butter and jelly sandwich from his backpack, neatly wrapped in cellophane, along with a sliced apple in a perfectly sized baggie.

"What happened in Contracts?" he says. "Your hypo about the impossibility defense was pretty far out there."

"Lots of people give wrong answers."

"Not you. I haven't heard you say something that off-base all semester."

If Olson said that, I'd want to kick him in the nuts, but this is probably Henley's idea of a compliment. "I've had a lot on my mind lately," I say.

A seagull lands nearby and Henley tears a piece of bread from his sandwich and feeds it to him.

Kind to birds, another good quality. Suzanne called last night and invited me to dinner this Friday. I don't want to go alone. Having Henley along would take off some of the pressure. "Henley, what are you doing Friday night?"

"Studying."

"Would you be interested in going to dinner with me at Professor Stafford's house?"

He sets his sandwich down on the cellophane. "You mean like a date?"

"No," I say too emphatically. "Just friends."

"Would it be okay with him?"

"I'll ask, but I'm sure it will be."

"Stafford's not my Legal Writing professor. I'm in Beck's section."

"He won't care. Professor Stafford is cool, and everyone says it's good to get to know your professors. References, research assistant positions, networking."

"Sure," he shrugs. "Do you want me to pick you up? I still don't know where you live."

I can't hide forever. "Seaside Apartments. It's—"

He laughs. "Really?"

"Why is that funny?"

"Because I live in Brooks Manor, the building right behind Seaside, just across the alley."

"No way. That's weird."

"Not really. Other law students live in my building. I assume that's true of most apartment buildings in walking distance of First Coast. What about yours?"

"I haven't seen any, but I just zip in and out."

"I actually called Seaside when I was looking for a place, but it was booked."

"Lucky for you. It's run by the worst property management company in the entire world."

"You know, being so close, maybe we could study at each

other's apartment sometime instead of just at the library. It would be much more efficient."

"Yeah, maybe."

* * *

Being back in Legal Writing after the cake debacle has been fine. I was apprehensive at first, but Bryce has been his usual funny, laidback self. I approach him at the end of class.

"Hey, Professor." I always call him *Professor* in school. "Do you guys want me to bring anything for dinner on Friday?"

"I'm sure we're covered. Suzanne loves to entertain. She's the extrovert in the family in case you didn't notice."

"Haha, I did. When she called to ask me to dinner, we ended up talking for like fifteen minutes."

"That's Suzanne."

"Would it be okay if I bring a friend? His name is Henley Oliver. He's my study partner."

"Absolutely! I'll tell Suzanne."

His enthusiasm for the idea reaffirms I completely misread everything. A little part of me was still wondering, or maybe just hoping.

My stomach cramps as I head upstairs after class for my weekly mentoring session with Nemworth. It isn't going to be pretty. I'm going to move the needle on the whole Christina thing one way or another. I can't just sit around doing nothing while she bleeds him dry. Need to be more strategic than I was in class, although I have no clue how.

He's in his same place and position, bent over a book under the banker's lamp. If anyone ever does an oil painting of him—which they should because he's a legend—this would be perfect.

"Knock, knock," I say. "Hi, Professor! Time for our mentoring session."

"Come in."

I move a small pile of books from my usual chair and put them in the chair next to it. Creature of habit.

"Sorry I missed last week. I had a visitor in town."

Closing one eye, "Ah, yes. I wondered about that." He obviously didn't notice or remember it.

And from this an idea emerges. Detective Roberson explained about *misinformation effect* due to memory decline, which can make it easy to implant false memories in elders. I did more research on it. One study showed old people are ten times more likely to have their accurate memories altered by subsequent misleading information than younger people.

I tell myself the end justifies the means, ignoring my old preacher's remonstration, *The road to hell is paved with good intentions.*

"How have you been, Professor?"

"Fine, fine."

"How is your friend Christina's cancer doing?"

He lowers his glasses. "How did you know about that?"

"You told me, remember?"

He hesitates and mumbles, "Yes, of course."

"What was it again? Thyroid cancer?"

"Kidney."

"Oh, right. Where does she get her treatment? They must be doing a good job. She sure seems healthy."

He ignores me.

"Professor, I'm just wondering, has she ever showed you proof she has cancer?"

"*Humph.* Now I see what you were poking at with that ridiculous hypothetical in class. Miss Calby, you know quite well I don't discuss personal matters with students, yet you continue to violate the boundaries of my privacy, and now Christina's."

"Only because I care about you, Professor."

Exasperated, "It's not your job to care about me. Your only job here is to master law and legal analysis. Here's today's mentoring lesson. Go home. Take out some paper and write five hundred times: *I will mind my own business.*"

I'm out of ideas. The only road left is straight to the heart of the matter. It's a big risk, but there comes a time when silence is betrayal. Martin Luther King, Jr. Lucas taught me that quotation when he took me to the Lorraine Motel, where Dr. King was shot.

I take a deep breath. "Professor, I need to tell you something. I wish—you have no idea how much I wish it—there was someone else to tell you. Would it be okay if I close the door?"

I don't wait for an answer. I reseat myself, unnerved by his glare. Last chance to slam on the brakes before I go over the cliff. *Fat* chance is more like it. "You're not going to like what I'm about to say. You'll probably hate me for it. I just want you to know it comes out of my deepest respect for—"

"Get to the point, and hurry."

"I believe Christina Smith, if that's even her real name, is a predator who is exploiting you for money in what's called a sweetheart scam."

He stone-faces me, no reaction whatsoever, and I wonder if he heard me. I'm about to repeat it when he says, "That is a serious defamatory accusation. Do you have facts to support it? Or do you simply make a habit of reckless character assassination?"

"Mostly I have inferences from facts. Professor LeMoy taught us that most fact determinations in law are based on circumstantial inference-drawing, not direct evidence. I could be wrong, and hope I am, but here's how I reached my conclusion."

Give your best objective analysis. Leave emotions out of it. Just like they've been teaching us.

"You lost your wonderful wife to cancer. Then Christina, a woman less than half ... a much younger woman, shows up. I'm not sure how you met her, but I've done a lot research about elder financial exploitation. She might have picked you out from somewhere she saw you, like in a grocery store or while you were taking a walk."

An eye twitch makes me think I hit a target.

"When I was taking care of your house while you were in the

hospital, I tried to clean things up, as you know. I was vacuuming your office and, um, accidentally saw a romantic card she wrote to you."

"Accidentally?"

"Sort of. I was straightening your desk."

"You snooped through my personal papers? This is outrageous," he bellows.

"Yes, sir. It is outrageous and I apologize. It gets worse, so if you'll just bear with me." Another phrase I picked up in court during my murder trial.

"I'm assuming you told Christina your wife died of cancer and, lo and behold, this young woman out of nowhere coincidentally says *she* has cancer and needs money for medical treatment. And you give her money. A lot."

His gray eyes narrow behind the greasy lenses. "How do you know about the money?"

"Because I accidentally—okay, that's a lie. Because out of concern for you, I grossly overstepped my boundaries and violated your privacy, just like you said."

I pause for a quick prayer before my funeral. "I looked at your checkbook one day, when you stepped out of your office. I saw a bunch of checks in large amounts written to Christina, all with a *cancer* notation."

I'd prefer red-hot rage to what I see. The legendary Professor Edgar Nemworth, a man I admire, revere even, staring at me with utter contempt. The truth can set you free, or bury you. He reaches for his cane and it slips to the floor. I'm tempted to retrieve it for him, but force myself to stay put. He pushes himself out of his chair without it.

"Miss Calby, do you suffer from mental illness?"

"Yes, sir." It's not the answer he was expecting. He meant it sarcastically. "Professor, there's one more thing."

"Stop. I do not want to hear one more word from your loquacious mouth. It is only because you assisted me when I was in the hospital that I am not going to have you expelled from law school. Our course of dealing, however, is terminated. There will be no more mentoring sessions."

A forlorn nod.

"Please gather your belongings and remove yourself from my office."

"Professor—"

"I said not one more word. Do not risk me changing my mind and ruining your legal career."

What was it I was thinking in class this morning, about the need to force the issue *without getting myself in trouble*? As if I could ever manage that.

I unzip my backpack and take out the domestic violence complaint. I unfold it and stick my hand out, but he leaves it hanging.

"What's that?"

I take the question as permission to talk. "It's the last thing I wanted to tell you. Christina told you the man she lives with—Cyprus Keane—is her brother. That's a lie. This is a copy of a domestic violence complaint she filed against him last year with the police. It's right here in her own handwriting. She calls him her husband."

He doesn't move, so I lay it on his desk and turn to leave, stopping at the door.

"I'm sorry, Professor." In so many ways. Sorry for what I did. Sorry for what's happening to him. Sorry there was no one else to tell him.

"Get out and shut the door behind you. And don't come back."

I stand in the corridor lost, like it's my first time here and I don't know which way to go. Professor LeMoy comes bouncing out of her office humming a tune.

"Emily! Meeting with Nemworth again, I see."

Tightlipped, "Yes, ma'am."

"Be careful, you know how rumors spread in law school."

I don't laugh.

"Sorry, bad joke, but you really do like him, don't you?"

"Yes, ma'am."

"Well, here's a little secret. I get the definite impression he's taken a shine to you too, and *that* is a first as far as I know."

With effort, I manipulate my lips into the shape of a smile before fleeing the building.

28

THE WEEK passed with merciful speed. It seems like the closer we get to final exams, the faster the clock goes. I hid behind my computer in Contracts, but it wasn't necessary. Nemworth acted like I didn't exist.

It's Friday evening and I'm getting dressed for the dinner at Bryce's, with Lucas on speaker, catching him up on the latest news. Most of it. I decided my incident with Bryce and Suzanne didn't fall within the scope of my promise not to hide things from him. It's personal, not to mention embarrassing.

I'm in the middle of telling him about Gabberman's odd warning in the hall. "He said *Be careful,* then went back in his apartment before I could ask what he meant. He wasn't saying like, *Be careful, the stairs are wet,* but it also didn't sound like a threat. It was more like *he* was afraid of something."

"Why didn't you just knock on the man's door and ask him?"

Because I was enmeshed in a public humiliation that will probably scar me for the rest of my life. I find it hard to talk to Lucas about guys, not that I've had a lot to talk about in that department. I'd probably feel the same way with my real dad.

"I did knock, later. He was in there. I could hear the TV. But he didn't answer. I think he smokes a lot of weed. I could smell it again. You two would probably be friends."

He asks if I've heard anything else back from Agent Forster and I say not yet.

"So that's about it, except I did have a bit of an incident when I went to visit Nemworth."

"Where's that?"

"Who, not where. My Contracts professor, the one I'm convinced is being exploited by that woman. I ran out of ideas to help him. The financial crimes detective I talked to said the best thing would be if the victim filed a complaint. So I went to Nemworth's office and ..."

The story set him off more than I expected. He ranted about how I'm lucky Nemworth didn't kick me out of law school because that's what he would have done.

"You can't keep stickin' your nose in people's lives just because you think they should be living 'em different. That professor's a grown man, entitled to make his own decisions, including bad ones. Mind your own fucking business."

"I don't have any choice now. He excommunicated me."

"Good," Lucas says and we end the call.

Almost time to meet Henley out front. I agreed to let him give me a ride to Bryce's, but didn't invite him up to my apartment. I put on a touch of lipstick as I gaze out the back window at the apartment complex behind me. Brooks Manor. Henley's building, not more than a hundred feet away.

What do I feel toward him? Definitely not the squirmy gut feeling I had for Ben at Pochachant, or Bryce. Maybe I'm just too picky or maybe desire's not the most important thing. Henley checks a lot of boxes. Can you learn to desire someone?

I do a last check in the mirror. I picked out the most boring outfit I could find. Long beige pants and a peasant-collar short-sleeve blue blouse that buttons up the front.

The neck knife tucked behind my bra makes a small bump. I un-lasso it and toss it on the bed. Just as well. Bringing concealed weapons to your professor's house is rude and probably against law school policy.

Waiting outside, I'm surprised when two girls in my class get out of an Uber car. We exchange greetings and it turns out they live at Seaside. I guess Henley was right. Law students are everywhere around here.

Henley's ride is a sensible Toyota RAV4, old but immaculate. The night got off to a rocky start when he came around to open the passenger door for me. I told him I can open doors by myself, then felt bad for being rude and added, "But I appreciate you being a gentleman."

The drive is awkward because it feels like a date even though it's not. We default to talking about law school, our go-to subject.

* * *

Suzanne is the perfect host. She made us feel welcome and relaxed from the second she opened the door. Dinner was delish. Angel hair pasta with jumbo shrimp and a light cream sauce. Watching Henley interact in a social setting has been interesting. He's more outgoing than I would have guessed.

I'm holding Marigold in my lap, terrified I might drop her. She's so tiny, like a little toy. Henley's asking Bryce about his year in *Biglaw,* the world of law firms with hundreds or even thousands of lawyers.

"It wasn't for me," Bryce says and starts talking about sixty-hour workweeks doing *due diligence* for mergers and acquisitions.

Suzanne comes to retrieve Marigold. "Bedtime, Mari. Come with us, Emily. I'll show you the rest of the house. Believe me, when Bryce starts waxing about mergers and acquisitions, it's time for a fast escape."

The house is small but super-cute, like a fairy tale cottage, with wood floors, peaked ceilings, even a fireplace. I didn't know they had them in Florida. Marigold's bedroom is the sweetest. A hand-painted night sky knitted with stars covers an entire wall.

"Did you paint that?" I ask. "It's really good."

"Thank you. I never did much with my art degree, but like to dabble."

"It's like something my mom would do," I say wistfully. Like something she did do. Becky was obsessed with butterflies, so Mom painted swirling monarchs and swallowtails on the wall above her bed, like they were coming from her dreams.

"I'm so glad you could come tonight. Henley seems awfully nice."

"He's alright."

Lowering Marigold into a frilly pink crib, "He seems to like you a lot."

"Really? How do you tell? I'm clueless about these things ... obviously."

"Just a vibe I get, nothing too specific, although I did notice him nudge his chair closer to yours."

She leans in and kisses Marigold, who coos. I wonder if I'll ever have a baby. Omigod. That is the funniest thought in the entire world. I'd be buying her rubber neck knives instead of rattles.

Back at the dining table, Bryce and Henley have switched from mergers and acquisitions to law school. Suzanne brings out a dessert tray of meringue shells filled with lemon curd and topped with berries. They're yummy.

"How are you liking it so far?" Bryce asks.

"As you know, it's a lot of work, but Emily and I are managing it."

"She mentioned you're in a study group together."

"Yes, sir. We make formidable partners."

I roll my eyes. *Partners?* That's a little strong.

"What's your favorite subject, setting aside Legal Writing, which is no one's favorite subject?"

"I like Property. Emily likes Torts."

"Excuse me. I can speak for myself," I say.

"So what's your favorite subject, Emily?" Bryce asks.

"Um, Torts."

Everybody laughs, including me. That's the way the night goes. Just what I needed to take my mind off my problems. By the end, I'm thinking I like Suzanne as much as Bryce.

We say our goodbyes around ten. I tell Bryce I'll see him tomorrow at work, although now that the spell is broken, reviewing documents doesn't grab me quite the same way.

On our way home, Henley turns down the radio and shocks me. "Emily, would like to go for a walk on the beach?"

"Just you and me?" I say.

"No, I thought we'd hit the next bus stop and see if we can pick up some more people."

"Smart-ass." But it was funny. He's been loosening up all night, definitely looser than I've ever seen. I'd say it was the wine, but he only had one glass.

I study Henley's profile. He really does have nice teeth.

"Okay. I'll go," I say.

* * *

I'm lying in bed thinking about the night, how much I enjoyed it, even the walk on the beach. Henley didn't talk a lot, which I appreciated. He's not one of those people who feel the need to fill every second of silence with blather.

Our hands brushed a couple times, but he didn't try to hold mine, or try to weasel up to my apartment when he let me off. They say that's what guys do. Having lived with Lucas since I was twelve, I never actually experienced it. The few guys I went on dates with were either black and afraid of Lucas because of his reputation as Big EZ or white and afraid to drive in South Memphis at night.

When we got back to Seaside and said goodnight, he gazed into my eyes and I thought he was going to try to kiss me, but he just said *See you in Contracts* and drove away.

I slept soundly for the first night in a while, no tossing and turning, no nightmares. In the only dream I remember, I was flying.

29

THE FIRST THING I do Saturday morning is sit down at the kitchen table with a pen and my embossed EBC stationary. I debated it all week, worried it might do more harm than good, that he'll see it as another intrusion, maybe change his mind and get me kicked out of school.

Dear Professor Nemworth,

I am deeply sorry for what I did. It was extremely wrong of me. Like I said, I only did it because I care about you. I could not stand the thought of someone hurting or taking advantage of you. If I was wrong in my conclusions, I also apologize to Christina, but I do not think I am wrong.

I cross out *but I do not think I am wrong.* It looks like crap so I get out another sheet and rewrite it.

I understand you not wanting me to come to your office anymore, but if I can ever be of assistance in any way please do not hesitate to let me know.

Respectfully,
Emily Calby

I read it over. Sounds okay. I'm licking the envelope when the camera alerts and I hear Gabberman's door open. I drop everything and run into the hall before he can escape.

"Lyle!"

He scowls, but stops.

"Hi, I've been trying to find you since you knocked on my door last week."

No reply.

"Why did you tell me to be careful?"

"Because I made a mistake," he says and starts moving toward the elevator.

"Hold on. You can't tell someone that and leave them hanging. Why should I be careful?"

His droopy eyes remind me of my childhood bestie Meggie Tribet's bassett hound. "Because it's a dangerous world."

"I already know that. Can you narrow it down?"

"It's a dangerous building. That's all I can say." He scoots around me and enters the stairwell.

"Who punched you in the eye? Was it Greg?" I shout after him, but the door thumps shut.

Dangerous building. I already knew that too. Toby rounds the corner and rubs against my ankle, spindly tail swishing as he walks me back to my apartment.

"Be careful, Toby. You heard the man, it's a dangerous building."

Henley and I spend Saturday afternoon at a Starbucks working on our Contracts outline, already fifty-six pages long. When I walked in, there was a single yellow rose wrapped in cellophane on the table.

"What's that?" I said, pointing.

"A yellow rose. I brought it for you."

I put it aside and unpacked my computer. "Thanks. Are you a, um, big fan of roses?" I had to ask even though I knew there was no way Henley Oliver would ever confuse *your* and *you're.*

He shrugged. "They're alright. Now, about the parol evidence rule ..."

If we ever did get together, Henley and I would be the dorkiest couple on earth.

* * *

In the afternoon I go to Bryce's office to look through more documents. As B.B. King sang, the thrill is gone. The intense stirring that kept me up at night popped like a balloon after the birthday cake incident. With it went any possibility of being excited about or even mildly interested in scrutinizing more reams of useless crap from Regal Estates. What's to keep defendants from just taking out all the bad documents before they turn them over?

Bryce comes in. "How's it going?"

Frowning, "Still nothing."

"Don't let it get to you. Maybe the next box will hold the magic smoking gun."

We order Chinese for lunch. The atmosphere between us is different. *Normal.* I like it much better. I don't think I'm cut out for romance. It's too exhausting.

Polishing off an egg roll, I raise the question I've been wanting to ask for weeks.

"Do you know Professor Nemworth very well?"

"No, not well. He was still teaching in the big leagues when I was a student, and we lowly adjuncts rarely interact with the regular faculty. But I remember studying his Contracts treatise in law school. Do the students appreciate they're being taught by a legal legend?"

"I do. I'm not sure about everyone else. He's kind of ... slipping." I almost say *losing it*. "I'm worried about him."

"How so?"

"I think he's in trouble and doesn't know it, or doesn't want to know."

"Trouble?"

The floodgates opened. I poured out everything I know about Christina Smith and Cyprus Keane, pausing only to take breaths and repeat my pleas to keep it confidential. Nemworth would kill me for dishing about his personal life to another professor. Bryce cringes when I mention snooping into Nemworth's checkbook and going to Christina's house.

"Now Nemworth has kicked me out of his life and Lucas tells me to just forget about it, that it's none of my business."

Shaking his head, "Emily, the passion-for-justice side of me is cheering your bold actions, but the lawyer in me is screaming that you need to listen to Lucas and stop acting so ..."

"Reckless? You can say it. It's one of my trademarks. Anyway, my question is, since the cops won't do anything, is there any way I could bring a civil suit against her on his behalf? Like a tort suit for fraud."

"Have you studied *standing* in Civil Procedure yet?" he says.

Shoulders slumping, "*Locus standi.* The requirement that a plaintiff show direct injury from the defendant's actions. So it all comes back to Nemworth not being able or willing to recognize he's a victim."

"That's a big roadblock in sweetheart scams, which are all too common in Florida. And keep in mind that while I agree what you described sounds suspicious, it's possible you're wrong about this Christina person."

"Nah," I say with a smirk. "My instincts are always right. Surely I've proved that much to you."

* * *

Come Monday, Professor LeMoy introduces us to our last major topic of the semester in Torts: proximate cause. She's in the middle of warning us that it's the most difficult concept in the entire course because the law is confusing and conflicting.

The first cases are a pair of golden oldies, the *Wagon Mound* cases. A ship leaked oil into a harbor and the water caught fire, burning up a dock and some ships. *Wagon Mound 1* said the ship owner wasn't liable because the fire wasn't foreseeable, but *Wagon Mound 2* said it was foreseeable.

LeMoy says, "Henley, how could the same fire be unforeseeable in one case and foreseeable in the other?"

Henley didn't raise his hand, but I've noticed the professors trying to speed things up as the end of the semester closes in, calling on people they know are reliable.

Without even looking at his notes, Henley says, "Because *Wagon Mound 2* focused on a risk-utility calculus. The court said there was no social utility in spilling the oil and the potential harm was great. So even if the fire was just a mere *possibility*, a reasonable ship captain would have taken steps to prevent it."

Dang, he's smart. Already talks like a professor. I love smart—more than looks, not that he looks that bad.

LeMoy raises her arms in triumph. "See? Just what I told you. Confusing and conflicting."

"Great job, Henley," I say as we walk out of class together.

"Thanks," he says. "Lunch in the courtyard?"

"I—" My phone vibrates. "Hold on a sec." A text from Agent Forster. *Call me when you can.* "I need to go check on something. I'll meet you out there if it doesn't take too long."

I find a quiet spot in the student lounge and call him back.

"Emily, how are you?"

"I'm good. How about you? What's going on?"

"Nothing earthshattering. Just wanted to update you on a couple things. First, the agent in Illinois went out to interview Roland Romansky at his last known address, but he wasn't there. A neighbor said he moved a couple years ago without saying where he was going. His probation expired, so he wasn't required to let us know.

"Number two is the forensics folks weren't able to make any headway on that text message or the pictures. The text came from a spoofed number and while it's possible to identify a smartphone by analyzing photos taken on it, we'd need to have possession of the phone."

He goes on to explain about *photo-response non-uniformity* or

PRNU. Lucas already told me about it. Every phone camera has unique microscopic imaging flaws in the pictures it takes.

"It's similar to matching bullets to guns using ballistics analysis," Forster says. "The problem is you have to have the gun. Same thing here. We'd need the phone."

My phone pings.

"I just texted you Romansky's booking photo. Does he look familiar?"

I study the image. Hollow eyes, unshaven, cold smile. Dangerous-looking, like a cannibal.

"No, but I'll keep an eye out."

"Any other incidents?"

"Thankfully not."

"Well, I'm sorry I couldn't be more help. Keep me posted if anything else happens. How's law school going otherwise?"

"Quickly. I can't believe we're already coming up on final exams."

"You know, the FBI hires a lot of agents with law degrees. Just saying."

"Haha. I'll keep it in mind."

As soon as we hang up, the phone vibrates again and I assume Forster forgot to tell me something, but it's another door camera notification. I open the app and, of course, see nothing because of the stupid privacy zone blocking Gabberman's door directly across from mine. But I hear something and raise the phone volume. Someone's knocking on my door.

I fumble to find the privacy settings to delete the privacy zone, but not in time. All I see is the back of a dark-haired man as he moves quickly out of the camera view. Frustrated, I find the setting and delete the privacy zone. Gabberman will never know.

30

ARRIVING HOME from school, I grab a protein bar and jump right into my books. Henley's sharp answer in Torts about the *Wagon Mound* cases bugged me because mine wouldn't have been as good. He also beat me on our Torts midterm exam, *A* to *B+*.

He's out-studying me. I've let my non-law school life take me off mission, interfere with my reason for being here. No more. I'm going to finish with better grades than him if it kills me, unless something else does first. Haha.

Three hours later the sky is darkening to the sound of my growling stomach. I'm wondering what I can scrounge together for dinner when the camera app alerts. I pull out my foam ear plugs and listen. What is that sound?

A tapping, soft and repetitive. I go to the peephole. It's Mrs. Alvarez, Toby's mom, bony knuckles rapping as light as a heartbeat. She's so short I can only see her from the shoulders up. Her hair is permed and she's wearing a gold pin, like she dressed up just to walk over here.

I open the door. "Hi, Mrs. Alvarez!"

"Hello dear. I apologize, but I've forgotten your name."

"Emily. Would you like to come in?"

"No, no. I'm looking for Toby. I thought I'd check with you because he told me he likes you."

"Told you?"

"Not in so many words." She pats my hand. "Don't worry, dear, I'm not quite that far gone—yet. Toby lets me know when he takes a liking to someone and he's come home more than once with tuna on his breath."

"That was me. Sorry. I shouldn't feed him. He's just such a sweet cat."

"Quite alright. He only accepts food from people he trusts. I was wondering if you've seen him today. He went out for his walk hours ago and didn't come back. I thought maybe you brought him inside for a visit."

"I haven't seen him, but I can go look for him. Maybe he slipped into the stairwell when someone opened the door."

"I couldn't trouble you like that."

"It's no trouble at all." And I mean it. I love that old cat. He's one of my only friends in St. Augustine. "Don't worry. I'll find him."

* * *

"*Toby, Toby.*" I shouldn't have promised Mrs. Alvarez I'd find him. I've searched all four floors, stopping every person I ran into with, *Have you seen a ginger cat wandering around?*

I've reached the basement, checking inside the washers and dryers in case he climbed in for a catnap. The broken washers haven't been fixed. Broken washers. Broken mailbox. Broken swimming pool. Entire building, broken.

I circle each floor one more time on my way back up. On the third floor I come to 312, Jurado's apartment. I stop and knock.

The door inches open, chain-lock attached like before. "What do you want?" he says. His face is still badly bruised, but at least it doesn't look like raw meat.

"I'm looking for a lost cat. Have you seen one?"

"No." He starts to shut the door.

"Wait. What happened down here a couple weeks ago?"

"Mind your own business." Again with the mind your own business. Maybe it should go on my gravestone.

Here Lies Emily Blair Calby
She Never Minded Her Own Business

"Who beat you up? Was it Greg?"

He slams the door. What's his problem? He was nice the day I met him. Back on the fourth floor I turn left, stopping at Mrs. Alvarez's. I knock lightly.

"Who is it?"

Bless her heart. She's too short to see out the peephole.

"Emily. Your neighbor."

The door opens wide. "Did you find my baby boy?"

"No. I'm sorry. I checked every floor twice. Are you sure he's not hiding in your apartment somewhere?"

"I looked everywhere I could. I'm not quite as spry as I used to be."

"Would you like me to check?"

"Could you?"

"Of course."

Her apartment is a tidy two-bedroom, elegantly decorated with a beige overstuffed sofa, Persian rug and Louis VI chairs. Above the sofa hangs an oil painting of a much younger Mrs. Alvarez and a man I assume was her husband.

My search for Toby takes me high and low, on my toes to inspect the closet shelves and on my knees scanning under the furniture. One bedroom is set up as an office. A diploma on the wall says, Marisol Alvarez. Escuela Latinoamericana de Medicina. Havana, Cuba. Wow, a doctor!

"No sign of him," I say when I return. "But don't give up hope. I don't see how he could have got out of the building. I'll bet he's around here somewhere. If I could borrow a picture of him, I'll put a sign up in the lobby."

"*Mi preciosa*. Such a lovely girl. I know your parents are proud of you."

Welded smile.

Her delicate fingers pick up a photo frame from a side table. “Use this one. It’s his favorite. He loves to gaze at it, fancies himself quite the ladies’ man.” She gives me her phone number to put on the sign.

“Do you want me to put *Dr. Alvarez* on it? I saw your diploma.”

“Marisol will be fine. And you call me that too.”

“What kind of doctor are you?”

“I was an internist.” Her eyes point to the painting. “So was Ova. My husband. He passed on four years ago.”

“He sure was handsome. Do you have any children?”

She shakes her head and I detect regret. It makes me think of Nemworth. If for no other reason, people should have children so they have someone to look out for them when they get old.

I return to my apartment and make the sign with a sheet from the same art pad I used for Bryce’s painting. *Have You Seen This Cat?* I put clear-wrap over Toby’s picture to protect it and travel downstairs once more to tape the sign next to the mailboxes.

Toby’s vanishing act cost me almost two hours of study time. He’s getting a stern lecture next time I see him.

31

I'M SIPPING a latte in a cute coffee shop on a rainy Thursday afternoon. Can't believe I waited this long to find one. It's cozy, with red-brick walls, strings of hanging lights and a chalkboard menu.

It brings back memories of *Otherlands,* my favorite coffee shop in Memphis, my refuge from the confines of Lucas's building. I spent a lot of afternoons there doing my online undergrad work.

Today's mission is to fill in the gaps in my notes from this week's thrilling Civil Procedure lecture on *joinder. Woohoo.* Can't wait for next week. *Interpleader!* But it's coming to an end soon. Final exams start a week from Monday, right after the Thanksgiving break.

Everyone at school is living in a state of caffeinated, sleep-deprived stress. Each exam is four hours and covers the entire fourteen weeks. One good thing about Legal Writing is no exam. Yesterday we turned in our final assignment, the *major memo.* What a silly name for a twenty-page research paper requiring ten million hours of labor. My idea of a *memo* is *Buy bread* or *Don't forget to feed the cat.*

Cats. Poor Mrs. Alvarez—*Marisol* as she insists I call her. Toby hasn't shown up and no one called about the flyer in the lobby. It's been four days. He must have escaped from the building somehow.

When I got home yesterday, a gift bag sat outside my door,

poking my panic button like a hot needle. I thought the secret admirer had struck again, but inside was a bottle of dark rum with a thank you note from Mrs. Alvarez for helping her.

I went to her apartment to say thank you, not mentioning I don't drink. She asked if I would stay for a cup of tea. I was swamped, but she looked so lonely I couldn't say no. She's really interesting. Not only was she a doctor, she taught classes at the medical school in Havana where she got her degree.

Except for exam pressure, my life has been peaceful the last few weeks. No threatening pictures or messages, no stolen underwear, not even a chocolate kiss. The more time that passes since Lucas's presentation, the more I think the pictures were a sick prank, unconnected to anything else.

Henley and I have been spending most evenings together, going over our outlines and working through practice exams. Last night I let him come to my apartment to study for the first time, a gigantic leap in our "relationship," a word desperate for air quotes.

I'm not sure what our situation is. I admit we do make good *partners*, as he said at Bryce's house, at least when it comes to studying. I still don't feel any desire, but something's different because I told Lucas about him and even sent him a selfie I let Henley take of us. I never let people take pictures of me.

Tonight's another first. Every Thursday the 1Ls gather at a local bar. Law students love to drink. This week's edition is at an Irish pub. Henley asked me to go with him, as *friends*, preempting my question as to whether it was a date.

I said yes, even though hanging out with drunk law students talking nonstop about law school isn't my idea of a great time. I also know that whatever Henley and I call it, our classmates will think it's a date. I consider canceling, but know I need to make more of an effort if I'm ever going to find and keep a friend.

* * *

Maybe I should take up drinking. Everyone around me seems to be having the time of their life, laughing, cheering and booing about—what else?—law school. Except Henley, who seems content to talk to me while sipping a glass of Scottish ale.

I'm wearing a dress. I bought it at the Target next to my new gym. I now own two hundred percent more dresses than my previous total in the last eight years. It's cute, a watermelon-colored fit and flare, but this one has sleeves and reaches below my knees. Some of the girls are dressed to the nines, spiked heels, the whole nine yards.

Henley told me I look nice. He's been unusually inquisitive tonight. Right now, he's asking about my past.

"I know you don't like to talk about it and I understand that. I was just wondering how you think it might impact you in a relationship."

I almost spit my water out. Leave it to Henley. Direct and to the point. Is he seriously wondering about our prospects together?

"I have absolutely no idea." That's a lie. I have some idea and Henley deserves honesty. "Okay, I can think of one thing. I'm probably, no, I'm *definitely* too guarded. I have a hard time letting people get close to me."

He takes a swallow of beer and nods. "How many serious relationships have you had? Is that okay to ask?"

"Like, romantic relationships?" The answer is none, unless I count Ben at Pochachant, and I don't see how that could legitimately count as serious. "How many have you had?"

He smiles. "I asked you first."

"*Serious* ones? Well, none. What about you?"

"Same."

"Really? Get out. That's surprising."

"Why?"

"Because you're a guy and two years older than me. Why none?"

He examines the bottom of his beer glass. "I know it sounds old-fashioned, practically Victorian, but I've been waiting for the right person."

Someone nearby is cursing Nemworth. I turn with flashing eyes, but it's just a guy complaining about tomorrow's thirty-page assignment in Contracts. I'm about to tell Henley I agree with his relationship philosophy when Dale Olson staggers up.

"Well, if it isn't Benedict Arnold and his trophy. Just want you to know, buddy, that our study group is doing fine without you. F-I-N-E, *fine*."

The rage-tiger stirs. I am not a fan of being called a *trophy*. You want to see a trophy? How about I sever your head with my neck knife and mount it on that wall?

"Glad to hear things are going well," Henley says amiably.

That's *it*? Olson calls me a trophy and Henley doesn't stand up for me?

With Brady Chapman attached to his shoulder, Olson glances down and says, "Be careful she doesn't slit your throat in your sleep. Or maybe her gangbanger boyfriend will *pop a cap in yo ass*."

That does it. Nobody mocks Lucas. I curl my fingers and start to stand, but Henley grabs my wrist and pulls me down, whispering, "He isn't worth it."

He's right, of course. I steady myself with deep breathing, attempt to, but Olson's standing over me, invading my space, which is not going to work. I shoot a sideways glance at Henley, who's busy arranging his beer glass in the center of a napkin.

I'm about to stand again when Julie pops out of nowhere and wedges between us. "Get the fuck away from her."

"Or what?"

She puts a finger to her chin. "Hm, for starters I think I'll throw this beer in your face."

"Go ahead," he says smugly. "Then prepare to get sued for battery."

I squeeze my forehead. *Law students.* Henley pushes his chair back and gets up. It's about freaking time. He raises his hands and says calmly, "Everybody settle down. Dale, could I talk to you for a second?"

I watch as Henley leads Olson to a corner of the bar. Henley's face remains a picture of serenity as they talk, while Olson's jawbone looks like it's going to pop out of its joints. Henley holds out a palm. A pause before Dale digs out his wallet, slaps cash into it and wheels out the door in a huff.

The server is asking if everything's okay when Henley walks up and hands her a twenty. "This is for that gentleman's tab," he says, pointing to the door. "The one who just left. He said keep the change."

She thanks him and walks away.

"What the heck happened?" I say. "What did you say to get him to leave like that?"

"I told him I had written down every malicious comment he ever made about our professors and classmates during our study group meetings and that if he didn't leave immediately, I'd post them all on social media."

"No way! Did you really write them down?"

"Nah."

"Haha. Love it!" Henley's full of surprises. You never really know someone until you really know them. He defused the conflict without conflict. Maybe I can learn from him.

I rest my hands on his lanky shoulders and give a little squeeze. "Thank you, my knight in shining IQ." Julie's laughing and hoisting a toast to Henley's negotiation skills. "You too, Julie," I say.

"You'd do the same for me. You already did."

We leave soon after, not because of the Olson mess. We were both bored out of our minds. When Henley pulls up in front of Seaside, he says, "I already know the answer, but do you want me to walk you to the door?"

"No, but thanks for asking."

He undoes his seatbelt and twists his body sideways. I know what's coming and try not to visibly wince. To his credit, being Henley, he says, "Would it be okay if I kiss you?"

I say, "I guess," and he does.

32

"WHY DIDN'T you introduce me to your boyfriend when I was there?" Lucas says.

It's the Monday before Thanksgiving. I'm standing outside my new gym, bathed in sweat, taking a break after an hour of high-intensity intervals. I check the time. Already four o'clock. It takes thirty minutes to get here, time I can't spare, the downside of avoiding spa music and Greg the roid-rager.

"Because he's not my boyfriend ... I don't think." What are the rules? I never learned.

"You have sex with him?"

"Lucas! Don't ask me questions like that!"

"Just trying to help you figure out if you got a boyfriend."

"Well, we didn't have sex and I'm not planning on it ... but I did let him kiss me."

"And you let him take that little lovebirds selfie of you two. Sounds like a boyfriend to me. What you like about him? Sure ain't his looks from the picture you sent."

"Ah, that's mean. He's cute in his own way. You know looks aren't the most important thing to me. He's very nice and a hard worker, and polite and respectful. And super-smart."

I explain how Henley handled Dale Olson at the bar. "He stayed calm the whole time. Kept me out of a fight."

"Bonus points for that."

I hustle home to get started on studying. Exams begin in six days. Two more days of class, then Thursday and Friday off for Thanksgiving, then the weekend. Monday is D-Day. First exam is Contracts at eight a.m.

Lucas wanted me to fly home for Thanksgiving. "I can't," I said. "That's two whole study days." He wasn't happy, but it turned out okay. He decided to go visit Kiona in Las Vegas, which he needs to do. I promised to come home for the winter break.

In the lobby, I run into Mrs. Alvarez getting her mail. The poster with Toby's picture still hangs on the wall. It's been an entire week.

"Um, hi Mrs. Alvarez," I say.

"Emilita," she says, reaching out and cupping my hands.

"Any word about Toby?"

She shakes her head, despair obvious.

"Maybe he'll still turn up," I say, but neither of us believe it.

I reach out to my mailbox, which still hasn't been repaired even though I've called three times to complain.

"*Cuidado,*" she says, pointing to the floor. "Don't trip over your package."

A box is parked at my feet, a little bigger than a shoebox. It says Amazon on the side, but didn't come from there. My name and address are printed on top with a marker. Sent first-class mail.

"Something you ordered?"

"Uh, no." I study the box. No return address. That's strange.

"Maybe an admirer," she says coyly.

I walk with her to the elevator, package under my arm, holding the door until she maneuvers inside. The top of her head barely reaches my shoulder. I've heard old people shrink. "Mrs. Alvarez, I'd be happy to pick up your mail for you, or help with anything else you need."

"You are an angel," she says.

God would take issue with that.

"And remember. It's Marisol."

Inside my apartment, I shake the box before setting it on the kitchen table. It's taped up like a mummy. What could it be? Something from Lucas? Maybe a pre-exam surprise. Or Kiona. She's always sending me gifts.

I pull my neck knife from under my blouse and start slicing. Every seam is sealed. When I finally open the flaps, a chemical odor hits me in the face and I pull away.

What in the world? I lean in to pick out foam packing peanuts. They cover a clear plastic bag with something brown inside. Looks like leather. Shoes? A purse?

I slit the bag and pull it apart. It contains a ... roasted turkey? For Thanksgiving? Shouldn't it be packed in dry ice? Those were my first thoughts. I carried the box to the kitchen window for more light.

Good thing, or I wouldn't have reached the sink before vomiting.

* * *

"Take a breath," Lucas says. "You sure it's a cat?"

"Pretty sure, and it's probably Mrs. Alvarez's. Toby. He went missing a week ago. Should I tell her? I can't."

"Slow down. Let's take it step by step. Is there anything else in the box, a letter or note?"

"I don't know. I closed it as fast as I could and stashed it on the balcony. The smell is revolting. Not a rotting smell. Chemical. I'm thinking formaldehyde."

"Someone went through a lot of trouble."

"Why? Why would anyone hurt Toby and send him to me? He's not even my cat. ... Unless the person thought he was mine. Toby used to wait at my door a lot because I always fed him and ... wait a minute! I just remembered something. The day Toby disappeared, I got a camera alert while I was at school. A man knocked on my door and then walked away. Maybe he took Toby."

"What'd he look like?"

"I don't know. I had a privacy zone set on my neighbor's door. Gabberman. He complained about the camera. Unfortunately, his door is directly across from mine."

"What good is a camera if you block the view?"

"Gabberman was really mad, threatened to break the camera or get his own and point it at my door. I turned off the privacy zone after I got that alert. Too late."

"So you didn't see nothin'?"

"Just the back of a man with dark hair moving away."

"Send me the video so I can analyze it."

"I never signed up for the cloud service. It was ten bucks a month. It was just a livestream."

Lucas groans.

"It *has* to be someone here at Seaside, right? It's a locked building. Maybe this is proof that everything is connected, maybe even all the way back to the sticky note and chocolate kiss."

"I don't know about that. Why send it by mail if they live in the building?"

"Not sure, but if it's Toby, the person had to have access."

"Alright, first thing to do is check what else is in the box. Can you handle that?"

"I'll probably puke again, but yeah. I'll check it and call you right back."

I take a spatula out to the balcony and use it to pry open the cardboard flaps. Lucas said try not to touch anything. Moving the bag around, I hold my breath, one eye closed. At the bottom lies a lavender envelope, like a greeting card. I pinch it with a paper towel and pull it out with my eyes closed.

Quit being such a wimp. You've seen plenty worse. I have to know if it's Toby. I force myself to examine the poor creature inside, on his back, bony paws curled in the air, like Toby used to pose when I rubbed his stomach. Then I see the charred collar and the ID tag, scorched black. I rub it clean with the paper towel. *My name is Toby. If I'm lost, call my mami ...*

I shut the box and take the envelope inside, washing my hands before calling Lucas back.

"It's Toby alright. And I found an envelope. I think it's a card."

"Open it. Try not to get fingerprints on it."

I slit the envelope with my neck knife and shake out a card with flowers on the front. *With Deepest Sympathy.* Inside is a folded sheet of paper.

"It's a sympathy card with a note inside."

"Read it."

"*Dear*—I can't say it. It's the C-word."

Sometimes I know Lucas's mood just by his phone breathing. Right now I hear a locomotive steaming down the track. Fury. "Alright," he says.

"*Dear blank. You and your kind have destroyed our lives and the lives of many.*" I pause to force down the bile bubbling up my esophagus.

"That it?"

"No. There's more. It's bad. *For that, you have been put on trial. The verdict was GUILTY. The sentence is DEATH.*"

"Sick motherfucker. Go on."

"*Don't worry. We will not overcook you like your cat. Tender is the flesh that satisfies.*"

"Anything else?"

"A postscript. I—I can't read it."

"Say it. I need to know."

"It says, *p.s. You've never ...*" I stop and wipe my eyes. "*You've never heard a cat screech until you throw him in the oven.*" Poor Toby.

Silence except for Lucas's thick breathing. "Any signature?" he says.

"No, and it's typewritten."

"Alright. I'll be there by morning."

"*No no no.* You're going to visit Kiona in Las Vegas for Thanksgiving, like you should have done a long time ago. I'll call

Agent Forster. This package came in the mail. That gives the FBI jurisdiction. Maybe it's Romansky. How many people out there have cannibalism fetishes?"

"You just got done saying it was someone in your building. Which is it?"

I scrunch my shoulders, stress bones crackling. "I don't know."

"Go ahead and call your Agent Forster. I'm still coming."

"No, please. You don't understand. Finals start next week. Everything in law school depends on first-year grades. I need to focus on them. You being here will be a distraction."

Lucas's laugh is definitely not of the *haha* variety. More like disgust. "Gettin' a dead cat in the mail ain't distracting to you?"

"Of course it is. I'm sorry. I didn't mean like a bad distraction. I wish I could come home tomorrow. But I can't, Lucas. Law school is important to me. You've been telling me to go since I was sixteen. I've worked my butt off for fourteen weeks, harder than I've ever worked on anything except training with you and Kiona."

"*Pfft*. What's more important to you? A grade on a piece of paper or your life?"

"You mean, like right now? Just kidding! There's nothing either one of us can do without outside help. We don't know who did it or even what it's about. It could be some kind of a scare campaign. Like you said at the beginning, if someone really wanted to hurt me, they wouldn't need to go through this much trouble."

"They are hurting you. Can't you see? They're tearing you apart from the inside."

I study the note again. "What could it mean? *You and your kind have destroyed our lives and the lives of many*. Who is *my kind?* Could it be a relative of Brooker? Or maybe tall man or stocky man. Maybe even someone who figured out what happened to Twiggs, the correctional officer at Pochachant."

"Maybe all of 'em. Maybe they formed an *Emily Calby Killed My Relative* support group and live in a commune on the second floor. What the fuck do I know? Go call your FBI. Then go study some more. I gotta go," he says and hangs up.

He's pissed. I find Agent Forster's number in my contacts.

33

I POINT into the darkness. "It's on the balcony." I'm in my living room with Agent Forster and an agent he brought from the Jacksonville field office. Margareth Magritte.

So tired. I hardly slept last night knowing poor Toby was curled up outside in the cardboard casket. I didn't tell Mrs. Alvarez, couldn't bear to. We passed in the hall today when I got home from school—where I was unprepared for every class for the first time. She asked me to come over for tea again. I told her I had to study and hurried away.

Agent Forster looks almost the same as the first time I met him eight years ago. His salt and pepper hair has more salt, but his tan cheeks are as buttery smooth as ever.

Agent Magritte is a statuesque black woman with short-cropped hair in a navy blue suit. I catch a glimpse of a Glock nine-millimeter on her belt as she turns to hand the evidence bag containing the card and letter to Forster. They exchange grim looks.

Forster explains that Florida is outside of his territory, which is why he asked Agent Magritte from the Jacksonville office to accompany him.

"Thank you both for coming," I say.

I run through the full chronology, starting at the beginning: the sticky note and chocolate kiss, the rose and love note, even the stolen underwear. Forster had already told Magritte about the photos sent during Lucas's presentation.

"On the day Toby disappeared, I got an alert from my door camera. A man was knocking ..." They were as disappointed as Lucas that I had the privacy zone turned on and the video wasn't stored.

"Could you show us the box?" Agent Magritte says.

I turn on the outside light and lead them to the balcony, Forster helping me wrestle open the sliding door, which is off the track again. The stars are bright. The fronds of my kentia palm dance in the ocean breeze. Another heavenly Florida night ... except for the box from hell. "There it is," I say.

Agent Magritte stretches on a mask and gloves and inspects it with a flashlight. An *umm* escapes when she opens the bag, but she doesn't flinch. She moves aside and Forster leans in for a look, shaking his head.

"Maybe you two should go inside while I bag and tag it," Magritte says.

I follow Forster in. He waits until we're seated before leaning forward with his elbows on his legs, hands clasped, wearing the same thick wedding band as the first time we met.

"Emily. What can I say? You've experienced more trauma in your young life than any person should ever have to endure." He knows me well enough not to add *I'm sorry,* even though I know he is. "Now this. How is Lucas taking it?"

"Not well. He wants to be here. I told him not to come."

"Have you thought about going home, where you'd be safer?"

"I can't. I have my final law school exams next week."

"Given the seriousness of the two events—the photos, then this—don't you think they'd let you postpone them? I'd be happy to talk to your dean."

"I don't want to postpone them and I don't want anyone to know about this. Some people already think I get special treatment and others think I'm a freak."

Agent Magritte comes in carrying the box sealed in a large clear bag. She sets it down and goes to the kitchen sink.

I say, "Nobody gets how important law school finals are, especially the very first ones. They can determine your whole future."

Magritte returns, wiping her hands with a paper towel. "It sounds crazy, Jeff, but she's right. I'm still scarred from my first year."

"See, Emily?" Forster says. "I told you the FBI likes to hire agents with law degrees. Agent Magritte here graduated from Georgetown law."

Magritte laughs. "Have you been trying to recruit her?"

"For years," he says. "First as a sketch artist."

Time to get serious. I see it in his eyes. He knows me well. He'll give me the unadorned truth, good or bad, knowing that's what I want.

"Agent Magritte and I discussed your situation driving here from Jacksonville. While we can't be sure, it certainly appears possible, maybe even likely, that the photos and deceased cat are connected. Would you agree?"

"Seems logical, especially since they both mentioned my *flesh*. Do you think everything could be connected? You know, from the beginning."

"Can't rule anything out. Could be a planned escalation."

"Or someone losing control," Magritte says ominously, more to Forster than to me.

"Part of me thinks it's someone in the building because you need a key to get in, but I can't stop thinking about Roland Romansky. The whole *flesh* thing."

"I filled Agent Magritte in about Romansky. She's already spoken with your property management company. No one by that name lives here."

"I'm surprised you got through. That company completely sucks, excuse my language."

Magritte says, "It helps when you can leave a voicemail saying you're calling as part of an FBI investigation."

"Maybe he's using a fake name."

She says, "That's hard to pull off these days without high-level professional help because they run credit checks on applicants."

I had high-level professional help changing my identity for four years. Lucas Jackson, expert document forger.

Forster says, "Anyone in the building who comes to mind?"

"Well, there's this guy named Greg. He's a personal trainer ..." I explain about Greg, that he got insulted when I rejected his flirtations at the gym and apparently beat up Jurado and Gabberman. "He would be my top choice."

Forster looks at Magritte. "What say we have a chat with Greg the trainer?"

She nods.

"I don't know his last name or what unit he lives in, but he works down the street at a gym called the Peaceful Moon."

"We'll find him."

"What do you guys think about the crazy letter?"

Forster says, "It's ugly, for sure, but impossible to draw any conclusions without investigation."

"Time to get the ol' *text analysts* on it, huh?" That's how the FBI identified me when I was twelve and on the run, pretending to be *Robert Williams* via email.

He smiles. "You got it. We'll also do a forensic workup on the note and, uh, package. In the meantime, my primary goal is to keep you safe. Any thoughts about that?"

"Can I borrow one of your Glocks?"

34

MY LAST Contracts class is loaded with uplifting announcements that the exam will be hard and several people will probably flunk it. Classic Nemworth. I'm going to miss him. I already do. He occasionally looks my way, but I'm not sure he can see me. One more thing I never got to do for him. Clean his glasses.

Agent Magritte laughed at my Glock comment last night, but Agent Forster knew I was only half joking. They were reluctant to leave me alone, wanting to notify the local police about the situation. I begged them not to, saying the worst thing that could happen to me (short of getting murdered, which I left out) would be more public attention.

"I'll be okay," I said. "I have a door camera and a new neck knife and—" I stop. There were people in the FBI who suspected me of killing tall man and stocky man. "Not that I know how to use it or anything. Mostly I have a lot of confidence in the FBI."

Forster cleared his throat, maybe to keep from laughing, while Magritte cautioned me about the dangers of neck knives and gave me her cell number. I thanked her again for coming.

"Happy to help," she said. "You probably already know it, but you have yourself a good friend here in Agent Forster."

"I do know. Thank you, Agent Forster, for *everything*."

I stayed up studying until almost two after they left, determined to be extra well-prepared for my last day of classes. I took breaks to check the peephole and practice pulling out the neck knife.

Covering my mouth, I yawn as our final Contracts class winds to a conclusion. I was clinging to a hope Nemworth would mark the occasion with some words of wisdom or inspiration, but he just thumps his casebook shut and reaches for his cane, same as always.

As he steps off the podium, I leap up and start clapping. Henley joins me. Then everyone does. We keep it up until he exits, which takes so long my hands are stinging. Henley glances back at me and raises a triumphant fist.

Exchanging my Contracts book for Torts, I run into Julie at my locker. "Hey, girl," I say. "Last day of classes. Congrats!"

"Thanks," she says like Eeyore. "I don't know if I'll even make it to exams. I've never been so stressed in my life."

I refrain from joking, *Try being stalked by cannibals.* "You'll be fine. Your answer in Torts about the *Wagon Mound* cases was spot on and they were hard. I know you can do it."

I take a different route home, hyperaware, scrutinizing every face. The only way to pump my vigilance any higher would be to spin in circles. I go two blocks past Seaside on a different street before circling back to make sure I'm not being followed.

I plot my exam study schedule as I walk. Four full days. They say to study for the later exams first because ...

Flashing blue lights ahead. Two cop cars.

That's my building! I pick up the pace. Across the street are two unmarked black SUVs with flashing red lights built into the grill. Did Forster and Magritte already solve my case?

OMG, sure enough, there they are, standing out front with two uniformed locals. A man in a dark suit is carrying a large box out the front door. Trailing behind him is a guy with thick arms and a bulging chest.

Greg. They got him. I knew it! *See?* You're not just paranoid. There's nothing wrong with you.

He stops to say something to Forster and Magritte. I break into a run.

"Agent Forster! Agent Magritte! You guys are amazing. I can't believe you solved everything in one day! Hello, *Gre-eg.*" Effing psycho cat-killer.

He glowers at me. Why isn't he in restraints? He mutters something as the front door bangs open and a big cop shoulders through. Behind him is a man in a blue blazer with slicked-back hair, wearing handcuffs.

WTF? It's Matt Jurado.

"No no no," I say. "You got the wrong guy. He's the one," stabbing a finger at Greg.

"Emily," Forster says.

"Agent Forster, he's the one I was talking about. He beat the crap out of this guy. Look at his bruises."

More firmly, "*Emily.*" A clear mandate to shut the hell up. "We will fill you in shortly."

I watch in bewilderment as the cops load Jurado into the back of a car. Greg gives me a disgusted look and goes inside.

I'm about to object when Agent Magritte lays a hand on my shoulder. "Let's go up to your apartment. We have a lot to tell you."

* * *

The first thing they do on entering is walk around examining the floor. I follow along. Forster points at a couple of spots and Magritte takes close-up pictures with her phone.

"What's going on?" I say. "Why did you arrest Jurado? Why not Greg? Did Jurado kill Toby? Why—"

Forster holds up a stop-sign hand. "Didn't I say she'd be good at cross-examination?"

We settle in the living room. Agent Magritte speaks first.

"Agent Forster told me you lead an exciting life. I don't need any more convincing. Prepare yourself for some disturbing information. He said you prefer the unvarnished truth."

"I do. I'm ready," I say.

"We tracked down Greg at the gym this morning. His last name is Toulian." She spells it for me. "He lives on the second floor, in unit two-seventeen. He was quite willing to talk to us."

I already want to butt in, but stitch my lips.

"He denied taking Toby. He did admit to seeing the cat one time, when he came to your floor to leave the rose and note you told us about."

"So it was him! He pretended to be coming in from the rain."

Magritte produces a small recorder from her shoulder bag. "How about we let him fill in the story? He agreed to let us record the interview." She sets the recorder on the coffee table and fiddles with the volume. I recognize both voices.

Magritte: So you had some kind of a thing for her?

Greg: I'm not sure what you mean by a thing.

Magritte: A crush?

Greg: I liked her. Well, I thought I did. Believe me, I don't anymore.

Magritte: She said you asked her on a date.

Greg: I just asked if she wanted to go for a drink or get coffee or something. That's it.

Magritte: Did you leave a rose and a note outside her door?

A pause.

Greg: Yes. It was immature. I admit it. I guess I'm not real confident with women. I didn't mean any harm.

Magritte: Anything else?

Greg: I put a chocolate kiss and note in her mailbox when she moved in. All it said was welcome to the neighborhood.

Magritte: How did you know it was her mailbox?

Another pause before, *Please don't get me in trouble with my job. I looked it up on her gym application.*

Again my freaking personal information gets violated! Jerk!

Magritte: Did you steal her underwear?

Greg: Huh? What are you talking about?

Magritte: Did you take a bra and pair of underwear that belonged to her from the washer or dryer in the laundry room? ... The recorder can't pick up a headshake. Can you answer yes or no?

Greg: Absolutely not.

She stops the recorder and speeds it ahead. "The next part is where I questioned him about Toby. He denied it emphatically. No point reliving the gruesome details. He also said he wasn't at your friend Lucas's presentation.

"Do you believe him?"

"His sign-in records at the Peaceful Moon confirm he was at work on both days."

"What about the underwear?"

"You heard him deny it. No way to verify."

"Well, that's two little mysteries solved. The chocolate kiss and the rose. But I'm still not getting where Jurado fits in."

"That's coming right up." She hits play.

Magritte: Did Emily reject your advances at some point?

Greg: I wouldn't call them advances, but she made it clear she didn't want anything to do with me.

Magritte: Did that make you angry?

Greg: It hurt my feelings.

Magritte: Did you want to hurt Emily?

Greg: No. Never.

Magritte: Emily described an incident that occurred in the apartment below her. The tenant's name is Matt Jurado. Do you know Mr. Jurado?

Greg: Oh, yeah. I know Mr. Jurado.

Magritte: She thinks you beat him up, and also her neighbor across the hall. Lyle Gabberman. Is that accurate?

Greg: Yes as to Jurado. Gabberman just kind of got in the way.

Magritte: Why did you beat up Mr. Jurado?

Greg: This could get me in big trouble.

Magritte: You may already be in big trouble. Why did you beat up Mr. Jurado?

Greg: I did it for Emily.

Magritte stops the recorder.

"What?" I say. "He did it for me? What does that mean?"

"Here's where things get crazy, and disturbing. You want to jump in, Jeff?"

Agent Forster says, "Emily, it turns out Mr. Jurado supported himself selling drugs. That's what he has been arrested for. He had quite the inventory, sort of a one-stop shop for connoisseurs." He opens his phone. "Let's see here. Approximately three pounds of marijuana, two ounces of cocaine, opioids, steroids ..."

Lucas was right about Greg being a juicer. He was in Jurado's apartment that night to restock on steroids. Gabberman was there buying pot.

"As Greg tells it, when he entered the apartment, Gabberman was already present," Forster says. "While waiting for them to transact their business, he caught a glimpse of Jurado's computer screen. Brace yourself. What he saw on the monitor was you, sitting at your kitchen table studying."

In Torts we learned about a doctrine called *res ipsa loquitur*, which translates from Latin to *the thing speaks for itself.* That's what my face is doing right now, broadcasting complete noncomprehension. "Me? On his computer screen? I don't get it."

"You saw us looking at your floor when we came in, right?"

"Mm-hm."

"That's because Mr. Jurado drilled holes through his ceiling and installed pinhole cameras in them."

I clasp my mouth. Talking through my fingers, "You don't mean."

"I'm afraid I do. He did it to watch you. Greg says when he figured out what was going on, he went berserk. Smashed Jurado's computer equipment, then did pretty much the same to Jurado.

"As for Mr. Gabberman, Greg called it an accident. Said he tried to play peacemaker in the middle of a right cross. We talked to him too. He admitted buying marijuana from Jurado, but swore he had no idea about the cameras."

"Why didn't Greg call the cops about Jurado and the cameras?"

"He was there buying illegal drugs. Gabberman gave the same explanation."

I get up and walk to one of the spots Forster and Magritte examined when they first entered. In the corner of the living room, a pencil-thin hole in the wood floor. *It's a dangerous building,* Gabberman said in the hall that day.

I return to my seat, anger rapidly supplanting shock. My first thought is *Kill Jurado.* "Does this mean my ... my entire ... everything?"

Forster hands the ball back to Magritte. "Not necessarily," she says. "Jurado didn't know your floor plan. He apparently was able to install two cameras, one in your bedroom and one in your living room. Fortunately, your dresser completely blocked the view from the one in the bedroom. So unless you walk around in your living room ..."

"Naked? I don't. I'm probably the most covered-up person in St. Augustine." Three cheers for modesty. "I doubt I've ever left my bedroom without at least a robe on."

"In that case, we think what he mostly saw was you studying at your kitchen table, same thing Greg saw the night he tore everything up."

Bad enough. I shiver at the thought.

"We confiscated what was left of his electronic equipment after Mr. Toulian's rampage," Forster says. "Which wasn't much. Jurado's in the county jail and barred from returning to the building even if he bails out. The crime scene is sealed off."

"You said he was arrested for drugs. Isn't it a crime to, you know?"

"It is, but the drug charges will bring harsher penalties under Florida's sentencing laws, and keep your name out of the proceedings. I was thinking of you in asking the locals not to tack on the video voyeurism charge, but we can probably get that changed if you disagree."

"I don't disagree. I hate to see him get away with it, but you're right. It's humiliating enough. Thanks for thinking about that. What about Toby? Could Jurado have killed him?"

"He's not talking, but it doesn't appear he had any animosity toward you, just a sick fantasy. There was nothing in his apartment suggesting he recently killed, cooked or packaged a cat."

"What about the presentation pictures?"

"Did you see him in the audience?"

"No, but it was really crowded."

"Well, we're still investigating. I think I explained PRNU to you."

Photo-response non-uniformity. "You did. That every phone camera has identifiable imaging flaws. Lucas explained it too."

"Maybe Lucas is the one I should be recruiting for the FBI," he says.

I laugh. "Now *that* I would love to see."

"We have Jurado's phone. I'll ask the folks in forensics to take some pictures with it and compare them to the presentation images. While we wait, you're safer operating on the assumption that whoever took the pictures and killed Toby is still out there."

"So you don't think it's Jurado, Greg's in the clear and I can't see Gabberman killing a cat. That would mean it's either someone in the building who I don't know or an outsider who found a way in."

"That seems to be the key question," Forster says.

"What happens to Greg and Gabberman?"

"Probably nothing. Based on what we know, their only crime is illegal drug possession. Jurado has no interest in pressing charges against Greg for assault."

"I definitely owe Greg an apology."

* * *

A cracked plastic rectangle says *217.* I knock. Greg answers wearing a black tank top that shows off his massive upper-body. A TV is on behind him, monster trucks crunching cars.

"Hi, Greg," I say.

"What do you want?"

"I came to apologize and say thank you."

"That it?"

"Um, yeah, but—"

He starts to close the door. "Hold on. I'd like to explain a little better, if that's okay."

"Go on."

"First, I wanted to say I'm sorry if I acted rude at the gym. It wasn't anything personal." Should I leave it at that? I decide I owe him more. "I go into protective mode when men approach me. I'm programmed to think they have bad motives. You didn't do anything wrong. You were just being nice to a girl you liked. Um, thanks for liking me." That sounded dumb. Don't get carried away.

"Apology accepted," he says, not exactly friendly, but the ice melted a little.

"As for the thank you, wow, you have no idea how much I appreciate what you did to Jurado and his computers. I'm *so* glad you beat the hell out of him."

This brings a laugh from his well-insulated neck. But it's true. Jail isn't enough for what Jurado did. If I were being faithful to the deserves-to-die philosophy Lucas taught me—and then made me abandon—Jurado would be at the top of the list with a bullet. Pun intended.

"You're welcome," he says.

"Anyway, I guess that's about it, except would you mind if I came back to work out at the Peaceful Moon?" I'm wasting an hour a day driving back and forth to the new gym.

"Fine with me," he says and shuts the door.

35

JURADO AND the cameras are gone, but I plugged the holes with tissue paper and scrutinized every square centimeter of the floor before calling Lucas to tell him what happened. He was on his way to the airport to catch his flight to Las Vegas.

He stayed silent the entire time. When I finished all he said was, "Trouble follows you wherever you go. Thing you're in is just a sac o'woe."

"Where'd that come from?"

"Look it up," he said. "Law school ain't the only education. Gotta go."

I barely got out *Happy Thanksgiving* before he hung up on me, obviously still upset about me insisting he not come to St. Augustine. I Googled the words. It's a song lyric from a couple of fifties jazz cats.

Can't argue with truth. *Why does trouble follow me?* asks the sac o'woe. Maybe I follow it. That's Lucas's theory. Once I said I wished I could lead a calmer life and he said, *Then make calmer decisions.*

I hope he knows how much I wish I could spend Thanksgiving with him. Instead, I spend it with Henley, camped in my living room in exam overdrive.

Only the first day of the study period and it looks like a tornado hit. Papers and books are strewn everywhere. Multicolored highlighters surround us like a school of neon fish. Extension cords wind like snakes across the crooked floor. My sink's already filling up with coffee cups.

Adding to the mess is the bankers box parked in the corner. The last box of documents from the Artiel Jones case against Regal Estates. Bryce told me to stop working during exams, but I wanted to finish the job so I brought it home. Maybe I can get to it tonight.

It's been a long day already. We started with Torts. Henley and I agreed to work six hours straight starting at eight a.m. before breaking for lunch. We're almost there. Good. I'm famished. I just finished my recitation of the doctrine of *negligence per se*.

I slap my computer shut. "That's it for Torts. Let's go to lunch. I'm starving."

"We have fifteen more minutes pursuant to our six-hour rule."

"Henley, it was a concept, not a fixed rule. And even if it was, I'd argue there's an implied emergency exception when one of us is dying of hunger."

"Okay, but next time it might be thirty minutes early, then forty-five."

I cannot believe Henley Oliver is *out-emily-calbying* me. "Fine. Let's just skip lunch, dinner too. And sleep. We'll study straight through until Contracts starts Monday morning."

"Come on. It's just fifteen minutes. Then we can go enjoy our first Thanksgiving meal together," he says, nudging me with his elbow.

First? Either a joke or another indicator he's way out in front of me in terms of how he views our course of dealing. I like Henley, but the more time we spend together, the more I know he's not *The One*. I've considered the possibility it's just another example of my default reaction to anyone who gets too close. Push them away. But there's more to it. He just doesn't light a fire in me.

Before we leave, I text Lucas. *I hope you and Kiona are having a great Thanksgiving! I've been studying all day and am finally going out to lunch.* I start to add *Wish you were here*, which is true, but that would probably just irritate him.

We find a cafeteria serving traditional Thanksgiving fare. Turkey, dressing, pumpkin pie, the works. All you can eat. I take them up on it. I'm halfway through my second helping when my phone chimes.

The camera app again. Probably just Gabberman, but I check it anyway. At least I'm back to having legit excuses for my hypervigilance.

Huh, just a black screen. Did the camera battery run out? No, I hear movement and what sounds like Gabberman's door opening and closing. Why no image?

* * *

I parted with Henley after our late lunch, wanting to squeeze in a quick workout and do some studying on my own. We agreed to reconvene at my apartment in the morning. I've still never been to his place. He's never invited me, which is fine because I prefer my own space.

Before we left the cafeteria, I bought a take-home meal and filled a plate with turkey and all the fixings. It occurred to me Mrs. Alvarez might be spending Thanksgiving alone. I still haven't told her about Toby. Agent Forster gave me an excuse not to, saying it was part of a confidential criminal investigation.

"Knock, knock," I say, tapping on her door. "It's Emily, your neighbor."

She greets me with an effusive *Emilita!* She's wearing denim shorts and a beachy short-sleeve blouse. She's the cutest little old lady in the world.

"Hi, Mrs. Al—Marisol. Happy Thanksgiving!"

"Come in, come in."

"I can't stay. Sorry. I'm studying for exams. But I brought you this in case you were hungry. I didn't cook it. It's from a cafeteria."

The aromas wafting from her apartment suggested she had already cooked up something much better, but she appreciated the gesture, saying she wanted to adopt me as her granddaughter. Not only did she understand why I couldn't stay, she said, *Estudia, estudia mucho!* Haha. Like listening to Nemworth in Spanish. They'd probably like each other.

He's been on my mind today. It's been three weeks since our "break-up." I'm conflicted because I don't want him to be alone on Thanksgiving, but I more don't want him to be with blood-sucking Christina.

Rounding the hall, I'm relieved there are no roses or dead animals or anything else in front of my door. My door camera looks undisturbed. I open the app and it's working perfectly. Must have been an internet glitch at the cafeteria. I'm looking straight into my own face, standing in front of Gabberman's door.

What the ... Over my shoulder I see a new peephole camera, the exact same model as mine! I pound on his door with a fist.

"Lyle. Oh, Lyle."

No movement. I guess I can't be mad at him for doing the same thing he's mad at me for. I also can't blame him for being careful after the Jurado ordeal, although you'd think he'd be more discrete about smoking weed. The hallway reeks. I guess that's his life, sitting around in his bathrobe smoking pot.

Lucas says it's relaxing. Maybe I should try it. My pressure-cooker brain is about to blow. I hate taking time from studying but need a workout to let some steam out.

Drive thirty minutes to the new gym or walk two minutes to the Peaceful Moon? Easy choice.

Entering, there's Greg, working with a woman doing sit-ups on a mat. I sheepishly ask Rayna, the girl behind the counter, if I can buy a guest pass. Ugh, ten dollars. I'm opening my wallet when here comes Greg. *Please don't make a scene.*

"Hi, Emily," he says mildly.

"Um, hi, Greg."

"She's good to go, Rayna," he says. "Complimentary. She's thinking about rejoining."

His voice sounds more normal, more confident, like he's not trying so hard. "Have a good workout," he says and returns to the woman in the corner.

He didn't bother me the entire time. I pushed myself to the edge for an hour, evoking memories of Kiona standing over me in Lucas's basement shouting, *Beast it up, beast it up!*

I limp home and microwave a frozen meal so I can dive back into the books. I work until my forehead bounces off the monitor. I nodded off. Enough.

But my eyes land on the bankers box stationed in the corner. I've kept Bryce waiting the entire semester for one measly project. I need to finish the job.

I refill my water bottle and set the box on the table. The first folder is same ol', same ol'. Eviction letters, Regal's most efficient function. No point studying them. I fan the stack, stopping only when the wavelike orange and aqua letterhead registers in my depleted brain.

Seaside Apartments
Paradise by the Sea

I riffle through the box. It's *all* Seaside. The discovery zaps me with energy, which lasts about five minutes, the time it takes to realize it's just one more incomplete mess of paper. A file labeled Leases got my attention, but there was no Romansky. Or a Jurado or Gabberman or Toulian, not even a Calby.

Even doing a slipshod job of skimming, it takes an hour to reach the back of the box, where I use both hands to pull out a thick brown expanding folder labeled *Repair Requests*. A thousand bucks says there's nothing in it about my mailbox.

It's unanimous! Everyone hates Regal Estates. Complaints about the broken washing machines, the elevator stopping between floors, a faucet twirling in circles. I laugh out loud when I come to a letter complaining about the pool.

Dear Dipshits Who Never Answer the Phone:

I moved here to enjoy the sparkling rooftop swimming pool pictured in the attached brochure. Instead I found a toxic waste pit that's been closed for "repairs" since I arrived eight months ago.

I'm writing to tell you I am breaking my lease ...

I study the brochure. The pictures must have been taken ten years ago. The inviting pool, fresh paint, groomed landscaping. Even the back of the building and alley look fresh and tidy. What a fraud.

The complaints go on and on:

Air conditioner blowing hot air.

Windows leaking and it's raining.

Toilet won't flush.

Balcony rail loose, uncle almost fell off

Broken lock on backdoor.

Pool still not fixed!

Whoa, wake up. Broken lock on the backdoor? A way for cat-killers to get in. Dated a month ago. But there's also a repair ticket, dated a few days later. *Checked backdoor. Lock working fine.*

I look at the time and sigh. I swore to myself I'd be in bed by midnight, but this can't wait. I put on my neck knife and head out the door, taking the elevator to the basement.

Everything is spookily quiet when I step out. The laundry room is to my right. I'm facing the backdoor.

I bang on it. Solid. A sign says, *For Deliveries Only, Keep Locked at All Times.* I twist the knob. The door doesn't budge. A double-keyed deadbolt holds it tight.

Another dead end, another waste of time. I take the stairs back up, still wearing the sweat of the longest Thanksgiving I ever spent. I'll shower in the morning. I text Henley to say I won't be ready until ten and turn off my phone in case he replies with another lecture.

I can't believe this is only my first day of exam studying. It seems like I should be getting ready to graduate by now. I can't even imagine what next week is going to be like. I wish I could blink my eyes and jump ahead.

Instead I close them and am asleep in one minute.

36

FRIDAY, ONE P.M.:

... In conclusion, because the risk of branches falling is the very risk that made it negligent to not maintain the tree properly, the lightning strike would not be a superseding Act of God relieving the State Parks Agency of liability.

Two minutes left. Four hours passed in a blink, just like the first two exams. I do a quick skim for typos and hit the submit button.

"That's it, folks. Exam's over," Professor LeMoy says. "No more writing."

I crack my back and rub my aching neck. *Woohoo!* Three down, one to go!

What a week. Things got off to a shaky start Monday when five minutes into Nemworth's exam, a guy ran out of the room screaming his head was on fire and never came back. I didn't think the exam was that bad, maybe because I studied harder for it than the others, or missed everything. I had hoped to see Professor Nemworth, but he sent a proctor.

Owusua's Property exam was intricate, but the nice thing about property law is the rules are concrete. If you know them, they're easy to apply, like solving a math problem. Most law exists in the fuzzy netherworld of *It depends.*

Torts was its usual crazy self. The main essay was about some campers who got caught in a storm at a state park. Calamity and bodily harm ensued, as they always do in Torts—including a rotted tree struck by lightning that fell on one of the campers. I think I spotted the issues, but you never know in law school.

My classmates file out in a zombie march. Olson strides past me wearing his usual self-congratulatory smirk. Brady Chapman looks shell-shocked. He spent the whole semester partying. *Guess what, Brady? You were supposed to study.*

Henley approaches as I pack up. "What did you think?" he says.

"Who knows? I thought it was fair. Tricky, but fair."

"Ready to start on Civ Pro?"

I laugh. "Right now?"

"Of course not. After lunch."

"No way. After a week like this I need more of a break than lunch. Civ Pro isn't until Monday. I'm taking the afternoon off to recuperate. We can jump back on it in the morning."

"As you like. Let me know if you change your mind. I'll be studying."

Watching him walk away, I'm not sure if I'm more annoyed at him or me, for taking a break. I give a wide berth on my way out to the clumps of classmates dishing about the Torts exam.

I text Lucas when I get outside. *Only one more exam!*

No response. I'm starting to worry about him, about us. He hasn't been checking on me, which is good in a way but definitely not the norm. I never thought I would miss it. When we talk, he keeps the conversations short, always saying he has something to do or somewhere to go.

I'm feeling abandoned when it occurs to me he probably feels the same way. I'll make everything up to him when I get home for the semester break. I need to think of a really great Christmas present.

My phone pings as I round the corner from the promenade onto the sidewalk. A text from Lucas: *Good.*

That's it? Staring at it, I smack headfirst into a man moving quickly down the sidewalk in the other direction. Tall and lean, in jeans and a gray t-shirt, wearing sunglasses and a black ballcap pulled down tight.

"Sorry," I say.

He's two steps past me when I hear, "Yublebee, Stacy," followed by a laugh and more words I can't make out.

Yublebee? Sounds like some kind of holiday greeting. Was he talking to me? He's wearing ear pods. Maybe he's on the phone.

I go to my new favorite coffee shop and splurge on a salmon and cucumber sandwich to celebrate the end of the first week of exams before heading to the Peaceful Moon for a light workout.

I rejoined. Greg's here. We wave to each other. It's still awkward, but anyone who beats the crap out of the guy who drilled holes in my floor to spy on me is A-okay in my book.

Back at my apartment, scowling at Gabberman's new camera, it dawns on me my camera app hasn't gone off much in the past few days. Maybe Gabberman went into seclusion after getting beat up.

I drop my gear and fall back into my sofa, reassuring myself I need this break to recharge. Sometimes you can work too hard. Henley should take a break too. His intensity overwhelms me sometimes, which is saying a lot since I'm not exactly Little Miss Mild.

Five minutes later I'm already fidgeting. I can't just sit here and do nothing. I spy the box of Regal Estates documents. I went through them slapdash. Definitely not up to my standards. If I'm going to flub my first legal job assignment, I'm at least going to do it on the merits.

This time I start at the back, with the repair folder. I re-study the complaint about the broken backdoor lock. That's exactly the kind of thing Bryce would be looking for because it presents a risk of physical harm to tenants. But it has the dang repair ticket. *Checked backdoor. Lock working fine.* I checked it myself. It was locked.

I come to the *Dear Dipshits Who Never Answer the Phone* letter about the swimming pool and laugh again. Too bad Bryce's claim against Regal isn't for misrepresentation. Seaside doesn't look anything like the pictures in the brochure attached to the letter.

I'm about to drop it back into the folder when a photo grabs my attention. The backside of the building and alleyway. Is that what I think it is? I snatch my keys and phone and head out the door.

I've never been in the alley. Henley's building looms to my left. I pad along the asphalt dodging potholes. I pass the metal door, the one that works, searching for the spot of green I saw in the picture.

There! Partially hidden in an alcove, made of wood with peeling green paint. A second door. I grab the handle and it pulls right open. There's a deadbolt lock, but the innards are missing. I stick my thumb in the hole where the bolt should be.

Inside is a musty storage room full of junk. An old radiator, some battered garbage cans, a stack of used paint cans—and another door leading to a corridor. I follow it, ending up in front of the elevator. The metal door is to my left.

The repair guy checked the wrong door. Negligent! Maybe this is how the cat-killer got in. I go back to the broken door and take pictures of it from every angle.

Back upstairs, I pound out a complaint letter to Regal Estates on my computer and print it. Four o'clock. Enough time to get to the post office and send it certified mail.

* * *

I'm stir-frying veggies I picked up on the way home from the post office. The sizzling pan makes my skin crawl. I think about Toby and my own *tender flesh*. I turn down the heat.

My Civil Procedure outline calls to me from the countertop. It printed out at seventy-one pages. I picture Henley hunched over his computer unraveling the mysteries of personal jurisdiction. I stash the outline out of sight in the living room. *You are taking a break tonight.*

I try to relax while I eat, but can't do it. Some dark thing in a corner of my mind keeps nagging at me, but there's too much traffic up there for me to make out what it is.

I turn on my computer and stream a romantic comedy on Netflix. Some mindless entertainment might help me decompress. But it's too mindless and gets boring in a hurry. Same ol' romcom plot. Brad and Stacy navigate amusing relationship pitfalls as they work their way toward having sex.

Stacy! The dark thing in my brain. The man I ran into leaving the law school said *Yublebee, Stacy.* I flash back to Lucas's presentation, to the round-faced kid with the cowlick standing outside the auditorium blocking the sidewalk. He called me Stacy, acted like he knew me. I told him I wasn't Stacy. *Oh, yes you are.*

Who the heck is Stacy? Do I have a doppelgänger in St. Augustine? I shut down the movie and open a browser window, searching for *Stacy, Stacey* and *Staci* in St. Augustine. None of the results with pictures look anything like me.

And what about *Yublebee? Yublebee, Stacy.*

Yu-ble-bee. You. Bull. Bee.

It's nothing. Let it go! You're being cuckoo again. You have plenty to worry about without inventing more.

I fold my computer shut and clear the dishes. I'm gazing out the window washing my plate, mind churning, when the plate slips and cracks into pieces in the sink.

The exchange didn't start with *Yublebee.* I bumped into the man—*or* he bumped into me—and I said *Sorry.* He said, *Yublebee, Stacy.*

You will be, Stacy.

I pick up my phone to call Lucas, but set it back down. I can already hear him. *Lemme get this straight. You ain't sufficiently worried about gettin' death threats and dead cats for me to come there, but you freaking out 'cause you think a man called you the wrong name.*

I put the phone in a drawer to avoid temptation and return to the sink to clean up the broken plate. *Cuckoo. Stop.* I'm repeating the words as I dry my hands, retrieve the phone and begin writing a text to Agent Forster.

Hi Agent Forster. It's Emily. This probably sounds stupid, but two different strangers called me Stacy, acting like they knew me. One of them happened right after Lucas's presentation. Then it happened again today when I was leaving the law school. I'm sure it's just a weird coincidence. I don't even know why I'm writing this. Feel free to delete.

I hit send and go back and reread it. Yep, sounds stupid. Oh, well. Too late now.

Only seven o'clock. What do normal people do at night when they're alone and not studying law? Part of me wants to call Henley, just to talk, but he'll be busy studying.

I consider calling Suzanne, Bryce's wife. We've texted back and forth a few times. But she is my professor's wife and we haven't got our grades in Legal Writing. I could call Julie, but then I really would feel like I was using her. I could call Nemworth, haha. *Hi Professor! It's Emily. What's up?*

There *has* to be something to help me unwind. Too bad I tossed the Xanax. Hm, that makes me think of something. The bottle of dark rum Mrs. Alvarez gave me. I stashed it in the closet. Why not?

I take the bottle to the kitchen and use my neck knife to cut the seal around the cork. I find a clean coffee cup and pour a shot. Maybe it's more than a shot. What do I know? I've never poured one. I swirl and sniff it. It's the color of coffee, but smells like medicine.

Arm out, I raise the cup above my head. "Here's to ...?"

To what? "Here's to my family and Lucas and safety and sanity and the FBI. And getting straight *As!* Cheers!"

OMG, it's burning a hole in my esophagus. Why do people like this stuff? But the fire is quickly replaced by a warm glow spreading through my chest. I recork the bottle. Not bad. Maybe I should drink rum every night.

I return it to the closet and see the bubble bath Kiona gave me for my birthday. I never used it. I haven't had a bubble bath in forever, not since Mom and Becky were alive. Again, why not? Live it up.

I crank up the hot water and squeeze blue glops from the bottle, watching glaciers of foam swell. I sync my phone to my speaker and skip the usual playlists, typing in *spa music*.

The rum buzz has my whole body lit up. *Whoopsy.* I almost slip getting in the tub and giggle at the thought of committing a self-tort. Contributory negligence, for sure.

I ease myself into the silky heat. The bubble mountains reach all the way to my eyes and ears. Pan flutes play on the speaker. Already, the noise in my head is quieter. So peaceful.

Peace. I think about Ben at Pochachant. A pacifist. We broke up over it. I wish I could have taken some of his serenity with me when I got released. Even better, the whole boy. I snort bubbles through my nose.

I should have thought of this a long time ago. I'm adding more hot water when the camera app interrupts the vibe. Gabberman must have finally emerged from his pot stupor. Ignore it.

The playlist switches to forest sounds. Closing my eyes, I let them open the vault to memories of the woods behind our house in Georgia, the ones I grew up playing in. I knew every inch of them ... including the gulley where I hid under the leaves as the stocky man was chasing me, where he stopped and said, like he knew I was there, *Little girl, if I ever get my hands on you, you're gonna wish you died with your mama and sister.*

I sit up too fast and smash my head on the dang faucet. *Oww.* Don't go there. *Don't live in the past. Think happy thoughts and make them new memories.* Dr. Laura.

Rubbing my skull, I slide back down and force myself to imagine a different woods, a happy place where no one could ever hurt me, or even find me unless I wanted them to, where I'd make friends with all these forest music makers. The trilling birds on lead vocals, mating frogs on bass and cicadas providing the rhythm section.

I sink farther into the suds and something approaching relaxation, content listening to Mother Nature's band, except the cicadas have gone way off tempo.

Click click click. Click click click.

That doesn't sound like insects. I pause the music.

Click click click.

It's coming from the living room. Now what? I get out and put my robe on, opening the camera app. What was that alert about? A black screen again, like happened on Thanksgiving. Great time for another malfunction.

I go to the living room, trailing wet footprints, and look through the peephole. *WTF?* Something's blocking it. I can hear someone out there and they're messing with my lock! That's what the clicking sound is coming from.

You're safer operating on the assumption that whoever took the pictures and killed Toby is still out there. Agent Forster.

Always expect the worst and be glad when it don't happen. Lucas Jackson.

I run to the bathroom and trade the phone for my neck knife. The knob on the deadbolt is jittering when I get back.

Please don't let that door open, Lord. Not a second time. It's not fair.

A woman's voice says evenly, *It's not fair, Emily, but we have to deal with it.* I know her. The calm girl who looks like me, but older. She came to help when I was young. I thought she was real. I know now she isn't. But I need her to be.

Time spins backward. I'm thirteen, sitting in the office of Dr. Townsend, my shrink in the hospital psych ward.

Emily, you seem to have a remarkable ability to dissociate. It's a common symptom of the disorders I mentioned.

Ability? So it's a good thing?

No. Poor word choice, but sometimes the brain uses dissociation as a tool for self-protection in response to trauma. Think of it as an internal detachment from self.

I'm detaching now. Splintering. Like the door frame.

37

TWO MEN burst in. Shadows, dressed completely in black. Balaclava masks hide everything but their eyes. One's tall and thin. The other's short and wide. Shall old acquaintances be forgot. *I know them.* Tall man and stocky man. They came back from the grave to get me.

Stay here, Emily, says the calm girl. *I need you. It's not the same men.*

The tall one moves toward me, raising a semiautomatic pistol with a noise suppressor attached to the barrel. Lucas taught me how to build a DIY version on a lazy Sunday afternoon when we didn't have anything else to do. This one looks more professional.

I hold out the piddling four-inch blade of the neck knife. They make the blades small to keep them concealable, the only thing I never liked about neck knifes. I always want a big blade. I feel completely exposed. Bare feet, water running down my ankles, wearing only the bathrobe.

"Drop it, Stacy," he says, muffled by the mask. Not even a mouth hole. "Condemned prisoners aren't allowed to have weapons."

Stacy. And the letter in Toby's casket. *For that you have been put on trial. The verdict was GUILTY. The sentence is DEATH.* They're connected.

Waving the knife and backpedaling, "It seems like what we have here is a clear case of mistaken identity. I am not Stacy. I don't even know any Stacy. If we could just discuss this reasonably, I'm confident we can work it out." Good ol' calm girl. Gotta love her.

"We know who you are."

"What do you want?"

"You," he says. "You're coming with us. Junior, get to work.

"Yes, sir."

Junior? The short one unfurls a duffle bag on the floor, a long one, big enough to hold a person, and pulls out a roll of duct tape.

There's no way I'm leaving in that bag alive. *Attack! Go for the carotids. Slash! Kill!*

The scary girl. She's back too. Easy for her to say. We both learned a long time ago a gun beats a knife. So does two against one. But she makes a valid point. We're not going down without a fight. Surrender has never been an option.

Junior unwinds the duct tape. The ripping sound of the adhesive is tattooed on my brain, an icepick from the past stabbing my eardrums. He makes a move.

"Stop right there, *June-yur.* I'd hate to have to slash your intestines open. Do you know what a colostomy bag is? Very unpleasant from what I hear."

Trembling inside the robe, fake it 'til you make it. Think of a way out. There's always a way. Isn't there?

Calm girl? Are you there?

I'm always here, Emily.

Any suggestions?

The man wraps both hands around the gun grip and extends his arms, fixing the sight on my forehead. "Drop the knife and do exactly what Junior here tells you to do—or else."

An option-reducing development. The man has gun skills. That's obvious. The tip of the noise suppressor barely quivers.

"I'm telling you. You have the wrong person. I'm not Stacy. Go look at my driver's license. It's in that backpack over there on the kitchen table."

If he turns to look, I'll charge. I think back to Lucas's

knife-fighting lessons. So long ago. The man is too tall to reach his carotid arteries reliably, but if I remember right, the abdominal aorta is just above the stomach and right below the ribcage. Dead center.

But he doesn't turn, keeping his dark eyes behind the mask locked on mine. "I'm counting to three," he says. "Drop the knife or die. Your choice. And don't think I won't do it. I didn't bring this noise suppressor for nothing. *One.*"

I take another step back and hit the patio door. I reach my free hand behind me and try to open it. Maybe I could hurdle the patio railing and swing down to the balcony below, like in the movies.

Not likely to work, but falling four stories beats getting shot in the head. Honestly, I don't that know for sure. Both sound bad. The idea is mooted by the fact that the friggin' patio door is off the track again! I hate Regal Estates!

"*Two.*" His finger constricts on the trigger.

Scary girl says, *What are you waiting for? Rush him!*

It's a bad strategy. He'll get his shot off and I'll die. But I've read stories of people with fatal gunshot wounds running as far as ten yards before dropping. Maybe I can at least take him with me. I'll die trying. *Mom, Dad, Becky, I'm coming home.*

"*Thre—*"

Gabberman's door bangs open across the hall.

"Gabberman! Help!"

I blink. The shadow filling the doorframe, blocking out backing light, does not look anything like slumpy Lyle Gabberman in one of his bathrobes. It looks more like a giant, a beast. In fact, it looks a whole lot like ... Lucas?

I don't have time to process it as he thunders across the hall into the living room swinging a short-handled baseball bat. It connects with the gun holder's head so viciously I can see the mask cave in. The sound of splintering bone clenches my teeth.

The man crumples and falls. Dead weight or just dead. The

calm girl observes helpfully that if not for the balaclava mask, our entire beachy living room would be splattered with blood. The scary girl does cartwheels, chanting a cheer from my sixth-grade pom squad. *Hit 'em high, Hit 'em low, Hurt 'em, kill 'em, Go go go.*

Hurt 'em, kill 'em? Don't remember that part. It's coming back how annoying she can be.

"Lucas?" I say in a small questioning voice. I'm not sure he's really here, that anything is real, that I even exist.

"Just a minute, Em," he says.

Junior is brawny, must weigh close to two hundred pounds, but Lucas stands him up like he's picking up a sack of potatoes. He's whimpering, "Daddy, daddy."

"Shut the fuck up and take that mask off."

"Ye—yes, sir."

He peels it back and I recognize the chubby face of the kid with the cowlick outside the auditorium the day of the presentation. The one on the floor must be *Yublebee*. Father and son cannibals?

"Em, kick that gun aside, just in case daddy starts moving again. Don't pick it up."

I do as he says.

"Open the balcony door."

"Why?"

"Just do it."

I lift it back on track and wrangle it open. He drags Junior onto the balcony and leans him over the railing.

"What are you doing?" I say.

"Junior here just decided to commit suicide by jumping after what happened to his daddy, or maybe because he didn't want to face the law. Who knows why folks do these things?"

Scary girl cackles, *Yes! Do it!*

Shut up!

"Lucas, no. Remember? Let the law get justice, although I *totally* agree he deserves to die. What you just did is called the *defense of others*. We learned it in Torts, but the same rules apply in criminal law. You acted lawfully to protect me from an imminent threat of deadly force. *Bu-ut* once that threat terminates—"

He halts me with a hand the size of the dinner plate I broke tonight. "Spare me the lecture, Professor. How's a splat on the sidewalk gonna testify against me?"

I look down at Junior, on his knees, craning to see his father, Lucas holding him by the back of his shirt.

"Junior," I say. "Look at me."

Good grief. In the orangey glow of the patio light, his tormented face looks ten years old.

"What's your real name?"

Tears stream down his puffy cheeks. "Fer–fer–fer–Frederick."

"Why are you here? Why did you try to hurt me?"

"My daddy. He told me to."

"Is your father's name Roland Romansky?"

He shakes his head. "No, ma'am. It's Steven."

"So your dad told you to abduct a woman for no reason and you went along with it?"

"He said you were bad, that you hate me and all the eighty percenters, because you're a St–St–Stacy. He said you killed the man in Louisiana for no reason and put Roland in jail for nothing." He buries his head in heaves of "Daddy, Daddy."

I look at Lucas and do a crazy twirl with my finger. He reads my look—pity—and releases his grip. Frederick sinks onto the patio like a lump of wet clay.

"Go ahead. Call nine-one-one," Lucas says grudgingly. "Maybe his daddy's still alive. Tell 'em you need an ambulance. Don't give any details. Just say a man collapsed."

I retrieve my phone in the bathroom and make the call. When I return Junior is parked against the wall with his hands taped behind him. Lucas is bent over, feeling for a pulse on the man. "He's alive, barely."

"We did the right thing, Lucas. The Law won."

"We see about that."

"And you saved me—again! This whole thing is unreal. You really are here, right? This isn't a delusion?"

"I'm really here, Em," his voice unusually gentle. The light's not good, but I swear I see tears shining in his eyes. That's never happened, not once in our eight years together.

"You have a lot of explaining to do. Where's Gabberman? How did—"

"Later. Go get some clothes on."

I wrap my arms around him until he says, "Go."

38

ON THE COUCH waiting for the ambulance, I imagine the scene from the point of view of an EMT responding to a call that a man collapsed in an apartment.

Frederick's father lies in the middle of the floor in a widening puddle of blood around his head, gurgling occasionally through his skull mask. Frederick sits against the wall with his eyes closed, sniffling, hands bound. On the coffee table, next to my Civil Procedure outline, rests the sawed-off baseball bat.

"The EMTs are going to call the cops the second they walk in," I say dejectedly. "It's going to be another Emily Calby scandal, another media circus. I'll have to quit law school and go underground again." I consider breaking out the bottle of rum.

"Not if Agent Forster gets here first," says Lucas.

"Agent Forster! I forgot to call him!"

"He's on his way. Should be here any second."

"Huh?"

A knock on the door before I can ask questions. I look out the peephole. It's still blocked. "Who is it?"

"Jeff Forster."

I open the door, spying a piece of duct tape covering the peephole and camera. I reach for it, but he stops me. "Evidence," he says.

This doesn't compute. "What are you doing here? I mean, come on in, but watch your step. There's a man over there leaking his blood all over my floor and it's running toward the door because the dang floors at these crappy apartments are crooked."

He arches his eyebrows. Easy does it, girl. Last time we met after a bloody crime scene he put me in a hospital against my will.

"Hi, Lucas," he says.

"Hey, Jeff," Lucas says. They bump fists.

What is going on? They're acting like old pals.

"Agent Magritte and her team are on their way from Jacksonville to process the crime scene. I met up with the EMTs outside. They'll be here any minute. I suggest you two vacate the premises until we get everything squared away."

Lucas nods. "Come on, Em."

"Will someone please tell me what's going on?"

* * *

"No way! You've been staying at Gabberman's since Thanksgiving?" The couple at the next table stop mid-bite, wondering what the commotion's about. I wave to them and lean forward, whispering, "Why didn't you tell me?"

I'm with Lucas and Agent Forster in the lobby bar of the Franklin Hotel, same place Lucas stayed last time. He just returned from reserving us adjoining accommodations for the night. A room for me, suite for him. We're at a table for four with a flickering blue LED candle in the center. Lucas sips a beer on my left and Forster drinks coffee to my right.

Lucas says, "'Cause you told me not to come. I didn't wanna be a 'distraction' while you studied." He actually uses air quotes.

"And you knew about it?" I say to Forster.

"I encouraged it. We were both worried about you, and it's always best to have boots on the ground, especially when they belong to this man. We've been in contact since the deceased cat incident."

I study his boyishly handsome face, stubble from the long day bristling on his usually smooth cheeks. It's late, but he's wearing a suit with the knot of his striped tie still pulled tight. When I met him eight years ago my first thought was *he looks exactly like the FBI*. That hasn't changed.

And big beautiful Lucas directly across from him, dark eyes glowing like pieces of coal in the flickering blue light of the electric candle. He seems content to sit back and take it all in. Hard to read his face. Pensive, maybe just tired.

What a pair, so different, what you might come up with if someone asked you to design complete opposites. The straight-arrow FBI agent and the take-no-prisoners former gang member.

"I still can't get over how unbelievable this is," I say. "Including that you two are like, hanging together. That is too funny. You have absolutely nothing in common."

"We got one thing in common," Lucas says.

Forster nods and they both look at me. "*Aw*, I love you both. I'm blessed to have you. Now, I have several questions, starting with you, Lucas. So you never really went to Las Vegas? I'll bet Kiona is *ma-ad*."

After I told him not to come, he contacted Gabberman and offered a generous sum to rent his apartment for two weeks. Agent Forster even gave him the phone number. That's why I haven't seen Gabberman. The marijuana I smelled was Lucas. Gabberman even left him some. Haha, I told him they could probably be friends.

"How did you move in without me knowing? The camera would alert. Ah, never mind. I just figured it out."

He did it on Thanksgiving after I texted him that I was going out for lunch. He drove in the night before, waiting at the Franklin for an opportunity. He put a piece of tape over the door camera, just like the criminals did tonight. That's why I got the black screen at the cafeteria. Hauled up a pile of groceries and installed his own door camera to keep an eye on me before I got home.

"You are amazing, as always. I'm sorry I hurt your feelings."

"It wasn't about hurt feelings. It was about you making me responsible for your safety since you was twelve, then making it fucking impossible to do, excuse my language, Agent Forster."

It's true. For eight years he's borne a burden he never asked for, all because some crazy girl from nowhere showed up at his building in search of a fake driver's license.

"I know. I'm sorry. What did you do in there for ... jeez, nine days?"

He said he slipped in and out, quick enough to be gone by the time I opened the camera app. Even played golf a couple of times. Spent most nights gaming.

Lucas credits video games with teaching him about computers when he was young. He still kicks butt on Call of Duty. That's what he was doing when the two men came. He was in a battle wearing headphones, which is why he didn't hear anything at first.

He orders another beer when the server comes over.

I say, "I'll have a shot of rum. Make it dark." Lucas looks at me with one eye closed. "It's been a stressful night," I explain.

"May I see your ID?" the server says.

"Never mind." I turn back to Lucas. "If you only knew how much I wanted to be with you on Thanksgiving. And to think you were right across the hall! *Crazy*. Everything's crazy."

I turn to Forster. "Like you being here. How did you just happen to be in the neighborhood when those two freaks came? And can someone tell me, *Who-Is-Stacy?*"

Agent Forster looks at Lucas and says, "Emily, have you ever heard of the *manosphere?*"

I shake my head.

"Incel?"

"Sounds like a tech company."

"It's short for *involuntarily celibate*. It's part of a loose online community of men who assert they are unable to, well ..." He pauses to twist his wedding band.

Lucas: "Get a woman to fu— have sex with 'em."

"What he said. These folks believe women, especially attractive women, are responsible for their sexless lives. They call them *Stacys* and see them as ..." He's having a hard time spitting things out, obviously embarrassed. Lucas isn't.

"Stuck-up bitches who look down on 'em 'cause they ugly."

"Um, basically," Forster says. "I wouldn't use those exact words, but that's the essence of it. They believe in something called the 'eighty-twenty' principle, that eighty percent of women will date only the top twenty percent of attractive men."

"Interesting," I say. "Frederick told me his father taught him I hate him and all the *eighty-percenters*."

"Some of the hardcore followers believe the *Stacys* of the world have ruined their lives and deserve punishment for it. If you dig into it—which I know you will—you'll see their ideology is pretty far out there."

"You're right. I will research it, but I've never heard of them."

"Unfortunately, they've heard of you. Most are probably harmless. Lonely introverts with a computer. But as you learned tonight, there are extremists out there."

"I think I heard from some of them after the news of my trial broke. Hold on. Is this connected to Roland Romansky? I just remembered something. I asked Frederick why he did it, why he wanted to hurt me. He said his dad told him to, in part because I *put Roland in jail for nothing*."

A grim nod. "It is connected. When major websites banned extremist manosphere forums, they migrated to more obscure platforms, making them harder to track. I didn't put it together that Toby and the letter were related to something like this. I'm sorry I let you down."

Bless his heart. He looks truly disappointed in himself. "There's no way you could have known," I say. "But it makes sense now. The letter. *You and your kind have destroyed our lives and the lives of many*."

"I made the connection when I saw the *Stacy* reference in your text, and caught the first flight to Jacksonville. On the way I got some help from an FBI analyst who specializes in these types of groups. He located a sub-thread on one of the alt social media platforms with the name *Rol Rom*."

"Roland Romansky."

"Yes. There's an entire thread devoted to him. The commenters consider him a martyr because of his prosecution, consider it evidence of male persecution."

"A martyr! For sending a recipe about how to cook me for dinner?"

"It's safe to say we're not dealing with rational people here. The thread also contains several comments about Scott Brooker. Same theme." He gets out his phone and scrolls around. "Here's an example. *Do you really think she would have got acquitted of murdering Brooker if she was ugly? Or a man? We would have got the death penalty.*"

Brooker. Like a bad penny, always coming back.

"How did they get in the building?"

"Through an unlocked backdoor according to the boy."

"I knew it! I discovered it just today and sent a certified complaint letter to Regal Estates. Is the father going to live?"

Forster shakes his head. "Magritte said he died on the way to the hospital."

"Great! I mean, oh, that's too bad."

Lucas rolls his eyes.

"What about the son? Frederick."

"Magritte said he's a wreck, waived his right to a lawyer and spilled everything. She said he shows signs of stunted development, thinks he may have been abused, probably by the father."

"Doesn't surprise me. Is Lucas going to be in any trouble for ... doing justice to daddy?"

The question gets Lucas's attention. He plants his enormous forearms on the table and leans forward.

"I can't imagine why he would. Lucas is the hero here. The physical evidence is overwhelming and the boy said it happened exactly like you described. They took and, um, prepared Toby, and came back to get you. God only knows what the father had in mind if they had succeeded."

"Do you think they're really cannibals?"

"I doubt it. Just followers of the Romansky thread, which has a lot of blustery chatter on it about cannibalism. By the way, we'll be taking down that forum, but right now we need it for investigative purposes. The only thing the boy denied was sending the pictures at the presentation."

"I don't believe that. That's where I ran into him. And the poetry caption on my picture talked about my *flesh,* like the letter that came with Toby."

"The boy insists he didn't attend the presentation. Said he waited for you outside. He could be lying, of course, but with everything else he's already admitted to, I'm not sure why he would hold back on that."

"Have you checked Matt Jurado's phone about the, what is it, PRNU non-uniformity match?"

"Just got the report today. The photos weren't sent from the phone we confiscated at Jurado's apartment. Of course, that only eliminates one phone. Emily, I know you want all the answers. We all do. But we're just beginning the investigation."

I saved my most burning question, biggest fear, for last, maybe because I'm afraid to hear the answer. "Is this thing going to go public?"

"Agent Magritte and I are meeting with a U.S. Attorney in the morning to discuss the importance of keeping the records sealed. We have a strong case for it. The FBI considers the extremist fringe of the manosphere movement to be a form of domestic terrorism. Several killings have already been linked to it, meaning that what happened to you is already part of a larger ongoing investigation."

"I hope it works. I'll keep my fingers crossed. Thanks again, to both of you. I owe you so much. I'll never be able to repay it. I wish I could." I've told Lucas that a hundred times.

"You can repay me by applying to the FBI after law school," Forster says with a wink.

I laugh. "I'll think about it."

Lucas says, "You can repay me by stayin' outta trouble. It's wearing me out."

"*Trouble follows me wherever I go.*"

39

THE LONG night ended with a tussle about me going back to the apartment to get my computer and Civil Procedure outline. "I need them. My last exam is on Monday."

Forster started out, maybe because he could feel the steam coming from Lucas.

"Emily, we know law school is important to you. But given the circumstances, don't you think this would be a good time to take a break from St. Augustine and go back to Memphis with Lucas? I can call your dean. I feel certain she would be open to granting you a leave of absence or—"

"Uh-uh. No leave of absence." I fix my pleading eyes on Lucas. "I can come home Tuesday. I'm safe now, thanks to you. Just three more days."

Lucas rubs his temples. "Em, it ain't just about safety. Think what you been through." He proceeds to list the presentation photos, Jurado, Toby, *poor Toby,* and *the fucking icing on the cake,* two men breaking into my apartment to kidnap and possibly grill me for dinner. "What's it gonna take to bring you around?"

"I can't give up now, Lucas. I've worked too hard. I'm almost at the finish line. I'm a warrior, a survivor, like you, like you taught me to be."

"Being a warrior don't include holding everything in and pretending like nothin' happened. It ain't normal."

"I know what happened. It was bad, horrible. But I've also seen worse. So have you." A sad truth we share, part of our bond.

"You need help. You was traumatized before you even got here. Now it's worse."

He's right, of course. The surprise appearances of calm girl and scary girl put any doubt about that to rest.

"I admit it. I'm traumatized. Again. But what can I do about it? Nothing. I can't make it go away. It's been there a long time and always will be. All I can do is deal with it. If I didn't suppress things, I'd crack up for sure."

"Emily," Forster interjects. "Please, listen to him."

Lucas drains his beer and claps the glass on the table. "Save your breath. She ain't gonna listen."

"It's just three days. *Please.*"

He gave in only because he knew I wouldn't change my mind, but on the condition he's staying in St. Augustine and driving us to Memphis on Tuesday. They reluctantly agreed to take me back to my apartment to retrieve my stuff.

At Seaside we squeeze into the elevator together. It's past midnight, but people in white hazmat-type suits are still in my apartment processing the crime scene. Agent Magritte meets us in the hall. Forster already told me I wouldn't be allowed inside. We exchange greetings and Forster explains I came to retrieve some of my belongings.

"Let me guess. Your Civil Procedure outline," Magritte says, trying to lighten the scene. "I thumbed through it. Impressive work. I wish I had it when I was taking my Civ Pro exam," she says.

Through a crack in the door, I see a coagulated rivulet of the man's blood that oozed across my sloping floor. "Thanks."

She asks what else I need and I start listing. Computer, backpack, clothes, hygiene stuff … "Oh, and my neck knife."

"Can't help you with that one. It's already sealed in an evidence bag."

She disappears inside and returns a few minutes later lugging my loaded backpack. "I stuffed as much in it as I could fit," she says.

"I have something else for you." She pulls an envelope from her pocket. "An elderly woman brought this by. Said she lives on the floor and got worried because of all the commotion. I told her you were okay."

Emilita is written on the envelope in large elegant script. A note inside says, *I am worried about you, my dear. Those people in your unit said they were Federales. Please telephone me when you can to let me know you are alright. I am praying for you. Love, Marisol.*

She is the absolute sweetest. I tuck it in my pocket. "One more thing," I say. "There's box of documents in the corner of the living room. They're from a case I'm working on in my law clerking job. I need to get them back to my boss."

* * *

I sleep until ten, waking to three texts from Henley.

Hi Emily, I'm here. Can you let me in?

Are you alright?

Okay, no answer. Maybe you're asleep. I'll be at the law library studying.

I text back. *Sorry! Crazy night. A pipe burst in my ceiling and I had to vacate the premises. Staying nearby at the Franklin Hotel. I'll meet you at the library in thirty minutes.*

I spring from the king-size bed. Never slept in one before. Like rolling around on a trampoline. I dump a clot of compressed clothes from my backpack and fish through it for my usual ensemble of jeans and double-tees. I bang on Lucas's adjoining door.

"Come in."

I find him luxuriating on the bed surrounded by room service trays. Cereal, waffles, eggs, bacon, fresh fruit. I smell coffee and zero in on an insulated pitcher.

"Can I have some of that?"

"I got this for both of us. You need to eat."

"I'm running late. I have to go meet Henley at the law library. I'm already two hours behind on our study schedule." I slosh coffee into a foam cup and grab a waffle that I bite into like a sandwich.

"Sit with me and have a proper meal."

"Loo-cas. I'm so sorry. I knew this was going to happen. This is why I didn't want you to come sooner. I can't give you the attention you deserve. But I will soon. Only three days."

I leave him muttering behind me as I bolt from the suite and fast-walk to the law school—looking over my shoulder, despite the threat having passed. I call Mrs. Alvarez.

Voicemail. Good. I have no idea how to explain why my apartment was full of FBI agents last night. "Hi, Mrs. Alvarez! This is Emily. Thank you for the nice note. Don't worry about me. Everything's fine."

"Glad you could make it," Henley says snidely when I join him at our usual study carrels.

"Sorry. I had a long night."

"Are you okay?"

"Mm-hm. Let's get started. I say we focus on personal jurisdiction first. Cricks *loves* personal jurisdiction."

"Agreed."

We work for two hours. More like an hour for me. I spent the other hour trying to lock up the images of the man's head caving in when Lucas hit him with the bat. That sound! I've heard people die by guns, knives, even a garrote, but a shattering skull is really something else.

You'd think it would ruin my appetite, but I'm ravenous. I should have eaten more breakfast than the waffle, like Lucas said. No wonder he's frustrated with me. I keep ignoring every piece of good advice he has. I'm glad when it's Henley who suggests lunch.

"Breezeway?" he says.

"I didn't have a chance to pack anything."

"Happy to share. I brought two exquisite peanut butter and jelly sandwiches."

"No one makes them better, or more often," I laugh.

"Not only. I have—*ta da*—grapes." He opens a baggie from his backpack and holds it out. "An *amuse-bouche* perhaps?"

"A what?"

"Sampling. Translates to amuse the mouth. Trying to spruce up the menu."

I appreciate him making me laugh. I pop a grape in my mouth. "Thank you, kind sir. So rich and succulent."

Henley smiles with his nice teeth and we go downstairs, sitting at the same picnic table where Julie and I used to sit. We're the only ones out here. Most of the upper-levels have already finished their exams and fled for the holidays.

"Excellent sandwich," I say, smacking my lips. The peanut butter keeps pasting my tongue to my palette. I forgot to ask Agent Magritte to pack my water tumbler. "I love the way the jelly and peanut butter are spread at the exact same thickness all the way to the corners. Very OCD of you."

He blushes. "I know I can be that way."

"I'm just teasing." He's more sensitive than he shows. "Hey, takes one to know one, right?"

"Actually," he says. "I wanted to talk to you about that. I'm sorry I've been pushing you so hard. I did it out of caring. I want us both to finish at the top."

"You didn't push me too hard. I probably could have used more of it lately. Usually I'm the one who pushes."

"Yes, I've noticed," he says with a smile. "I guess we're both obsessive-compulsive control freaks."

"A perfect match," I say.

40

MONDAY, NINE A.M. Waiting for the greenlight to start the Civil Procedure exam. *What a long strange trip it's been.* The Grateful Dead. One night at the height of my Bryce crush, I tried to speed-master jam bands.

I'm glad Agent Magritte included my hoodie in the crime-scene haul. It never occurred to me Florida could get cold, but the mid-December day is chilly and they haven't turned the heat on in the law school. With the hood up and wearing a pair of plaid stretch Dickies I forgot I owned, I look like a skate punk.

Around me, everyone's ready to end this thing. No more excited tension, just droopy eyes, slumped shoulders and sloppy clothes.

Only Henley looks the same, alert and dressed in a freshly starched gingham button-down. Olson is eager too. Swaddled in gray sweats, he has that forward lean going, like when he's about to pounce on someone in class. He gained weight during the semester, growing from Beanie Baby to bean bag furniture. Across the room, Brady Chapman repeatedly finger-combs his hair. Probably too much Adderall.

I don't see Julie and get concerned before spotting her in the back row, dressed in her University of Georgia tee. Same one she wore on the first day of class and to every exam. Russell's band t-shirt for exams has been Jimi Hendrix.

We all have our good luck charms. Mine is the bracelet Lucas gave me when I was twelve, the one that saved my life. It's seen better days. The medallion is scratched and tarnished and the leather strands that hold it together are either hanging by a thread or already broken.

"Ready, set, begin," Professor Cricks says.

I flip through the exam. Three essay questions. The first one is worth fifty percent. I guessed it. Even a quick scan reveals it's a personal jurisdiction question.

I'm only halfway through reading the question when people start typing. Tempting, but I force myself to outline the issues first. Nemworth said most exams he reads these days are *word vomit*. ... Poor Professor Nemworth.

No time for it! Focus!

* * *

Henley is waiting in the hall when I come plodding out of the classroom. "We're done!" he says, giving me a half-hug that I return.

"Man," I say, shaking my head. "That was the hardest exam by a hundred miles. I think I botched it." I couldn't concentrate. My tornado brain was spinning from the weekend's events.

He cocks his head. "Really? I thought it was relatively easy, except for that subject matter jurisdiction issue Cricks hid in the first question."

"Thanks, Henley. I didn't spot that."

"Sorry. I'm sure you did fine. You know what they say. It's impossible to predict how you did on a law school exam. Up for lunch? I promise not to talk about the exam."

"Um, I'm going to try to find Professor Nemworth to say goodbye." When did I make this eventful decision? In the middle of my stroke-inducingly complex Civil Procedure exam. *Nice focus, Emily.*

"How about dinner then? To celebrate! We have to after all we've been through. At my place. I'll cook my special dish—and no, there's no peanut butter in it."

"I don't know. Lucas is probably expecting me to celebrate with him."

"He's here again?"

"Yeah." I leave it at that.

"Come on. I won't see you for almost a month and you've never even been to my apartment. I always come to yours."

"Because you never asked me."

"I was waiting for you to suggest it, being a gentleman."

Sometimes I swear Henley was transported here from the 1950s.

"I have a surprise for you. I didn't want to tell you in advance."

"What kind of surprise? I don't like surprises." I *hate* them. My whole life has been filled with surprises—bad ones.

"It's nice. You'll like it. How about it? Seven o'clock?"

"Alright." It's the least I can do. Henley's been a good friend all semester, my only one. "But I can't stay late."

He gives me his apartment number and I head for the faculty wing. My slapping footsteps echo in the empty stairwell.

The professors have already bailed for the break. All the offices are dark with the doors closed, except Nemworth's.

I creep up and peek around the doorframe. There he is, bent over a book under the lamp, his unruly hair longer than the last time I saw him. The oldest professor by decades and he's the only one here working.

I step into view, careful not to cross the threshold. He told me to never return. "Knock, knock," I say.

He looks up and squints. His glasses are as filmy as ever. "Is that you, Miss Calby?"

"Yes, sir."

"Come in," he motions. "Sit."

I collapse in my regular chair. The musty smell of the old books triggers good memories from the days before he banished me.

"I just came to say ... Professor! What happened to your eye?" He has a black eye! I can see it even behind the smeared lenses.

"Just a broken blood vessel. These things happen to old people."

Bullshit. I know a bruise when I see one. One more lie, you out. Last warning. What Lucas said the day we met. He asked what happened to my eye and I said, *Just purple blush. I'm not very good at makeup yet.*

"You were saying?" he says.

I'm still staring at his eye. "Well, I just finished my last exam and came to say goodbye."

"You're leaving?"

"Just for the winter break." I hope. I'm still not convinced the attack in my apartment won't go public. "Also, I wanted to thank you in person for being my professor. It was an honor and privilege."

Fossilized silence.

"Anyway, I guess that's it."

I stand, but he waves me back down with a liver-spotted hand. "Miss Calby, could you spare an extra minute?"

"Uh, sure."

"I'd like to tell you a story."

"Story?"

"Yes. About the man who knew everything. Have you ever heard it?"

"I'm not sure, sir. I don't think so."

"One day the man who knew everything visited a town with which he was unfamiliar and got lost. He wandered the streets for hours, never asking directions because, of course, he was the man who knew everything."

I'm not sure where this story's going, but there's obviously a reason for it.

"My, my, he was exhausted. Every street led to a dead end. It was late afternoon by the time he passed a young girl on the sidewalk. He must have looked lost because the girl simply looked up and said, *That way.* The man scoffed. What could a child know that he didn't? Do you know what he did?"

"No, sir."

"The damn fool went in the opposite direction and fell into a hole."

"Everyone makes mistakes," I say.

"Ah, but that's not the end. So prideful was the man that even after he fell in the hole, he convinced himself he was right and the child was wrong. He climbed out and kept walking in the same direction, and guess what?"

"I don't know."

"He fell into a deeper hole. By the time it occurred to him that maybe he didn't know everything—that the child was right all along—he found himself in a hole so deep he couldn't get out of it."

With a lump in my throat, "That's, um, a sad story, Professor."

"Do you understand the point?"

"I think so."

He claps his hands on the desk. "Very well then. I hope you have a nice holiday break."

I've been dismissed but the pain in his eyes rips at my heart. Pain of what's happening to him and pain of telling me in the only way he could.

I should let it go, should go home to Lucas. I already tried. That's what he'd tell me. *You already tried. It ain't your job to save the world.*

"Sir, I don't want to butt in, since that's what got me evicted in the first place." A nervous laugh. "But if someone helped the man, lowered a ladder into the hole, he could climb out."

"Someone like who?"

"The police. I even know the right person to call. Detective Roberson. He's with the Financial Crimes Unit in the Sheriff's Office."

Another silence. When he speaks again, his voice breaks. "Miss Calby. *Emily.* If a man is too weak of mind and judgment to help himself, too blind to acknowledge the truth even when he knows it, he doesn't deserve help."

"But—"

"Congratulations on finishing your first semester of law school. Please go now. And thank you."

I didn't even make it out of the law school building before calling Detective Roberson. He said he remembered me, but I recapped the story of Nemworth and Christina to make sure he understood.

"I just talked to him. He's finally facing up to the truth, but having a hard time admitting it."

"We talked about that. It's a common issue in sweetheart scams. Especially for an educated, intelligent—"

"Brilliant."

"Okay. Especially a brilliant person like your professor. I worked on a case where a son asked his father, the victim, why he couldn't face up to the truth that he was being exploited. You know what he said? *Because I'd have to kill myself.* That's how powerful the threat to self-image is from acknowledging you've been suckered in such a cruel way."

"That's why I'm calling. Today, he did acknowledge it, but said he didn't deserve help. I think if you went out and talked to him in person, he's at the point where he might crack and spill everything, agree to file a complaint."

When he hesitates, I add, "It's gotten worse. He has a black eye. I just saw it. He said it was a broken blood vessel, but I don't believe him. I think Christina might be physically abusing him."

My hair is corkscrewed so tight around my finger it looks like the tip is about to burst. I loosen it only when he says, "Alright. I'll go out today and try to talk to him."

"Promise?"

"I promise I'll give it a shot. No guarantees it will work. He might slam the door in my face. It's happened before. Where can I find him?"

I suggest he wait until late afternoon and give him the home address. Nemworth would be mortified if a detective showed up at the law school looking for him. He will be anyway. "Can you call me back and tell me if it worked?"

He starts to explain that police investigations are confidential and because I'm not a relative—

"Detective, please. I'm all he has."

He pauses before, "I'll text or call tonight."

"Great, thank you."

"Don't get your hopes up."

41

LEAVING CAMPUS, I turn and wave good-bye with mixed feelings. I'm excited about finishing exams, but my conversation with Professor Nemworth cast a cloud over everything. And that black eye! Now he won't have even me around to help, not that I was much help. That detective better follow through on his promise.

My phone pings. A text from Suzanne. *Hi Emily. Bryce said today was your last final. Congratulations!*

I write back: *Thank you!!! Tell Professor Stafford to go easy on us grading our major memos. :) Can you also tell him I'm going to drop off the last box of documents from the Artiel Jones case today? Thanks!*

Stepping out of the elevator at the Franklin, I hear laughter coming from Lucas's room. A woman's laugh. Definitely not Kiona. She doesn't laugh like that. She doesn't really laugh at all. He gave me a keycard. I'm supposed to knock but I throw open the door.

Busted! He's at the cafe table with a trim black woman in a white blouse with her back to me. Danisha from the pool! He's going to hear about this. But then the woman turns.

"Agent Magritte, what are you doing here? I mean, hi."

She reads the alarm on my face. "No worries. Just took a statement from Lucas. SOP. I'll need one from you too. Lucas was just regaling me with some of his favorite Emily Calby stories."

"Hm, I see. Well, when you have a few hours to spare, I'll regale you with some of my favorite Lucas Jackson stories. Any news?"

"As a matter of fact, yes. First, congrats on finishing your exams. I still remember that day."

"It's a great feeling. Even with ... everything."

"Like I told you," Lucas says. "Glass-half-full girl."

"I see that." She pats the chair next to her. "Come join us. Here's what we've learned ..."

The FBI discovered that Frederick's dead daddy wasn't just a follower of the Rol Rom forum, but a contributor, posting comments like, *Can anyone send me Roland's recipe?*

"Gross," I say. "What about Romansky? Does he run the forum?"

"That's something else we learned. We finally tracked him down, to a cemetery in St. Louis."

"Dead? Maybe he cooked himself, or chewed his arm off."

A chiseled look from Lucas. *Watch your mouth.* I thought it was funny.

"Less dramatic than that," Magritte says. "He died of a heart attack, a year ago. One more thing. We confirmed the father and son did indeed enter the building through the broken backdoor you discovered. The boy admitted it and they left behind footprints and other evidence."

"Good old Regal Estates," I say.

"Analysis of the father's phone shows they started tracking you shortly after the newspaper article came out about you being a law student here."

"I figured that was it."

She asks if I'm ready to give a statement and I say might as well get it over with.

"Would you like to have a counselor present?"

"A lawyer? Do I need one?"

"A mental health counselor. We have an excellent victim specialist in Jacksonville."

"I'm fine," I say and Lucas grumbles.

Magritte notices. "Emily, I first heard about you from Agent Forster. We worked on an investigation together. One day on a long drive to meet a witness we got into exchanging war stories. He told me about a case involving a young victim who suffered unspeakable tragedy, yet somehow managed not only to survive, but thrive. He said she was the strongest person he ever met."

She pauses like she's waiting for a response.

"Um, if he was talking about me, it was nice of him to say that."

"However, he also said this young victim fought so hard to be strong she couldn't see when she truly needed help."

"Really, I'm fine." As long as no one pokes a hole in my armor.

The interview lasts an hour. When Agent Magritte leaves, Lucas pats my back. "I ain't saying I agree with your decision, but I'm glad you got to finish your exams. I know it was important to you. Look over here. I got you some presents."

He points to his gigantic bed. Two small boxes with gold bows are perched on a pillow in the center.

"Aw, you didn't have to do that. It's only one semester."

"Not just for that. For bein' you, Emily-the-Powerful. A warrior and survivor ... and 'cause I love you, even when you annoy the shit outta me."

I've known he loves me for a long time, but this is only the second time I remember him actually saying the words. The first time, near the beginning, I had to ask.

"I love you too, Lucas. More than anything."

"Hey, no crying allowed at a celebration. Open your presents."

I tear into the first one. "A new neck knife? Yay! What happened to *no weapons*? The threats are over."

"Yeah, well, I've thought that before."

I slip the cord over my head and drop the Kydex sheath inside my shirts. The second box rattles when I shake it. Something metallic. "A garote? Brass knuckles?"

"Just open the damn thing."

"Omigod!" It's a bracelet—an exact replica of the one on my

wrist, the one he gave me for my thirteenth birthday. Same silver medallion, same black leather strands bundled with silver rings, all shiny and new. "How did you do it? Did James make it?"

He shakes his head. "No GPS in this one. Took your old one to a jeweler while you was still in Memphis and asked him to recreate it. Was gonna wait for your twenty-first birthday until I found out law school is more important to you. Just a regular bracelet."

"There's nothing regular about it. It's spectacular. And I needed it." I hold up my wrist. "This one's hanging by threads. That's why I don't wear it more."

"One other difference. Turn over the medallion," he says.

In tiny script: *Yesterday. Today. Tomorrow. Always.*

When the two men took Mom and Becky from this world, there was nothing left. Nothing worth living for, no reason to keep going. I was ready to give up when God led me to Lucas, although he doesn't believe that.

"How can you expect me not to cry now?" I blubber. "These words are beautiful. Did you make them up?"

"Didn't I tell you? I took up writin' poetry as a hobby since you left."

"Really? You did?"

He starts laughing.

"Liar." I punch him in the arm.

"Found it on the internet," he says. "But I did add the *Always*."

"That's the best part!"

* * *

"Sorry it took so long to get this back to you." I'm at Bryce's, returning the last box of documents from the Jones case. We're in my *office*, handwritten name plate still adorning the door. "Things have been kind of ... busy."

"No apology necessary. I'm the one who told you not to work during exams. Find anything useful?"

"Not really. Well, there is this one thing. I found another broken lock in my building, and not just a mailbox."

I show him the request to fix the broken lock on the backdoor. "And look. Here's a repair ticket that says someone checked the backdoor three days later and found the lock to be working fine. I went down and checked it myself."

"Okay," he says. "Now don't take this as criticism, but in terms of legal analysis, that probably works in their favor. They received a request to repair a risk of unauthorized entry, went and checked it and it was fine. That sounds like *reasonable care*."

"That's because you didn't let me finish. They checked the wrong door. A few days ago I found a second backdoor where the lock was broken. Not just broken. There wasn't even a lock, just an empty hole. Anyone could walk in right off the alley. I have pictures of it on my phone. I already sent Regal Estates a complaint by certified mail."

"Impressive investigative work. Have they fixed it? That really is a dangerous condition in an apartment complex. Thank God nothing bad happened."

"Well, actually ..." Driving here, I debated whether to tell him about daddy and junior. I've worked all semester trying to help in the Artiel Jones case and came up with zilch. It's relevant, even though it's still not going to help. Thanks to Forster and Magritte, a federal judge sealed the records.

"Cannibals?" he says when I finish. If he didn't already know me, he'd think I was a crazy person making it up, as opposed to a crazy person telling the truth.

"Probably just wannabes. The FBI doesn't know what the dad would have 'cooked up' for me if they succeeded." Bryce winces at the pun. "They did kidnap and roast my neighbor's cat."

Shaking his head, dazed, "Emily, that story is ... I can't even think of a word. And they came in through that broken backdoor?"

"Yep. The FBI confirmed it."

"And you took your Civil Procedure exam today? I'm thankful

they didn't hurt you physically, but how are you doing otherwise? Are you getting help? Counseling?"

"I'm fine." Maybe *that* should go on my gravestone.

Here Lies Emily Blair Calby
She's Fine

I say, "Unfortunately—well, fortunately for me, but not for Mr. Jones—the case records are sealed. We can't use them as evidence."

I expect him to be disappointed, but he's stupefied by my wild tale.

I say, "Is Mr. Jones still in the hospital?"

"Um, they released him a few weeks ago. He's convalescing at his daughter's house."

"That's good. I'm really sorry I couldn't help him."

* * *

"Your boyfriend?" Lucas says.

It's almost seven o'clock. I'm going to be late to Henley's. I laid down to rest for a second and crashed for two hours. I'm standing in front of the mirror in Lucas's suite scrambling to make my hair presentable.

"Study partner. He was never really my boyfriend. I tried to make myself like him that way, but he's just not the one." I wonder if there will ever be a *one* for me.

"Then why's it so important to have dinner with him? I thought we was gonna do something."

"We still can. I'm not going to stay late. He's been a good, loyal friend all semester. My only one—besides you, of course. We studied together almost every day and I won't see him for a month. I owe him."

"Where's he live?"

"Only a couple blocks from here. His building is directly behind mine, right across the alley."

"Where's this boy from?"

"Not sure. I asked once and he said he didn't want to talk about it. Said his parents had an ugly divorce when he was young and bounced him from place to place. Painful memories."

"How old is he?"

"Twenty-two."

He flips me off with a wave of his hand. "Go ahead. Abandon ol' Lucas again."

"Don't worry. I'm going to be spending every second of the next month with you."

"Thanks for the warning."

42

HENLEY'S APARTMENT is on the fifth floor. I'm standing outside, a tingly sensation running up my spine. Not excitement or anticipation. Just nerves. Twenty years old and I've never knocked on a guy's door before. Embarrassing. I squish my lips and knock. The door flies open.

"Emily! Come in. Welcome." Henley's face is aglow above the collar of yet another button-down shirt, this one blue and white stripes. Maybe I'll peek in his closet, see if he owns any other type of clothing.

"Hey, Henley." I step inside. "Sorry I'm late. Man, something smells good. What are you cooking?"

"My special dish. You'll see. Did you get a new bracelet?"

How does he notice something like that? "I did. Lucas gave it to me for finishing the first semester."

I hold it out, but he turns and says, "Well, this is my place."

"Nice," I exaggerate. It's tidy but plain, like Henley. The mottled gray carpet is worn. The walls are bare. There's a lumpy brown sofa that looks like something you'd pluck off the curb and stacks of metal shelves full of books organized by size. But the apartment is huge compared to mine.

"Thanks. I'm not much at decorating, as you can see. How about a tour?"

"Sure."

"Do you want me to take your jacket for you?"

I'm still wearing the hoodie. "No, thanks."

"Well, this is obviously the living room and dining area. Across that counter is the kitchen from where yond marvelous smell cometh. And down this hall ..."

I follow him. I've never seen him so pepped up. Probably as nervous as I am.

"Those doors go to a bathroom and closet and here is my bedroom-slash-office."

We enter a good-sized bedroom, unfurnished except for the bed, a floor lamp and a large desk made from a door resting on two metal file cabinets. It's loaded with tech gear.

"Impressive computer set-up," I say. "Three monitors. All I have is a laptop."

"You'd be shocked at how much student loan money Henley Oliver, aka Mr. Logical, can justify wasting on tech junk. Computer science was one of my majors. I think I told you."

"I remember. You and Lucas would probably get along. He's a genius techie."

"And this is my view. Which, of course, is your view in reverse," he says.

Above the desk, out a bay window, stands the Seaside Apartments, shrouded in darkness. "Wow, I never realized we were this close."

"Um, have you ever looked out your window?"

"Very funny. I knew our buildings were close, but not ... you." My apartment is just slightly to the left and one floor lower. The FBI left the lights on. The blinds are closed. I wonder what it looks like when they're open.

Henley's phone starts chiming. "My masterpiece is ready. Hungry?"

"Always. You know me."

The dining table is meticulously prepared. White cloth napkins, long-stem wine glasses, even fresh flowers in a vase.

"So what is this masterpiece of yours? The smell is making my mouth water."

"Mango chicken," he says with pride. "A far cry from peanut butter and jelly, yeah? Bet you didn't expect this."

No, I didn't. Mangoes. "Henley, you're not going to believe this. I'm allergic to mangoes. They're the only food I'm allergic too."

His taut face somehow manages to droop, like I just told him he flunked all his law school courses.

"I'm sorry. I guess I should have told you. It never occurred to me you would make something like this."

A flash of something in his eyes passes and he bounces back. "That's okay. I made asparagus and mashed potatoes as sides. Are you allergic to those?"

"Uh, no. Those sound good."

They're actually tasty, and filling. I tell Henley he should eat his mango chicken, but he says he's fine with the sides. When we finish, he stands and announces, "And now for the surprise."

He retreats to the kitchen where I hear him banging around in cupboards and drawers.

"Need any help?"

"I got it. You're the guest of honor. Just relax."

He marches out carrying a double-layered cake with white icing and two thick candles standing side by side like pillars.

"*Miss Calby*," he says. "I present you with our end-of-the-first-semester congratulations dessert." He sets it in the middle of the table and runs back to the kitchen.

I stare at the perfect cursive script of purple icing on top. He asked my favorite color once. It's been purple since I could name colors.

The icing doesn't spell *Congratulations* or *We Did It*.

Study Harder would have been a funny Nemworth joke.

It says *Henley + Emily* drawn inside a heart, one burning candle above each name. I'm still looking at it when he returns with an uncorked bottle of red wine.

Waving it away, "No, thanks."

"Come on. Just one toast."

The cake is weird, but I already ruined his special dinner. "Okay, one toast." I let him pour me some wine. "That's enough," I say.

He raises his glass. "To the end of our first semester."

"Hear, hear," I say. I take a tiny sip and put the glass down.

"And here's your first-semester graduation gift." He pulls a tiny square box from behind his back, wrapped in white paper and squiggly red ribbon.

"Gift? Whoa. I didn't get you any gift."

"No problem. I didn't expect you to. Open it."

I do it reluctantly. Not many gifts would fit in a cube this small. I rip away the paper and put the top off. "What–is–this?"

"A ring."

"I can see that, Henley." Not only is it a ring, it looks like a frigging engagement ring. There's a tiny diamond in the middle. "What's it for? Why are you giving me a ring?"

"Because I like you."

"Okay, well, I like you too, but, uh, not in a ring way."

I try to hand it back, but he won't take it. I set it on the table.

"But we're a perfect match. You said it yourself, at the library."

"I was making a joke."

"We spent almost every day and night together. All semester."

"That was schoolwork," I say.

"We ate lunch in the courtyard and went to Professor Stafford's for dinner. We walked on the beach. You made fun of my peanut butter-spreading."

"And that was all fun," I say. "But it wasn't 'ring' stuff."

"We kissed."

"Only once."

He squeezes his eyes shut. "I'm sorry the diamond's so small. It's all I could afford."

Like *that's* the issue! Is this my fault? I knew he *liked*-liked me. He made it clear. Why wasn't I more clear? For a while I was conflicted. Then I didn't want to hurt his feelings ... or lose my only friend.

"Will you at least have a piece of cake with me?" he says. "I made it myself."

I know how he feels. Embarrassed and hurt, like I felt standing in Bryce's office holding the birthday cake while being introduced to his wife and baby. What is it with cakes?

"Of course," I say.

He takes the cake back to the kitchen and returns carrying slices on two small plates.

I take a bite. "Yum. This is so good. I didn't know you were a chef, but I should have figured Henley Oliver is smart enough to be good at anything. I wish I could have tried the chicken." So want to boost his spirits, but it's not working.

"Thanks," he says, eyes downcast.

"Henley, I'm really sorry if I gave you the wrong impression. I *do* like you, a lot, as a friend." I almost add, *I tried to like you more,* but decide it would come out wrong. "Honestly, I don't think I'm fit to be more than a friend to anyone."

He looks up. "Except Lucas." An edge on the words.

"Lucas?"

"You're fit to be more than a friend with him."

O-key dokey. I take a last bite and push the plate away. Need a minute to figure things out, end this as gently as possible. "I know this is bad timing, but could you excuse me for a sec? I really need to use the restroom."

"Down the hall. On the right."

"I'll be right back."

The hallway lighting is bad, made worse by the dark wood paneling. I find a gold doorknob as my phone starts vibrating. I reach inside for the light.

The flare blinds me as Henley shouts, "Hey! Not that door."

43

CONFUSION GRABBED me first, before the shock and horror. It all happened in a blink. *That's me. That's my underwear? WTF?*

The pink bra and panty set that disappeared from the laundry room. They're pinned to the wall like a department store display, bra on top, underpants below.

If it was only that. Mounted strategically around them are photographs—of me—taken through my apartment windows. In one I'm holding the freaking laundry basket. It's an entire wall of *me*.

Henley's standing behind me. I hear his heavy breathing and reach under my shirts. *Thank you for the new neck knife, Lucas.* My phone keeps vibrating. Need it to stop so I can concentrate. I wrap my fingers around the rubber grip.

Legally, it will come down to whether I'm in imminent fear of death or serious bodily injury. They almost got me on that with Scott Brooker. Do I think Henley is going to *imminently*—almost immediately—inflict death or serious bodily injury on me? It's possible. For all I know he's holding up a machete, ready to split my skull open. Do I actually *believe* that? Not really.

Then there's the philosophical question. Does Henley Oliver deserve to die? Scary girl would say, *Duh, of course. Look what he did.* Calm girl would say, *Not necessarily.* Hiding girl would be as useless as ever, on her knees praying.

He's a freak—obviously, but that doesn't mean he's dangerous.

Keep it together. Try to not kill Henley. I let go of the knife and turn to face him, arms bowed, knees bent, ready for anything.

He's leaning against the doorframe, looking more defeated than dangerous. "You don't need to worry, Emily. I don't want to hurt you."

"You stole my underwear? And put them up as ... a *shrine?*"

Sheepishly, "Your crappy property management company, the one you always complain about, made it easy. There's a broken backdoor where you can walk right in."

"Henley, listen. I don't want to hurt you either, but you have about two seconds to explain what's going on."

A sardonic laugh. "*You're* what's going on. Isn't it obvious? Go ahead. Take a better look at your tribute. I spent a lot of time on it. A whole lot."

Keeping Henley in my vision, I twist sideways and scan the collage. There I am in my kitchen washing dishes, and sitting on my balcony with a casebook. Scattered among the photos are printouts of news articles about me and screenshots from my national television interview. *Gawd,* he even painted the wall purple.

I gawk in disbelief, struggling to take it all in. I'm opening my mouth to rip Henley a new one when my eyes float to the bottom, near the baseboard, where an eight-by-ten photograph grabs me by the throat.

It's a blonde girl. She's seated at a table behind a laptop, sipping coffee from a mug. *Otherlands.* My favorite coffee shop in Memphis. My home away from home.

The picture is me, but of course it can't be, because the girl is just a teenager. She's wearing a t-shirt from the Beale Street Music Festival, brown with yellow lettering, like the one I got when I was sixteen.

Next to it is another eight by ten. Me and Lucas at Central Barbecue. Kiona's there too, half obscured by a stack of presents. My seventeenth birthday party.

"They're in reverse chronological order," Henley says. "New on top, old on the bottom."

Waves of dizziness prick me like Taser darts. "How did you get those pictures?"

"Later," he says with a wave.

"Later? There isn't going to be any later."

"Have faith, Emily. *Jack shall have Jill, Nought shall go ill.* Shakespeare. A Midsummer Night's Dream."

It's all I can do to not pull out the neck knife and ram it into his abdomen.

"Remember our first lunch?" he says wistfully. "You laughed when I told you my other major was English Lit, the *dead white male poets.* That was a fun time. I still like poetry, not just the English dudes. There have been plenty of great American poets who are also white, male and dead. Robert Frost, T.S. Eliot ..."

His eyebrows pull together as his eagle eyes burrow into me. "Walt Whitman."

My brain's working slow. It takes a few seconds to sink in. Walt Whitman? *And your very flesh shall be a great poem.*

"What the fuck? You sent the pictures at the presentation?" Slurring in my words. I can hear it. What's happening? The wine? I only had a sip.

He raises his hand like he's in class. "Guilty."

"I thought you were my friend. You put an effing rifle scope on Lucas's head and called him the N-word!" I stumble, holding the wall to steady myself. *Keep it together.*

"You're not going to need Lucas anymore."

"That's it. Get out of my way or *you* will be a dead white male poet."

I take a wobbly step forward and pitch onto the floor. A black curtain drapes my brain. The last thing I feel is my vibrating phone. The last words I hear: "I promised you a long time ago we'd be together, one way or another." My last thought: *Some Cupid kills with arrows, some with traps.*

44

I'M COLD. That's my first realization as consciousness returns. My second is I can't move my hands or feet.

I pry my eyes open. I'm outside on a blanket. The moon shines through pine branches rustling in the night breeze. Chorusing tree frogs and percussive insects bring back a memory of lying in my bubble bath listening to the forest sounds before daddy and junior broke in. Henley sits directly across from me on another blanket, his law school backpack beside him.

"Are you okay?" he says.

I might laugh if I could. *Fine and dandy, Henley. Thanks for asking.* I look down to see what's binding me. Nylon ties on my wrists and ankles. I wriggle myself upright. Henley reaches to help.

"Don't touch me," I say groggily.

"I'm really sorry I had to drug you. Gamma-hydroxybutyrate, better known as GHB. I poured it on your cake. Don't worry, I didn't touch you. Not in that way."

I try to swallow, but my throat's too dry. "Where are we?" I murmur.

"About an hour from St. Augustine, in Clay County, not far from the state prison in Starke."

Anger swells, helping to push some of the fuzziness away. Need to suppress it and focus. *Think.* Whatever's going on, he's got me right now. Stay calm, keep him calm. Learn more.

"Why are you doing this, Henley?"

"Simple. I love you. I'm devoted to you. I always have been."

"O-kay," I say with impressive self-restraint. "What does 'always' mean?"

"Well, not always, but since the first time I saw you."

"When was that?"

"In person? At your press conference in Memphis, after your trial."

"That was four years ago. You couldn't have been there."

"Didn't you see the picture in your tribute room? That's what I call it. It was the first one I ever took of you. Photography is a side hobby of mine."

"How is that possible? I was only sixteen. Help me understand."

"It's going to sound crazy."

"Oh, really? What an effing shock." *Zip it. Listen, learn.*

Henley's unfazed. "After I saw your national television interview, everything changed for me. You captured me. I don't mean to be ironic, but I don't know any better word for it. Your beauty, intelligence, strength. I loved that laugh of yours and the way you twirled your hair. *On the first view to say, to swear I love thee.* Also A Midsummer Night's Dream."

"Spare me the Shakespeare."

"Anyway, that's when I moved from Houston to Memphis."

"*Whoa whoa whoa.* Stop there. You moved to Memphis just to—" The darkness lights up to my right. My first thought is someone's out there with a flashlight. I'm about to cry out when I see my phone, flashing on a tree stump.

"Probably Lucas again," Henley says. "He's texted and called about a hundred times."

My brain is still swirling, from the drug or each new revelation, I'm not sure, probably both. Need to make it stop. "Could I have some water?"

"Of course. Anything you want. I don't want you to be uncomfortable."

"Then cut these ties off me."

"I wish I could, but can't risk it."

"Do you have another blanket? It's cold."

"Hold on. There's one in the car."

When he gets up, I press my hands to my chest, relieved to feel my neck knife still in place tucked behind my bra. It's going to be hard to reach with my hands tied, and impossible to use unless I can get free. I barely manage to wriggle my fingers beneath my shirts before he returns.

He spreads the blanket over my shoulders and holds out a bottle of water, asking if I need help with it.

"No," I snap, holding it in clamshell hands, ties cutting my wrists. I slowly drain the whole thing, taking slow deep breaths between swallows, feeling my wits returning.

I consider whether the plastic bottle can be used as a weapon, decide it can't and toss it aside. "So let me get this straight. You've had a crush on me since I was sixteen and moved to Memphis to be near me?"

"Basically, yes. I enrolled at the University of Memphis. That's where I got my undergraduate degree. I suppose it sounds impulsive, especially for me, but I gave it a lot of thought."

It sounds friggin' insane, which he obviously is. "Did it ever occur to you to just tell me you liked me?"

"Oh, but I did. Many times in my letters. I finally gave up on them. Remember my last one?"

Some Cupid kills with arrows, some with traps. I don't answer.

"I didn't want it to be this way. I swear."

"Why didn't you come up and talk to me in person? You obviously saw me at the coffee shop."

An enigmatic smile. "Those were my favorite times with you—until law school, of course. I'd sit in the corner while you worked on your computer and imagine all the clever things I would say to you."

"While you took pictures of me," I say, unable to disguise my disgust. "So why didn't you ever say any of those *clever things*?"

"I knew someone as beautiful as you would never like anyone who looks like me."

"Henley, you keep forgetting, I *did* like you. There's nothing wrong with the way you look. Don't tell me you're one of those involuntary celibate freaks."

"Not at all. I'm the opposite of them. They hate you. I love you. I saw the things they wrote about you. I've collected every reference to you on the internet ever made, thousands of them. I'm *voluntarily* celibate because I was saving myself for you."

I know it sounds old-fashioned, practically Victorian, but I've been waiting for the right person. That night at the Irish pub.

Movement in the trees.

"Help!" I shout. "Help me! Help!"

He reaches calmly into his backpack and pulls out a pistol. Henley with a gun? Does he even know how to use it? With my luck, it's another *side hobby*.

"Probably just a raccoon," he says, setting the gun on the blanket. "There's no one out here but you and me. I put a lot of thought into selecting this spot. Still, I would appreciate you not yelling. I'd hate to have to tape your mouth because I like talking to you."

A bug is crawling up my calf inside my jeans. I roll my leg to smush it.

"Even if I'd been able to summon the courage, Lucas was always hovering around, even at the coffee shop. My plan was to meet you in college, away from him. I thought for sure you'd go to Memphis, to stay near Lucas, but you messed that up by getting your undergraduate degree online."

I pull the blanket around me as a cloak, twisting my hands beneath it, trying to figure how to grab the neck knife and cut the ties. It's going to be impossible with him sitting right there.

He says, "Fortunately, patience is one of my strongest qualities. So I made a new plan. It's strange, because I really like law school. I never even considered it before you applied. By the way, the admissions office didn't tell me your LSAT score. Your coffee shop did, and also that you were planning to attend First Coast."

Deadpan, "My coffee shop told you." Crazier by the minute.

"Indirectly. You should never use public WiFi on a guest

network. It's easy to intercept the traffic if you're nearby. All you have to do is put your WiFi card in promiscuous mode and use a program like Wireshark to collect the data."

The coffee shop is where I filled out most of my law school applications. "You took the LSAT and went to law school just so you could follow me?"

"Like I said, devotion. One-hundred percent. You should at least appreciate that. I doubt most people ever reach even fifty percent. And it worked. I couldn't believe it. It was like a miracle. Even tonight, you coming to dinner ..."

His face crumples. "Then you rejected the ring. I saw it in your eyes before that, when I brought out the cake. Even when you said you were allergic to mangoes. That was an early warning sign. I knew everything was about to come apart. Everything I worked so hard for."

He picks up the gun and examines it. A Glock. Striker-fired. Just one trigger pull.

"Poof," he says. "Four years. *Gone*. I couldn't throw them away and couldn't go on without you any longer. There was nothing left in me. I used it all up. Part of me always knew it was too good to be true."

The moon illuminates his tortured face, brown eyes distant. "So that's the prologue to how we ended up out here. I had a backup plan. You know me, always well-prepared." A forced laugh. "I bought a plastic trunk with wheels at a container store. I felt terrible putting you in it, but promise I was extremely careful taking you to my car."

"You put me in a trunk?" If I ever get out of this, he is *dead dead dead*.

"Yes, and interestingly, it technically wasn't a false imprisonment because you were unconscious. Remember the *Parvi* case in Torts? To constitute a false imprisonment, the plaintiff must have present awareness of being confined."

I raise my bound hands. "Look at me. I'm still confined. It's a false imprisonment." Along with about a million other crimes and torts. "Come back to earth, Henley. You're a good person. I know you. This isn't worth it. I'm not worth it. There are lots of other girls. No need to ruin your life." Or mine.

"It's too late now."

"No, it's not. Let me go and I won't tell anyone about this."

"Please. Don't insult my intelligence."

"Then don't make it worse. You could spend the rest of your life in prison. Lucas knows I was going to your apartment tonight. He's probably already called the cops."

"*Lucas Lucas Lucas*," he says in a mocking little boy voice. "I'm so *sick* of him. I hate him. Not because he's black, by the way. It's not a racial thing. That slur on his picture was just to throw you off. I hate him because he has you and I don't."

I give up trying to surreptitiously reach the neck knife. It's going to require a prolonged shoulder-scrunch while I chicken-wing my elbows, and he's staring right at me.

"Anyway, I'm not going to prison, Emily."

"Oh, really."

"Yes, really. Because I'm not going to live through the night." He reaches into the backpack and extracts a small black case. "Unfortunately, either are you. I'm sorry." He opens the case and removes a syringe and clear glass vial.

"What's that?"

"Cyanide. For both of us. It will be like Romeo and Juliet. I hate to keep harping on Shakespeare, but it is a fitting end."

Juliet took her own life, psycho. "You said at your apartment you didn't want to hurt me."

"I don't. I wish there was another choice."

"Of course there's another choice. Don't do it!"

"Please don't yell. I'm trying to concentrate."

He's wiping the rubber stopper of the vial with an alcohol pad. He's about to kill us and worried about bacteria. Totally whack. I estimate it will take at least a full minute of alone time to remove the knife and free myself without slitting my wrists.

"Henley, could you at least do me one last favor? Every night I say prayers before I go to sleep. My faith is very important to me, especially right now." That's an understatement. "Could you leave me alone for a minute to pray in private ... before I die?"

He pokes the syringe into the vial and starts drawing from it. "I'd like to, but again, too risky. I can put my hands over my ears if that helps."

When I don't respond, he says, "I guess it's time then." He taps the syringe and pushes the plunger until a tiny fountain sprays from the needle.

"Wait! You don't want to do this. Think back. Think about all the fun we had, like you were saying in your apartment. Remember the time we got in an argument about *in rem* jurisdiction at the Starbucks and the barista had to ask us to shut up?"

A crooked smile. "That was a good time. I was right about that, by the way."

He's moving closer, holding the needle pointed at the sky.

"What about our kiss?" That stops him.

"Our kiss. I've relived it a thousand times. It was probably the best moment of my whole life."

He looks like he means it. Sad. "Then how about this? Let's do it right. Like Romeo and Juliet. One last kiss and embrace. Wouldn't that be a lot more poetic?"

"Do you expect me to believe you want to kiss me?"

"The thing you still don't get is I really did like you, and I don't want to die alone."

"How would we do it?"

"Well, you'd have to take these ties off my wrists, obviously, for an embrace."

"Nice try. I know you can kick my ass. Remember, I've studied you for four years."

"Okay, just the kiss then."

"What kind of trick do you have planned?" I can see he wants it, wants to believe so bad. Love clouds the mind. He could probably recite a Shakespeare quote about it.

"No tricks. Um, could you at least remove the ties from my

ankles, so I can stand and do it properly? I wouldn't be able to run far from a gun."

"You'd probably knee me in the nuts. But I'll help you stand."

"Alright."

He removes the blanket and pulls me to my feet. The drug's still in my system and my pogo-stick balance isn't too great right now. I teeter and he holds me up.

"I'm still woozy. Can I put my wrists over your head to steady myself. And I'm still cold. You could you warm me up. No one wants to die cold."

I see his brain analyzing whether I could do any damage that way. "Okay," he says. "Don't bite me. I'm warning you. It will just make me mad."

"I won't."

He steps in close and I drape my wrists over his head, resting them on his neck. His breathing quickens. He's excited, quivering.

"Close your eyes," I say. "It's not a real kiss if our eyes are open," says the expert on kissing. "Don't worry. There's nothing I can do with my ankles and wrists bound."

Well, *nothing* is an overstatement. Interestingly, Kiona, not Lucas, taught me about headbutts, during a boxing lesson. She showed me a video of Evander Holyfield destroying some guy with one and getting disqualified. "They're illegal," she said. "But when all else fails ..."

All else has failed. I reconstruct the lesson: Use the crown of the skull. Three inches above your eyebrows, not too far toward the top. Compress low, aim and shoot up like a missile. Element of surprise is everything. I'll only have one chance.

I wait until his lips part, launching for his cheekbone as I yank his neck forward. *Crack.*

Sweet Mary, that hurt, but not as much as it hurt Henley. He's tumbling backwards with a cry, taking me with him. We hit the ground hard, but I have him to cushion me. I unloop my arms from his neck and scramble to my feet.

Contorting my hands, I slide out the neck knife while he rolls on the ground with his face buried in his hands. The headbutt smashed his glasses, gashing his forehead.

I work the knife between my wrists, forcing myself to go slow so I'm not the one who bleeds out. It isn't easy when your heart's pounding two hundred beats a minute. The new blade is sharp. A minute later I'm a free person.

Claws out, fangs bared, I pounce on Henley. He looks up at me, ghostly pale in the moonlight, a sadness in his eyes so deep it threatens to pull me under. No time for sentimentality. I raise the knife high, aiming for the throat.

A loop is playing in my head. *The Law, The Law ...*

Whatever. What good is it? Where was *The Law* for Mom and Becky? Where was it when Scott Brooker picked me up hitchhiking? When the guards at Pochachant were hurting the girls? Where was it tonight?

"Go ahead, Emily. Do it," Henley says, face an ugly smear of blood and tears. "I deserve it."

I respect him for recognizing it. *Deserves to die.* As the knife plunges down, a lost girl in the woods silences the tree frogs and insects with a howl like a rabid wolf.

45

THE BLADE disappears into the damp dirt all the way to the hilt, an inch from Henley's neck. I push myself up, wipe the knife on my pants and return it to the sheath. I couldn't do it. I'm not sure why.

I find the zip ties in the RAV4 and use them to secure his hands and feet. He doesn't resist, even offers to help. He's shivering so I spread my blanket over him. Ever the gentleman, he thanks me twice. Silent and motionless on his back with only his head sticking out, he looks asleep in bed.

I retrieve the Glock and eject the magazine. Empty. I clear the chamber and a cartridge pops out. Only one bullet. I wonder who he intended it for.

I grab my phone from the stump. Henley wasn't lying. A long string of texts from Lucas. The first one says, *Leave wherever you are right now and call me!* Below it:

The pictures match. PRNU. Came from the same camera.

The selfie and presentation pics.

Get out now!

On and on. And nine voicemails. I don't waste time listening to them. I hit the call button. It picks up before the first ring finishes.

"Em?"

"It's me, Lucas. I'm okay."

* * *

I'm waiting for Lucas and Agent Magritte to find us. I sent them my GPS location. Magritte warned me she had to notify the local authorities in Clay County, said they might get here first.

I start the car and turn on the lights to make us easier to spot. The interior reminds me of our trip to Bryce's and walk on the beach, and the kiss. I never should have let that happen. Maybe an earlier rejection would have jolted him back to reality when there was still a chance. I doubt it though. Four years! I can't believe he wasted four years of his life stalking me. Sick.

I ponder my own mental illness. I didn't split tonight, not like I started to do when the *Rol Rom* boys busted in. Not sure why. There were definitely some extreme triggers. Maybe the GHB. Maybe because I had more time to think. The apartment attack was so sudden.

But I think Henley was the main reason. Through it all, part of me didn't believe he would hurt me, even after he got out the cyanide.

A half hour passes. Henley hasn't moved an inch. Antsy, pacing and listening for cars, I check my phone. Nothing new. This is where I could really use a shot of that rum Mrs. Alvarez gave me. Henley says something I can't hear over the car motor. I walk over to him.

"What'd you say?"

"I said you're fidgeting."

"Yeah, so?"

"It's something you always do. I don't mean it as a criticism, just an observation from someone who's studied you for a long time. You fidgeted in the coffee shop when you were sixteen. I always thought it was cute."

"Henley, here's some advice. Don't tempt me to cut your heart out by reminiscing about your stalking me."

"Sorry," he says.

"And you're the one who should be fidgeting. You said we're near the state prison? Maybe they can drive you straight there."

A beetle lands on his face. I sweep it away with my foot.

"Thanks. At least I'll get to know my exam grades. You won't believe this. I missed the *rescue doctrine* issue on the Torts exam. It hit me last night in bed. It was *so* obvious."

I don't know whether to laugh or cry. Law school. The only topic he ever seemed at ease talking about.

"Happens to everyone," I say.

"I guess. I still wouldn't be surprised if we finished one and two in the class."

"Anyone but Olson. That's all I hope."

And that's how we pass the time, talking about law school. Bizarro-world, but listening to the Henley I once knew makes me glad I didn't kill him, even gives me second thoughts about calling for help. Then I see the cyanide bottle and syringe glistening in the headlights on a bed of pine needles.

The growing rumble of a car engine sets my heart racing. Please don't let it be the local police. A large black shape roars into view.

Lucas. He grinds to a stop and jumps out of the SUV, breathing fire. I run to position myself in front of Henley.

"You alright?"

"Mm-hm."

Nodding toward Henley, lying straight as a board under the blanket, "What about him? He dead?"

"No. He's fine."

"Not for long." He skirts me.

"Lucas, no! *The Law!*"

* * *

It hurts my heart watching them load Henley's limp body into the back of the cop car. I run over as they're about to leave.

"Can I say something to him?" I don't wait for an answer. "Henley," I whisper. "Tell me one thing. Were you really going to kill me—or just you?"

"I wouldn't lie to you, Emily, not even to help myself. I can't swear one way or the other."

I back away.

Through glazed eyes, like his soul already died, he says, "Goodbye, Emily," and they drive him away.

A van showed up a few minutes earlier, occupied by a detective and crime scene investigator. The detective comes over and pulls a recorder from his pocket, saying he needs to take my statement. He's a big guy with a lumpy face, but not anywhere near as big as Lucas, who stands at my side like a bodyguard, not saying anything.

"Who's this?" the detective says with a jerk of his head. The dismissive way it comes out makes me instantly dislike him.

"Ask him yourself. He's standing right here."

"Who are you?" he says.

"A friend."

I say, "More than a friend. As for a statement, I'll let the FBI handle it."

He looks to Magritte, who arrived shortly after Lucas. She pulls us aside and explains the jurisdictional complexities of the case, which started in one county and ended in another. "As for the FBI, I'm not sure we have jurisdiction over anything except the presentation pictures."

"No interstate transportation," I say.

"You got it."

If Henley had driven north, we would have crossed into Georgia. "So I have to talk to that guy? A lot of the things are personal, and I thought he was rude to Lucas. And I know it sounds strange, but I don't want to get Henley in trouble ... more trouble."

Lucas looks up like he's saying a prayer.

Magritte says, "At some point you'll have to talk to them, but if you happened to be feeling too traumatized at the moment, which would be totally understandable ..."

I take the hint. "I definitely am. *Completely* traumatized."

"I'll talk to the detective and suggest we arrange another time."

"Thank you, Agent Magritte."

"Fair notice, I have to go give him a rundown on the night's events based on what you told me."

I cringe. "Could you at least leave out my underwear?"

She says she can, for now.

"If the FBI doesn't have jurisdiction, does that also mean you don't have control over whether this goes public?"

"I'm afraid not, although it's state law to redact the names of sexual assault victims in public records."

I almost defend Henley, explain he was a gentleman who didn't and wouldn't try to sexually assault me. Instead I puff my cheeks and sputter, "I guess that means my law school career is over. I could never come back if this gets out. I'm not sure I can even if it doesn't."

"This isn't the time to make any big decisions. Go home to Memphis with Lucas tomorrow. Take a break, from everything. Even strong people need a break, Emily."

46

POUNDING ON the door between our rooms wakes me, Lucas yelling, "Time to get movin'. We're headed home." A groggy glance at the nightstand. Two o'clock? Can that be right?

"Okay," I say in a fog. I stumble into his suite in my PJ's. "I have to take a shower and pack. Do you have any coffee?"

"Coffee came with breakfast. That was six hours ago. You can use that." He points to the in-room coffee maker.

I add some water and a coffee pod. "Why did you let me sleep so long?"

"You needed it."

I take the foam cup back to my room and crank up the hot water in the shower. It insulates me like a warm blanket as I struggle to process last night. I asked Lucas on the drive home how he knew I was in trouble.

"I called James. Asked if he knew how to do PRNU photo comparisons. He said he didn't have the software, but would *acquire* it."

Acquire is James's word for hack. "I thought he went legal."

"I told him you was in trouble and it was an emergency. He didn't hesitate."

"Aw, I love James."

"The selfie of you and your psychopath friend showed the same imaging flaws as the pictures from the presentation. They came from the same camera."

"What made you decide to go through all that trouble? How did you know?"

"Just a hunch. Didn't you think it was strange that boy lived right next to you? You're suspicious of everyone."

"I did at first, but thought it was a coincidence. Other law students live there too. Same with my building."

"And you said he wouldn't tell you where he was from."

"He said it was painful to talk about. I don't like talking about my past either. If you knew him, you'd understand why I wasn't suspicious. I know it sounds crazy, but he's a really nice person, a good person."

"Yeah, fine person. Let's review the events. He stalked you for four years, took secret pictures of you, stole your underwear—"

"I know, I know."

"I'm just gettin' started."

"I know what happened. He's messed up, obviously. Isn't everyone in some way? I still don't think he would have injected me. And the gun only had one bullet. I think he intended to use it on himself. That's my hunch."

I turn the water up even hotter. I'd stay here the rest of the day, but Lucas keeps hollering to hurry up. I dry off and throw on more crumpled jeans and tees, cramming everything else in the backpack.

"Come on," Lucas says.

"Almost ready." I unplug my phone and it flashes with new messages.

One from Agent Forster: *Sorry I couldn't be there for you last night. I'm out on another case. Magritte filled me in. We'll talk soon.*

One from Agent Magritte: *Hope you're hanging in there. I gave the locals your contact info so they can arrange for a victim statement. Now go home and rest!*

The last message is from a number I don't recognize: *This is Detective Roberson. I went out to see your professor last night. He wouldn't talk to me.*

Oh, frick. I forgot all about Professor Nemworth. Lucas is haranguing me to get my butt in gear, voice growing louder.

"Just a second." I push the callback button.

"Financial Crimes. Roberson."

"Detective, this is Emily Calby. I'm calling to find out what happened with Professor Nemworth?"

"Like my message said, he didn't want to talk to me. Do you happen to know if he drinks a lot? His words were slurred."

I didn't see any alcohol when I cleaned his house. "I don't know for sure, but I don't think so."

"Well, he definitely was under the influence of something. I believe the woman was there too. Dark hair, much younger?"

"Yeah, like, by about a million years."

"What kind of car does she drive?"

"An old white Nissan."

"There was a new BMW in the driveway."

"She probably bought it with the *cancer* money she got from the professor. Did you ask him about the black eye?"

"He said he broke a blood vessel."

"I don't believe that. Can't you make him talk? What about the law?"

"Miss, I'll be completely honest. The bottom line is that the law doesn't always work in these cases. I left him my card. If he changes his mind and wants to talk, I'll be more than happy to follow up. As of now, there's nothing the law can do."

We disconnect. *The law doesn't always work ... there's nothing the law can do.* At the Pochachant detention center, Miss Mava, my boss at the library, asked why I was so determined to learn the law. I said, *Because the law never loses. Everyone loses sometimes, every single thing in the world loses, but not the law.*

I was wrong.

Lucas storms into my room. "What's taking so long? It's a twelve-hour drive."

"*Wel-ll,* there's a little problem I need to take care of before we leave."

He looks to the ceiling. "Can't you set aside even one minute in your life where you ain't got a new problem? What is it now? Aliens landing? Zombie attack? You used up every other kind."

Poor Lucas. I don't know how he puts up with me. I tell him about my meeting with Professor Nemworth after the Civ Pro exam, about the black eye and his fable of the man who knew everything.

"Lucas, it was the saddest thing in the world. It would have broke your heart. He basically admitted that Christina—that woman—was exploiting him, but said he didn't deserve help."

"That's the man's choice, Em. He ain't a child."

"That's what people don't understand. In a way, he is like a child. Remember when you saved me? I was alone and vulnerable and not in my right mind. It's the same with him. It could be you or me or any of us some day."

"You tried. Let the law handle it. Let's go."

"That's the problem. The law won't handle it. I just talked to a detective. He went out to see the professor last night, but Nemworth wouldn't cooperate. The detective said there's nothing the law can do. Those were his exact words."

"Yeah, so?"

"If the law can't get justice, I have to do it myself ... unless you want to help me. She needs to go away. Once I leave, he has no one."

"Fuck no. We ain't stopping off to kill some lady on our way outta town."

"Not kill. *Persuade.*"

"How?"

"Fear. Scare her away. If you help me with this, I'll never ask you to help me with anything else, ever."

I expect him to go ballistic, threaten to stuff me in a trunk like Henley did and cart me back to Memphis in the back of the SUV. Instead he gives me his trademark snort with the half-shoulder roll. "Put that in writing under oath. Gimme one good reason why I should."

"Because he's an innocent victim of a predator. Like I was. And he doesn't have anyone else to help him. Like I didn't until I met you. And because the strong have an obligation to protect the weak. It's even in the bible."

He mutters something about religion, picks up the room phone and says, "This is Mr. Jackson. We need to extend our stay another night. Thank you." He sets down the receiver.

"Seriously? You'll help?"

"Somethin' I ain't told you. I had an aunt once. Gussie. No sweeter woman ever lived. She met a man at church who pretended to like her and stole all her money. Not that she had much."

"What did you do about it?"

"Use your imagination."

"So you'll help?"

"Only because of somethin' else I learned." He proceeds to explain that while marooned in Gabberman's apartment, he took a deep dive into Christina Smith and Cyprus Keane on the web, including the dark web. From public records, he pieced together that *Christina Smith* is one of at least seventeen aliases for a woman with at least three criminal complaints filed against her for elder financial exploitation.

"The first one was more than ten years ago. She's made a profession of preying on old men. Never prosecuted for any of 'em. One man even died. She was a suspect because they found a handwritten will leaving the victim's money to her. But he never signed it."

"*Hol-ee!*"

"That ain't all. Your friend Mr. Keane? Also a fan of aliases. That man has some deep women issues. He likes to hurt 'em."

"That doesn't surprise me. You know how you can tell some people are mean just by looking at them? He's one of them. When I went to their house, he came out punching his fist, saying if I trespassed again I'd be leaving in an ambulance. And I told you about the domestic violence complaint Christina filed against him."

"She was lucky. He beat one woman so bad she spent two weeks in the hospital. Served time for it."

"Why didn't you tell me all this?"

"I just did. Let's make a plan."

* * *

"It's ringing."

"Put it on speaker," Lucas says.

I'm on one of his burner phones. He's holding up a second one to record the call. He brings a couple wherever he goes and they never fail to come in handy. We're sitting at the cafe table in his suite. Out the window over his mountainous shoulder, the afternoon sun looks like an orange gumball.

"Remember, your goal is to get her to incriminate herself."

He's hoping we can scare her away with evidence, threaten to give it to the cops if she doesn't leave town. I don't think it will work. I researched it and Florida is an all-party consent state when it comes to recording phone calls, so nothing she says can be used in court. More fundamentally, she's already shown she's not afraid of the law. She knows it doesn't work here. But he's helping me, so I didn't argue.

I give an *Okay* sign as she picks up. "Hi! Do I have the pleasure of speaking with Christina Smith?" Lucas moves his phone closer.

"Who is this?" Already wary.

"Emily. Nemworth's student. And I wouldn't hang up if I were you."

Muffled voices. "What do you want?"

"I guess you'd call it a cut. Nemworth just flunked me out of law school, after all I did for him. Gave me a big fat *F*, just like you wanted."

"A cut of what?"

"Come on, you know. The money you've been stealing from him."

I wait. Nothing.

"I'm moving back home. All I want is two thousand dollars. Cash. Pay me and you can keep robbing that old fart blind forever as far as I'm concerned." *Forgive me, Professor.*

"I had nothing to do with your grade. I did you a favor. I never even mentioned your coming to my home and harassing me."

"I believe that. You had too much to hide. It would have been stupid. If you rob a bank, you don't walk in the next day and say, *Someone accused me of robbing your bank.*"

She shushes an angry man's voice in the background. Cyprus Keane, speaking the language I don't recognize.

"Two thousand is a bargain," I say. "I saw Nemworth's checkbook. Give me the money and you'll never have to worry about me again."

Still nothing. She's too smart. A worthy adversary. I give her credit for that. Most of my enemies are dumbasses. Lucas signals it's time to fire our best shot.

"If Christina Smith doesn't want to give it to me, could I please speak to Christina Green? Or Christina Williams? I'll even settle for Cristina, without the h, Taylor." Aliases Lucas discovered in his internet search.

Come on, incriminate yourself! But light static is the only sound. "How's your cancer doing? Nice BMW, by the way. Wonder where the money for that came from."

Muted background conversation before, "I have no idea what you're babbling about, but I do think we should meet. Come to my house at eight."

I look at Lucas. A grudging nod. "I'll be there," I say. "Just be sure you have the money."

"Come by yourself."

I disguise my laugh as a cough. "Who else would I bring?"

47

WE DEBATED the next steps for an hour. I said I should go in alone because I've already put him at risk too many times. He said they might be planning to kill me and he should go in alone because they don't know him. I said they weren't going to invite him inside and that he could get shot busting in, which happened eight years ago in Pensacola. In the end, we decided to both go.

Another complication arose, both operationally and in terms of nearly causing Lucas to have an aneurysm, when I said scaring them out of town wasn't enough justice. I wanted to get Nemworth's money back, at least some of it.

"Anything else?"

"Well, it would be nice if we could collect some evidence that she exploited him. In case we need it later."

"This ain't gonna be a slumber party. It's got to go down in a hurry."

The streetlights came on a few minutes ago. We pass a twenty-something in flip flops walking a golden retriever. He looks at us, but the SUV's windows are tinted darker than the night.

Lucas wheels into the shadow of an enormous white oak and turns off the lights and motor. He's dressed completely in black. We went on a shopping spree before coming.

"I can't believe I let you talk me into this," he says, adjusting the spooky virus mask we got at a dollar store. Black with a red nose and clown grin on the front.

"Don't worry," I say. "It's a good plan and no one will get hurt.

Think about your Aunt Gussie. Oh, and don't forget the hatchet."

I insisted we buy one when we stopped at a home improvement store for zip ties and duct tape, must-haves for any home invader, a lesson I learned the day my family was murdered. Lucas argued we didn't need a hatchet because he brought a nine-millimeter semiautomatic, the only gun he kept when he disarmed his building.

"The hatchet will make a fantastic visual!" I argued. "I can't imagine anything scarier in this world than big, bad Lucas Jackson bursting through the door wearing a clown grin and carrying a shiny new hatchet. Hold it up high for maximum effect."

"I know what I'm doing, Mr. Hitchcock. Remember who the apprentice is."

I look at my phone. Five 'til eight. "It's time." I push open the passenger door. We're parked around the corner a block away. "Be careful," I say.

"*You* be careful and remember what I said."

"I remember. You told me five thousand times."

"Repeat it."

"No one gets hurt. Stick with the plan. Don't do anything except act my part. Control myself."

"And?"

"Make it real. No lapses." The whole plan depends on them believing it.

"And?"

"No matter what, unless my life depends on it, *Don't take out that fuckin' neck knife."*

I climb out and pull my hood over my head. It's another nippy night. Orion's sword dangles above me in the twinkling sky. He always seems to be around on nights like this. Rounding the corner, I glance back to see Lucas carrying a black canvas bag, keeping a safe distance.

I turn up Christina's driveway and pass a shiny silver BMW that gets my blood boiling. *Control yourself.*

I rap on the door. The curtains are drawn, but a face peeks through. Moths party around a yellow porch light. The doorknob turns. I press my hand to my chest to still my pounding heart, tracing the outline of my neck knife.

"Hi, Christina!" I say. "Nice to see you." Cyprus Keane's pug face pops up behind her. "What's he doing here? You said to come alone. I thought you'd be alone too."

Need her to keep the door open for at least a minute. That's the plan. They have to believe Lucas and I don't know each other, that we're not connected.

"He lives here," she says. "Come in."

"I'm not sure about this. What if you're planning to hurt me?" It's obvious from their malignant stares they would like nothing more.

"No one's going to hurt you," she says.

I press the issue with more questions until she cuts me off. "You'll be fine. Now please come in."

"Do you have my money?"

"Get the hell inside. I don't want to be having this conversation in public."

"Alright. I just—hey!" Something hits me from behind.

Lucas shoves me through the door, into Christina, who backs into Cyprus. I land hard on a terrazzo floor.

Dang, he looks scary. A giant black Pennywise with a gleaming hatchet in one gloved hand, raised high, pistol in the other.

"You two. Join the girl on the floor. *Now.* One word, I'll hack you to fuckin' pieces. All three of you."

I was right about the hatchet. Their eyes are glued to it. I turn to Christina. "What's happening? Who is this man?"

A shake of her head, caught between fear and shock. Cyprus looks more angry than scared. Need to keep an eye on him.

"You deaf, blondie?" Lucas says, thumping me in the ribs with his foot. "I said no talking."

"Hey, that hurt!" He sticks the gun in my face, fiery eyes screaming, *No lapses.*

"I—I'm sorry, sir."

He collects everyone's phones and puts them in the black bag, pulling out the ties. "Blondie. Take these and bind that man's hands behind his back."

Gladly! "Ye—yes, sir. I'll try."

I touch Cyprus and he roars to life, knocking me down with a punch to the face. He makes it halfway to his feet before Lucas smashes him in the temple with the gun butt.

He leans down and presses the barrel against Cyprus's forehead. I see his finger twitching on the trigger and know he wants to pull it. The fire in his breathing burns loud and clear even through the mask. I clear my throat to telegraph, *Don't do it. I'm okay. Stick with the plan.* I hold my breath until his finger relaxes.

"You like to hit women, tough man? You don't get your hands behind your back in one fucking second, you a dead man."

Cyprus complies, but I see the devil in his snaky eyes.

Tasting blood from a split lip, I pull hard on the nylon strips, then give them a couple extra yanks. His hands are already plum red.

Lucas plops into an armchair, sending bits of foam stuffing spewing into the air. His eyes move from Cyprus to Christina to me, seated in a row at his feet like he's Mr. Rogers about to read us a story.

"Blondie, what the fuck you doing here? My client said there was gonna be two people. A man and a woman."

"I'm just here on an errand. I don't even know these people."

He clicks his tongue. "Wrong place, wrong time. Bad luck. But I may need you. Do exactly what I say, maybe I let you live."

"Yes, sir. I want to live."

"*You.*" He points to Christina. "Where's the money?"

"What money? We're poor immigrants. You have the wrong house."

"I know exactly who you are. Where's the money? Last time I'm gonna ask."

"No money."

"Blondie, take that woman's right hand and flatten it on the floor."

Yes! "What are you going to do? Please don't hurt her."

"No questions."

"Yes, sir. I'm sorry, Christina," I say, wrenching her wrist and pressing it against the cool terrazzo.

Lucas tucks the gun in his waistband and raises the hatchet. Cyprus starts shouting in the foreign language. Every word sounds like a curse word. A thwack to the jaw with the axe handle silences him. "Ain't no one talkin' to you, ugly."

Ouch. Watching it reminds me that for all his newfound philosophy of no violence, Lucas didn't get to be Big EZ in a South Memphis gang by being nice.

"Spread your fingers," he says.

Christina balls up her hand.

Lucas says, "Your choice. Keep 'em that way and you lose the whole hand. Do what I say, you only lose one finger. That's all it's gonna take to tell me. Trust me."

"In the bedroom," she blurts. "Top of the closet. Shoebox in the corner."

"Blondie, go find me that shoebox."

"Yes, sir. Which room?" I say to Christina.

A flicker of suspicion in her eyes, the first one. Lucas sees it.

She doesn't answer.

He winds his arm back. "How 'bout I chop off your whole head? You wasting my time. Which room?"

"Master bedroom," she says.

"Blondie, go get the box. No tricks. Your one and only warning."

Christina's voice trails behind me. "I wouldn't trust that girl if I were you."

The master bedroom furniture looks new but cheap. Some kind of fancy French Colonial or something, all curly and white with gold trim. Everything else is maroon. Carpet, paint, everything except a discordant yellow blanket with a red smiley face on it spread on top of the maroon bed comforter. A painting of a unicorn in an ornate gilded frame hangs on the wall.

The box is where she said it would be. I have to stand on a chair to reach it. It's heavy and ... omigod, completely filled with cash.

I spy another bedroom on the way out, an office. An open laptop sits on a desk. Jackpot. Proof of *everything* is on a person's computer, and Lucas knows how to find it. I lay it on top of the cash box.

I hear Christina. "It shouldn't take her this long. The box is where I said it would be. Aren't you worried she's trying to escape?"

Definitely suspicious. We're ready for it. *Plan two steps ahead, three if possible.* Another basic survival lesson from Lucas.

"Blondie," Lucas shouts. "Hurry up. I'm countin' to five and you better be back before I get there. *One, two ...*"

I creep down the hall, halting at the threshold to the living room.

"*Four, five.*"

I count *six, seven* in my head before barging in, breathlessly lugging the money box and computer.

"You're late," Lucas says. "That the box?"

"Yes, sir. There's money in it."

"What's that on top?"

"A computer. I thought maybe you could sell it."

Even with the mask on, I can read his dirty look saying, *Stick with the plan.* Why would a home invader want a stolen computer that might bring a hundred bucks on the street?

"You're late and I didn't say nothin' about a computer. Put that shit down."

I set the box and computer on a dining table.

"Now move over there," he says pulling out the nine.

I do as he says. "What are you going to do? Please don't hurt me. I was only trying to help."

"I'm *sick* of you people not listening."

I thought I was mentally prepared. I was wrong. The flashing barrel and concussive boom shake loose memories of too many real gunshots entombed in the concrete of my past.

Ears ringing, I clutch my left arm and sink to my knees, popping blood-red paintballs taped under my t-shirts. We had to buy a bag of a thousand. The sporting goods store didn't have any blank nine-millimeter cartridges, so Lucas made one, pulling the bullet from a regular cartridge with pliers and packing the tip with Styrofoam.

Dropping to the floor, I glimpse Christina and Cyprus. Their wide-eyed frozen looks say any suspicion is gone. Even Cyprus is scared now. Lucas comes over to inspect me. Streams of red trail down my arm. I may have used too many paintballs.

"You'll live," he says, tossing me a dishtowel from the dining room table and pulling out the duct tape. "Wrap it in this and don't ever *not listen* to me again."

I think he's enjoying this, the tormenting-me part, maybe a way to take out his frustration for all the trouble I've caused by not listening. I gulp fake tears while fumbling with the tape.

"Pipe down. I got to talk to these people," he says. "You two. Pay attention. I'll make it simple. Someone wants your asses to disappear. Someone who really don't like you."

Unintelligible growls emanate from Cyprus. He doesn't look quite right. Probably concussed from the hits to the head.

"Disappear?" Christina says. "What does that mean?"

"Up to you. You got ten minutes to pack your shit, get in that luxury automobile before they repossess it and drive north. Don't stop 'til you at least five states away. I'll be tracking it."

"Ten minutes! That's not enough time."

"I wasn't fucking finished. Your other choice is to die. From what my client says, you deserve it."

I nod involuntarily.

"Call the police or ever set foot back in the Sunshine State, I will hunt you down and kill you without wasting one more word. You won't even know it's comin'. Now get off your sorry ass and pack. I'll stay here with ugly."

"I can't do it in ten minutes. We need a moving truck for our furniture."

"Don't need no furniture. You about to start a new life. Down to nine minutes now. You saw what happened to her when she was late. Blondie, go with her. She does anything except pack, and I mean *anything*, you shout. You do that, I let you live."

"I've lost too much blood," I whimper. "I feel dizzy."

"For fuck's sake, quit being such a baby. Get up."

I make a big deal of wrangling myself off the floor with my right arm and follow Christina down the hall, gripping the duct-tape bandage and concentrating on keeping my dominant left arm limp.

One step into the master bedroom, she says, "Why does that man trust you to watch me?"

Right shoulder shrug. "I guess he believed me when I said I wanted to live."

She grabs a suitcase from the closet and starts jamming clothes in it. I keep my eyes glued to her hands. Could be a gun stashed somewhere. She says, "Does this mess have anything to do with Nemworth?"

"How would I know?"

"Seems awfully coincidental he showed up the same time you did."

"I guess he could have followed me, although I can't see Nemworth hiring anyone to do this. Maybe he has relatives."

"That senile old fuck's been more trouble than he's worth."

The rage-tiger growls from somewhere deep. *No lapses.* I say, "Yeah, he was a pain in the ass. Believe me, after he flunked me, I wanted to give him a black eye too."

Holding a handful of bras and underwear, she stops and appraises me, finally taking the bait. "It was just a slap. He was getting increasingly irritable and uncooperative. We had to start drugging him a few weeks ago to keep him calm. I blame it on you for interfering. Everything was fine before you came along."

Yeah, it's my fault. Hit an eighty-four-year-old man in the eye?

Drug him? I'll bet that's why his words were slurred when the detective went to see him.

She finishes filling the suitcase and I follow her into the bathroom where I catch a glimpse in the mirror of my fat lip and bruised cheek where Cyprus hit me. *Fucker!*

Christina shovels pill bottles, cosmetics and hygiene supplies into a laundry bag. "That old windbag actually believed I loved him. Get real."

I picture the card on the professor's desk. *Edgar, my love for you grows deeper every day.* They're called sweetheart scams for a reason. The rage-tiger claws closer to the surface. *Control yourself. Don't blow everything.*

I say, "How much money did you steal from him?"

"Steal? He gave it to me to help pay for my cancer treatment."

Because he cared about you and didn't want you to die like his poor wife did. *It was a long, painful journey, the most terrible thing I've ever witnessed.*

"Except you don't really have cancer, do you?"

"Details, details." She flips me off and opens the bottom drawer of the vanity, fishing around in the back. I tense, ready to pounce in case her hand comes out holding a gun.

It's a scarf, but wrapped around something solid. I'm still thinking gun and start to reach when the scarf slips and I catch a glint of a shimmering green stone on a silver chain. She quickly thrusts it into the laundry bag.

Well, what do you know? Professor Nemworth's memory is better than I gave him credit for. *I promised her I would take care of it ... I failed her.* He didn't misplace his wife's necklace after all. It really did *disappear.* Need to get it back.

She says, "They're all alike. So desperate for companionship. It's pathetic. Edgar's thing was wanting to hold hands. I was like, seriously? I laughed my ass off."

Picturing Professor Nemworth reaching out and getting laughed at by this piece of shit ... I can't even. Stealing his money is bad enough. Stealing his wife's cherished heirloom worse. Robbing his dignity, unforgivable.

I grit my teeth and flex my hands, both of them. Maybe I could smash her skull on the terrazzo, tell Lucas she slipped and fell. His shout that she has four minutes left snaps me out of it. *No one gets hurt.*

She sets the laundry bag next to the suitcase and crosses the hall to the second bedroom, pausing to call me the C-word for taking her computer. She picks up a pair of scissors from the desk and glances over her shoulder.

Go for it!

But she tosses them aside and starts cramming manila file folders into a plastic utility bin. I wonder what's in them. How many people has she exploited? She's probably too savvy to keep paper records. I can't wait to get into that computer.

"So what was your angle?" she says. "Before you turned on him. I know you had one."

The thought that someone could genuinely care about another person is foreign to her. "I didn't have any angle."

"Bullshit. I know a predator when I see one."

Valid point. "Takes one to know one."

"So what was it? Just kissing his ass for a good grade? Obviously that didn't work." She laughs. "Maybe something bigger, daughter-up to him and get in his will?"

Lucas again: "Blondie, she still packing?"

"Yes, sir."

"Tell her to hurry."

"He said—"

"I heard," she snaps.

"I have a question," I say. "I get stealing. I've done plenty of it, but what about the heart part?" An image of the professor trying to hold her hand keeps puncturing my brain.

"What about it?"

"When you, uh, do what you do, do you realize you're tearing a human being's heart apart?"

She laughs. "The only way I'd care about that geezer's heart would be if he put *me* in his will, which he would have if you hadn't interfered. Once that happened, I'd care that it stop beating."

Soulless, no conscience at all. The voice saying *Control yourself* is getting weaker.

From the living room, "Two minutes."

"Quit wasting my time talking," she says. "You're going to get me shot."

"Well, if I were you, I'd be careful not to contact the professor ever again. You know, just in case that's what this is all about."

"No reason Edgar can't help his 'sweetheart' long distance."

A tiger claw breaks through, raking my skin. The blood streaks on my arm startle me until I remember the paint balls. "Allow me to rephrase," I say. Another lawyer saying I learned during my murder trial. "Stay away from Professor Nemworth."

"Fuck off. You've been nothing but trouble since the first time we met. Here's a little secret. Cy and I had a plan to make *you* disappear tonight."

"Oh, did you now? And how did you expect to accomplish that?"

"Let's just say getting shot by that spade in the living room would be a much easier way to go than what Cy had in store for you."

Control yourself is eclipsed by *Do it! Do it!* If she intends to keep exploiting the professor, this whole plan was for nothing. I lift my left arm and slip it inside my shirts. She notices.

"What are you doing? A second ago that arm was limp."

"Fast healer. Good genes." I pull out the neck knife. Too fast. The shiny blade pierces my shirts. Out of practice. *Be careful. Control yourself. No one gets hurt.*

I raise the blade to her face, slowly so I don't accidentally stab her in the eye. She flares back.

"You think that man out there is scary? Listen to me. If you *ever* contact Professor Nemworth again, in any way, I will cut your eyeballs out and make you eat them. I'll push your jaws together until I hear them pop like cherries."

Pop like cherries? Oh, brother. Scary girl is back. I guess all that cannibalism stuff got stored in her dark closet.

Hands raised, mouth agape, she backs against the wall. "Are you fucking crazy?"

"It depends." *Sometimes the law doesn't work.*

48

WE REACH Jacksonville and head west on I-10, toward the panhandle. Lucas has his window down, probably to keep me quiet. Wind buffets the inside, loud as a jetliner. He hasn't spoken since we left St. Augustine.

Christina's scream brought him running from the living room, dragging Cyprus with him. When he saw her face and hands bathed in blood, he gave me a look of total disgust, puckering his lips and shaking his head.

"Um, she attacked me," I said sheepishly.

"Lie!" Christina screeched through dripping red fingers clamped to her mouth. "She tried to murder me. Completely unprovoked."

That was a lie. *A*, I didn't try to murder her, just cut her. *B*, she provoked the crap out of me. Said they were planning to kill me! And called Lucas a spade!

Mostly though, it was about the professor. They hit him and drugged him. Stole his money and his heart. Even his wife's precious necklace, the one she died wearing. Then she had the nerve to say she was going to keep exploiting him even after we ran her out of town. That's not provocation?

Still, I tried. *Control yourself. No one gets hurt.* I chanted it in my head like a mantra. It was the mocking that pushed me over the edge.

I had no intention of using the knife when I took it out, just wanted to threaten her to stay away from Nemworth. Then she held up those hands and all I could think was, *Those are the hands the professor wanted to hold.* The hands he thought belonged to someone who cared about him—because she manipulated him into believing that. And she laughed at him!

I snapped. Two quick slashes, one slice for each palm, clean and straight. I should have stopped there. Well, of course, I never should have started. I knew that even while it was happening. But things might have ended better if I stymied myself at that point.

I didn't, couldn't. I crisscrossed those laughing, mocking lips. From a technical standpoint it was pretty good work. I guess knife-fighting is like riding a bike. Once you learn, you never forget.

Lucas took my knife and ordered me to sit in the corner. He told Christina to quit screaming so he could wrap her hands and mouth with strips of sheets and duct tape, getting Cyprus to help. She kept crying and Lucas kept shushing her, trying to calm her down. "Just relax," he said. "Everything gonna be alright."

Then he made them lie down on the floor on top of the maroon bedspread and the yellow blanket with the red smiley face and shot them in the back of the head.

We pass under a lit-up green sign. *Pensacola, 350 miles.* Life comes full circle. More accurately, death. Pensacola is where we got justice for Mom and Becky. Maybe it's the memory that prompts Lucas to finally speak—through gritted teeth.

"Your impulsiveness ruined the whole damn plan. I'm supposed to be relaxing and playing golf in my old age."

"I'm sorry."

"Cannibals and psychopath boyfriends ain't enough for Emily Calby. Oh, no. You got to up the ante, keep your life at DEFCON-one."

Kneading my hands, "I know. I'm sorry."

"Sorry," he sputters. "*Sorry sorry sorry.* You always sorry."

"I'm still not sure she would have gone to the cops, even after I cut her. You should have seen the look in her eyes. She was convinced I'm a psycho."

Struggling to keep his voice even, "That woman needed to go to the hospital and they would've called the police as soon as she walked in the door. What, you thought she was gonna just get in her car and drive off into the fuckin' sunset with her hands and half her head wrapped in bloody sheets and duct tape?"

"Even if they did call the cops, I could have lied and claimed self-defense. Look at my busted lip. She even said they were planning to kill me. I would have been willing to take my chances. You didn't have to shoot them."

He hammers the steering wheel. "Oh, really? That's nice. Take your chances, huh? Well, you forgettin' one thing. I was there too. And I didn't wanna take my chances. You tell me, how was I gonna explain to the police why I broke into their house?"

"Um, maybe because ..."

"And stole their money and threatened 'em with a hatchet and beat ugly senseless? Come on, law student, tell me. What's the legal defense to that? Would have taken the cops two seconds to connect you and me and we'd both be on our way to the penitentiary. You left me no fucking choice but to get rid of 'em."

"You're right, you're right. I'm sor— You're right."

We pass a towering gas station sign with a digital clock. 3:05 AM. It took a while to scrub down the house and load the bodies in the trunk of the BMW. Then it took another hour to find a remote canal to drive the car into, me following Lucas in the SUV while he drove the BMW.

We sank everything except the box of cash and emerald necklace. Suitcase, plastic bin, laundry bag, anything with blood on it, all weighed down with cinderblocks I swiped from a construction site on the way. Lucas even tossed in his last gun, untraceable, like all of his guns. Stolen with an obliterated serial number.

He made me deep six the computer too. I didn't fight him over it. He was already madder at me than I'd ever seen him. I just politely suggested we hang onto it to see if we could get into Christina's bank account and get back more of the professor's money. Lucas responded, not so politely, "Connectin' the computer of a dead person to the internet is how fucking dumbasses end up on *Dateline.*"

Before we left the house, Lucas used his burner—which also went in the drink—to set up a spoofed account on a neighborhood app. He posted a message in the *Free* category:

Emergency Home Foreclosure Tomorrow.
All house contents FREE.
Everything must go! First come, first served.

Then he doxed the address and taped a sign to the door. *COME ON IN! ALL CONTENTS FREE.*

"People love free shit," he explained while refusing to look at me. He predicted an invading swarm would empty the house and contaminate the crime scene beyond reconstruction if and when the cops find the car, which could take years. Florida's web of canals are the dumping place of choice for bodies and stolen cars.

At five, we stop for breakfast at an IHOP outside of Tallahassee. Lucas orders a *Family Feast* and the server asks if we're expecting more people. I sip coffee from a chipped ceramic mug, needing but not wanting to stay awake. My head hurts.

"Lucas, are you ready to talk?"

"If I have to."

"I have a question. And I want you to be honest with me."

"Have I ever not been?"

"No. Do you want me to go away?" I say.

"Go away where?"

"Just, you know, away. From you. I would *totally* understand it. Ever since I showed up at your building when I was twelve, I've caused you nothing but trouble."

"Trouble follows you wherever you go."

"That's the problem. It doesn't just follow me. It always ends up involving you, and putting you in danger. It's so unfair. And you're right. All I do is keep saying *I'm sorry,* over and over like a broken record. I really mean it though. I swear to God. I'm so, so sorry."

Subdued, "I know you are, Em."

Voice breaking, "I just can't control myself sometimes. I try really hard, then something just snaps. I don't know why you put up with it. You shouldn't have to. You should get rid of me. I'm a plague."

He hands me a napkin. "Don't cry in here. We already look like the odd couple. First, you ain't a plague. A pain in the ass for sure, but no plague. Second, I put up with it 'cause *you* got snapped as a kid."

Every once in a while, not often, I try to imagine myself as a normal person, as someone whose family didn't get slaughtered two weeks after her sixth-grade *We're Just Getting Started* graduation dance. What would my life be like? What would *I* be like? It doesn't work. My brain refuses to go there, like it's telling me there's no point wondering what might have been. It will just break your heart and defeat you.

Lucas says, "Course I don't want you to go away. We family. You know that. And I know you'd be there for me too."

"I would! If you ever need help killing anyone or disposing of a body or anything else, I am *so* there. I would die for you, Lucas."

He massages his eyelids and says softly, "I believe you, but how about we start lookin' at things a different way? Stead of plannin' for a future of mayhem, we agree to do everything possible—*every single thing*—to avoid situations where there's any risk, even a hint, of you or me or anyone else dying. Can we do that?"

"Sure!" I say.

"*Pfft*. Yeah, okay. *Sure*. I wish it was that fuckin' easy."

"I'm going to try harder than ever before."

The waitress asks if we need anything else. Lucas says just a check.

Back on the interstate, the sky blazes orange behind us. A new day. I tell myself it has to be better than the last few, then immediately look around for some wood to knock on. I end up using my thick skull.

"Lucas, do you remember that night at the restaurant, by the ocean? You said it wasn't normal for a person to be able to kill without a conscience. Does your conscience bother you, about Christina and Cyprus?"

"No, but I never claimed to be normal. I ain't crazy about the legal risks, I tell you that. But my conscience is good."

"I'm glad." During the drive from St. Augustine I told him—in a monologue since he wasn't speaking to me—everything that happened in the room with Christina, all the terrible things she said.

"But don't think that gets you off the hook for fucking up so bad."

"I know. I shouldn't have lost control, but we did justice. They'll never be able to hurt anyone ever again. And for the record, I did try to let *The Law* handle it. I went to the police and talked to Professor Stafford about a civil suit. I tried to get Professor Nemworth to go to the cops."

"You tried," he concedes. "Although once again, it wasn't your job to get involved in the first place."

"You know, it's funny," I say, twirling my hair. "I've been telling myself for years *The Law* always wins. It's not true. Sometimes it doesn't work. I guess that's the biggest legal exception of them all."

"What's that mean for your legal life?"

"Hm." I gaze out the window as we fly past cows in pastures. They remind me of my days riding the trains before I met Lucas, before he uttered the words that changed my life. *Justice. Always comes too late, but it's still justice.*

"Good question," I say. "I guess it means that if you're truly committed to doing justice, you need a dual skillset."

"Such as?"

"*The Law* and ... *Not The Law.*"

Epilogue

"PROFESSOR, DID I tell you Marisol was a doctor *and* a professor?" I say, passing him a wicker basket of sweet-smelling biscuits nested in a red and white checkerboard cloth napkin.

"Three times, if I'm counting correctly," Nemworth says.

Marisol chuckles. The three of us are seated around his dining room table for a Saturday lunch. Playing matchmaker was near the top of my *To Do* list when I returned to St. Augustine. With me working as her assistant, Mrs. Alvarez cooked up a feast.

The two of them look so cute together. Professor Nemworth is wearing a suit and tie, same ones he wears to class. Marisol is styling in a flowing blue blouse and white linen pants. Even I dressed up—in a dress! Kiona got it for me for Christmas. Now I own three. I'm on a roll.

They seem to really like each other. The professor has a sparkle in his eyes I can actually *see*. Within five minutes of being introduced, Marisol said, "Edgar, dear, would you mind if I clean those glasses for you? I'm surprised you can see anything through them." She gently lifted them off his nose and he didn't make a fuss. Amazing. I love her!

I never expected to be back in St. Augustine—especially after the walls came crumbling down when Lucas and I arrived home in Memphis.

It's happened before. I bottle things up, sealing off the hiding girl's cries for help, feigning confidence and strength and *I'm fine*-ness. Then I land in a safe place and everything falls apart. That safe place is usually Lucas's building.

I didn't shatter any mirrors or cut myself this time, but I stayed in my room with the door closed for a week. I barely talked or ate. Sometimes I slept twelve hours straight. Dr. Laura, who Lucas made me see almost every day, suggested meds to *balance me out*. It wasn't the first time. Lucas agreed with her. Also not the first time.

I said no, again. The doctors forced them on me when I was a kid locked up in the psych ward. I felt more anesthetized than balanced. I don't always like the way I am or act. Sometimes I hate myself for it. But I can't be someone else, which is how the meds made me feel.

Dr. Laura and I talked a lot about whether I should, or even could, return to St. Augustine and the First Coast College of Law. Safe in the confines of her pillow-filled office, we roleplayed the likely triggers.

Returning to my apartment at Seaside. No way. Everyone agreed. Last week Lucas helped move me into a newer and nicer building three blocks away. I insisted for the umpteenth time on taking out student loans to pay for it, but he brushed me off again.

My old apartment smelled like bleach when we went to clear out my stuff. A faint outline of daddy's blood was still visible on my crooked wood floor. I stood at the back window gazing at Henley's apartment across the alley until Lucas said it was time to go.

Matt Jurado. The Law not only worked in his case, it did so in a hurry. He already entered a guilty plea to the drug charges in return for a five-year sentence at the Lake Correctional Institution in Clermont. Didn't even contest them. He was anxious to avoid the video-voyeurism charge and risk being labeled a sex offender. My name never appeared in the case records. I told Dr. Laura that with a new apartment and Jurado locked up a hundred miles away, I didn't think he would be a problem.

The Rol Rom boys. Good news! Daddy's head-bashing by Lucas was ruled justifiable. Less good, Frederick is in a federal institution after being declared incompetent to stand trial. The doctors confirmed Agent Magritte's initial suspicion. He's developmentally disabled and was abused by his father. I feel sorry for him. I'd feel it more except for Toby.

"On a scale of one to ten, how much do you think the events of that night affected you?" Dr. Laura asked during one session.

I said I couldn't put a number on it. The first night I wake up in the middle of a nightmare with the shakes, I'll give it a ten. On most days I'll probably suppress it like everything else. I conceded only that it was *a memorable evening*. Sometimes Dr. Laura gets as frustrated with me as Lucas.

Christina and Cyprus. I never mentioned the formerly alive elder exploiters, having learned long ago that therapist-patient confidentiality doesn't extend to crimes. The first thing I did on returning to St. Augustine was drive by their house. A blue minivan sat in the driveway. Two kids kicked a soccer ball around the front yard. New renters. A relief.

In my prayers, I ask God—in deciding whether to send me to hell—to take into consideration that we not only protected Professor Nemworth, but probably a lot of other poor souls. Their future victims.

That left Henley, the biggest trigger and question mark of all. They piled the charges on him, enough for a life sentence. The case made the news, which was thankfully thin on the dirty details. I'm just *VICTIM* in the public records, as in *VICTIM managed to escape and call for help.*

As days passed, I found myself wishing I hadn't got the cops involved, that I tried to force Henley to get help instead. Threaten to expose him, beat the crap out of him, whatever it took.

Lucas never understood why I cared about someone who did so many terrible things to me. The look on his face was classic when I tried this explanation: "Lucas, you have to admit, it's kind of a compliment for someone to like you so much they spend four entire years of their life stalking you."

Of course, I didn't understand it either. I used to add people to my deserves-to-die list just for being rude.

I tried to look past it, lock it in my brain warehouse of black boxes (compartmentalization being my dissociative disorder's best feature). It didn't work. I couldn't see going back to First Coast knowing Henley was rotting in a cell in the next county.

I looked into transferring to another school, but you have to finish a full year first. I thought about asking for a leave of absence from Dean Trapano. I probably could have got it, but worried I'd lose the energy to return after a year off. And what would it accomplish? Henley would still be there.

I told Lucas I was seriously considering quitting law school.

Then one morning we were at his kitchen table eating cereal and talking about the Memphis Grizzlies' big win the night before over the Lakers. Well, Lucas was talking. I was pretending to listen. His phone rang. I looked down and saw *Agent Magritte*.

"Hey, Margareth. What's up?"

First name basis? I was concocting a warning about how he'd better not get sweet on her or I'll tell Kiona when his face screwed up. "Alright," he said. "I'll let her know. Thanks for calling."

He set the phone down and scratched his head. "Em, I got some news."

The *more bad news* trigger fired and I froze. "Good or bad?"

"It depends."

I almost made a nervous joke about him going to law school because he already knew the answer to every legal question.

"Your friend Henley committed suicide in jail last night."

"Huh?" I felt the color drain from my face. "No. Uh-uh. That's not possible."

"I'm afraid it is. He hung himself in his cell with a piece of wire."

I just sat there, wagging my head in denial. Lucas stayed quiet. I finally looked to the ceiling and whispered, "Why, Henley?"

Lucas's phone pinged. "You really wanna know? He left a letter with your name on it. Margareth said she'd send a picture of it. That's probably it."

I said I wanted to know. I've read the letter a hundred times, never making it through without tearing up.

> *Dear Emily:*
>
> *I'm not sure what to say. Res ipsa loquitur, right? The thing speaks for itself. Just like Professor LeMoy taught us.*
>
> *I have no excuses for my acts and the only explanation is there's something wrong with me. "Non compos mentis." It's in my notes from when Nemworth was discussing the incapacity defense to a breach of contract action.*

Pure Henley to the end, defaulting to law school talk even in his final hours.

> *By the time you see this, I will be gone. Do not feel bad for me. I know you're sick of Shakespeare, but as Hamlet said, to die is nothing more than to sleep and end the heartache and thousand natural shocks that flesh is heir to.*
>
> *My biggest heartache is I lacked the courage to do this before I caused you so much pain and trauma. I'd give anything to go back in time, to your favorite coffee shop in Memphis, and walk up and introduce myself. Be a normal person.*

But I'm not. I don't belong in this world. I never fit, not since I can remember.

My only wish, my dying wish, is that you become the kick-ass lawyer you were always meant to be. Goodbye, Emily.

Your friend and study partner,

Henley Oliver

p.s. I hope you finish number one in our class.

I learned Henley lied to me about his parents divorcing. They died in a terrible car accident in Texas only two months before he moved to Memphis at age eighteen. A tractor-trailer rammed them from behind on the interstate and their car exploded. He was an only child.

Maybe that contributed to me becoming his fixation. Trauma can make you do weird things. Exhibit A: me.

The jail released a death certificate stating the cause of death as asphyxia. With no family, no one claimed his remains. There was no funeral. They buried him in a plywood box in a prisoner cemetery.

The suicide sent me into an even deeper funk and cemented my decision to quit First Coast. I wanted to run a million miles in the opposite direction. I asked Lucas if we could drive to St. Augustine to get my stuff. The sooner I could disconnect from that place the better off I would be, I said.

He acquiesced and two days later we were nearing the end of the twelve-hour drive, jetting east on I-10, closing in on Jacksonville, when Lucas took an exit at State Road 301.

"Gas?" I said.

He shook his head.

"Gotta pee?"

He shook it again and turned south.

"Then what?" It couldn't be lunch. We stopped a couple hours earlier at a Cracker Barrel, our old favorite when we were living on the bus.

"Thought we'd stop by the prisoner cemetery."

"The what? *Whoa,* I don't know about that. I need time to think about it."

"Think fast. Agent Magritte set it up for this afternoon."

He wasn't doing it to pay his respects to Henley. He never said so, but I knew he was glad Henley was gone. He did it to help me, drove all this way. I felt gratitude even though I didn't want to go. My muscles tensed tighter with each bump in the road until they felt like frozen rods. We drove in silence past fields, farms and warehouses.

I sensed we were getting close when Lucas took a sharp turn onto a gravel road, slamming me against the door of the SUV and snapping me out of my paralysis.

A minute later we came to a stop. "This is it," Lucas said.

I couldn't see it because my eyes were squeezed shut. The diet coke in my hand was overflowing because the can collapsed under my grip.

I expected the absolute worst, a Dickensian horror show of scattered bodies and leftover parts buried under piles of rocks. Such a relief when I opened them and saw we were parked next to a well-kept green field surrounded by pine trees and enclosed by a split-rail fence. That alone made me glad we came.

"You go on," Lucas said. "I'll wait here."

His grave was easy to find because the dirt was fresh. The grave marker didn't do him justice, just a small square stone reducing Henley's complex existence to name, prisoner number and date of death. I wished I had brought something, maybe a yellow rose like the one he gave me that day at the Starbucks.

I kneeled in the dirt and prayed. *Lord, please forgive and take care of Henley. He was a lost soul, mentally ill. Like so many of us. In pain ... like so many of us.*

That's as far as I got before the damn broke and my emotions flooded me. Sorrow. Grief. *Depletion.* I cried so hard my eyes ached. The longer it went on, the more I knew it wasn't just about Henley. I was crying for me, and my family, for *Loss.*

Face buried against my knees, curled in a ball, I felt myself sinking into a sea of depression, drowning, fighting the can't-breathe feeling that has always terrified me. I thought I was choking and wondered if Lucas could see me.

Then the strangest feeling washed over me, lifting me like a warm wave. Out-of-body, otherworldly. I could never explain it rationally. I can't rule out it was endorphins released from all the crying, but I'll go to my own grave believing it was more.

Henley's letter played in my head, like he was reading it to me. *My only wish, my dying wish, is that you become the kick-ass lawyer you were always meant to be. Your family would want that.* The last sentence is what really got to me. The weird part is it wasn't in his letter. I don't know where it came from or who or what appended it. I just knew it was true.

On the way back to the car, mopping tears and snot with my shirts, I decided to return to law school. To not run away. Stay and be the warrior and survivor Lucas always proclaimed me to be, that my damaged life taught me I had to be. Follow my dreams, like my mom told me a hundred times starting when I was a little girl.

And so here I am, eating lunch in Professor Nemworth's dining room, a week before classes start.

"Emilita," Marisol says. "Edgar told me you wrote the best exam in his entire class. That is so wonderful."

When I got my grades and saw an asterisk next to my Contracts grade, I assumed it meant something bad, like *Pending* or *In Review.* But I got the top paper award. They give one in every course for the best exam. Since grading is anonymous, I know it's legit. I did well in my other classes too, all As, except for a *B* in Civil Procedure. I knew I messed up that exam.

"I was only able to do it because Professor Nemworth is such a great teacher!"

Nemworth laughs. I never saw it happen until today. I love it so much I start laughing myself.

We've chatted in his office a few times since I got back. If he missed Christina, it didn't show. Just the opposite. He seemed happier and more relaxed, definitely less grouchy. As a test, I asked during one visit, "How's Christina doing?" He said, "She disappeared," adding after a long pause, "Just as well."

Then he surprised me by opening up. "Apparently, the cancer treatment checks you so outrageously snooped through were not enough for her."

The words didn't come out in anger, more like a wistful confession. He explained that in the last few weeks—before Lucas and I disappeared her—Christina used his banking credentials to set up online bill-paying on his computer, probably while he was drugged, transferring money to herself until she emptied the account.

That afternoon I wrapped up the shoebox from the closet and his wife's necklace and left the package on his porch. The shoebox contained twenty-two thousand dollars. I rang the doorbell and hid in the hibiscus shrubs to make sure he came out and got it. I included a typed note I rewrote twenty times. In the end, I kept it short.

Edgar — I'm leaving town. I never had cancer. I'm sorry I took so much of your money and your wife's jewelry. Here is the necklace and as much as I can pay back. Christina.

When we finish dessert, I insist on doing the dishes so the professor and Marisol can talk. I was shocked on arrival to find the house spotless, with all the curtains open and yard mowed. It looked and felt like a different place, a happier one.

I'm not sure what made the professor decide to get it all done. Maybe the date with Marisol played a role. Overall, I see the signs of a person emerging from depression. I know them. And it all correlates with Christina *leaving town*. Please take note of that on my send-to-hell checklist, Lord.

I return to the table to find a slim gift-wrapped box sitting on my placemat. "What's this?" I say.

"A gift, for all your help," Nemworth says.

"Aw, you didn't have to get me anything. Should I open it?"

"Please do."

"*Regalos!*" Marisol says, rubbing her hands together. "So exciting."

I pull off the bow and unwrap the paper with no idea what to expect. I can't picture Nemworth going gift shopping. I'm thinking something school-related, maybe a pen or bookmark.

When I open the box, I just stare. I look up at Nemworth, bewildered.

It's Mrs. Nemworth's necklace. The emerald glistens in the sun streaming through the windows. I'm lost. Is it some kind of joke? What would it be? Maybe he gave me the wrong box by mistake. I could see that happening.

"Professor, um, do you know what's in this box?"

He coughs up a laugh. "I should hope so."

"What? What is it?" Marisol says, leaning in.

I show her the box then shift it to Nemworth, stretching my arm out to make sure he can see it.

He turns to Marisol. "It's a necklace that belonged to my wife, Claire."

"*Magnifico*," she says.

"Not just any necklace," I say. "Her favorite. A family heirloom. She—" I almost say *died wearing it*. I've been doing better about restraining my impulses to *almost*. No harm, no foul. Only been a few weeks, but it's a start.

"Professor, I don't understand."

With crinkled smiling eyes, "Oh, come now. It's not difficult. A *gift* is a voluntary and gratuitous transfer of property from one person to another. I would expect the top student in the class to recall at least that much."

Marisol chuckles. Now he's a comedian? What is going on?

I say, "It's way too valuable. You said the insurance company wanted you to keep it in a safe deposit box."

"Indeed. It is quite valuable, but not based on what an insurance company says. They place the value on the emerald, which is simply a piece of rock. The value of this necklace lies in what it meant to Claire."

"Exactly. That's why you shouldn't give it away. She wouldn't want you to."

Shaking his head, "You're wrong. She wanted it to be worn, not kept in a drawer or safe deposit box. I told you that before. And what would happen to it when I pass? Sold at an estate auction? That would break her heart."

I look to Marisol, pleading for an assist, but her chin is keeping up a slight nodding motion that says, *Accept it.*

Nemworth says, "Trust me. Claire would want that necklace to be worn next to the beating heart of a young woman full of ambition and vibrancy and hope. A good heart, one that reaches out with kindness to others. Like she always did. Someone like you."

"Professor. I am *so-oo* touched by this. You don't even know. But I don't deserve it. I really don't."

"Ms. Calby, let this be your final mentoring lesson. You *do* deserve it."

An image of Christina flashes, hands and lips bursting with blood as I slash her with the neck knife. "No, sir. I–I'm not a good person like Mrs. Nemworth. I'm ... just not."

He looks to Marisol. "What do you think, Dr. Alvarez? Good person? Deserving?"

She reaches across the table and touches my cheek, eyes welling. "*Emilita,*" she says, and that single word brims with such warmth and love it overpowers me. Whether I deserve it or not, I sure like the feeling. I'm sniffling as the professor removes his sparkly clean glasses and dabs his eyes with a napkin.

And that's how our get-together ends. With all three of us

crying. I will never in a million years understand how *The Girl Who Never Cried* became such a crybaby.

I reluctantly accepted the necklace, on the condition he can have it back anytime if he changes his mind. I'm terrified of losing it, but won't let Mrs. Nemworth down. What he said about her rings true. I would want the same thing. Marisol comes around the table and helps clasp it around my neck.

After lunch, I give Marisol a ride back to Seaside, promising to stop by for tea next week. She wants me to meet her new kitty. I never told her what happened to Toby. I don't know if it was the right decision. I'd want to know. In the end, I didn't see the point of hurting her.

I wait until she's inside and zip across town to Bryce's. He texted me about a new case he wants to discuss. No answer when I knock, but his Audi is out front. I use my key for the first time.

Such an odd feeling being back here. Nothing is the same in my life yet everything seems normal and familiar. The only difference is the reception area has more boxes.

Bryce waves me into his office where we sit facing each other across his desk, messy with files as usual. Over-the-ear headphones and a CD by some band named Khruangbin lay on top. I ask about Suzanne and Marigold.

He says they're fine, that Suzanne wants me to come back for dinner and Marigold spoke her first word yesterday. *Dada*. "Honestly, it could have been indigestion, but I'm sticking with *Dada*. How was your break?"

Something's off. He keeps twisting a paperclip into a pretzel and then restraightening it.

"Um, fine," I say.

"Good, good. Congrats on your Legal Writing grade. Excellent major memo. No surprise."

"Thanks. You mentioned a new case. More documents to review?"

"No, nothing like that." The paperclip breaks and he sets the pieces down. "Emily, when you told me about the horrific events at your apartment the last time I saw you, sympathy and shock clouded out my legal brain."

"What do you mean?"

"As soon as you left, it hit me that you have your own negligent security lawsuit against Regal."

"Hm, I'm surprised I didn't think about that."

"Probably a good thing. Maybe law school hasn't completely brainwashed you to see everything in life exclusively through a legal lens—yet. It will."

Not so sure about that. "It makes sense," I say. "We even have proof they had notice the lock was broken."

"That's right. But when you say *we*, I want to emphasize I'm not suggesting you retain me as your lawyer."

"Are you kidding? Of course I'd want you to be my lawyer. Do you think it would be a good case?"

"Honestly, while it's impossible to predict, getting what happened to you in front a jury, especially given your background ... well, let's just say I wouldn't want to be the defense attorney."

"Everything would have to come out?"

"I'm afraid so. Civil cases are a matter of public record."

I wave my hand like I'm washing a window. "No can do. It would be another media carnival. The missing Calby girl, cannibals ... I can't even imagine."

"You could be giving up a lot. Maybe millions."

Millions is right. Millions of private things in my life exposed to the media savages. Talk about cannibals. Just picturing myself on a witness stand being asked what I was wearing when daddy and junior busted in makes my skin itch. Not to mention that everything else could come out. Jurado, maybe even Henley.

"You know I would *love* to see Regal pay, but no."

"I understand and respect that, but felt I had an obligation to tell you."

"I appreciate it. I have another idea though ..."

Which was: A plan to help Artiel Jones, who's permanently

disabled from the attack at the Regal Estates property and already has more than a million dollars in medical expenses.

Step 1: Ask Agent Magritte to write a letter to Regal informing them of a negligent premises condition at the Seaside Apartments—to wit, a broken lock on a backdoor—that resulted in a serious physical attack on a tenant.

Step 2: Get her permission to let Bryce use the letter along with the repair records I found showing prior notice as leverage to force a good settlement in the Jones case. Surely Regal is smart enough to not want a jury to see a letter from the FBI accusing them of negligent security at their properties.

The letter wouldn't have to give names or details. It could say the *gravity of the case* required the records be sealed. Truth. Regal obviously knows something about what happened that night. When Lucas and I returned to move my stuff, I went to the alley to check the green door. Not just a new lock. A brand new metal door.

Bryce says, "That could be a powerful negotiating tool. Do you think your FBI friend would be willing to do it?"

"Maybe. It's worth asking. She's super-cool."

I called Agent Magritte who said she'd be more than happy to send the letter. "I told Regal's president the same thing on the phone. He kept dancing and dodging until I said, *Just get off your butts and secure your properties!*" I love Agent Magritte!

Bryce escorts me to the door. "This could really help Mr. Jones. Great legal thinking, Emily."

"Not really," I say glumly. "My main accomplishment was being a victim—again."

He opens his mouth at the word *victim* and I'm certain he's going to ask about Henley. He must read the reticence on my face because instead he says, "Whatever happened with Professor Nemworth and that woman you were worried about?"

"Um, I'm not exactly sure. I think it worked out."

* * *

My first stop the next morning is the law school. Dean Trapano emailed to ask if we could meet. I told Lucas I'll be back soon. He's been staying at the Franklin again. Wanted to make sure I got settled before going home to Memphis. He's leaving this afternoon. I'm going to miss him more than ever.

Whenever I feel a trigger coming on, I turn over the medallion on my new bracelet and get strength from the inscription. Solid invincible Lucas. My forever defender and companion.

I polish the medallion now as I enter the dean's suite.

"Thank you for coming, Emily. Have a seat," Dean Trapano says with an effusive over-smile as she wriggles in her chair like she has ants in her pants. I seem to be making everyone nervous these days. The building's mostly empty, but she's dressed in a turquoise suit, her hair and makeup perfect.

"What did you want to talk to me about?" I say. As if I didn't know.

"I assume you've heard the sad news about your friend, Henley Oliver."

Unblinking, "Yes."

"I'm so very sorry. People tell me you two"—she struggles between past and present and it comes out—"*arwere* close."

A tightlipped nod.

"A detective from the Clay County Sheriff's Office came here to visit with me."

I gave them a statement over the phone while I was still in Memphis, keeping it as brief as possible. Jungle cat senses tingling, "What did he tell you?"

"Not much that wasn't already in the news. He asked some questions about Henley ... and you." I scrutinize her for tells, wondering if she knows I'm *VICTIM*.

"What did you tell him?"

"I didn't know Henley. I wish I had, but with nearly five hundred students, I–I just ..."

"It's not your fault. Henley was quiet. He flew under the radar on purpose. What did you tell the detective about me?"

"Only good things, of course. What a wonderful student you are and how glad we are to have you here. Speaking of which, I have exciting news for you. Class ranks haven't been released yet, but you finished number one in the first-year class. Congratulations! That's a huge accomplishment and honor."

"Really? Wow, thanks. Um, could you tell me how Henley did?"

She hesitates. "I'm afraid I can't because of—"

"FERPA." The federal privacy law for student records. "I respect that." Especially since I spent the whole semester blaming the law school for telling Henley my LSAT score. "But grades were really important to Henley and he'd want me to know. I swear. We studied together every day."

"Well, Henley actually finished with a perfect four point."

My GPA came out at 3.82, thanks to the *B* in Civ Pro. "Then there's been a mistake. I couldn't be number one because I only had a three-eight-two. Henley should be number one."

"I understand, but because he's no longer, um, here, he isn't eligible for class ranking. I'm sorry if that sounds insensitive."

"But he earned it."

"That's the rule. It's in the Academic Regulations."

I ask her to show it to me. The rule is clear as day. *Only currently enrolled students are eligible for class ranking*. Airtight, but there's always an exception. I know that now.

"I can't be ranked number one when I didn't earn it."

Her face puckers. "I'm not sure you have a choice."

"How about this? You could rank me number two through the Spring semester and keep the number one slot blank, in memory of Henley. You wouldn't be ranking him, so it wouldn't violate the rule."

She studied the wording and gave in, adding it would be a nice gesture.

We did it, Henley. Number 1 and 2, like we always talked about.

I meet Julie for lunch at Calo's, the same seafood joint we went to at the beginning. She called me in Memphis after seeing the news about Henley, but I couldn't talk. Things were too raw.

I get the broiled grouper sandwich again. Julie goes with a bowl of lobster bisque. The food is as scrumptious as our first time. Small talk so far.

"What'd you do over the break?" I ask.

"Not much. Hung out with Addie and relaxed. It's weird. After a couple days off I didn't know what to do with myself not having to study."

"I know what you mean."

She raises her arms like a football ref signaling touchdown. "The big news is I'm still here. *Woohoo!* I didn't flunk out. Not bragging, but I got all *B*s except for a C in Contracts."

"That's awesome! I told you."

"How about you?" she asks. "I'll bet you killed it."

"I did okay." I leave it at that.

The big unstated hangs in the air, making it hard to breathe. I keep gulping water to loosen my throat. I'm actually relieved when she breaks the ice.

"So sad about Henley."

"Mm-hm."

"Some people made fun of him for being a nerd, but I liked him. You could tell he was smart, but he didn't show off. And I loved the smooth move he pulled on Olson that night at the pub."

"I liked him too." I blink and a tear breaks free. I wipe it with my finger.

"So, like, what happened? Were you the *victim* in the news stories? That's what everyone thinks."

"Everyone?" The news reports never said the victim was a law student.

"Well, I don't know about everyone. I've only talked to a few classmates, but you know how it is. Same old law school gossip machine. It's only because you two were together all the time. I've been telling people it wasn't you, that there's no way you could have been a victim of Henley."

"Why do you say that?"

"First, it's hard for me to picture you being a victim of anyone, especially Henley. He didn't exactly strike me as UFC fighting material. On the other hand, I can't picture him doing any of the things they say he did, so who knows? But also, I always had the feeling he loved you. I can't imagine him trying to hurt you."

"I—I can't talk about it. I'm sorry." Our friendship broke up over me not being able to open up. Now I'm doing it again. But it's the truth. I *literally* can't talk about it. If I started, I'd melt down right here in the restaurant.

"That's okay. I understand. Hey, would you like to join our study group? I already asked Russell and he's totally down with it."

"That's sweet of you, but I think I'm going to study on my own this semester."

Here I go, shutting out another person. This time the same person. I've been doing it forever it seems. Where has it got me? *Alone.*

"You know, on second thought, I would really like that. Thank you, Julie." I reach out and touch her hand. She squeezes my fingers and it feels good.

* * *

"Well, here we are again," Lucas says. We're outside the Franklin loading up his SUV. He's wearing the Memphis Grizzlies sweatshirt I got him for Christmas. It was a good Christmas, considering the circumstances. Kiona came and we were like a little family again.

My big present for Lucas was an honorary doctoral degree. I made the diploma the week I spent in my room, meticulously penning the Gothic calligraphy.

The Regents of The University of Life hereby confer upon
Lucas Ellington Jackson
the Doctorate of Greatness, Summa Cum Laude.

A little cheesy, but it touched him. I could tell. He tried to cover it up by joking that *Some-a Cum Loud,* as he pronounced it, sounded like the name of a porn star.

"You gonna be alright?" he asks.

Déjà vu all over again. "I'll be fine."

He doesn't look convinced. Again. "Don't forget your promise to consider transferrin' to Memphis at the end of the school year."

"I won't."

He hoists a jumbo-sized suitcase into the back. "Before I go, tell me somethin'. You learn anything valuable during your adventurous first semester?"

"Of course. I wrote the top paper in Contracts. I had to learn a lot to get that."

"Not law school. I'm talkin' life lessons."

I knew that. "Oh, for sure. First *and foremost,* I am going to try my brains out to control myself and not be so impulsive."

"Excuse me if I don't hold my breath."

"You just wait. Second, and related, I learned I need to work much harder on avoiding trouble because it follows me wherever I go and I'm tired of being stuck in a sac o'woe."

"That makes two of us."

"Third, I learned I can believe in *The Law* while also recognizing it doesn't always work. In which case—"

"In which case you go back to lessons one and two. Control yourself and stay out of trouble. Anything goes wrong this semester, you're comin' home. We ain't playing this game again."

"Wrong?" I spread my arms and tilt my face to the sun, lower in the sky than when I arrived in August. "What could possibly go wrong in a beautiful place like this?"

I laugh and twirl in circles as he palms his massive forehead.

What did you think of *Target: The Girl*?

THANK YOU for reading *Target: The Girl* (Emily Calby Book 3). We know you have lots of reading and other entertainment choices, so we really appreciate it. If you liked the book, please consider posting a review on Amazon and Goodreads to help spread the word. And thanks again!

Have you read *The Hiding Girl* and *The Girl in Cell 49B*?

TARGET: THE GIRL is the third book in the Emily Calby Series, which tracks Emily's perilous life forward from the day two men broke into her rural Georgia home when she was twelve years old and murdered her family. Each book is spaced four years apart in Emily's life (*The Hiding Girl*, ages 12–13; *The Girl in Cell 49B*, age 16; *Target: The Girl*, age 20).

The Hiding Girl
(Emily Calby Book 1)

TWELVE-YEAR-OLD Emily Calby was a good girl from a religious family in rural Georgia. She loved softball, her little sister and looking up words to get her allowance. Then two men came and murdered her family. Only the killers know she survived.

On the run, surviving by wits and animal instinct, she makes an unlikely ally in an ex-gang member who lost his own family to violence. He takes her in and trains her in “self-defense” before more tragedy launches her on a terrifying journey for justice. Nothing will stop her—not cops or creeps, not even her own splintering mind. Through it all, Emily fights to hold onto the girl she once knew, kept buried deep inside.

Dark and gritty, but filled with heart and hope, *The Hiding Girl* is a twisty, fast-paced coming-of-age story and testament to the boundless limits of love, sacrifice and the will to survive.

Order it on Amazon

The Girl in Cell 49B
(Emily Calby Book 2)

EMILY CALBY disappeared at age twelve, the only survivor of a notorious home invasion. Three years after her terrifying odyssey in *The Hiding Girl*, she's safe, living in anonymity with her mentor, ex-gang member Lucas Jackson—before life blows up again on her Sweet Sixteen birthday. Arrested for carrying her birthday gift (an illegal handgun), a fingerprint scan shows her to be the missing Calby girl and worse: she's wanted for murder in another state.

Extradited to a corrupt juvenile prison, Emily struggles to adjust to a new code of survival while battling a vindictive prosecutor willing to resort to any means to convict her. As *The Law* thwarts her every move, she begins to appreciate its awesome power. She discovers a hidden prison law library and buries herself in the books, casting her destiny.

As she fights for her life in court, the dark secrets behind the prison walls close in. Her cellmate, a spookily prescient drug addict, is in grave danger. So is her first love, a gentle boy sentenced to life without parole. Emily's desperate to help them, but how can she, when her explosive trial brings a new disaster every day? A legal thriller like no other.

Order it on Amazon

Locations and Entities in *Target: The Girl*

ALL CHARACTERS and events in *Target: The Girl* are fictional, but the *Emily Calby Series* is set in real cities, so some elaboration about specific locations and entities mentioned in the book may be helpful. The First Coast College of Law is fictional. There is no law school in St. Augustine. "First Coast" is a term coined, originally for marketing purposes, in the 1980s to describe Florida's northeast Atlantic coast. There is a Florida Coastal School of Law in Jacksonville, about an hour north of St. Augustine, but it bears no resemblance to the fictional First Coast College of Law.

If you Google "Regal Estates"—the name of the less-than-stellar property manager of Emily's apartment building—you'll find real estate companies, apartment buildings, mobile home parks, assisted-living facilities, even sandwich shops bearing that august title, including some in Florida. The name is used fictionally and generically in this book and bears no resemblance to any real entity. Similarly, and not surprisingly, there are numerous "Seaside Apartments" in the United States, including some in Florida, but none of them bear any resemblance to Emily's building.

In addition to the FBI, local city and county law enforcement agencies are referenced in *Target: The Girl*, but they are all used fictitiously.

A Note About Elder Financial Exploitation

THEY ALWAYS SAY, "Write what you know." In the case of elder financial exploitation, my knowledge is personal and painful because our ninety-four-year-old father was the victim of a "sweetheart scam" shortly before he passed away. A veteran con artist stole ninety-thousand dollars from him after targeting him as he took a walk, leaning on his cane, near his South Florida home.

The facts of his case were somewhat similar to those of the fictional Professor Edgar Nemworth. On learning our father had recently lost his wife (our stepmother) of thirty-five years to lung cancer, the exploiter preyed on that vulnerability. She said she had cancer and that the doctors would only treat her if paid up front. She called the money loans, saying she owned a building in New York and would be able to repay him once she sold it. There was no building. There was no cancer.

It was difficult for my sister and me to comprehend how an intelligent, independent, college-educated, frugal person like our father could fall for such a ploy, and even harder to understand why he was unable or unwilling to acknowledge the truth when confronted with it. Some of the cognitive and psychological explanations for this phenomenon are mentioned in the book.

My sister and I were lucky to hook up with a detective who understood elder financial exploitation and was willing to put in the time and effort to pursue our dad's exploiter. Like all economic crimes, elder financial exploitation cases consume substantial resources that many local police departments lack.

We're indebted to this detective. He didn't blow us off with the insult heard by so many family members who report elder exploitation, that "It's not a crime to give your money away." As he summarized the case in the arrest affidavit:

> *The lies and fictitious stories [the defendant] continually tells [the victim] are clearly designed to prey on his affections and loneliness for the sole purpose of stealing [the victim's] money. This detective, relying on experience and training, clearly views this incident as a classic "sweetheart scam."*

The result was a rare success story. The defendant pleaded guilty to a felony and paid partial restitution. Most victims are not so fortunate. As explained in the book, elder financial exploitation, which can assume many forms, is grossly under-prosecuted despite the fact that the crime is widespread and growing. With seventy-eight million baby boomers in or nearing retirement, it has been given the label, "The Crime of the 21st Century."

Keep an eye on your elderly loved ones. Never make the mistake of assuming they're immune to financial predation. We thought that about our father.

About the Author

DORIAN BOX is an award-winning author and former law professor. His nonfiction books include an Amazon Editors' Favorite Book of the Year. In his fiction, he likes to blend dark themes with heart, hope, and humor. His novels have received honors and awards from Publishers Weekly, Writer's Digest, Readers' Favorite, IndieReader, BestThrillers.com, Feathered Quill, and the National Indie Excellence Awards.

In his academic life, Box won numerous awards for both teaching and research and wrote thousands, possibly millions, of scholarly footnotes. He's been interviewed as a legal expert by National Public Radio, the PBS Newshour, the New York Times, and many other sources.

Dorian lives out his childhood rock star fantasies playing in cover bands that earn tens of dollars sweating it out in dive bars until two a.m.

Follow Dorian at dorianbox.com and on Facebook and Goodreads. Drop him a line at dorianbox@outlook.com.

Also by Dorian Box
Psycho-Tropics

A HIGH SCHOOL reunion in a South Florida beach town unburies the past (literally) in this dark mystery of revenge and redemption. Lottery-winning surfer Danny Teakwell seems to be living the life, but he's been hiding a terrible secret, punishing himself for two decades.

Now he's hit rock bottom. So he thinks. The ghosts from his past show up at the reunion, launching him on a mayhem-filled race through the Sunshine State to save a missing woman, and his soul.

The odds aren't good. He only has three days and his main allies are a pill-popping lawyer, crusty barkeep, and seven-year-old embalming expert. Heart and dark humor combine with page-turning action and a twisty plot that will keep you guessing until the end.

Order it on Amazon

Editorial Reviews of *Psycho-Tropics*

"Marrying humor with suspense is not easy, but it comes across masterfully ... A truly enjoyable read." — *Writer's Digest Award for Genre Fiction*

"An engaging thriller with plenty of humor, good characterization, and a memorable villain." — *Kirkus Reviews*

"Clues are tossed out like bait, twisting and turning the storyline along ... The characters are brilliantly constructed ... The dark humor serves to lessen the tension in all the right ways before it heightens again ... Effortlessly captures the wonderful eccentricities of life in South Florida." — *IndieReader (Official Seal of Approval)*

"A genuinely creepy sadist is the high point of Box's dark thriller set in Florida in 1995." — *Publishers Weekly*

"Psycho-Tropics is like riding Pipeline with a hangover. It's jaw dropping, heart thumping and addictively exhilarating, but with a hint of disorientation, dizziness and an unsettled stomach. But by the end you'll be smiling ear to ear and bursting to tell your mates how good it was." — *Surfer Dad UK*

Amazon Reviews of *Psycho-Tropics*

"A twisted, hilarious mystery with heart ... When a seven-year-old embalming expert and James Garfield, the twentieth president, play roles in solving the case, you know something different is up."

"It's got it all: action, humor, pulse-raising suspense, pathos and warmth."

"Lots of writers have stories to tell—but can't. Box has stories to tell—and can."

"I thought this was going to be a typical crazy Florida book ... what a huge surprise. ... Great story and great characters, well told and believable."

"This book drew me in from the first sentence ... Every time I thought I figured out what was going on, I was wrong. Every time I wanted to finish a chapter and put it down, the dramatic ending would propel me to the next chapter."

"Finished the damn thing in two days. I could not put it down. This is one of the best books I have read in a long time ... The pacing was balanced, the characters were rounded and complex. Just when I thought I knew what was going to happen, the author threw a curve ball. The ending was truly a surprise."

"Carl Hiaasen on steroids."

"I am drawn to books with heavy character development. If there also happens to be a compelling story, all the better, but I've come not to expect it. It seems like most authors can't do both. This book has marvelous, complex characters, but also moves along at a fast pace and is completely unpredictable.""My daughter heard me laughing from across the house as I read this one. Don't let the humor fool you, though. This book has serious messages about forgiveness, redemption and self-examination."

"Wonderfully off-beat characters ... Suspense and comedy are hard to make work in novels, but Dorian Box has pulled it off beautifully."

"A brilliant mystery thriller, masterfully written."

Order it on Amazon

Made in United States
North Haven, CT
21 December 2024

63188591R00212